About the Authors

Annie West has devoted her life to an intensive study of charismatic heroes who cause the best kind of trouble in the lives of their heroines. As a sideline she researches locations for romance, from vibrant cities to desert encampments and fairytale castles. Annie lives in eastern Australia with her hero husband, between sandy beaches and gorgeous wine country. She finds writing the perfect excuse to postpone housework. To contact her or join her newsletter, visit www.annie-west.com

Initially a French/English teacher, **Emma Darcy** changed careers to computer programming before the happy demands of marriage and motherhood. Very much a people person, and always interested in relationships, she finds the world of romance fiction a thrilling one and the challenge of creating her own cast of characters very addictive.

Since her first venture into novel writing in the mid-nineties, **Kristi Gold** has greatly enjoyed weaving stories of love and commitment. She's an avid fan of baseball, beaches and bridal reality shows. During her career, Kristi has been a National Readers Choice winner, Romantic Times award winner, and a three-time Romance Writers of America RITA finalist. She resides in Central Texas and can be reached through her website at http://kristigold.com

Mavericks

Mavericks: Her Playboy Prince Charming

ANNIE WEST

EMMA DARCY

KRISTI GOLD

MILLS & BOON

First Published in Great Britain 2020
By Mills & Boon, an imprint of HarperCollins*Publishers*
1 London Bridge Street, London, SE1 9GF

MAVERICKS: HER PLAYBOY PRINCE CHARMING © 2020
Harlequin Books S.A.

Passion, Purity and the Prince © 2010 Annie West
The Incorrigible Playboy © 2013 Emma Darcy
The Sheikh's Son © 2014 Kristi Goldberg

ISBN: 978-0-263-28212-2

MIX
Paper from
responsible sources
FSC™ C007454

This book is produced from independently certified FSC™ paper to ensure responsible forest management.

For more information visit: www.harpercollins.co.uk/green

Printed and bound in Spain
by CPI, Barcelona

PASSION, PURITY AND THE PRINCE

ANNIE WEST

CHAPTER ONE

'HIS HIGHNESS will be here soon. Please remain in this room and *do not wander*. There are strict security controls and alarms in this part of the castle.'

The prince's aide spoke in clipped English and gave Tamsin a stern look. As if after finally passing the barriers of royal protocol and officious secretaries she'd run amok now she was within the royal sanctum.

As if, after weeks working in the Ruvingian royal archives and living in her suite on the far side of the castle courtyard, proximity to flesh and blood royalty might be too much for her! She'd never seen the prince. He never deigned to cross the courtyard to the functional archive room.

She stifled an impatient sigh.

Did she look the sort of woman to be overcome by pomp and wealth? Or be impressed by a man whose reputation as a womaniser and adventurer rivalled even that of his infamous robber baron ancestors?

Tamsin had more important things on her mind.

Secret excitement rippled through her and it had nothing to do with meeting a playboy prince.

This was her chance to rebuild her reputation. After Patrick's brutal betrayal she could finally prove herself to her colleagues and herself. Her confidence had shattered after the way he'd used her. He'd damaged her professionally but far worse, he'd hurt her so badly she'd wanted only to crawl away and lick her wounds.

She'd never trust again.

Some scars wouldn't heal. Yet here, now, she could at least kick start her career again. This was a once in a lifetime opportunity and she was ready for the challenge.

For ten days Prince Alaric had been too busy to meet her. His schedule had been too full to fit her in. Clearly an expert on old books didn't rank in his priorities.

The notion ignited a shimmer of anger inside her. She was tired of being used, dismissed and overlooked.

Had he hoped to fob her off by seeing her so late in the evening? Tamsin straightened her spine, clasping her hands in her lap, ankles crossed demurely under the massive chair.

'Of course I won't leave. I'll be content here until His Highness arrives.'

The aide's dubious expression made it clear he thought she was waiting her moment to sneak off and gape at the VIPs in the ballroom. Or maybe steal the silverware.

Impatient at the way he hovered, she slipped a hand into her briefcase and pulled out a wad of papers. She gave the aide a perfunctory smile and started reading.

'Very well.' His voice interrupted and she looked up. 'It's possible the prince may be…delayed. If you need anything, ring the bell.'

He gestured to a switch on the wall, camouflaged by the exquisite wood carving surrounding the huge fireplace. 'Refreshments will be brought if you need them.'

'Thank you.' Tamsin nodded and watched him bustle away.

Was 'delay' code? Was the prince busy seducing a glamorous beauty from the ball? If gossip was right Prince Alaric of Ruvingia, in line to the crown of Maritz, was a playboy *par excellence*. Pursuing women would be higher on his priorities than meeting a book curator.

Tamsin ignored a fizz of indignation.

Her gaze strayed to the ceiling height bookshelves. The inevitable spark of interest quickened her blood. Old books. She smelled the familiar scent of aged paper and leather.

If he was going to be late…

Not allowing herself second thoughts, Tamsin walked to the nearest bookcase. It was too much to hope it would yield anything as exciting as what she'd unearthed in the archives, but why sit reading documents she knew by heart?

Her reluctant host was probably hours away.

* * *

'You must excuse me, Katarina. I have business to attend to.' Alaric disengaged himself from the countess's clinging grasp.

'So late? Surely there are better ways to spend the night?' Her ruby lips parted and her silvery eyes flashed a familiar message. Sexual promise, excitement and just a touch of greed. She swayed forward, her barely covered breasts straining against her ball gown, her emerald-strewn cleavage designed to draw the eye.

Acquiring lovers had always been easy for Alaric but he was tired of being targeted by women like Katarina.

His rules were simple. First, no long term commitment. Ever. Emotional intimacy, what others called love, was a mirage he knew to be dangerous and false. Second, he did the chasing.

He needed diversion but on *his* terms.

Katarina, despite her genuine sexual desire, was another who'd set her sights on marriage. Permanency. Royal prestige. Wealth. Right now he had more significant concerns than satisfying the ambitions of a grasping socialite.

'Sadly it's a meeting I can't avoid.' Over her head he caught the eye of the steward hovering at the entrance. 'Your car is here.' He lifted her hand, barely brushing it with his lips, before leading her to the door.

'I'll call you,' she whispered, her voice sultry.

Alaric smiled easily, secure in the knowledge she wouldn't get past his staff.

Five minutes later, with the last guests gone, he dismissed his personal staff and strode down the corridor, his mind returning to the recent conversation with Raul.

If anyone else had asked him to stay here, cooped up through winter, Alaric would have ignored them. The need to be out and doing something, keeping busy, was a turbulent tide rising in his blood. The idea of six more months tied to his alpine principality gave him cabin fever.

It might be home, but he felt hemmed in. Constricted. Prey to the darkness clawing from within.

Only constant action and diversion kept him from succumbing. Kept him sane.

Alaric forked a hand through his hair, impatiently flicking his cape off one shoulder. That was another thing to thank his distant cousin and soon-to-be monarch for. An evening wearing the outmoded uniform of two centuries ago.

Yet he'd given his word. He must help Raul.

After decades of peace, the recent death of the old king, Raul's father, had reignited unrest. Alaric's principality of Ruvingia was stable but elsewhere tensions that had almost led to civil war a generation ago had reopened. With careful management danger would be averted, but they couldn't take chances.

He and Raul had to ensure stability. In their nation of Maritz, clinging to monarchical traditions, that meant a calm, united front in the lead up to his cousin's coronation and the reopening of parliament.

So here Alaric was, cutting ribbons and hosting balls!

He swung into another corridor, itching for action. But this wasn't as simple as leading a commando squad to disarm combatants. There was no violence. Yet.

Alaric's belly twisted as the ghosts of the past stirred, a reminder of how suddenly tragedy could strike.

With an effort he shoved aside the lingering pain and glanced at his watch. He was miles late for his last obligation of the day. As soon as it was over he'd escape for a few hours. Take the Aston Martin over the mountain pass and try out its paces on the hairpin bends.

Alaric quickened his step at the beckoning sense of freedom, however temporary.

Another twist in the ancient passage and there was the library door. Automatically he slowed, acknowledging but not yielding to the frisson of discomfort feathering his spine.

This would never be his study, no matter what the staff expected. It was his father's room, his brother's. Alaric preferred the mobility of a laptop he could use elsewhere. Preferred not to be reminded he walked in dead men's shoes.

Too many dead men.

Fragmented images rose. At the forefront was Felix, his talented, capable, older brother.

The one who should be here instead of Alaric.

Who'd died because of Alaric.

The frisson of awareness froze into a gut-stabbing shaft of ice. Familiar guilt engulfed him. Pain tore his chest and throat with each breath.

He accepted it as inevitable. *His punishment.* The weight he would always bear.

Eventually he forced his breathing to slow and his legs to move.

The room was empty. Logs burned in the fireplace, lamps glowed but no expert waited to harangue him about the state of the archives. If the matter was so urgent surely she'd have stayed.

All the better. He could be on the open road in ten minutes.

He was turning away when a stack of papers caught his attention. A battered briefcase sagged on the floor. Immediately he was alert, his gaze narrowing.

Then he heard it, an almost imperceptible swish from above. Instincts honed on the edge of survival sharpened. He flexed his fingers. An instant later, hand on the hilt of his ceremonial sword, he faced the intruder.

For long moments he stared, then his hand fell away.

The room had been invaded by a…mushroom.

On top of the ladder fixed to the bookshelves perched a shapeless muddle of grey-brown. A long granny cardigan the colour of dust caught his eye and beneath, spread across the ladder top that now served as a seat, a voluminous grey skirt. It was a woman, though her clothes looked like something that had sprouted on a damp forest floor.

A wall sconce shone on dark hair, scraped back, and a glint of glasses above a massive book. White-gloved hands held the volume up, obscuring her face. And beneath…his gaze riveted on the rhythmic swing of a leg, bare to just above the knee.

One seriously sexy leg.

Alaric paced closer, his attention gratefully diverted from sombre remembrances.

Skin like moonlight. A shapely calf, trim ankle and neat foot. Toes that wriggled enticingly with each swing.

Masculine appreciation stirred as his gaze slid back up her leg. Even her knee looked good! Too good to be teasing a man who was restless and in desperate need of distraction.

He crossed to the base of the ladder and picked up a discarded shoe. Flat soled, plain brown, narrow and neat. Appallingly dowdy.

He raised his brows. Those legs deserved something better, assuming the one tucked beneath that horror of a skirt matched the elegant limb on show. They demanded heels. Stiletto sharp and high, to emphasise the luscious curve of her calf. Ankle straps. Ribbons, sexy enough to tease a man till he took them off and moved on to other pleasures.

Alaric shook his head. He'd bet all the jewels in the basement vault the owner of this shoe would be horrified at the extravagance of footwear designed to seduce a man.

A tingle of something dangerously like anticipation feathered his neck as he watched her leg swing and her foot arch seductively. This time the little wriggle of her toes seemed deliciously abandoned as if the drab clothes camouflaged a secret sybarite.

Alaric's mood lightened for the first time in weeks.

'Cinderella, I presume?'

The voice was deep and mellow, jolting Tamsin out of her reverie. Warily she lowered the volume enough to peer over it.

She froze, eyes widening as she took in the man gazing up at her.

He'd stepped out of a fantasy.

He couldn't be real. No flesh and blood man looked like that. So mouth-wateringly wonderful.

Numb with shock, she shook her head in automatic disbelief. He could have been Prince Charming, standing there in his elaborate hussar's uniform, her discarded shoe in one large, capable hand. A bigger, tougher Prince Charming than she remembered from her childhood reading. His dark eyebrows slashed across a tanned face that wasn't so much handsome as magnetic, charismatic, potently sexy.

Like Prince Charming's far more experienced and infinitely more dangerous older brother.

Eyes, dark and gleaming, transfixed her. They were… aware.

Meeting his unblinking regard she had the crazy notion that for the first time ever a man looked and really saw *her*. Not her reputation, not her misfit status but the real flesh and blood Tamsin Connors, the impulsive woman she'd tried so hard to stifle.

She felt vulnerable, yet thrilled.

A lazy smile lifted one corner of his mouth and a deep groove creased his cheek.

Stunned, she felt a squiggle of response deep in her abdomen. Tiny rivers of fire quivered under her skin. Her lungs squeezed her breath out in a whoosh of…of…

The book she held shut with a snap that made her jump. Instantly the other volumes in her lap slid and she grabbed for them. But they were cumbersome and she didn't dare let go of the precious herbal in her hands.

In dry mouthed horror she watched a book tumble out of her grasp. It fell in slow motion, turning over as it went. Even knowing it was too late to save the volume she scrabbled for it, barely keeping her precarious perch.

'Don't move!' The authority in his voice stopped her in mid lunge.

He strode forward a step, stretched out his hand and the book fell into his grasp as if it belonged there.

Dizzy with relief, Tamsin shut her eyes. She'd never have forgiven herself if it had been damaged.

How had he done that? The volume was no paperback. It weighed a ton. Yet he'd caught it one-handed from a fall of twelve feet as if it were feather light.

Tamsin snapped her eyes open and saw him turn to place the book on the desk. The indigo material of his tunic clung to his broad shoulder and muscled arm.

That formidable figure wasn't the result of tailored padding.

She swallowed hard, her gaze dropping to long powerful thighs encased in dark trousers. The crimson stripe down the side drew attention to the strength of those limbs.

No pretend soldier. The straight set of his shoulders and the contained power of each precise movement proclaimed him the real thing.

Abruptly he turned, as if sensing her scrutiny. His gaze pierced her and she shivered, overwhelmingly aware of him as *male*.

She worked with men all the time, but she'd never met one so undeniably masculine. As if testosterone radiated off him in waves. It made her heart race.

'Now to get you safely down.' Was that a glint of humour in his eyes?

'I'm OK.' She clutched the books like a lifeline. 'I'll put these back and—'

'No.' The single syllable stopped her. 'I'll take them.'

'I promise you I'm not usually so clumsy.' She sat straighter, annoyed at her stupidity in examining the books here instead of taking them to the desk. Normally she was methodical, logical and careful. It was no excuse that excitement had overridden her caution.

'Nevertheless, it's not worth the risk.' He walked to the foot of the ladder and looked up, his face unreadable. 'I'll relieve you of your burden first.'

Tamsin bit her lip. She couldn't blame him. She'd almost damaged a unique volume. What sort of expert took such risks? What she'd done was unforgivable.

'I'm sorry, I—'

Her words cut out as the ladder moved beneath her, a rhythmic sway as he nimbly closed the distance between them.

Tamsin became excruciatingly self-aware as his ascent slowed. Warm breath feathered her bare ankle then shivered against her calf and to her horror she couldn't repress a delicious little shudder.

A moment later a dark head appeared in the V between her splayed knees. Something hard and hot plunged down through her abdomen as she met his gaze.

From metres away this man was stunning. Up close, where she could see the twinkle lurking in midnight-blue eyes and the sensuous curve of his full lower lip, he stole her breath. Tiny lines beside his mouth and eyes spoke of experience and a grim endurance at odds with his easy humour. Yet they only accentuated his attractiveness.

Her heart beat a rapid tattoo that pulsed adrenaline through her body and robbed her of coherent thought.

'Allow me.' Large hands reached out and scooped the book from her lap, barely ruffling her skirt. Yet his heat seared through her clothing and suddenly she felt dizzy. She clutched the herbal to her breast.

Then he was gone, swarming down the ladder with an ease that spoke of supreme fitness and agility.

Tamsin drew a deep breath into constricted lungs, searching for composure. She'd never been distracted by male beauty before. She dismissed as irrelevant the knowledge that she'd never seen anyone so magnificent.

She shook her head. He's just a man, just—

'This one, too.' There he was again. She'd been so caught up in her thoughts she hadn't noticed his rapid ascent. He reached for the book in her arms.

'It's all right. I can carry it.' For suddenly, close enough to inhale his subtle spice and forest and man scent, she didn't want to relinquish the barrier between them. She clung to it like a talisman.

'We don't want to risk another accident,' he drawled in his easy, perfect English. 'Do we, Cinderella?'

'I'm not…' She stopped herself. Despite his mock serious expression there was amusement in his eyes.

Anger welled. Self-consciousness tightened her stomach. Patrick laughed at her too. All her life she'd been a misfit, a figure of speculation and amusement. She'd learned to pretend not to notice but still it hurt.

Yet this was her fault. She'd put herself in this ridiculous position because she'd been too curious to sit meekly waiting. She'd never be taken seriously now. Just when it was vital she win confidence and trust.

Had she single-handedly wrecked her chance of success?

Summoning the scraps of her dignity she unclamped stiff fingers and lowered the volume into his waiting hands.

Calloused fingers brushed hers through the thin gloves she'd donned to protect the books. An electric shock shot up her arm and across her breasts. She jerked her hands away.

Tamsin bit the inside of her cheek and looked away from his knowing gaze, her emotions too raw for comfort.

He stood still. She felt his stare, tangible as a trailing touch, move across her face to her throat then back up again. Her breathing shallowed.

She told herself she was used to being a curiosity, out of step with her peers. Stubbornly she ignored the hurt lancing her chest.

An instant later he clattered back down the ladder and she let out her breath in a sigh.

Time to climb down and face the music. She unfolded the leg tucked beneath her. Pins and needles prickled, proof she'd sat here longer than she'd realised. Gingerly she wriggled, pulling the bunched hem of her skirt down where it had rucked up. Grasping the ladder she rose, ready to turn.

His appearance before her prevented her moving.

'I need space to turn around.' Her voice was betrayingly uneven.

Instead of descending, he rose, his hands grasping the top of the ladder so his broad shoulders and powerful arms surrounded her.

Something fluttered in Tamsin's chest at the sensation of being caught within his embrace, though he didn't touch her. The force field of his presence engulfed her. It made her feel small and vulnerable and edgy.

Her breath hissed in.

His head was at breast height now. She leaned back towards the shelving, trying to put space between them.

'Whoa. Easy now.' His deep voice lowered to a soothing pitch, as if steadying a fractious animal.

'I can climb down alone.' Her words were sharper than she'd intended, betraying her embarrassment at the storm of inexplicable reactions bombarding her.

'Of course you can.' His lips pursed ruminatively, drawing her eyes. Heat washed her neck and cheeks as she stared. In a less rugged face that perfect mouth would look almost feminine. But on him those lips simply looked sensuous and dangerously inviting.

Like the deeply hooded eyes that steadily surveyed her.

Tamsin swallowed and felt her blush burn hotter. Could he read her thoughts? He must be accustomed to women gaping. The realisation didn't ease her embarrassment.

'But accidents happen and I wouldn't want you losing your footing.'

'I won't lose my footing,' she said in a horribly breathless voice.

He shrugged those wide, straight shoulders, mesmerising her with the movement. 'We hope not. But we won't take chances. Think of the insurance claim if you're injured.'

'I wouldn't—'

'Of course you wouldn't.' He rose further and she backed so her shoulders touched the bookshelf and there was nowhere else to go. 'But your permanent employer might sue for damages if you're injured due to our negligence.'

'It's not your negligence. I climbed up here.'

He shook his head. 'Anyone with an ounce of understanding would realise what temptation this ladder is to a woman who loves books. It's asking for trouble.'

Something flickered in his eyes. She was sure he was laughing but his sympathetic expression couldn't be faulted. 'It was irresponsible to leave it here, just begging to be climbed.'

He conveniently ignored the fact that the ladder was fixed top and bottom to the rails placed around the walls.

'You're talking nonsense.'

His eyebrows arched and a flash of something that might have been approval lit his eyes.

'Very probably,' he murmured. 'The tension must be getting to me. Heights can affect people like that, you know.' His lips curved up in another one of those half-smiles that melted something vital inside her. 'Take pity on my nerves and let me get you down from here.'

Tamsin opened her mouth to end his games. She refused to be the butt of his jokes. But before she could speak large hands pulled her towards him, warming her through several layers of clothing and jamming the words in her throat. For a moment panic threatened as she plunged forward, but an instant later she was draped over one solid shoulder. He clamped her close with his arm and then he was moving, descending the ladder with her firmly in his hold.

'Put me down! Let me go, *right now!*' She couldn't believe he'd grabbed her.

'Of course. In just a moment.'

To her horror Tamsin *felt* his deep voice rumble through his torso and hers.

Tamsin shut her eyes rather than look at the distant floor, or, more disturbingly, the intriguing sight of muscles bunching in the taut backside inches from her face.

But closing her eyes heightened other senses. She felt him against the length of her body, his strength undeniably exciting as ripples of movement teased her breasts and thighs. Disturbing warmth swirled languidly in the pit of her stomach.

She shouldn't be enjoying this. She should be outraged. Or at least impervious. She should…

'There.' He lowered her into a chair and stepped back. 'Safe and sound.'

His eyes weren't laughing now. They were sober as he stared down at her. His mouth was a firm line, his brows tipped into a slight frown as if the joke had turned sour. His jaw clamped hard and she had the fleeting impression he was annoyed rather than amused.

Tamsin wanted desperately to conjure a witty quip. To redeem herself as clever and insouciant, taking the situation in her stride.

Instead she gazed helplessly, enmeshed in a web of unfamiliar reactions. Her breasts tingled from contact with him, her nipples puckering shamelessly. Her thighs were warm from his touch. Her gaze caught on his black hair, now slightly rumpled. Heat sizzled inside like a firecracker about to explode.

It wasn't the sexy cavalry uniform that made him look so good, despite the gilt braiding that moulded his tapering torso, the cut of clothes that made him look every inch the fairy tale hero. What unnerved her was the flesh and blood man whose shadowed eyes glowed like an invitation to sin.

She tried to tell herself he was vain enough to have a uniform designed to enhance the incredible colour of his eyes. But the gravity of his expression when he wasn't smiling told her he didn't give a toss for his looks.

Tamsin's breath sawed as he dropped to one knee and took her bare foot in his hand. Tremors rippled up her leg and she felt again that strange molten sensation pooling low in her belly.

She squirmed but he didn't release her. Instead he fished something out of his pocket and slid it onto her foot. Soft, worn familiar leather. Her discarded shoe.

'So, Cinderella. Why did you want to see me?'

Tamsin's pulse faltered. For the last ten minutes she'd pretended he was a guest, even a member of staff. Yet deep inside she'd known who he was.

Prince Alaric. The man who held her career and her reputation in his hands.

Already she amused him. How he'd laugh if he knew that in ten minutes, without trying, he'd seduced one of Britain's last dyed in the wool virgins to mindless longing.

Tamsin swallowed convulsively. She shot to her feet and stepped away, busying herself by stripping off her gloves and stuffing them in a pocket.

'It's about the archives I'm cataloguing and assessing for conservation.' A cache of documents recently discovered when a castle cellar had been remodelled.

She turned. He stood by the chair, frowning in abstraction. Tamsin lifted her chin, breathing deep.

'They include some unique and valuable papers.'

'I'm sure they do.' He nodded, his expression blandly polite. Obviously he had no interest in her efforts.

'I have a copy of one with me.' She reached for her briefcase, grateful for an excuse to look away from his hooded gaze.

'Why don't you just tell me about it?'

Cut to the chase, in other words.

He'd had plenty of time to dally, amusing himself at her expense, but none to spare for her work.

Disappointment curled through her, and annoyance.

'One of the documents caught my attention. It's a record of your family and Prince Raul's.' She paused, excitement at her find bubbling up despite her vexation.

'There's still work to be done on it.' Tamsin paused, keeping her voice carefully even. 'I've been translating from the Latin and, if it's proved correct…'

'Yes? If it's proved correct?'

Tamsin hesitated, but there was no easy way to say it. Besides, he'd surely welcome the news.

'If it's genuine you're not only Prince of Ruvingia, you're also the next legitimate ruler of Maritz. Of the whole country. Not Prince Raul.' She paused, watching his expression freeze.

'It's you who should be crowned king.'

CHAPTER TWO

ALARIC'S body stiffened as her words sank in with terrible, nightmare clarity.

Him as ruler of Maritz!

The idea was appalling.

Raul was the crown prince. The one brought up from birth to rule. The one trained and ready to dedicate his life to his country.

Maritz needed him.

Or a man like Alaric's brother, Felix.

Alaric wasn't in the same mould. Even now he heard his father's cool, clipped voice expressing endless displeasure and disappointment with his reckless second son.

Alaric's lips twisted. How right the old man had been. Alaric couldn't take responsibility for the country. Bad enough he'd stepped into Felix's shoes as leader of a principality. Entrusting the wellbeing of the whole nation to his keeping would be disaster.

He, whose conscience was heavy with the weight of others' lives! Who'd failed them so abysmally.

Horror crawled up his spine to clamp his shoulders. Ice froze his blood. Familiar faces swam in his vision, faces distorted with pain. The faces of those he'd failed. The face of his brother, eyes feverish as he berated Alaric for betraying him.

He couldn't be king. It was unthinkable.

'Is this a joke?' The words shot out, harsh in the silence.

'Of course not!'

No. One look at her frown and her stunned eyes made that clear. Tamsin Connors wasn't kidding.

He'd never seen a more serious, buttoned-up woman. From her tense lips to her heavy-framed glasses and scraped-back hair, she was the image of no-nonsense spinsterhood.

Except for that body.

Hard to believe she'd felt so warm and lithely curved. Or that holding her he'd known a curious desire to strip away that fashion crime of an outfit and explore her scented femininity. A desire completely dormant in the face of so many blatant sexual invitations from tonight's beauties!

Beneath her bag lady clothes Tamsin Connors was only in her mid-twenties. When she forgot to prim them her lips were surprisingly luscious. He looked into her frowning face and knew he was avoiding the issue. The impossible issue of him being king!

'What exactly is in these papers?' His voice sounded rusty, as if his vocal cords had seized up.

'They're old records by a cleric called Tomas. He detailed royal history, especially births, deaths and marriages.' She shifted, leaning imperceptibly closer.

Did he imagine her fresh sunshine scent, warm in a room chilled with the remembrance of death?

With an effort he dragged his focus back to her.

'Take a seat, please, and explain.' He gestured to one of the armchairs by the fire then took one for himself.

'According to Tomas there was intermarriage between your family and Prince Raul's.'

Alaric nodded. 'That was common practice.' Power was guarded through alliances with other aristocratic families.

'At one stage there was a gap in the direct line to the Maritzian throne. The crown couldn't pass from father to son as the king's son had died.'

Her words flayed a raw spot deep inside him. A familiar glacial chill burned Alaric's gut. The knowledge he was a usurper in a better man's shoes.

That he was responsible for his brother's death.

'There were two contenders for the throne. One from Prince Raul's family and...' Her words slowed as she registered his expression. Some of her enthusiasm faded.

'And one from mine?'

She shifted as if uncomfortable, but continued.

Two rival princes from different branches of intertwined families. A will from the old king designating one, the eldest by some weeks, as his successor. A tragic 'accident' leading to the accession of the alternate heir and a desperate decision by the dead prince's widow to send her newborn son to safety far away. The suppression of the old king's will and a rewriting of birth dates to shore up the new monarch's claim to the throne.

It was a tale of treachery and the ruthless pursuit of power. But in his country's turbulent history, definitely possible.

How was it possible she'd found such a contentious document?

The likelihood was staggeringly remote. For centuries historians had plotted the family trees of the royal families in each of the neighbouring principalities.

Yet her earnestness, her straight-backed confidence caught his attention.

Obviously she'd found something. This woman was no one's fool, despite her up-tight demeanour. He remembered reading her CV when she had been recommended for the job of assessing and preserving the archives. Multiple qualifications. Glowing references. Her first degree in her teens and a formidable amount of experience since then.

It was tempting to believe this was a mistake, that she'd jumped to the wrong conclusion. Yet she didn't strike him as a woman prone to taking risks.

'You're not pleased?' she ventured, her brows puckering. 'I know it's a shock but—'

'But you thought I'd be thrilled to become king?' His words were clipped as he strove to suppress a surge of unfamiliar panic. He had to fight the rising nausea that clogged his throat.

He shook his head. 'I'm loyal to my cousin, Dr Connors. He will make the sort of king our country needs.'

Alaric succeeding in his place would be a nightmare made real.

Hell! The timing couldn't be worse. The country needed stability. If this was true…

'Who else have you told?' Alaric found himself on his feet, towering above her with his hands clamped on her chair arms. She shrank back as he leaned close.

In the flickering firelight she looked suddenly vulnerable and very young.

The pounding thud of his heartbeat slowed and he straightened, giving her space.

No need to intimidate the woman. Yet.

'I haven't told anyone.' Wide eyes stared at him from behind those ugly glasses and a twist of something like awareness coiled in his belly. 'I had to tell you first.'

The tension banding his chest eased and he breathed deep. 'Good. You did the right thing.'

Tentatively she smiled and he felt a tremor of guilt at having scared her. Even now one hand pressed to her breast as if her heart raced. He followed the rapid rise and fall of her chest. An unexpected trickle of fire threaded his belly as he recalled her feminine softness against him.

'When I get the test results back we'll know if the papers are what they seem to be.'

'Results?' He stilled. 'What tests are these?'

'There are several,' she said slowly, her expression wary. Alaric thrust his hand through his hair, fighting the impulse to demand she explain instantly.

Instead he took another deliberate step away from her and laid his forearm along the mantelpiece. Immediately the tension in her slim frame eased.

'Would you care to enlighten me?'

She blinked and blushed and for a moment Alaric was sidetracked by the softening of her lips as they formed an O of surprise. She looked charmingly female and innocently flustered in a way that threatened to distract him.

An instant later she was brisk and businesslike. 'I've sent pages for testing. We need to know if the parchment is as old as it appears. That it's not a modern forgery.'

She'd sent papers away? Who had them now? This got worse and worse.

'Plus the style of the text is unusual. I've sent copies of some pages to a colleague for verification.'

'Who gave you permission to do this?' His voice was calm, low, but with the razor edge honed on emergency decisions made under fire.

She jerked her head up, her body stiffening.

'I was told when I started that, so long as the usual precautions were taken, testing of documents found in the archives was allowed.'

'If you're right these aren't just any documents!' His hands fisted. Had she no notion of the powder keg she may have uncovered?

'That's why I was particularly careful.' She shot to her feet, hands clasped before her; chin lifted as she met his gaze. 'None of the pages I sent for testing were, by themselves, sensitive.' She paused then continued with slow emphasis. 'I realise this information must be kept confidential until it's confirmed. I followed the protocols set out when I took on the job.'

Alaric let out a slow breath. 'And if someone put those pages together?'

'No.' She shook her head then paused, frowning. 'It's not possible.' Yet she didn't look so certain.

Alaric determined to get his hands on the pages as soon as possible.

'It would have been better to keep this in house.' Even if it turned out this was a mistake, rumour could destabilise a delicate situation.

Fine eyebrows arched high on her pale forehead.

'Ruvingia doesn't have the capacity "in house" to run such tests.' She paused and he watched her drag in quick breaths, obviously battling strong emotion.

'I apologise if I've overstepped the mark.' Her tone said he was being unreasonable. 'I would have checked with you earlier but it's been hard getting an appointment.'

Touché. Meeting to discuss the royal archives hadn't been on his priorities.

'How long before you get the results?'

She launched into detail of how the document would be authenticated, her face growing animated. All the while he was busy reckoning the risks posed by this discovery. The need to verify her findings and keep the situation under wraps.

Yet he found himself watching her closely as she shed that shell of spiky reserve. There was a fire in her that had been lacking before. Or had it been hidden behind her starchy demeanour?

Despite the gravity of the situation, something in Alaric that was all male, functioning at the most primitive level, stirred.

Behind her dowdy appearance he sensed heat and passion in this woman.

He'd always been attracted by passion.

Alaric wrenched his mind back to the problem at hand.

'A short wait, then, before the results come through. In the meantime, who has access to this chronicle?'

'Only me. The assistant from your national museum is working on other material.'

'Good. We'll keep it that way.' Alaric would personally arrange for it to be kept under lock and key.

'I'm also keeping my eyes open for other papers that might confirm or disprove what I've found. There's still a lot to investigate.'

There could be more? Even if this document conveniently disappeared there might be others?

Damn. A simple solution had been tempting. An accident to destroy the evidence and remove the problem. Yet it would only make precautions around the remaining documents tighter and subsequent accidents more suspicious.

Self-knowledge warred with duty. The former told him the country would be better off in his cousin Raul's hands. The latter urged Alaric to face his responsibility no matter how unpalatable.

He speared a hand through his hair and paced, his belly churning. In thirty years he'd never shirked his duty, no matter how painful.

He'd warn Raul. They'd develop a contingency plan and make a discreet enquiry of the royal genealogist, a historian known for his expertise and discretion. Alaric needed to know if this far-fetched story was even possible.

Genuine or not, the papers were dynamite. If spare copies existed, and if Tamsin Connors was the innocent, earnest professional she appeared, he needed her onside.

If she was what she appeared.

Was it possible forged papers had been planted for her to find and disrupt Raul's coronation? Unlikely. Yet how convenient she'd found them after just a couple of weeks.

Too convenient?

He narrowed his gaze, taking in her heavy-framed glasses and appalling clothes. The way her gaze continually slipped away from his.

His gut tightened at the idea she was hiding something. A link to those stirring discontent? It was preposterous, but so was this situation.

He'd get to the bottom of it soon.

Meanwhile Tamsin Connors had his undivided attention.

'Of course, I understand,' Tamsin murmured into the phone.

She should be disappointed by the news she'd received. She *was* disappointed, but she was distracted by the man prowling the confines of the workroom. His long stride gave an impression of controlled impatience, at odds with his meticulous interest in every detail.

Intently she watched every move, miserably aware Prince Alaric didn't need a splendid uniform to show off his physique. In dark trousers, plain T-shirt and a jacket, he was compelling in the afternoon light.

Until last night she hadn't known she had a weakness for tall broad-shouldered men who looked like they could take on the world. For men whose eyes laughed one minute and clouded with grim emotion the next as if he saw things no man should.

She'd thought she preferred men driven by academic pursuits, preferably fresh faced and blond, like Patrick. Not sizzling with barely suppressed physical energy.

How wrong she'd been.

Her skin drew tight, every nerve end buzzing, as he paced.

'Thank you for calling. I appreciate it.' Carefully she put the phone down.

'A problem?' He approached, eyes watchful.

Tamsin dragged in a breath and placed her hands on the desk. She'd prayed her reaction last night had been an aberration. But seeing him in the flesh again scotched every hope that she'd imagined her response to his potent masculinity. His vitality, that sense of power and capability, were as fascinating as his stunning looks.

With his black hair, midnight-blue eyes, high-cut cheekbones and strong nose, he looked every inch the powerful aristocrat. Yet his mouth was that of a seducer: warm, provocative and sensual.

Tamsin blinked. Where had that come from?

'Dr Connors?'

'Sorry. I was…thinking.' Frantically she tried to focus. 'I've just heard the date test will be delayed.'

He frowned and she hurried on. 'I'd hoped for an early result on the age of the parchment but it will take longer than I'd hoped.'

The reasons she'd just been given were plausible. But the embarrassed way Patrick's assistant repeated herself made Tamsin suspicious.

Wasn't it enough Patrick had stolen the job that was by rights Tamsin's? He'd been the first man to show any interest in her, cruelly using her naïve crush to string her along. All those extra hours she'd put in helping him and he'd passed her work off as his own. He'd been promoted on the basis of it then dumped her unceremoniously. Pride had stopped her revealing his duplicity and her own lack of judgement. Instead she'd withdrawn even further into herself, nursing a bruised heart and vowing never to risk it again so readily.

Was he low enough to stymie this project, too?

Once it would never have occurred to her. Now she wondered if the whisper she'd heard was right and he saw her as a professional threat.

Would he really let ego get in the way of scientific research? The idea sickened her. How had she not seen his true character?

'They're returning the papers?' The prince's eyes sparked indigo fire and she watched, fascinated.

'Not yet. Hopefully it won't be a long delay.'

Tamsin watched his mouth compress. He was impatient. Despite what he'd said last night, he must be excited at the possibility of becoming king. Who wouldn't be?

'These are the rest of the newly found documents?' He gestured to the storage down one side of the long room.

'A lot of them. Some of the less fragile ones we've left until we can assess them properly.'

'Yet there may be more sensitive papers among them?'

'Possibly. But not many people would be able to read them. Even with my expertise, some of the texts are hard to decipher. It's time consuming and difficult.'

'That doesn't matter. We need secure storage for them all.' He strode restlessly down the room, assessing the set-up. Despite her intentions she followed every step, drinking in the sight of his powerful body. 'I want you to calculate exactly what you need and tell me today. They'll be locked with access only on my approval.'

Tamsin shook her head. 'It's not just a matter of space, it's about a properly regulated environment and—'

'I understand. Just let me know and it will be done.'

'It will be expensive.'

The prince waved a dismissive hand. He was notoriously wealthy. Money was no object now his self-interest was engaged.

Tamsin strove to stifle a pang of disappointment, recalling how her work had been virtually ignored earlier. She supposed his proprietorial attitude was justified. After all they were talking about proof of kingship. And if it meant proper care for the archives, all the better.

She stood. 'In the meantime, could I have the text to work on? I'll translate some more this evening.'

Late last night, after hearing her news, the prince had insisted on accompanying her here to see the original document. Then, without warning, and despite her protest, he'd taken it away. It worried her that he didn't fully appreciate how fragile it was.

'Certainly.' He glanced at his watch, obviously eager to be elsewhere. 'But not today—it's late.'

'But—'

He crossed the room to stand close, too close. She felt his heat, inhaled the spicy clean scent of his skin and wished she were still sitting.

'But nothing. I gather you've done little except work since you arrived. By your own admission this is taxing work.' He looked down at her with eyes that sparkled and a tremor rippled down her legs. Desperately she locked her knees, standing straighter.

'I'm not a slave driver and I don't want you making yourself ill working all hours.'

'But I want to!' What else did she have to do with her evenings?

He shook his head. 'Not tonight.' He turned and headed for the door, pausing on the threshold. 'If you could send me those storage requirements…'

'I'll see to it straight away.'

He inclined his head and left. Tamsin stood, swaying slightly and staring at the place where he'd been.

She'd hoped to spark his interest with her discovery. She hadn't thought to be sidelined in the process.

Sternly she told herself that wasn't what he'd done. She was allowing her experiences with one deceitful, good looking man to colour her judgement.

It was good of Prince Alaric to be concerned for her welfare. It was sensible that he took an interest in storing the documents properly.

So why did it feel like she was being outmanoeuvred?

Mid-evening Alaric headed for the gym on the far side of the castle compound. He needed to work off this pent up energy. His sleep patterns were shot anyway, but last night Tamsin Connors had obliterated any chance of rest.

The genealogist had warned today that proving or disproving a claim to the throne took time. Alaric wanted it sorted, and preferably disproved, *now*. It went against the grain to wait, dependent on forces beyond his control.

Plus, infuriatingly, his investigators had turned up little on the Englishwoman.

Surely no one had such a straightforward past? They'd reported on her academic achievements, her reputation for hard work and a little on her quiet childhood with elderly parents. But nothing about boyfriends. Any friends for that matter. Only an unconfirmed hint of some affair with a colleague.

In other circumstances he'd take her at face value: a quiet, dedicated professional. But he couldn't take chances. Not till he knew she was what she seemed.

She *seemed* too innocent to be believed.

He slowed as he passed the viewing level for the squash court. Lights were on and he paused to see which of the staff were playing.

There was only one. A woman, lithe and agile as she smashed the ball around the court in robust practice.

Alaric frowned, momentarily unable to place her. She lunged, twisting, to chase a low ball and for a moment her breasts strained against her oversized T-shirt. An instant later she pivoted on long legs with an agility he couldn't help but applaud.

His eyes lingered on the shapely length of those legs below baggy shorts. A sizzle of lazy heat ignited inside and he smiled appreciatively.

There was an age old remedy for insomnia, one he used regularly. A pretty woman and—

She spun round and a spike of heat drove through Alaric's torso, shearing off his breath.

He tensed instantaneously, hormones in overdrive.

It was Tamsin Connors. Yet not.

He should have guessed it was her, in those ill-fitting outfits. Yet she looked so different.

His mouth dried as he registered the amount of bare skin on view. Skin flushed pink and enticing from exertion. She really did have the most delicious legs. When that shirt twisted he realised her breasts were fuller than he'd guessed in her granny clothes. Her hair was soft around her face, escaping a glossy ponytail that swung like a sexy invitation to touch every time she moved. She breathed hard through her mouth, her lips not primmed any more, but surprisingly lush. Her eyes glittered—

Her eyes! No glasses.

Suspicion flared as he saw her face unmarred by ugly glasses. Maybe she wore contact lenses? But why hide the rest of the time behind disfiguring frames?

Had she tried to disguise herself? She'd done a remarkable job, concealing the desirable woman beneath a drab exterior and prickly professionalism.

Why? What had she to hide?

It was as if she deliberately tried to look like an absent-minded academic, absorbed in books rather than the world around her. She seemed too honest and serious to deceive. Yet instinct niggled, convincing him this was deliberate camouflage.

Alaric catapulted down the nearby stairs. On a bench beside the door to the court were an ugly cardigan and a case for glasses.

He flipped the latter open and held the glasses up to his face. Realisation corkscrewed through him and he swore under his breath. They gave only minuscule magnification.

Why did she wear them?

This time suspicion was a sharp, insistent jab. She was a stranger, in disguise. What a coincidence that she'd uncovered papers that could shatter the peace of the nation.

Tamsin Connors wasn't what she seemed. Was she part of a plot? An innocent dupe?

He'd just put the glasses down when she emerged.

Her thickly lashed eyes widened to bright dazzling amber, snaring his breath despite his anger. Amazing what those glasses had obscured. Her lips rounded in a soft pout of surprise and instantly fire exploded in his belly.

Slowly she approached.

Conflicting messages bombarded his brain. Caution. Distrust. Curiosity. Lust. *Definitely lust.*

His jaw hardened as he reined in that surge of hunger. This was no time to let his libido override his brain.

One thing was for certain. He wasn't going to let Tamsin Connors out of his sight till he got to the bottom of this. Already a plan formed in his head.

He smiled slowly in anticipation.

He and Dr Connors were about to become much more intimately acquainted.

CHAPTER THREE

TAMSIN'S steps faltered.

This man had invaded her thoughts, even haunted her dreams last night. Yet she'd forgotten how overwhelming he was in person.

So big. So vibrant. So powerfully *male*.

The air seemed to swirl and tickle her sensitised flesh as he subjected her to a short, all-encompassing survey. Heat blazed in her stomach and her skin tightened.

His eyes glittered and his mouth curved in welcome and her heart danced faster than it had on the squash court.

Would he look so welcoming if he knew she'd exhausted herself trying desperately to banish him from her thoughts? That she felt *excited* by his presence?

No. He paid her salary while she worked on loan here. He was her employer, an aristocrat living a glamorous, privileged life. A man with no interest in her or her work except that it made him eligible for the crown.

He'd be horrified by her reaction to him.

Even now her befuddled brain told her his smile wasn't a simple welcome. That it signified a deeper level of pleasure, a hint of danger. The sort of danger a sensible woman would ignore.

See? Her instincts were awry. She couldn't trust them.

Quickly she looked away, scared he'd read her thoughts. Patrick had read her longings like a book. She couldn't bear to reveal her weakness to this man, too.

The fact that she felt any weakness at all after the events of the last six months astounded her.

'Dr Connors.' His deep voice rippled like ruched velvet across her skin. She shivered, unable to suppress voluptuous pleasure at the sound.

Seeking distraction she reached for her cardigan and glasses, holding them close to her heaving chest.

'I hope you don't mind me using the court,' she murmured. 'Your steward said I could but I hadn't realised you might...'

'Of course I don't mind. It's good to see it in use. If I'd known you played I'd have invited you to a match.'

Startled, Tamsin looked up, straight into clear indigo depths that seemed warm and inviting.

He looked serious!

Her gaze strayed across muscled shoulders, down to the deep curve of a solid chest outlined against a black cotton T-shirt. She swallowed, her mouth drying at the latent power of him. His arms, tanned and strong, reminded her of the way he'd hoisted her over his shoulder as if she weighed nothing. Of how, despite her outrage, she'd revelled in his effortless he-man act.

He looked mouth-wateringly good in gym gear. As good as in uniform! It wasn't fair.

She stepped back, her eyes flicking away nervously.

'I don't think I'd be in your league.' Fervently she hoped he'd put her breathlessness down to her workout.

'I watched you play. You're quick and agile and know how to use your body.' His smile changed, became almost intimate, sending tendrils of heat winding around her internal organs. 'I'm sure we'd be very well matched.'

Tamsin's mind filled with an image of them matched in another way altogether. Tanned skin against pale. Hard masculine muscle against female softness.

Heat exploded, scalding her throat and face at the lurid, unfamiliar picture. Horrified, she ducked her head to fumble with her glasses case.

He couldn't know what she was thinking.

That didn't stop her embarrassment.

'It's kind of you to say so,' she mumbled. 'But we both know it would be an uneven match.'

She cast a furtive glance at his muscled arms and wished he'd cover himself up. It was hard not to stare.

'You underestimate yourself, Dr Connors.' His words sliced through her thoughts. 'Why is that? You struck me as a very confident woman when we discussed your work.'

Confident? She'd talked too much last night as they'd visited the archives. Nerves and guilt about the risks she'd taken with his books in the library had made her overcompensate. Anxiety had made her garrulous.

'That's different.' Reluctantly she lifted her chin and met his gaze. Even braced for the impact, the connection sent shock waves of pleasure racing through her. 'I've worked hard to develop my expertise. My work is what I'm good at. What I love.'

Tamsin had buried herself in work for years. At first because immersing herself in books had been an escape in her lonely childhood. Then from habit, especially as a student, when her age had set her apart from older colleagues. More recently it had been easier to be a workaholic than cultivate a personal life. She shivered. Her one foray into romance had been disastrous.

She waved a hand at the court. 'I lead a sedentary life. This is just a way to keep fit.' And a welcome outlet for troubled emotions.

He tilted his head, his gaze shrewd. 'Yet your focus was impressive. And your speed. You'd be a formidable opponent.'

The lazy approval was gone from his face, replaced by a seriousness that made her still.

Like last night Tamsin again had the suspicion he saw *her*: not just her academic reputation, but *whole*, talents and doubts, confidence and uncertainties. Saw the real person.

The notion thrilled yet made her feel oddly vulnerable.

She shoved an arm into her cardigan, pulled it round and slid her other arm in. Its familiarity steadied her, a reminder of her everyday world, devoid of handsome princes with dark chocolate voices.

She opened the case in her hands to take out her glasses. She felt naked meeting his scrutiny without them. But the sudden intensity of his stare arrested her. She closed the case with a snap.

'Hardly formidable, Your Highness. But thank you for the compliment.'

She made to turn away then stopped. This might be her only chance to talk to him. After today he'd probably be as elusive as before.

Steadfastly Tamsin ignored a sudden pang of disappointment. They had nothing in common. What did it matter if she never saw him again?

'Tomorrow, could I work on the text again? I'm eager to make more progress.'

'I'm sure you are.' Yet there was no answering enthusiasm in his face. If he was excited about the possibility of becoming monarch he hid it. His expression was flinty.

Had she said something wrong?

Finally he nodded. 'It will be brought to you tomorrow so you can pursue your…investigations.'

Tamsin sat absorbed, one bare foot tucked beneath her.

The more she delved into this manuscript, the more it fascinated. The choice of words, the phrasing, it was unique, even without the bombshell revelation that generations ago the wrong heir had become king. The intricate detail about life at court was incredible.

Take this word. She tilted her lamp to better view the idiosyncratic spelling. It should mean…

She paused, frowning as her thoughts strayed.

There was no sound, no movement on the periphery of her vision. Yet suddenly her focus was shot. The hairs on her arms prickled in atavistic awareness. Did she imagine a change in the atmosphere?

Tamsin focused again, trying to fathom the meaning of a convoluted sentence. Yet the more she tried to concentrate the more aware she became of…something else.

Finally in exasperation she looked up. And saw him.

The overhead lights were on against the fading afternoon. He stood under one, his black hair glossy in the spill of light. He was motionless, feet apart and hands in pockets in a masculine stance that reinforced the air of tough capability she'd noticed from the first.

Her heart throbbed an agitated tattoo. How long had he silently watched her? Why did he look so grim?

More than that, she wondered, as she sat back in her seat, what was he doing here?

'You've been working since seven-thirty this morning and you barely paused for lunch.' He dragged his hands from his pockets and approached. 'It's time you stopped.'

Tamsin frowned. 'You're keeping tabs on me?' She didn't feel indignant. She was too busy grappling with surprise.

He shrugged those superb shoulders and she stifled rising awareness. 'My staff have upped security given the importance of your find. I asked them to keep me informed.'

Informed of her meal breaks? Surely he had more on his mind than that? She opened her mouth to question him.

'You're translating?' He leaned over, one broad hand on the desk just inches from the manuscript.

Unaccountably heat washed her as she stared at his long fingers splayed close to hers. His masculine scent made her draw a deep, appreciative breath.

'Yes.' She sat straighter. 'It's a fascinating document, even apart from the succession issue.' She looked at the closely written text but all her attention was on the man who'd casually invaded her space.

'And now you've finished for the day.'

For a long moment Tamsin debated. It wasn't a question. She could contradict him and stay, working on the translation. Normally she worked much later. Yet her concentration had shattered. She found herself stretching, cramped muscles easing as she moved.

'Yes. I've finished.' She shoved her chair back and stood, busying herself packing up. By rights she should feel less over-

awed by him now she was on her feet. Instead, she inhaled his
fresh scent as he leaned close and became aware of the way his
body hemmed her in. It made her edgy.

'Good. You're free to come out.'

'Out?' Her brow knitted.

'How long since you left the castle?'

'I…' There had been her walk down to the river a few days
ago. Or had it been a week? She'd been too busy to count days.
'I've been occupied lately.'

'As I thought.' He nodded. 'Come on. Pack that up.'

'I'm perfectly capable of getting fresh air myself.'

Eyes of dark sapphire held hers as he leaned across the
desk. 'I'm sure you are. You're a most capable woman, Dr
Connors.'

His mouth kicked up in a smile that lit his face and made her
suck in her breath. The way he spoke her name, using her formal
title as if it were an endearment, made her ridiculously flushed.

A warning bell clanged crazily in her head.

'Why are you here?' She braced her hands on the desk rather
than lean towards that stunning smile. 'What do you want?'

She was no bedazzled fool, no matter how her pulse pattered
out of control and illicit excitement shimmied along her backbone. Men like Prince Alaric didn't waste time on women like
her. Women who weren't glamorous or sexy. She'd learned the
hard way where she stood with the opposite sex and she wasn't
making that mistake again.

'You don't pull your punches. I like your bluntness.'

Did he have any idea how gorgeous he looked, with laughter
lines crinkling from his eyes and that conspiratorial grin turning
rakishly handsome into devastatingly irresistible?

No wonder he had a reputation as a rogue. He'd only have to
ask to get anything he wanted from a woman. The knowledge
shored up her sagging defences.

She turned away to slip her notebook into a drawer.

'I do want something. I have a proposition for you.' She
looked up, startled, and he raised a hand before she could inter-

rupt. 'But not here. It's late. You need a break and I need to eat.
I'll show you some of our Ruvingian hospitality and we can
discuss it after we've eaten.'

Instinct warned her something was amiss. There was no reason
for a prince to take an employee to dine. Yet the sparkle in his
eyes invited her to forget her misgivings and take a chance.

Curiosity gnawed. What sort of proposition? Something to
do with the archives?

'If you'd like someone to vouch for me…' he began.

Her lips twitched. 'Thank you, but no.'

Despite his easy charm there was a tension about his jaw that
hinted at serious intent. Maybe what he had to say was important
after all, not just a whim.

'Some fresh air would be welcome. And some food.' Suddenly
she realised how hungry she was.

'Excellent.' He stepped back and the fragile sense of intimacy
splintered. 'Wear warm clothes and comfortable shoes. I'll meet
you by the garages in twenty minutes.'

'I'll see to this.' But as she reached for the text he pulled
cotton gloves from his pocket and picked it up.

'I'll take care of that. You go and get ready.'

He didn't trust her to keep the chronicle safe. Last night he'd
taken it away, saying he wanted it locked up. Disappointment
was a plunging sensation inside her.

If he didn't trust her with that, how could he trust her to do
her job? And why would he have a proposition?

Tamsin felt completely out of place in the luxurious, low-slung
car as it purred out of the cobbled courtyard and over the bridge
that connected the castle with the steep mountain spur. A last
glimpse of the castle, a floodlit fantasy with its beautiful, soaring
towers, reinforced her sense of unreality. She slid her fingers over
the soft leather upholstery, eyes wide as she took in the state of
the art controls. She'd never been in a car like this.

Or spent time alone with a man like Prince Alaric.

In the confines of the vehicle he was impossible to ignore. So
big and vital. Electricity charged the air so it buzzed and snapped.
It was hard to breathe.

She told herself lack of food made her light-headed. She should have eaten lunch instead of skimping on an apple.

He nosed the car down a series of swooping bends and she risked a sideways look. A smile played around his mouth as if an icy road after dusk was just what he loved. His powerful hands moved easily on the wheel, with a fluid sureness that hinted he enjoyed tactile pleasures.

Tamsin shivered as an unfamiliar yearning hit her.

'You're cold?' He didn't take his eyes off the road. How had he sensed the trawling chill that raked her spine?

'No, I'm warm as toast.'

'So it's the road that bothers you.' Before she could answer he eased his foot onto the brake.

It was on the tip of her tongue to protest. He hadn't been speeding. She'd enjoyed the thrill of the descent, instinctively sensing she was safe with such a capable driver. Disappointment rose as they took the next bend at a decorous pace but she didn't contradict him. She didn't want to try explaining the curious feelings that bombarded her when she was with him.

'What's this proposition you have for me?'

He shook his head, not looking away from the road as it curved one final time then disappeared like a dark ribbon into the forest at the foot of the mountain. 'Not yet. Not till we've eaten.'

Tamsin tamped down her impatience, realising her companion had no intention of being swayed. For all his light-hearted charm she sensed he could be as immoveable as the rock on which his castle perched.

'Tell me why you took this position. Being cooped up here in the dead of winter hasn't got much to recommend it.'

Was he kidding? Tamsin slanted another glance his way and saw nothing but curiosity in his expression.

'The place is beautiful. Its heritage listed for outstanding scenic and cultural significance.'

'But you've barely been out of the castle.'

Tamsin stiffened. Had his staff been reporting her movements? Why? The unsettling discovery didn't sit well with the sense of freedom she'd enjoyed.

'I'd planned to explore. But once I got engrossed in my work and found Tomas's chronicle, I never found time.'

'You came to Ruvingia for the views?' Disbelief edged his tone.

'Hardly.' Though the picturesque setting was a bonus. 'It was the work that fascinated me.'

'You don't mind spending an alpine winter so far from family and friends?'

Tamsin looked away, to the dark forest crowding close. She was grateful for the heating which dispelled any chill. 'My parents were the first to urge me to apply. They know how important my work is to me.'

They didn't care about her not being home for the festive season. As far as her father, a single-minded academic, was concerned the holidays were simply a nuisance that closed the university libraries. Her mother, wrapped up in her art, found it easier catering for two than three. Theirs was a distant kind of caring. They were dedicated to their work and Tamsin, an unexpected child after years of marriage, had fitted between the demands of their real interests. She'd grown self-sufficient early, a dreamer losing herself in a world of books.

'What about your friends? Surely you'd rather be with them at this time of year?' He probed the sore point, making her want to shrink inside herself.

Tamsin had friends, but none were particularly close.

Except Patrick. She'd expected to see a lot of him over the holidays. Had expected their relationship to blossom into something wonderful.

Before she'd discovered what a gullible idiot she'd been.

She turned to find Prince Alaric watching her closely. In the dim interior light she sensed an intensity to his stare that surprised her. Why did this interest him so?

'You don't understand how exciting this job is.' With an effort she pinned on a bright smile. 'A previously unknown hoard of documents. The opportunity to be of real value, preserving what might otherwise be lost. Not to mention the excitement of discovery. The chance to...' She hesitated, unwilling to reveal how important this job was at a more personal level.

This had been an escape route she'd gratefully seized. She couldn't bear Patrick gloating over his success and sneering at her naivety. Plus there'd been her colleagues' pitying looks.

It was also an opportunity to shore up her battered self-esteem. To prove that despite her appalling lapse of judgement with Patrick, she was good at what she did. Even, she admitted now, to show those who'd doubted her abilities they'd made a mistake promoting Patrick instead of her. His work was inferior but he had the charm to make the most of every opportunity. They'd soon realise their mistake but Tamsin wouldn't be human if she didn't want to banish her growing self-doubts with a coup of her own.

'The chance to…?'

Tamsin dragged herself back to the conversation. What had she been saying? 'The chance to be part of this exciting discovery. It's a once in a lifetime opportunity.'

'But you can't have known that when you applied for the job.' His riposte was lightning fast. He speared her with a penetrating look before turning back to the road.

'No, but I…'

She couldn't tell him how desperately she'd needed to escape. Escape Patrick lording his new position over her; Patrick with his old girlfriend on his arm again. Her forlorn heart had shredded whenever she'd seen them.

'I wanted a change. This sounded too good to miss.' She sounded stilted, falsely bright, but she wasn't about to bare her soul.

'Too good to be true, in fact.' His voice deepened on a curiously rough note. In the streetlights of the town they'd entered he looked stern.

Had he grown bored? He was probably used to more scintillating conversation. Tamsin was more than happy to change the subject.

'Where are we going?' They were in the old town, where roads narrowed and cobblestones glistened. Lights were strung between lampposts, giving the streets a festive air as pedestrians strolled, looking at decorated shop windows.

Tamsin wished she could be one of them. Away from prying questions. Away from memories that taunted her.

'The winter market is on,' he said. 'We'll eat and you can see some of the sights.'

Tamsin felt a flicker of excitement. The town looked quaintly romantic with half-timbered houses, brightly painted shutters and steep, snow-capped roofs.

But with a prince by her side relaxation was impossible. Instead she fretted over his mysterious proposition and the growing sense of something wrong. Why this interest in her?

A couple strolled hand in hand across the street, catching her eye. They were barely aware of anyone else, completely absorbed in each other. She felt a small pang of envy. Once she'd hoped she and Patrick...

Tamsin had never been close to anyone like that. Never experienced all-encompassing love, even from her parents. Never even fitted in, finishing school before her age peers and being so much younger than her university colleagues.

She turned away, setting her mouth firmly. She refused to pine for what she'd never had. One perilous venture into romance had proved what she'd always suspected. Love wasn't for her. She just didn't inspire that sort of affection.

But she had her work. That was compensation enough.

Alaric viewed the woman beside him with frustration. Two hours in her company and she was still an enigma.

On one level she was easy to read. Her peal of laughter at the antics of children on the outdoor ice-skating rink. Her enthusiasm for markets filled with local handcrafts and produce. She was pleased by simple delights: watching a woodcarver create a nutcracker dragon, or a lace-maker at work, asking questions all the time.

Most women he knew would complain of the rustic entertainment!

It was tempting to believe her innocent of deception.

But she'd prevaricated in the car and he'd sensed there was more to her reasons for coming here. Her tension when he pushed for answers, and the way she avoided his gaze made him suspicious.

She was back in disguise, hiding behind thick-rimmed glasses and a scrunched up bun, with an anorak the wrong colour for her complexion and a pair of shapeless trousers.

Was she trying to banish any memory of her in shorts?

His mouth twisted grimly. That particular image was emblazoned on his brain.

With rapt attention she watched a stallholder cook pancakes and fill them with dark cherries, walnuts and chocolate. It was pure pleasure watching her. Her face was blissful as she bit into the concoction, oblivious to the sauce glistening on her bottom lip or Alaric's testosterone-induced reaction as it dripped to her chin.

She swiped her lips with a pink tongue. To his horror his groin tightened and throbbed as if she'd stripped her ugly clothes away and offered him her soft body.

Right here. Right now...

What was going on? She was nothing like his usual women. He wasn't even sure he could trust her.

Yet her combination of quick mind, buttoned up formality, prickly challenge and hidden curves was absurdly, potently provocative.

She was like a special treat waiting to be unwrapped. The perfect diversion for a man jaded by too many easy conquests. Too many women seeking to trap him with practised seduction and false protestations of love.

Someone bustled past, bumping her close and branding her body against his. His mouth dried. He had to force himself to let go after he'd steadied her.

'Come,' he said abruptly. 'Let's find somewhere quiet.'

Tamsin looked up at his brusque tone, pleasure waning as she read his stony expression. Clearly he'd had enough.

She couldn't blame him. He'd gone out of his way to show her sights that must, for him, be unremarkable. Plus all evening he'd been approached by citizens eager to talk. He'd had no respite.

To her dismay her hackles had risen at the number of women who'd approached him, simpering and laughing when he turned his blue eyes in their direction. What did that say about her? Hastily she shoved away her petty annoyance at them.

She'd watched fascinated as he handled requests with good humour and practicality. He made his royal obligations look simple. She noticed he didn't have any obvious minders with him but mixed easily with the crowd. Perhaps his security staff blended in.

'Of course,' she murmured. 'Somewhere quiet would be—'

A crack of sound reverberated, then a shout. Her breath caught as a young boy raced in front of her, skidding on the cobbles and catapulting towards a vat of simmering spiced wine. She cried out, instinctively reaching for him.

A large figure plunged forward as the cauldron teetered. It overturned just as Alaric hauled the youngster away. There was a crash, a sizzle of hot liquid and a cry of distress, then a cloud of steam as the boy was thrust into her hands.

In the uproar that followed Tamsin lost sight of the prince as the crowd surged forward. Then, out of the confusion he appeared, pocketing his wallet and nodding to the smiling stall-holder. He accepted thanks from the boy's parents but didn't linger. Moments later he propelled Tamsin across the square and into an old hotel.

Only when they were ushered into a private dining room did Tamsin see his face clearly. It was white, the skin stretched taut across sculpted bones, his lips bloodless.

'Are you all right?'

It was clear he wasn't. Rapidly she scanned him, looking for injury. That's when she noticed the large splash staining his hand and her stomach turned over.

Tamsin propelled him to the bench seat lining one wall. He subsided and she slid in beside him, moistening a linen napkin from a water carafe and pressing it to his hand.

He sat silent and unmoving, staring ahead.

Tamsin washed the wine away, revealing a burn to the back of his hand. She pressed the wet cloth to it again.

'Is it just your hand? Where else does it hurt?'

Slowly he turned his head, looking blankly at her. His eyes were almost black, pupils dilated.

'Your Highness? Are you burned elsewhere?' She cupped his hand, reassured by the warmth of his skin against hers, though the chill distance in his eyes worried her. Frantically she patted his trousers with her other hand, testing for more sticky wine.

Finally he looked down.

Her hand stilled, splayed across the solid muscle of his thigh. Suddenly her eagerness to help seemed foolish.

'I'm fine. No other burns.' He threw the wet cloth onto the table, drawing a deep breath as colour seeped along his cheekbones. His free hand covered hers, sandwiching it against living muscle that shifted beneath her palm.

Fire licked Tamsin's skin. Something curled tight inside her at the intimacy of that touch.

Ink blue eyes surveyed her steadily and long fingers threaded through hers, holding her hand prisoner. Tingles of awareness shimmied up her arm to spread through her body.

'In the circumstances you can forget the title.' His voice was as smooth and seductive as the cherry chocolate sauce she still tasted on her lips. 'Call me Alaric.'

His mouth lifted in a tiny smile that made Tamsin's insides liquefy. A smile that hinted at dangerous intimacies, to match that voice of midnight pleasures.

Abruptly she leaned back, realising she'd swayed unthinkingly towards him.

'You're sure you're not hurt?' Her voice was scratchy, as if it were she who'd lunged in to save the boy, not him. The blankness had gone from his face as if it had never been, yet she couldn't help wondering what secrets lurked behind his apparently easy smile.

'Positive. As for this…' he flexed his burned hand '…it's fine. Though thank you for your concern.' He leaned forward, eyes dancing. Had she imagined those moments of rigid shock? It had seemed so profound. So real.

'Now we're alone, we can talk about my proposition.' He was so close his breath feathered her hair and cheek. Tamsin had to fight not to shiver in response.

'Yes, Your…yes, Alaric.' She strove for composure, despite the wayward excitement that welled, being so close to him. 'What did you have in mind?'

His fingers flexed around hers. His strength surrounded her. It was strangely comforting despite the way her nerves jangled at the look in his eyes.

His smile broadened and her breath snared.

'I want you to be my companion.'

CHAPTER FOUR

'YOUR...companion?' Tamsin snapped her mouth shut before she could say any more.

He *couldn't* mean what she thought.

Companion could have all sorts of interpretations. It was shaming proof of the way he turned her brain to mush that she'd immediately thought he meant *lover*.

Her heartbeat ratcheted up a notch and her breathing shallowed as, unbidden, another graphic picture filled her brain. The two of them, stretched naked on the carpet before the fire in his library. Limbs entwined. Lips locked. His hard, capable hands shaping her body.

Was that answering heat in his eyes? He watched her so closely. Could he guess her thoughts?

Tamsin forced her breathing to slow and sat straighter. She reminded herself she was known for her analytical mind. Not flights of fantasy.

He kept her hand anchored against him. Foolishly she couldn't bring herself to pull it away.

'That's right.' He nodded.

Companion to Prince Alaric of Ruvingia. Women would kill for time with Europe's most notorious bachelor. For the chance to persuade him into marriage or just to experience his vaunted expertise as a lover.

Desperately Tamsin told herself she wasn't one of them.

'You've mistaken me for someone else.' She lifted her chin, bracing for the moment he told her this was a joke.

Instead he shook his head.

'No mistake, Dr Connors.' He paused, his lips pursing ruminatively. To her horror, Tamsin couldn't take her eyes off his mouth. 'Perhaps I'd better call you Tamsin.'

A delicious little shudder tickled every nerve ending as he said her name like that.

As if it pleased him.

As if he looked forward to saying it again.

Reality crashed down in a moment of blinding insight. *He was playing with her.* A man like him would never view a woman like her in that light.

'Feel free.' She forced her voice not to wobble. 'What is it you're proposing?'

One straight brow lifted, giving him a faintly superior air. 'Exactly what it sounds. I need a companion and you'd be perfect. There'd be benefits for you too.'

Tamsin resisted the impulse to shake her head to clear her hearing. She'd watched him speak. She knew what he'd said. The excited patter of her pulse was testament to that.

No man had described her as *perfect* before.

'My invitation this evening wasn't totally altruistic,' he continued.

Did he realise he'd begun absent-mindedly stroking the back of her hand with his thumb as he clamped it to his leg? 'I wanted to see if we're compatible.'

'Compatible?'

His lips stretched in a brilliant smile that made something flip over inside. Only the hooded intelligence in his bright stare hinted this wasn't as simple as it seemed.

Sternly Tamsin told herself to be sensible. Logical. All the things she didn't feel when he touched her, smiled at her like that.

'I need a companion who won't bore me in the first half-hour.'

'I take it I passed muster?' Anger ignited at the notion of being assessed. Had it occurred to him she might have better things to do with her time?

She was sure she'd think of them in a minute.

She tugged her hand but he didn't release it.

His expression sobered. 'I needed to be sure you'd handle it, too. It's not necessarily fun keeping me company while I play prince-in-residence for all comers.'

Tamsin stared, curious at the bitterness in his voice as he spoke of his princely role. Was it real or feigned?

'I wasn't bothered.' She'd felt privileged to be with him and to see the able way he'd dealt with requests from the light-hearted to the serious. He had an easy manner with people. She envied that. 'But I still don't understand.' She took a deep breath and willed herself to concentrate. 'Why do you need a companion? And why me?'

'Ah, I knew you'd go to the crux of things.'

Alaric watched her troubled face and realised he'd have to do better. He'd only aroused her suspicions.

He supposed it was the shock of rescuing the boy that had done it. The initial explosion of sound: probably a firecracker but for an instant so like the report of a firearm. The need for urgent action combined with the feel of those small, bony shoulders beneath his hands, the distress on the kid's face. The huge, fearful dark eyes that for a moment had looked so hauntingly familiar. Together they'd triggered memories Alaric usually submerged beneath the everyday demands on his time.

It had only taken seconds, but that was enough to tip the balance and slide him into a nightmare world of guilt and pain. In an instant he'd been back in another time, another place. To another life he'd been unable to save.

Only the touch of Tamsin's hands, the concern in her voice and her insistence had dragged him out of a state he'd prefer not to think about. It was a condition he usually managed alone, never sharing with others.

That was the way it would stay.

'Commitments mean I'm staying in Ruvingia for a while.'

She nodded, wariness in every line of her face.

'And…' He paused, wondering how best to phrase this. How to appeal to this woman he couldn't read? 'While I'm here I need a companion.'

Amber eyes regarded him unblinkingly through the lenses of her glasses.

'Why? You can't be lonely.'

Couldn't he?

No matter how frenetically he'd pursued pleasure through Europe's glittering capitals, no matter how many lovers warmed his bed, Alaric remained profoundly alone. And when he was alone the memories came. Hence his constant need for action, for diversion.

She didn't need to know any of that.

'Not lonely, precisely.' He favoured her with a smile that had won him countless women.

She appeared unmoved, staring back with a slight frown as if she couldn't quite place him in a catalogue. Irritation surfaced. Why couldn't she be like the rest and fall in with his wishes? Why did she have to question everything?

Yet there was something about her seriousness, about the fact that she held herself aloof, that appealed.

'It would make my life easier if I were seen out and about with the same woman. A woman who didn't expect that to lead to a more permanent arrangement.'

As he said it, Alaric realised how weary he'd become of socialites and trophy mistresses. It would be a relief to be with someone who didn't fit the conventional mould of glossy beauty and vacuous conversation.

She tilted her head to one side, her mouth flattening primly. 'You want a decoy? Because you're tired of being chased by women out to snare you?'

'You could say that.' He shrugged and watched her gaze flicker away. 'There's something about a royal title that attracts women eager to marry.'

'I'd have thought you could cope with that.' Her words were tart. 'You've got a reputation for enjoying yourself in short term relationships. Surely you don't need to hide behind any woman.'

He read the stiffness in her body and realised he'd have to offer more. There was no sympathy there. If anything she looked disapproving.

'These are delicate times, Tamsin.' He lingered on her name, liking the sound of it. 'Power blocs are jockeying for position and they include some aristocratic families who'd love to cement their status by linking to royalty.'

'Marriage to you, you mean?'

He nodded. 'I've had aristocratic ladies paraded before me for months and it's getting harder to avoid them.'

'You're an adult. You just have to say you're not interested!' She tried to withdraw her hand but he refused to relinquish it. This wasn't going as he'd anticipated.

'It's not so simple. Even a rumour that one contender is favoured over another could change the perceived balance of power. My cousin Raul is under the same pressure.'

Alaric leaned forward, using his most cajoling tone. 'All I'm asking is some help to keep them at a distance. Is that unreasonable?'

Her lips thinned and she surveyed him coolly.

Impatience spiked. He was tempted to cut through her questions and demand acquiescence the easy way.

He'd drag her glasses away, cup her head in his hand and kiss her till her mouth grew soft and accommodating and she surrendered to his wishes. Till she blushed a delicate pink all over as she had on the squash court, this time with pleasure and anticipation.

Till she capitulated and said she'd do whatever he wanted.

Anything he wanted.

Heat poured through him as he remembered her parted lips, ripe with cherries. The swipe of her tongue licking up sauce in a move so innocently sexy it had tugged him towards arousal. The feel of her breasts against him as he carried her down the library ladder.

Alaric's pulse quickened, his hold on her hand tightening.

'I can see it might be useful to have someone to keep other women away.' Her tone told him her sympathy was limited. 'But what's that got to do with me?'

'You're already here living at the castle. You're not impressed by my position.' Despite the importance of persuading her, Alaric's lips twitched as he saw her flush. Few women could have made it clearer his title and money meant nothing. She had no notion how refreshing that was. To be viewed as just a man. 'You won't get ideas about companionship turning to something more.'

He raised her hand to his lips and kissed it, inhaling the summery fragrance of her satin skin, enjoying the little shiver of awareness she couldn't hide. Tamsin was different from other women. He couldn't remember any of them intriguing him so. Protecting his country had never coincided so well with personal inclination.

They said you should keep your friends close and your enemies closer. Alaric wasn't sure yet if she was an enemy or an innocent, but he'd enjoy keeping Tamsin Connors close. Very close.

Tamsin's heart faltered and seemed to stop as his lips caressed her hand in a courtly gesture. The trouble was, to her overwrought senses it felt provocative, not courtly, evoking reactions out of proportion with the circumstances.

There was no mistaking the amusement in his eyes. He was laughing at her. Did he take her for a fool?

She yanked her hand away, anger and hurt bubbling in a bitter brew that stung the back of her throat.

'No one would believe it.'

'Why not? People will believe their eyes.'

She shook her head, wishing he'd stop this game.

'Tamsin?' He frowned and she realised she was blinking eyes that felt hot and scratchy. Hurriedly she looked away at the old mural of convivial wine makers on the far wall.

'I'm not the sort of woman to be companion to a prince.' Even if it was make-believe.

'I know my record with women is abysmal but surely you could make an exception in the circumstances.'

'Oh!' She shot to her feet. 'Just stop it!' Tamsin paced the room then whirled to face him. 'No one would ever believe you'd really taken up with someone like...' The words choked as her throat constricted. 'Like me.'

He rose, eyes fixed on hers. 'Nonsense.'

Tamsin felt like stamping her foot. Or shouting.

Or curling up in a ball and crying her eyes out.

All the weak, emotional things she'd wanted to do when Patrick had revealed he'd only spent time with *a woman like her* because she was useful to his ambitions. All the things she hadn't let herself do because she'd been busy pretending it didn't matter.

'Look at me.' She gestured comprehensively to her practical, unglamorous clothes. 'I'm not…' But she couldn't go on. She knew she wasn't attractive, that she didn't inspire thoughts of romance or even plain old lust. But she refused to say it out loud. She had some pride.

'I see a woman who's intelligent and passionate and intriguing.' His words snapped her head up in disbelief.

When had he moved so close?

He loomed over her, making the room shrink so it seemed there was only her and him in a tiny, charged space.

Tamsin's throat worked as anger roiled. 'I refuse to be the butt of your joke.' She swung away but he caught her elbow, turning her implacably to face him.

'It's no joke, Tamsin. I was never more serious.'

She angled her chin higher. 'I don't think my clothes would pass muster for consorting with royalty, do you?' Easier to focus on that than the shortcomings of the woman who wore them.

'I don't give a damn about your clothes,' he growled, a frown settling on his brow. 'If they bother you replace them. Or let me do it if you don't have the cash.'

'Oh, don't be absurd!' As if it was just the clothes. Tamsin knew how men viewed her. No one would believe she was a sexpot who'd snared the interest of a playboy prince!

'Absurd?' The single word slid, lethally quiet into the vibrating silence, raising the hairs on her nape.

His eyes sparked fire. Suddenly the danger she'd once sensed in him was there, staring down at her.

A frisson of panic crept through her.

She backed a step. He followed.

'You don't believe me?'

Silently she shook her head. Of course she didn't believe him. She had no illusions. She—

In one stride he closed the gap between them. His hands cupped her face, fingers sliding into her hair, dislodging pins. The sensation of him tunnelling through her hair, massaging her scalp was surprisingly sensual.

Tamsin stared up into eyes darkening to midnight-blue, so close she could barely focus. She told herself to move away but found her will sapped by the look in his eyes. The floor seemed to drop away beneath her feet as she read his expression, his fierce intent.

That look bewildered her. She'd never seen it before.

'I—'

Her words stopped as his lips crushed hers. She gasped, inhaling his scent and the spicy taste of his skin. Her thoughts unravelled.

Taking advantage of her open mouth Alaric devoured her. He was determined, skilful, dominant. He overwhelmed every sense, blotted out the world. Stole her away to a place of dark ecstasy unlike any she'd known.

He held her so firmly she couldn't move. His body was hard, awakening unfamiliar sensations that rippled and spread, a trickle turning into a torrent of excitement.

Dimly Tamsin realised she didn't want to move. That in fact her hands had crept up around his neck, linked there to stop herself falling. Neither did she mind the sense of him surrounding her, legs planted wide to anchor them both. Her eyes closed as her thoughts scrambled.

Bliss beckoned.

This was nothing like Patrick's lukewarm attentions. Or the hesitant clumsiness she'd felt in his embrace.

For the first time Tamsin felt passion burst into scorching life. All she could do was acquiesce. And enjoy.

His kiss was fervent, almost angry, yet Tamsin had never known such delight. He ravished her mouth so fiercely she trembled with the force of it, bowed backwards as he surged forward, seemingly unable to slake his need.

And she welcomed him.

Despite his sudden aggressive ardour she wasn't afraid. Instead it made her feel...powerful.

Vaguely she wondered at that, but her mind refused to compute the implications. She simply knew that with Alaric she was safe. Even if it was like stepping off a skyscraper into nothingness. His strong arms hauled her close and she gave herself to delight.

She kissed him back, revelling in the warm sensuality of their mouths melding. He licked her tongue and she moaned, her knees quaking at the impact of this sensual onslaught.

The kiss altered. He didn't bend her back quite so ferociously, though he still strained against her. His hungry ardour eased into something more gentle but no less satisfying.

She breathed deep as he planted kisses along her jaw. Sensation bloomed with each caress. Her skin tingled and her breasts grew heavy. She thrust herself against him, needing his hardness just there. Her breath came in desperate gasps as she struggled to fill air-starved lungs. She clung tight, wanting more.

He moved to kiss her on the mouth again and bumped her glasses askew.

Instantly he froze. As if that simple action reminded him who he was kissing. Not a svelte sophisticate but plain Tamsin Connors.

He stilled, lips at the sensitive corner of her mouth. Tamsin held her breath, desperate for him to kiss her again. Craving more of his magic.

His steely embrace loosened and firm hands clasped her shoulders, steadying her as if he knew her legs felt like stretched elastic. He pulled back and she swayed, bereft of his heat and strength.

A protest hovered on her swollen lips but she swallowed it. She would not beg for more. Not now she saw the dawning horror on his face. The unmistakeable regret in the way his gaze slid to her mouth then away.

'Are you OK?' His voice was gruff, his expression stern. He was embarrassed, she realised.

Pity had provoked the kiss, but the reminder of who it was he embraced had stopped him in his tracks.

The lovely, lush taste of him turned to ashes on her tongue. The thrill that had hummed through her with every caress died.

There was no magic. It had been a kindness gone wrong. *An act of charity from a man who felt sorry for her.*

Anger and regret chased each other in a sickening tumble of emotions. At least, she told herself, he hadn't deliberately set out to dupe her, like Patrick.

She'd duped *herself* into believing that kiss was real.

Now she had to pick up the pieces. Pretend it didn't matter that he'd unthinkingly awoken heart-pounding desire in a woman who'd never known its like before.

Tamsin wanted to howl her despair.

But she had the torn remnants of her dignity. She might only be suitable as a decoy, not wanted for herself, but he needn't know he'd shredded her self-respect.

Deliberately she lifted a hand to set her glasses straight on her face. It was a gesture of habit, but never had it held such significance.

'I'm fine, thank you, Alaric. How are you?'

Alaric stared at the cool-eyed woman before him and struggled with his vocal cords. They'd shut down, just like his brain when he'd hauled her into his arms and slammed his mouth against hers.

Even now he was barely in control of himself! One moment of madness had turned into something more. Something that threatened the boundaries he used to keep from feeling, from engaging fully in the world around him.

He'd kissed countless women but not one had made him *feel*. Not like this.

Who the hell was she? What had she done to him? Passion was a pleasure, a release, an escape. Never had it overwhelmed him like that.

'You're sure?' He sounded strangled, like an untried teen, hot and bothered by his first taste of desire.

'Of course.' Her brows rose in splendid indifference. As if being accosted by lust-ridden strangers was an inconsequential distraction.

Alaric scrubbed a hand over his face, annoyed to note the slight tremor in his fingers.

Tamsin Connors might dress like someone's ancient maiden aunt but she kissed with all the generous ardour any man could want. The feel of her lush body melting against his, her mouth hot and welcoming, had driven away the last shred of his sanity. Their passion had been volcanic.

Hard now to believe her apparent hurt and self-doubt had appalled and angered him. It had provoked him into doing what he'd wanted for so long now: kiss the woman silent. When he'd dislodged her glasses he'd come to his senses and been horrified at the idea he'd taken advantage of her. Possibly scared her.

Had her earlier pain been real? Or had she played on his sympathies?

It infuriated him that he was no closer to understanding her. She was a bundle of contradictions. Fiery yet reserved. Confident in professional matters yet still vulnerable. Thrilled by a rustic fair but unimpressed by his title. A siren who shattered his control like no other.

He wanted to rip away the façade she presented the world and uncover the real Tamsin Connors.

He wanted to run from what she made him feel.

But mostly he wanted her back in his arms.

He drew a deep breath. One thing he knew for certain. *She was the most dangerous woman he knew.*

'I apologise,' he said stiffly. 'I shouldn't have done that.'

'No, you shouldn't.' She glared at him and it was all he could do not to reach for her again. With her eyes snapping gold fire, her hair in tumbled waves around her shoulders and her lips reddened and full she was too alluring. Even the glasses couldn't hide that now.

How had he ever thought her ordinary?

'As I said, Tamsin,' he lingered appreciatively over her name, 'clothes are immaterial.' He watched colour flush her cheeks and felt savage pleasure that she wasn't as unmoved as she pretended. 'I look for more than fashion in a woman.'

'I'm not *anyone's* woman.' Her chin angled up.

'Just as well,' he murmured, as something primitively possessive surfaced. 'We wouldn't want the complication of a jealous boyfriend, would we?'

'No fear of that.'

She looked away. Her expression didn't change but suddenly he regretted baiting her to salve his pride. Whatever had happened, whoever she really was, Tamsin had been caught like him in the conflagration erupting between them. At least he hoped so. The alternative was unthinkable.

'You're surely not still serious about this?'

'Never more so.' He watched her turn. She drew a slow breath as if gathering herself.

'You said if I spent time with you there'd be a benefit in it for me.' Her voice was crisp, her demeanour completely business-like. 'What did you mean?'

Disappointment reared at her about-face; her obvious self-interest. Alaric told himself it was easier to deal with her now than when she was warm and willing in his arms. A pity he didn't believe it.

'I've been thinking about the job we've contracted you to do. It would be easier if you had more staff.'

The light in her eyes told him he'd finally snared her interest. He squashed a spark of annoyance that he came second in her priorities to a pile of mouldering books.

'Not easier, but there's a chance of further damage in the time it takes us to assess what we've got.' She chewed her lower lip. Heat scorched Alaric's lower body as he focused on its softened contours. In repose Tamsin's mouth was a perfect Cupid's bow of invitation.

'The offer only applies if I become your *companion*?' The twist of her lips and her chilly look told him how little she liked the prospect. 'That sounds like blackmail.'

Alaric shrugged. His gaze drifted to her mouth and he remembered her moan of delight as they'd kissed. She only feigned disinterest.

'If you agree it will mean some time away from your work. Putting extra resources into the archives will compensate. Two qualified full time staff.' He watched excitement light her face.

'And you may want to come with me when I open a new wing of the national museum. There's a collection behind the scenes that may interest you. Illuminated gospels that I believe are noteworthy.' Those treasures had never been outside the country. Neither had foreign experts viewed them.

Her eyes widened eagerly. In other women it was the sort of look reserved for a gift of emeralds or rubies.

Tamsin Connors was unique. In far too many ways.

'This…arrangement would only interrupt my work occasionally?'

Alaric gritted his teeth. Women vied for his attention. He'd never needed to bribe one to be with him!

'That's right.'

Still she hesitated. She clasped her hands before her in a gesture he'd come to realise signalled vulnerability.

'We're not talking about anything more than spending time together? Being seen in public?'

He nodded curtly.

'Then…' She paused and licked her lip as if her mouth had dried. Alaric's groin tightened as he remembered her lush sweetness. 'Then I accept. On one condition.'

'Yes?' He hauled his gaze from her mouth.

The glacial expression he found in her eyes would have frozen a lesser man.

'No more kisses. Nothing…intimate.'

Alaric bowed stiffly, all dignity and insulted pride.

'You have my word that I won't take advantage. Nothing *intimate* except at your express request.'

She pretended to abhor his touch?

She'd soon be on her knees begging for his kisses.

CHAPTER FIVE

'I'M SORRY, ma'am. You can't go this way.'

Tamsin looked at the burly man blocking the path and drew her jacket close. His wide stance and implacable stare made the crisp morning feel chillier. Or was it that he automatically spoke in heavily accented English? As if he knew who she was and had been waiting for her?

'Why not?' This was the path to the village and she needed a walk to clear her head. After days working long hours she was no closer to finding the peace she'd always taken for granted in her job.

That peace had been missing since *he'd* taken her out four days ago. Since he'd kissed her till her head swam and her senses reeled and she'd forgotten she was plain Tamsin Connors. Since he'd proposed a fake relationship then promptly disappeared, leaving her wondering if she'd conjured the idea as a wish-fulfilling fantasy.

Each day she'd waited, nerves on edge, for him to summon her. Only to learn today he was away in the capital.

It rankled that he'd left without telling her. As if he had to report his movements! Yet after what he'd said she'd expected to see more of him.

Not that she was disappointed.

It was just that she wanted to work on the chronicle. She couldn't access it in his absence. *That's* what frustrated her.

'A landslip has taken part of the path.'

The stranger didn't move his eyes off her, neither did he smile. Tamsin's gaze strayed to his walkie-talkie. He didn't look like a groundsman, more like heavy duty security.

'How far along? Maybe I could take a detour.'

'Sorry, ma'am, but the surface is unstable. I couldn't allow it.' Steel threaded his voice for all his deference.

'I see.' She scanned the wooded hillside. There must be other tracks.

'If I might suggest, ma'am?'

'Yes?'

'There's an easy circuit walk above the castle.'

Tamsin repressed a sigh. She needed more than a tame stroll. This restlessness demanded a better outlet. She'd avoided the squash court in case she met the prince again. Perhaps she should try to work off her excess energy there.

'Thanks. I'll think about it.' She smiled, acknowledging his nod, and turned uphill.

The track curved and she looked back. He was still there, watching, as he spoke into his walkie-talkie.

She shivered. It was nonsense to think he was reporting her movements. Yet the claustrophobic feeling that dogged her intensified. In the archives the new staff meant she was never alone and whenever she left her rooms she seemed to run into staff.

Tamsin paused as the castle came into full view. A thrill sped through her as she took in the circular towers, crenellated battlements and banners fluttering black, blue and gold against the bright sky.

Just the place for tales of romance and derring do. For princes on white chargers rescuing damsels in distress.

Cradled by snow-capped peaks, its grey stone rose sheer from the mountain, high above the dark forest. It had an eagle's eye view down the valley to lands its owners had ruled for generations.

A nineteenth-century fad for gothic architecture had turned the once-grim stronghold into a fairy tale showpiece.

Yet below were grim dungeons where enemies had languished. The prince's word had always been law here and the ruthlessness of Ruvingian princes was legendary. They always got what they wanted.

Shadows moved beneath the portcullis. Tamsin's pulse danced and her breathing shallowed as she recognised the man in the lead: tall, powerfully proportioned and aristocratic with his confident stride and strong features. He matched his home perfectly.

Then it was too late to stand gawking. He'd seen her. He turned and dismissed his staff.

And all she could think of was how it had felt cradled tight in his arms. The intensity of his kiss. The passion that had ravaged her senses and left her craving more.

Every night she'd tossed in her bed, remembering. Imagining things that left her feverish and unsettled. Furiously she tried to repress the blush staining her cheeks, hoping he'd put it down to the chill wind.

'Tamsin.' He stopped a few paces away.

Despite her embarrassment her lips curved in response when he smiled, a dimple grooving his cheek.

She could almost believe he was pleased to see her, though she told herself he didn't really care. She tried to dredge up anger. He'd kissed her out of pity.

'Alaric.' She liked saying his name. Too much. 'How are you? I thought you were away?' Too late she realised she sounded far too interested in his activities.

'Business kept me away until today.' Was that a cloud moving over the sun or had his bright gaze shadowed?

'We need to talk about my work.' She drew herself up straight, reminding herself that was all that mattered. Not her shocking weakness for indigo eyes. 'I haven't been able to access the chronicle to continue my translation. Your staff claim not to know where it is.' Indignation rose that he didn't trust her with her own find!

'My priority is ensuring absolute secrecy till we confirm it's genuine.' His expression grew stern.

Tamsin opened her mouth to protest that it shouldn't stop her work. 'However, arrangements will be made to enable you access while maintaining security.'

'Thank you.' Her indignation fizzled, leaving her feeling wrong-footed.

'Now, would you like to come out with me tonight?'

He sounded like a polite host, entertaining a guest. Except he'd bought her cooperation, bribed her with staff for her project.

The knowledge stopped her pleasure in his smile. The staff had turned up days ago and now it was time to deliver on her part of the bargain.

'Where are we going?' She might as well be gracious about it.

His smile broadened and her lungs squeezed. He really was the most stunning man.

'To a ski resort.' He named a town famous for exclusive luxury that drew the world's most prestigious VIPs. 'There's an event I must take part in then we'll stay for dinner.' No mention of her role as decoy. The man was a diplomat when he wanted to be.

'Fine.' She stepped forward and he turned, shortening his stride to match hers.

'Watch the icy path.' He clasped her elbow and she tensed. Heat rayed from his touch, countering the wintry air.

He held her arm even when they reached safer ground. Tamsin didn't fuss by telling him to release her. He'd think she read too much into the gesture. Hurriedly she searched for something to say.

'What should I wear?'

He slanted her a piercing glance and the air sizzled between them. He was remembering, too.

I don't give a damn about your clothes, he'd said.

And then he'd kissed her.

Tamsin's pulse accelerated painfully as she watched his impassive face. Or had their kiss meant so little he'd forgotten it?

'Some will be in ski gear and the rest dressed for an evening out. Take your pick.' Heat shimmied through her as their gazes collided and she felt again that sensation like chocolate melting, deep inside.

Spending time with Alaric had to be the biggest mistake of her life! Yet despite her doubts, Tamsin couldn't resist the invitation in his smile and the intriguing mystery of his cool, blue eyes.

Even when he annoyed her, Alaric made her feel alive; brimming with an effervescence she'd never known.

* * *

Tamsin stood on the terrace of an exclusive resort hotel, huddled into the soft luxury of the full length faux-fur coat that had been delivered just before she left.

She'd been about to object, uncomfortable with accepting clothes Alaric had bought when she'd seen his note.

To keep you warm tonight. This was my mother's. I'm sure she'd approve its loan.

He'd lent her something of his mother's? Ridiculous to feel such pleasure that he'd trust her with the gorgeous garment. Yet she couldn't dispel delight that he'd thought of her comfort. Without being obvious, he'd also ensured she wouldn't look too out of place in this A-list crowd.

Tamsin glanced at the glamorous, beautiful people surrounding her, some of the faces familiar from press reports. They quaffed vintage champagne as if it were water. And the jewels—even by lamplight some of the women almost blinded her with their casually worn gems.

She stroked the soft coat. For now it didn't matter that beneath its elegant lines she wore a chain store dress and a pair of plain court shoes, her best, which she'd bet none of the sophisticated women here would be seen dead in.

'Here they come!' Excitement rippled through the gathering and Tamsin turned to look up at the blackness of the mountain looming above.

Butterflies danced in her stomach. It was hunger, not excitement at the idea of Alaric joining her.

'There they are.'

Now Tamsin saw it. A flicker of colour high on the mountain. As she watched the flicker became a glow then a tiny jewel-like thread of colour trailing down the slope.

The moon emerged from behind clouds to illuminate the imposing outline of one of Europe's most famous peaks. Its cool brightness intensified the scene's magical quality.

She couldn't take her eyes from the ribbon of rainbow colours descending in swooping curves through the silver gilt night. She'd never seen anything like it. Excited murmurs in a dozen languages buzzed in her ears and she found herself grinning, rapt in the spectacle.

Her spine tingled as a clear chorus of voices rose. A cluster of people, many in traditional Ruvingian costume, waited on a flat area beside the hotel.

The singing stopped and in the silence Tamsin heard the whoosh of skis. The stream of colour descended to the clearing, resolving into dozens of skiers, each holding a coloured lantern in one hand and a basket in the other.

'They skied that slope with no hands?' The mountain was notoriously dangerous.

'It's tradition,' said a woman in cherry red ski clothes and scintillating diamonds. 'Didn't you know?'

Tamsin shook her head, her gaze on the lead skier. Alaric. Her knees gave a little wobble as she took in his proud, handsome face and his easy grace as he slid to a flourishing halt. He handed the basket to a blonde who curtseyed and blushed. Each skier delivered a basket and was rewarded with a goblet.

'Mulled wine,' said the woman beside her.

There was a bustle as Alaric stepped out of his skis and headed purposefully through the crowd. It parted before him and Tamsin wondered what it would be like to have that effect on people.

His progress wasn't entirely easy. Others moved towards him, all women, she noted, frowning.

No wonder he had a reputation as a ladies' man. He didn't even have to search them out!

Some smiled, others greeted him and still others reached out to touch. A twist of something sharp coiled through Tamsin's stomach as she watched a beautiful redhead kiss him on the cheek.

Tamsin's sense of not belonging rushed back full force. Why was she here? Companion indeed! This was a farce.

'Your Highness.' The woman beside her bobbed a curtsey then Tamsin forgot her as she looked up into eyes like midnight. Black hair flopped roguishly on his brow and his lips curved in an intimate smile that sent shivers of longing scudding through her.

'Tamsin.' He lifted the silver goblet in his hand. She had a moment to notice its intricate design, then the scent of spiced wine filled her nostrils and its sweet pungency was in her mouth.

Heat exploded within, surging through her blood. An instant later it exploded again as she watched Alaric lift the goblet to his lips, turning it deliberately to drink from the same place she had. His eyes held hers as he tilted it and drank. Not a sip like hers but a full bodied swallow.

Fire sparked across Tamsin's skin at the blatant sexual message in his eyes. She told herself it was an act.

Yet a crazy part of her wished the message she read in his stare was real. She must be losing her mind!

Seated at a quiet table by a window overlooking the resort, Tamsin tried to relax. It was impossible with Alaric, like a sleek, dark predator, on the other side of the table.

The taste of spiced wine was on her tongue but it was the taste of *him* she remembered. Why couldn't she get that kiss from her mind? Heat flooded her cheeks as she sought for something to say, convinced his brooding eyes read too much of her inner turmoil.

'Tell me about the night ski. Is it an old tradition?'

Alaric settled back in his chair and stretched his legs. Tamsin shifted as they brushed hers.

'Since the seventeenth century. The locals have re-enacted it ever since.'

'Re-enacted what?' Maybe if she focused on this she wouldn't react to his lazy sensuality.

'It was the worst winter on record. Avalanches cut the valley off and crop failure meant the villagers were starving. In desperation some young men set off through near blizzard conditions to get supplies, though everyone believed the trek doomed.' Alaric's voice was as dark and alluring as the rest of him. Tamsin felt it curl around her like the caress of fur on bare skin.

'Fortunately one of the avalanches also brought down rock and opened a new route out of the valley. Weeks later they returned with supplies. Ever since the locals have commemorated the feat, and the salvation of the village.'

'And the wine?' She couldn't shake the idea there'd been hidden significance in the way he'd shared that goblet.

'Just to warm the skiers.' His eyes gleamed.

'That's all?'

He leaned forward, his gaze pinioning her till her only movement was the pulse thudding at her throat.

'You think I've deviously tied you to me in some arcane
tradition? That we're betrothed, perhaps?'

Her cheeks grew fiery. 'Of course not!'

His brows arched disbelievingly but she refused to admit how
the simple act of sharing his wine had taken on such ridiculous
significance in her mind. If only he hadn't looked so sinfully
sexy and dangerous as he'd deliberately drunk from her side of
the cup.

'Don't fret,' he purred, reaching out to cover her hand in a
blatantly possessive gesture. 'Our companionship has a purpose
and my actions were designed to achieve that purpose. They
succeeded, don't you think?'

'Admirably! Everyone got the message.' She tugged her hand
free and placed it in her lap, conscious of the interest emanating
from the rest of the restaurant. There were celebrities aplenty
here but Alaric was the man drawing every eye.

He raised a glass of delicious local wine in a toast. 'To more
success.'

Reluctantly she lifted her glass. 'And a speedy resolution.'

Alaric smiled as he watched her sip the wine. Not the usual
practised smile that he'd learned to put on like a shield from
an early age. But a smile of genuine pleasure. Tamsin Connors
pleased him, and not just because she was refreshing after so
many grasping, eager women.

He enjoyed her company, even when she was prickly. And
tonight the glow in her cheeks gave her a softness at odds with
the strict hairstyle and unimaginative dress.

His silence unnerved her. He saw it in the way she shifted
in her seat. Yet he didn't try to ease her tension. If she was on
edge she was more likely to reveal her true self. He needed to
understand her, find out how far he could trust her.

'You know,' she mused, her eyes not quite meeting his,
'there's a way out of your problem. Fall in love with a nice,
suitable princess and marry. Women won't bother you then.'

Instantly Alaric's sense of satisfaction vanished. He stiffened, fingers tightening around the stem of his glass. 'I'm in no hurry to marry. Besides,' he drawled, aiming to cut off this line of conversation, 'the princes of Ruvingia never marry for love.'

For an instant he allowed himself to remember his brother, the only person with whom he'd been close. Love had barely featured in their lives and when it had it had been destructive. Felix had been ecstatic in his delusion that he'd found the love of his life. He'd been doomed to disappointment.

Ruthlessly, Alaric clamped a lid on the acrid memories.

'What about the princesses?'

'Pardon?' Alaric looked up to find Tamsin, far from being abashed by his offhand response, was intrigued.

'Do princesses of Ruvingia ever marry for love?'

'Not if they know what's good for them,' he growled.

The hint of a smile curving her lips died and she sat back, her expression rigid and her eyes wide.

Damn. He felt like he'd kicked a kitten when she looked like that. He speared a hand through his hair and searched for a response that would ease the hurt from her eyes.

'Royal marriages are arranged. It's always been that way.' Until Felix had made the mistake of thinking himself in love.

Love was an illusion that only led to pain.

'Even your parents?' she said wistfully. 'That wasn't a love match?'

Clearly Tamsin Connors had a romantic streak. She'd probably grown up reading about princes rescuing maidens, falling in love and living happily ever after. Obviously she had no idea how far from the truth her fantasy was.

'My parents married because their families arranged a suitable match.'

'I see.' She looked so disappointed he relented.

'I was too young to remember but I'm told my mother was besotted with my father, though it was an arranged match.'

'She died when you were little? I'm sorry.'

Alaric shrugged. You didn't miss what you'd never known. Maternal love was something he'd never experienced.

'It must have been hard for your father, left alone to bring up his family.'

Alaric watched her sharply but she wasn't fishing for details, just expressing genuine sympathy.

'My father had plenty of assistance. Staff. Tutors. You name it.'

Looking back on his boyhood it seemed his remote, irascible father had only appeared in order to deliver cutting lectures about all the ways Alaric failed to live up to his golden-haired brother. For a man who, according to under stairs gossip, had only slept with his wife long enough to conceive a spare heir, he'd been remarkably uninterested in his younger son.

'Still,' she said, 'he must have missed your mother. Even if he didn't marry for love, he would have grown to care for her.'

Alaric shook his head. No point letting her believe some fairy tale when the truth was publicly known. 'My father didn't waste any time finding another woman.'

'He married again?'

'No, he simply ensured there was a willing woman warming his bed whenever he wanted one. He was a good-looking man and he had no trouble attracting women.'

People said Alaric was like him.

Hadn't the disaster with Felix stemmed from Alaric's too-easy success with women?

There was no disputing the fact Alaric, like his father, had never fancied himself in love, possibly because he'd never experienced it. Ice trickled down his spine. Maybe it was a character flaw they shared. That they were incapable of love. Unlike Felix. Unlike Alaric's mother who'd reputedly died of a broken heart.

'I see.'

He doubted it. Tamsin, he was beginning to suspect, had a naïve streak a mile wide.

He'd bet she'd be horrified to learn the first girl to profess love for Alaric had simply been aiming to meet his father. That *love* had been code for sex and expediency in a quest for the power and riches she'd hoped to obtain in the bed of a man old enough to be her own father.

Alaric had learned his lessons early. If there was one thing he'd never be foolish enough to do, it was to give his heart.

CHAPTER SIX

'THANKS for coming, Alaric. It was good to talk before I put the expansion plans to the rest of the board.'

Alaric turned. He didn't let his eyes flicker to the scar disfiguring Peter's cheek and neck. He'd long ago trained himself not to, knowing pity was the last thing his old comrade wanted. But nothing could prevent the sour tang of guilt in his mouth.

'My pleasure.' He forced himself to smile. 'You know I always have time for the youth centre. I just wish there'd been something like it when we were kids.'

Peter shrugged. 'The army saved us both from turning into feral teenagers.'

Alaric thought of his rebellious teens, chafing at his father's aloof authoritarianism and his own sense of uselessness, kicking his heels between royal duties.

'You could be right. Just as well the military is royalty's accepted profession for superfluous second sons.'

'Hardly superfluous.'

Alaric shrugged. It was the truth, but he wasn't interested in discussing his family.

'I like your Tamsin, by the way. A bit different from your usual girlfriends.'

It was on the tip of Alaric's tongue to say she wasn't his, *yet*. 'She is different.' That's why she fascinated him. She was an enigma. Once solved she'd lose her allure and finally he'd get a full night's sleep.

They walked into the large indoor sports hall to find a crowd clustered below the climbing wall. There was no sign of Tamsin. Last time he'd seen her she'd been engrossed in some new computer programme with a couple of lanky youths.

Then he saw her—halfway up the towering wall.

Bemused, he stared. He'd left her without a qualm, seeing her so involved and with his staff to look after her while he attended his meeting. Had she been pressured into scaling the massive wall? The teens often challenged visitors in a test of courage.

'Way to go, Tamsin!' called one of the youths holding the rope that kept her safe.

Alaric strode over, fury pumping in his veins. At them for forcing her into this. At himself for allowing it to happen.

He slammed to a halt as he realised, far from being petrified, she was making steady progress up the wall.

She wore a helmet but her feet were bare and her trousers rolled up, revealing those shapely calves. The harness she wore outlined the lush femininity of her derriere and made his blood pump even faster.

Tamsin moved with the grace of a natural climber. Another metre and she reached the top. Roars of approval erupted, almost obliterating her exultant laughter.

Who'd have thought it? Prim and proper Dr Connors had the makings of a thrill seeker! He watched her climb down.

'That was fantastic,' she called over her shoulder. 'I...' Looking down she saw him. Her foot jerked beneath her.

'I've got you.' Alaric stepped close. 'Let her down.' They obeyed and a moment later she filled his arms.

She was soft and intriguingly curvaceous for such a slim woman. The warm puff of her breath hazed his neck and his grip tightened.

She fitted snugly in his hold, her breast soft temptation against his chest, the sunshine scent of her enticing. His pulse accelerated but he kept his eyes on her flushed face, rather than linger on the pronounced rise and fall of her breasts.

'Thanks. You can put me down.' She sounded delightfully breathless. Free of her glasses, there was nothing to hide the amber glow of awareness in her eyes. Alaric felt he was falling into sunshine.

He had an intense vision of her looking up at him like that, lips parted invitingly, eyes dazed. But in his mind she was sprawled beneath the royal blue canopy of his bed, naked on silk sheets, awaiting his pleasure.

Alaric's breathing grew choppy as he fought the most primitive of physical reactions. His lower body locked solid at the force of abrupt arousal. The sound of applause and excited comment faded as fire ignited his blood.

Tamsin moved, dragging her gaze from his and fumbling at the strap of her helmet. It dropped away before she could stop it and her hair frothed over his arm in a dark cloud.

The scent of wildflowers hit him.

Forget the bedroom. He wanted this woman on sweet alpine grass. He wanted to watch her eyes light to gold as he plunged deep inside and took her to ecstasy.

'Alaric.' Her voice was deliciously throaty. He wanted to hear her calling his name as she climaxed. 'Please…'

Reluctantly he lowered her to her feet. But holding her had cemented his resolve. Amazingly, for those few moments she'd banished the dark shadows. He'd been utterly consumed by sexual need. Just as when they'd kissed.

It was no longer enough to satisfy his pride by making Tamsin Connors beg for his kisses. Alaric craved the release he knew he could find in her sweet, supple body.

And he intended to have it.

'A moment of your time before you go in.'

Tamsin halted at the door to the castle's staff quarters. Slowly she turned, schooling her face to polite interest. They were alone, the security men melting away when they arrived back from the youth centre.

In the late afternoon gloom of the castle courtyard, Alaric's face was unreadable but the way he towered above her, his shoulders blocking her vision, reminded her of the night he'd kissed her.

Of the way it had felt an hour ago when he'd held her in his embrace.

A shiver tingled to her toes as she recalled the heat in his eyes and the answering fire in her belly, and lower, at the message that had passed wordlessly between them.

No! Her imagination ran riot. Prince Alaric would never look at her with desire. Her hormones made her see what wasn't there. He'd played at intimacy for their audience.

'Yes?' At least her voice was steady.

For a moment he simply gazed down. She sensed the intensity of his regard, despite the way his eyelids dropped to half-mast. That gave him a dangerously seductive look that made her pulse race into overdrive.

He leaned closer, his breath tickling her forehead.

'Why wear those glasses? You don't need them.'

Stunned, she stepped back, only to find she'd already backed up against the door. He followed, lifting a hand idly to rest on the wall near her head. Instantly Tamsin was torn between unease at the sense of being trapped and, worse, delight at being so near him.

Beneath her jacket her breasts felt fuller. She wanted his hand there, she realised with a stifled gasp, on her breast, moulding her flesh.

This was worse than anything she'd felt for Patrick. Far worse. Surely it wasn't normal to feel this lick of heat between her legs or the heavy swirl low in her belly?

'Tamsin?'

Flustered, she grappled for the thread of the conversation. 'My glasses?' She touched them, gaining a moment's reassurance from their familiarity. 'For magnification. I do a lot of close work.'

'They don't magnify much.'

How did he know that?

'You don't need them now. You took them off to play squash and to climb. Why not remove them when you're not working?'

'I'm used to them.' Even in her own ears it sounded lame, but it was true. 'I've worn them for years.'

'Then perhaps it's time you came out from behind them.' Alaric leaned forward, his words a whispered caress that tantalised her bare skin.

He lifted a hand and for a moment she thought he was going to grab her glasses. Instead he stroked her hair from her face.

After taking it down to fit under the climbing helmet, she'd only secured it quickly and now strands escaped. She felt them tickle her neck.

Or was that his warm breath? He'd lowered his head and they stood close.

'What difference does it make to you?' Her voice was uneven, as if she'd run up the zigzag road to the castle.

'None.' Again his fingers stroked as he tucked hair behind her ear. Did she imagine his touch lingered? 'I just wondered why you hid behind them.'

Tamsin stiffened. 'I'm not hiding!' She'd acquired the glasses when she'd worked on a particularly difficult manuscript at university. The text had been so tiny she'd suffered eye strain until she'd got them.

She watched one dark eyebrow rise questioningly. She was about to reiterate her words when something stopped her.

The memory of how comfortable she'd felt behind her new glasses. How easy not to notice when older students pointed and dug each other in the ribs as they whispered about her. How hurtful it was when they'd gone to the pub after lectures leaving her, the young kid, behind and alone.

When had she decided to use her glasses all the time? Had it even been a conscious decision?

Or had she slipped into the habit the same way she'd filled her wardrobe with clothes that were functional rather than fashionable? *Because there was no point pretending to be what she wasn't.* Because she was what she was: a brain rather than a face. Known for her intellect, never invited out or pursued for her looks or personality.

Was he right? Had she been hiding? Isolating herself as a defence mechanism?

'Tamsin?'

'Was there anything else…Alaric?' She stood straighter, looking him in the eye, her brain whirling with the implications of his words. She'd think about it later. She couldn't think when he was so close, so…distracting.

'As a matter of fact there is.' He smiled and her heart jerked as if pulled on a string.

Tamsin swallowed, telling herself it was a trick of the fading light that made his expression seem intimate, as if he wanted nothing more than to stand here with her.

'Yes? You have another outing planned?' It didn't matter that she'd enjoyed her afternoon. That she'd revelled in the company of the teenagers, seemingly antisocial and yet so enthusiastic. Alaric had only invited her to be seen with him. Because she was a decoy.

He must have been ecstatic when she'd swooned in his arms, reinforcing their fictional relationship. Heat rocketed to her cheeks at the memory.

Would he be angry or amused if he realised how she felt about him? That the thought of him touching her made her long for things far beyond her experience?

'Not an outing.' He paused. 'I'm hosting a winter ball. It's an important event on the calendar.'

'*Another* ball? But you just had one!'

His mouth lifted in a lazy smile that softened her sinews and made her slump, grateful for the solid door behind her. In the gathering dusk Tamsin read the amused glitter in his eyes.

'How puritanical you sound. Do you disapprove?'

'It just seems a little…'

'Excessive?' He shrugged. 'Last week's was a small affair, only eighty or so guests to meet a new consul. The winter ball is something different. In four hundred years it's been held as regular as clockwork every year but one.'

'During war?'

Alaric's expression sobered. 'No.' Tamsin waited what seemed a full minute before he continued. 'There was no winter ball the year my brother died suddenly.'

Tamsin's flesh chilled as his words, sharp as shattered crystal, scored her.

'I'm sorry, Alaric. So sorry for your loss.' When he'd spoken briefly of his family the other night she'd had the impression they weren't close. Except his brother. The way Alaric spoke of him she sensed a special bond there.

She lifted her hand to reach for him, then dropped it. He wouldn't welcome her touch. He'd never looked so remote.

'Thank you.' He nodded curtly. 'But the point is this event, above all, is one where I'd be grateful for your presence.'

'Of course.'

It didn't matter that attending a ball was the last thing she wanted, that she'd be way out of her comfort zone. She'd seen the pain behind Alaric's cool expression. For a moment she'd seen anguish shadow his eyes and the sight hit her a body blow.

If he wanted her, she'd be there.

She didn't pause to question her decision.

'Good. Thank you.' His lips tilted in a ghost of his usual smile and something seemed to unravel, deep inside her. 'A dresser will attend you tomorrow and you can make your selection to wear to the ball.'

'But I—'

'Let me guess.' This time his smile was real and her heart tumbled. *Oh, she had it bad.* 'You're going to insist on buying your gown?'

'Well, yes.'

'You'd only buy a ball gown as a favour to me.' He stroked a finger down Tamsin's cheek, effectively stifling the objection rising in her throat. That simple caress held her still, breathless with pleasure.

'Consider it a work-related expense. I need you there and you need a dress. Unless you have one with you?'

Tamsin shook her head. She'd never owned a ball gown.

He leaned in. For a heart-stopping moment she wondered if he'd kiss her. She should object but her willpower seeped away. Her damp palms spread on the door behind her for support and her pulse juddered madly against her ribcage.

'Leave it to me.' His lips were so close Tamsin almost felt them against her skin. She sucked in a difficult breath as he spoke again in that deep, seductive whisper.

'All you have to do is relax and enjoy.'

CHAPTER SEVEN

TAMSIN lifted a hand to her hair then changed her mind and let it fall. She didn't want to disturb the softly elegant knot with its glittering pins or the artfully loose tendrils caressing her neck.

The dresser who'd returned this evening had done far more than zip up the dress. She'd transformed Tamsin into a woman she barely recognised. A woman who looked attractive in a way Tamsin never had before.

At first she'd thought it was simply the ball gown that made the difference. Of red silk shot with amber and gold, it was unlike anything she'd owned. From the moment she'd put it on she'd felt…special. The last of her scruples about accepting it disintegrated as she twirled before the mirror.

The bodice, cut high and straight above her breasts to leave her shoulders bare, made her look feminine and elegant. Even the fact that she'd had to go braless, relying on the dress's hidden support in lieu of a strapless bra she didn't own, didn't dampen her excitement.

It was shallow of her to feel wonderful because she looked good. But Tamsin didn't care. It was such a novel experience! Excitement bubbled in her veins. She felt she could take on the world!

For weeks Tamsin had featured in newspaper and magazine articles beside Alaric. Worst of all, the ones that made her cringe, were the 'then and now' pieces. Showing Alaric with previous girlfriends, all gorgeous and sophisticated. Those photos were set against pictures of Tamsin, looking anything but chic, her expression startled or, worse, besotted as she stared up at the powerful man beside her.

She wasn't besotted. She wouldn't let herself be.

The theme of each article had been the same. What did Alaric see in her? Those pictures had confirmed every doubt she'd harboured about herself, especially since Patrick.

More than once she'd been tempted to call a halt to this charade. She didn't, not simply because she'd given her word, but because being with Alaric, the focus of his glowing looks, made her feel good.

Even it if was a sham, she *enjoyed* being with him. It was balm to her wounded soul. Was it so wrong to enjoy the pretence that he genuinely liked her?

Yet the temptation was dangerous.

Now for the first time Tamsin knew she looked like a prince's companion. Delight filled her that this time there'd be no snide conjecture, no damning photos. This time she looked... attractive.

Tonight she'd learned so much. Things she'd always told herself she was too busy to bother with. Things her mother, so profoundly uninterested in fashion, hadn't thought to teach her. Like what shade of eye shadow accentuated the colour of Tamsin's eyes without being too obvious. Like how to tame her hair into a sophisticated style.

Yet the dresser said it was the glow in Tamsin's skin, the sparkle in her eyes that made her look so good tonight.

Surely that had been a pep talk to give her confidence. Apart from the clothes and light make-up, she was the same. As she turned before the mirror, feeling the silk swirl around her legs, Tamsin experienced a prickle of unease. The colour in her cheeks was because of the dress, that's all.

For there was only one other possible explanation. That her inner sparkle was anticipation at the idea of spending the evening with Alaric, maybe even dancing in his arms.

She stopped abruptly, letting her long skirts settle around her. No! She wouldn't let it be so. To Alaric she was a convenient companion. She wouldn't spin fantasies about him. These past weeks as his companion had been surprisingly delightful. She enjoyed his company. *But that's all.*

The phone rang and she snatched it up, grateful for the interruption to her disturbing thoughts.

'Tamsin? How are you, darling?'

Instantly her spine stiffened. She'd hoped not to hear that voice again for a long, long time. She'd crossed Europe to avoid this man. To pull herself together after he'd hurt her so badly. Now he had the temerity to call her darling!

'Who is this?'

'Ah, sweetheart, it's Patrick of course. Are you still upset about the way we parted?' He paused as if waiting for her to speak. 'Didn't I apologise?'

He'd apologised all right, while smirking at his success and her gullibility in believing he could ever interest himself in a plain Jane like her! As apologies went it had been a masterpiece of form over sentiment. He hadn't been sorry and in that moment Tamsin had finally realised how blind she'd been to his true personality.

In love with the idea of love, she'd fallen for him like a ripe peach. Or from his perspective, like a dried up prune! Too late she'd discovered his taste really ran to curvy blondes who dressed to reveal rather than conceal.

'It's late for a business call.' She was proud of her nonchalant tone.

'You're assuming it's business?'

'What do you want, Patrick?' He thought he was God's gift to women but he surely couldn't believe her weak enough to care for him after what he'd done.

His sigh might have moved her once but now she merely felt a burst of impatience.

It was only when he mentioned the date testing on the sample she'd sent to her home institution that Tamsin grew interested. By the time he'd finished speaking her scalp prickled with excitement.

She'd *known* this was special! Now the dating proved it.

Yet doubt lingered. On the face of it she now had proof that Alaric should be Maritz's next king. But caution warned her to make absolutely sure. Just because the document's age was right didn't prove the content.

Besides, Alaric wasn't as eager as she'd expected. Did he really not want to be king? Look at the strict security he'd instituted around the chronicle. It was locked away the minute she'd finished work each day.

'Tamsin? Are you still there?'

'Of course. I'll look forward to reading the report when you email it. Thanks for calling.'

'I said it seems you've got an interesting cache of documents. I hear on the grapevine the prince himself gave you extra staff for the project. Plus old Schillinger says you've sent him copies of some fascinating pages.'

'That's right.' She frowned. There was no way Patrick or anyone else could guess the explosive revelations in the manuscript. Those pages were kept here under lock and key. Dr Schillinger's interest in the rest was purely linguistic.

'Perhaps if it's such a find you'd feel better with another expert there. Someone you know you can work with.' He paused as if waiting for her to speak. 'I have a lot on at the moment but for you'd I'd tear myself away and...'

'No! That's not necessary.'

Did he think she was still so besotted that she'd invite him here after the way he'd treated her? Had she really been such a pushover?

'Tamsin.' His voice deepened to a cajoling note. 'I hurt you and I've regretted it ever since. I made a mistake and I'm not too proud to admit it. If I came over there we could pick up where we left off. I'm worried for you. Sometimes on the rebound people behave impulsively.'

Was he referring to the press reports linking her and Alaric? He had a hide!

How had she fallen for his oily charm? The only person Patrick cared about was Patrick. It made her sick to realise she'd been so needy she'd let him walk all over her without seeing his selfish opportunism.

As for his wet kisses and perfunctory embraces... Tamsin shuddered. How had she ever thought him appealing?

She remembered Alaric's demanding, exciting kiss. The combustible heat that consumed them and made her feel like she soared close to the sun.

In comparison Patrick's pallid caresses faded to insignificance. Now so did he: a mean, conniving man who wasn't worth her time or emotional energy.

'No, Patrick. I appreciate your offer to *tear yourself away.*' Her lips curled at his attempt to muscle in on what he thought was a project to further his career. 'It's all under control. The staff are excellent and we've gelled into a great team. Of course, if ever we need further support I'll be sure to let you know.' *When hell froze over.*

'But I—'

'Sorry, Patrick. I can't talk. I have to go.'

She put down the phone then stroked unsteady hands along the soft fabric of her dress, trying to conjure again her earlier pleasure.

Her stomach churned from hearing his voice. Not because she missed him, but at the knowledge of how close she'd come to making a complete fool of herself. She'd once considered *giving* herself to that…toad of a man!

Tamsin was fed up with being second best. Being *used.*

First Patrick and now Alaric, who only wanted her as a decoy. It didn't matter that Alaric also made her feel exciting, dangerous, unfamiliar things. That he brought her to tingling life like a sleeper waking from long slumber.

She was tired of being manipulated by men who wanted her for their schemes. Men who saw her as a convenience to be exploited.

Not a real woman of flesh and blood and feelings.

She stared in the mirror, taking in the reflection of a woman who was her and yet not her. Same nose, same eyes, same person, but so different from the old Tamsin everyone took for granted.

She was tired of hiding. Of not being noticed as a woman.

The idea of leaving the protective comfort of her usual role, of daring to pretend to be feminine and desirable, filled her with trepidation. Yet Alaric was right. Tamsin had isolated herself.

She owed it to herself not to hide behind her work and her past any longer. She might be out of her depth tonight but she was no coward.

Deliberately she lifted her hand and removed her glasses, dropping them onto a nearby table. Straightening her shoulders she left the room, her head high.

Alaric viewed formal balls as a necessary evil. Until he turned from greeting an ambassador and her husband to see the next guest in line and the air punched from his lungs.

She was breathtaking.

Among the bejewelled and bedecked glitterati she was unadorned, yet she glowed with a radiance that set her apart. She didn't need diamonds and platinum. Her skin was flawless, her lips a glossy pout that turned his blood molten hot with instant hunger. Her dark hair was a sensuous invitation to touch. It looked like she'd just pinned it up after rising from a bath or bed. As if it would tumble down at any moment around her bare shoulders.

And her eyes. She'd removed the glasses and her amber-gold eyes were even more vibrant, more beautiful than he remembered. They blazed with an expression he'd never seen.

He'd *known* she was hiding her real self. But nothing had prepared him for this.

The ambassador moved away and Tamsin approached.

Alaric stiffened. She was fully covered, more fully than many of the women present. Yet he knew an almost overpowering impulse to unbutton his military tunic and toss it around her bare shoulders.

He didn't miss the arrested glances from the men nearby. He wanted to growl out a warning to keep their distance. To look away.

'Tamsin.' His voice worked, though it emerged brusquely from frozen vocal cords. 'It's good to see you.' If his muscles weren't so stiff with shock he'd have laughed at the enormity of that understatement. He bowed over her hand, resorting to punctilious formality to prevent himself shepherding her straight out the way she'd come. Away from those admiring stares.

His gaze dropped to her bodice, tightly fitted to show off her slim frame and full breasts. Flaring skirts accentuated Tamsin's narrow waist and for an insane moment he found himself distracted, musing whether he could span her with his hands.

'Hello, Alaric.' Her voice was low and throaty, yanking his libido into roaring life.

His hand tightened around hers and he wondered what would happen if he swept her away right now and didn't come back. He was within an ace of scandalising everyone, had moved closer, when she spoke again.

'I'm sorry I'm late.'

Reluctantly he dropped her hand and stepped back, removing himself from temptation.

'You're not late at all.' His voice was unnaturally clipped. 'Please, go on in. I'll join you soon.'

She nodded and he turned away, forcing himself to greet the next guests in the reception line. Never had it been so hard to focus on duty.

It was easier than she'd expected to mingle at a royal ball. Tamsin smiled as she sipped a glass of champagne and listened to the conversation around her.

'You're enjoying yourself?' asked Peter, the friendly community centre coordinator she'd met just over a week ago.

'How could I not? I've met so many fascinating people and I love dancing.' She'd only discovered that tonight, as partner after partner had whirled her round the mirrored ballroom, her dress swishing about her and her blood singing in her veins. It had been heady and delightful.

She turned. Peter wore an officer's dress uniform. The gold braid and the neat row of medals across his chest gleamed in the light of the chandeliers. He looked the model of a dashing soldier of a couple of centuries ago, except for the scar on his neck and cheek.

He laughed. 'It's true, then, that all the girls love a uniform.'

'Sorry. Was I staring?' His smile dispelled any embarrassment. 'It's just so unusual. Uniforms have changed since the Napoleonic Wars.'

'Not in Ruvingia. Not for formal occasions.' He winked. 'Especially as they make us so popular with the ladies. But in the field we wear khakis like everyone else.'

A pair of dancers swung by: Alaric looking like he'd stepped from the pages of a fairy tale in a uniform like Peter's only with more medals pinned to his chest, and in his arms a delicate blonde woman glittering in azure silk and sapphires.

Something struck Tamsin in the ribs. Jealousy? The possibility appalled her.

Despite promising to join her hours ago, Alaric had only danced with her once. He'd held her at arm's length, propelling her around the floor as if she were an elderly maiden aunt. Not close in his embrace as he smiled down into her face like he did with the gorgeous blonde.

The pain in her ribs twisted, intensifying.

'The prince, too? Surely he doesn't have to wear khaki?'

'Alaric? You don't know—?'

The surprise in Peter's voice made her swing round to meet his suddenly sombre face.

'Don't know what?'

He shrugged and she had the impression he was buying time before answering. The instinct she'd always trusted with her work sent a tiny shiver down her backbone.

'You mean Alaric is a real soldier, too?' If Peter was surprised by her use of the prince's first name he didn't show it. 'I thought the uniform might be a perk of position. Like being a royal sponsor rather than a member of the regiment.'

Yet even as Tamsin spoke she recalled her first impression of Alaric. His controlled power and athleticism proclaimed him a man of action, not a tame administrator.

'Some perk!' Peter shook his head. 'He won his commission through talent and hard work. Much good it did him.'

Tamsin put her glass down. 'What do you mean?' Peter's grim expression spiked foreboding through her.

'There was nothing pretend about our work. Alaric was our commanding officer and a good one, too. But with command comes a sense of responsibility. That can weigh heavily on a man who genuinely cares, especially when things go wrong.'

He half lifted his hand towards his scarred face and Tamsin's heart squeezed in sympathy. She wished she'd never started this conversation.

'I'm sorry,' she said breathlessly. 'I shouldn't have brought it up.'

He smiled. 'Because of this?' He gestured to his face. 'Don't be. There are worse things, believe me.' He looked at the dance floor as Alaric and his partner swung by again. 'Not all scars are on the outside, you know. At least mine have healed.'

Tamsin's gaze followed the prince. So handsome, so powerful, standing out effortlessly from every other man here. The focus of so many longing female glances.

Yet Peter hinted at hidden scars. Could he be right?

She thought of the way Alaric's shadowed eyes belied his easy charm, hinting at dark secrets.

Out of nowhere came the recollection of Alaric's ashen face after he'd saved that boy from serious burns. The prince's expression had been stark with pain or shock. He'd frozen rigid, eyes staring blankly as if looking at something distant that horrified yet held him in thrall.

'Tamsin?'

'Sorry?' She turned to find Peter holding out his hand.

'Would you like to waltz?'

She met his friendly dark eyes and tore her thoughts from the man even now bowing to some aristocratic lady on the other side of the ballroom.

She spent far too much time fretting about Alaric.

'I'd love to.'

For the next hour she danced with partner after partner, revelling in the exquisite venue, the glamorous crowd, the pleasure of the dance. Resolutely she tried not to notice Alaric dancing with every pretty woman in the room. Finally, pleading exhaustion, she let her partner lead her to a relatively quiet corner for champagne and conversation.

He was an editor from a national newspaper, good looking and full of entertaining stories that made her laugh. Tamsin saw the openly admiring light in his eyes and felt a warm glow inside. Here was one man at least who didn't look on her as second best!

Plus he was flatteringly interested in her work, suggesting a feature article on the archives and preservation work.

'May I interrupt?'

At the sound of that deep voice her companion halted in mid-sentence. 'Your Highness, of course.'

Reluctantly Tamsin turned. She'd told herself she was glad Alaric hadn't shown her off as his fake companion tonight. She'd wanted to be her own woman, hadn't she?

Yet his lack of interest stung.

Had he finally decided she wasn't up to the job?

Piercing indigo eyes met hers and heat sizzled through her, making the hairs on her arms stand up as if he'd brushed fingertips along her bare skin.

She searched for the shadows she'd seen in his gaze once before, the shadows Peter had hinted at, but there was nothing wounded about this man. If anything there was a hint of steel in his stare, a tautness about his mouth. He was commanding, assured, supremely confident.

He bowed. The epitome of royal hauteur from his severely combed hair to his mirror polished shoes.

'Tamsin, I believe this is our dance.'

She tried to tell herself she didn't care that he'd come to her at last, but her heart gave a little jump.

'I'll be in contact later, Tamsin.' Her companion smiled and took her wineglass, urging her forward. She had no excuse but to go with Alaric.

A strong hand closed around hers and her heart hammered. Ridiculous! She'd danced with the prince earlier. But then he'd barely looked at her, his formality quenching her excitement.

Now his gaze pinioned her, so intent it smouldered.

What had she done to antagonise him?

'You've made a new friend,' he murmured as he curled long fingers around her waist. His touch evoked a tremor of primitive anxiety. As if she'd stepped too close to a slumbering predator.

Taking a deep breath Tamsin placed an arm on his shoulder, let him clasp her other hand and fixed her gaze on his collar. This was just a dance. For show.

'Yes, several. Everyone's been very pleasant.' Despite the heat flooding her veins as Alaric guided her on the floor, something in his tone chilled her.

'So I saw. You've flitted from man to man all evening.' His voice was harsh and she raised surprised eyes to his. Blue fire flashed like lightning in an approaching storm.

'Your instructions were just that I attend the ball.' Her breasts rose in indignation, straining at the taut fabric of her bodice. 'I hadn't realised I wasn't allowed to mingle.' After ignoring her most of the night, how dare he complain she'd socialised with the other guests?

'Is that what you call it?' He spun her faster till the room whirled around them. Yet in his firm hold Tamsin felt only a heady rush of excitement. As if she were on the edge of something dangerous that nevertheless called to her.

'Do you have a problem, Alaric?' She told herself she was breathless because of the speed with which they circled the room. Her skirts belled out around her and her breath shallowed but she didn't feel nervous. She felt…exhilarated.

'Of course not. Why should I?' He kept his gaze fixed over her shoulder. 'Though I'd be sorry to see you hurt.'

'Hurt?' The music ended and they spun to a halt, yet Alaric didn't let her go. They stood in the centre of the dance floor, his grip holding her still.

'We Ruvingians are hospitable to guests. I wouldn't want you to misunderstand and interpret friendliness for something more.'

Tamsin's breath hissed between her teeth as pain lanced her. 'What are you insinuating? That no one would normally want to spend time with a woman like me? That I'm too uninteresting? Or perhaps I'm too plain?'

All the pleasure she'd felt in the evening shattered in that moment, like fragile crystal smashed underfoot. She told herself she didn't believe him, but suddenly the brilliant glare of the antique chandeliers seemed to flicker and dim. The heady excitement of the evening faded to something tawdry and shallow.

She stepped back to break his hold but his grip tightened.

'Of course not. You're misinterpreting my words.'

The music struck up again and around them couples took to the floor, a throng of glittering, designer clad, beautiful people.

She didn't belong here.

'You can let me go, *Your Highness*. You've done your duty dance.' She primmed her lips rather than say any more.

He didn't move, though she saw his chest rise as he took a huge breath.

'I said—'

He muttered something savage under his breath in the local dialect. Something she had no hope of understanding. A second later he pulled her close and twirled her round into the dancing crowd.

This time there was nothing prim or proper about the way they moved. Gone was the staid distance between them. Instead Tamsin was plastered to Alaric's torso. His arm at her waist didn't steady her, it welded her to him. His breath feathered her forehead. His hard thighs cradled her then shifted provocatively between her legs as they danced, evoking a strange hollow ache in her womb.

This close she felt his every movement, partly because her hands were trapped against his chest. His heart pounded fast and strong beneath her palm and despite her anger and hurt, spiralling excitement rose.

'I've had enough dancing,' she gasped as he swung her round and back down the long ballroom. This was too much, too dangerous.

'Nonsense. You love to dance. I've seen the smile on your face all night.'

All night? That implied he'd watched her which he hadn't. He'd been too busy squiring so many socialites onto the floor or engaging them in close conversation.

'You may find it hard to believe, Your Highness, but not all women long to dance with you.' The room flashed by and her heart pounded faster and faster. 'I want to stop.'

'I told you to call me Alaric.'

His body moved against hers and she bit her lip at the surge of pleasure she felt. At the powerful throb building inside. She was pathetic. This was just a dance and with a man she assured herself she didn't like. Though as his arm dropped low on her back, pulling her even tighter, it felt like something altogether different.

'Alaric.' The word was barely audible. Whether from the pulse pounding in her ears or because she couldn't seem to catch her breath, she didn't know.

'That's better.' His voice was rough as his lips moved against her hair. 'I like it when you say my name.'

With one final turn he spun them off the dance floor. Before Tamsin could catch her breath he'd shoved aside a hanging tapestry and hustled her through a door into a narrow passage. A few steps on and another arched door opened on their left. They were through it and in a dimly lit chamber before Tamsin could get her bearings.

A key scraped in the lock, loud as the thrum of her heartbeat. Then she felt a solid wall behind her and Alaric's powerful body trapping her against it.

'What do you think you're doing?' It was meant to sound outraged. Instead Tamsin's voice was uneven, weak with the force of conflicting emotions.

She should abhor this forced intimacy, the press of his body. Yet a secret thrill of pleasure ripped through her.

'Getting you to myself.' Alaric cupped her face in warm palms and lifted her chin so she looked deep into eyes the colour of a stormy night sky. 'I spoiled your evening. I didn't mean to.'

He leaned forward, touching his forehead to hers, hands tunnelling her hair, sending threads of shivery sensation down her spine and across her shoulders. Suddenly it wasn't him holding her prisoner, but her body's response.

'Why?' she croaked, her mouth too dry for speech. How had they come to this?

She should move but she made no resistance as he caressed her scalp and rubbed his nose against hers.

Where was her anger? A deep shuddering sigh rose and she strove to stifle it.

'Because I was jealous.' Shock slammed into her. Yet she felt the words as well as heard them as his lips caressed her eyelids. He really had said it. 'From the moment you appeared tonight I wanted you with me. Only me.'

This couldn't be. Tamsin shook her head, or tried to. He held her so close she couldn't move.

'I don't understand.' She hated her shaky tone but she was at a loss. 'You avoided me most of the night.'

'Displacement activity. I either spent the evening glued to you, or I kept my distance, acting the polite host. There was no happy medium. In the circumstances I thought my self-control admirable.'

His hands moved, slid down her throat and spread across her bare shoulders. Something about his powerful hands touching her so tenderly made her breath catch. His palms circled back to her throat, warming her skin and making her pulse race.

'Every time I saw you smiling at a dance partner I wanted it to be me you smiled at. No one else. Do you have any idea how gorgeous you are tonight?'

He couldn't be serious!

She couldn't think logically when he caressed her like that. She needed to think, to understand.

'Please. Alaric, I…'

'Yes, let me please you. Like this?'

His hands dropped, skimming the silk of her bodice, down the sides of her breasts, till her nipples tightened and the breath seared from her lungs.

Logic didn't matter when his mouth was a mere inch away. She craved him with every fibre of her yearning, untried body. As if this were what she'd secretly waited for. Without volition she raised her face, hungry beyond rational thought for his passion.

His mouth hovered, a breath away from hers.

'I promised I wouldn't.' His husky voice stroked like suede, dragging at her senses. 'So ask me to kiss you, Tamsin.'

CHAPTER EIGHT

ALARIC'S heart slammed against his ribs as he awaited her response. Every nerve, every sinew strained at the need for control.

Part of him was furious that somehow, without him knowing how, she'd cracked the wall he'd built around himself. The wall he'd reinforced the day he'd learnt the need to keep his affairs short and uncomplicated by emotion.

Surely he knew the dangers of reckless affairs!

But this was different.

More than dalliance to hold other women at bay. Far more than a ruse to keep an eye on someone who might, though it surely wasn't possible, be in league with those wanting to undermine the government.

This was an urgent, blood deep hunger.

Somewhere in the ballroom he'd crossed an unseen boundary.

Had it been when he bundled her from the room in full view of scandalised eyes? Or when he'd hauled her close in contravention of every protocol, staking his unmistakeable claim on her? No, it had been earlier. When he'd read the shattered hurt dulling her eyes and known himself the cause. His pain then had been as sharp as any physical wound.

He'd never felt this intensely about a woman.

He didn't *want* emotion. He didn't *want* to feel. Emotions were dangerous, deceitful. Yet for now he functioned on a more primitive level. Raw instinct not reason drove him.

He inhaled deeply, intoxicated by the scent of her. Unthinking, he bent to the delicate curve where her shoulder met her throat, nuzzling flesh so soft it made him feel like a barbarian, demanding her acquiescence.

But he didn't care. Desperation smoked off his skin, clamoured in his pulse, clenched his belly.

From the moment she'd arrived, a demure siren among a crowd of overdressed mannequins, he'd hungered for her.

As he'd watched her laugh and whisper and dance with all those other men he'd experienced a completely alien sensation. A roiling, dangerous, possessive anger.

Jealousy.

The sight of her with that journalist, known as much for his feminine conquests as his provocative editorials, had been a red rag to a bull.

Alaric told himself he'd acted to break up any potential leak of sensitive information. They'd looked like conspirators, their heads close together, their voices lowered. The last thing he wanted was news of her theories about his inheritance splashed across the newspapers.

But in truth he'd stalked across to claim her because he couldn't bear to watch their intimate *tête à tête.*

He laved her skin with his tongue, filling his mouth with her essence. Tamsin shuddered against his hardening body and he did it again, unable to stop. She was delicious.

'Alaric!' Fleetingly he registered her trembling sigh was probably a protest, though it sounded more like encouragement.

'Mmm? I'm not kissing you.' His mouth moved on her skin, trailing up to just below her ear. 'This isn't a kiss.'

He closed his teeth on her lobe in a gentle, grinding bite that made her spasm and fall further into him. Fire flickered through his veins.

So responsive. So incredibly attuned to every caress.

Escalating desire bunched each muscle into lockdown. The press of her belly against his erection was exquisite torture. If she moved again…

'Alaric. No.' It was a throaty whisper that incited rather than protested.

This time he grazed his teeth against the tender flesh below her ear and was rewarded with a shuddering sigh as her head lolled back against the wall. She'd stopped trying to push him away, her fingers curling instead into his tunic as if to draw him closer.

He nipped his way down her throat, revelling in the sinuous slide of her body against his. Unable to resist any longer, he levered away a fraction so he could cup her breasts. High, ripe, lush, they fitted his palms perfectly.

Suddenly slim hands bracketed his jaw, urgently dragging his face up. An instant later Tamsin's lips met his, hard and frantic, delightfully clumsy in her ardour.

When her tongue invaded his mouth it was Alaric's turn to groan at the sheer intensity of sensation. She kissed like a sexy angel. Half seductress, half innocent. For a moment the illusion hovered that she'd saved herself for him alone. That he was her first, her only.

Then he sank into bliss as their tongues slid and mated and thought became impossible. She melded to him with a supple sensuality that drove him to the edge.

He caressed her nipples and she growled in the back of her throat, a decadent purr of pleasure that had him thrusting his knee between hers, parting her legs. In response she arched into his hands, pressing as if she too couldn't get enough.

He needed her. *Now.*

Tearing himself from her grasp he looked down. The gown's neckline was high across her breasts, and tight enough to make them inaccessible. But locating the fastening at the back was the work of a moment. As was lowering the zip enough to loosen the bodice.

He heard her suck in her breath but she didn't protest. Seconds later he peeled the bodice down enough to reveal her cleavage. Her breasts rose and fell rapidly, silently inviting.

With a swift yank of the silky fabric he bared her breasts, watching blush pink nipples bud in the cold air. Not even a strapless bra. Who'd have thought it of prim and proper Dr Connors?

Alaric wasn't complaining. He drank in the sight of pure white skin, full breasts, perfectly formed and deliciously uptilted as if begging for his attention.

His erection pulsed and he almost groaned aloud when she rocked her hips, her thighs widening suggestively. He needed that pelvis to pelvis contact, was desperate to sheath himself inside her. But first…

He lowered his head to her breast, skimmed a caress across her nipple and felt her hands claw his shoulders as if she could no longer stand without support.

He smiled as he kissed the impossibly soft skin around her aureole, revelling in her responsiveness as she gasped and shifted beneath his ministrations.

'Stop teasing.' Her voice was hoarse and uneven. Alaric looked up to see her brow furrow as she watched him. 'Just…' She paused and swallowed hard. 'Do it.'

Despite the wobbly order, Tamsin's eyes were dazed and her skin flushed with arousal. The combination of prim command, desperation and luscious wanton was delicious.

Eyes holding hers, he covered one nipple with his lips, enjoying the way her eyes widened as she watched him draw her into his mouth. Heat shot through him, catapulting him into a world of sensual pleasure as he devoured her sweetness. He sucked hard and she jerked like a puppet on a string, head and neck arched against the wood panelling. Her lower body moved restlessly against him, mimicking his own edgy need to thrust into her.

Not yet. Tamsin was pure delight. He couldn't get enough of her.

He moved to her other breast, daring a tiny erotic bite. She keened her pleasure, her body stiffening around his as if he'd generated an electric current. He breathed deep the sweet scent of feminine arousal and his blood surged south.

She was so hyper-sensitive, was it possible he could bring her to orgasm like this? The notion was almost too much for his threadbare self-discipline.

Another graze of his teeth, this time at her nipple, and another jolt ripped through her. Hungrily he suckled, feeding the demon inside that demanded more, demanded everything from her.

Fumbling, he scrabbled at her skirts, the slippery fabric sliding through his unsteady hands.

He couldn't wait any longer.

Rising, he plastered his mouth over hers, revelling in her kisses as finally his questing fingers found silk clad thighs. Stockings! He found the upper edge, the line where material met bare, smooth flesh and he faltered, heart pounding at the image his mind conjured.

He wanted to spread her on a bed and leisurely inspect the sexy picture she'd make before taking his fill. But he didn't have time, his need was too urgent. His erection throbbed so needily he wondered if he'd be able to get out of his trousers without injury.

He drove her head back with hungry kisses as he hiked her skirts. In a perfect world she wouldn't be wearing panties.

But this was no fantasy. His hands encountered cotton. Despite the sexy gown and stockings, Tamsin had chosen no-nonsense underwear. Underwear damp with arousal.

Spreading his hand to cup her mound, feeling her push hard into his grip, Alaric decided cotton panties were far sexier than silk, more of a turn on than Lycra or lace. Tamsin didn't need frills. She was potently, earthily sexy.

Her hand insinuated itself between their bodies to grapple with the fastening of his dress trousers.

She'd send him over the edge in a moment. He clamped an iron hand round her wrist.

'Don't!' he growled, his voice thick. He forced her hand back, high against the wall and kissed her again. He wanted this to last more than ten seconds. He'd bring her to climax, enjoy watching her take pleasure at his hands, and only then find release in her body.

His fingers slipped beneath cotton, drawn by her heat.

A roaring explosion cracked the night sky, penetrating his fog of sensual arousal. He stiffened, muscles freezing at what sounded like artillery fire. Dread engulfed him as adrenaline spiked in his blood.

By the time the second reverberating boom rent the air he'd opened his eyes and registered the flash of coloured light. Relief surged so strongly he felt weak.

Reality buffeted him and he dropped his head, gasping, trying to force down raw, conflicting emotions. Relief that he was no longer in the nightmare world of armed conflict. And lust—the almost insuperable need for completion. If only willpower could shift blood from his groin to his brain! Never had he so completely lost control.

'What is it?' Tamsin sounded as shaken as he.

Another couple of minutes and he'd have had her, ankles locked round his waist while he shuddered his climax into her. Even now he craved it. The effort of not taking her made him tremble all over.

If he did her gown would be rumpled and stained, proclaiming exactly what they'd been doing.

There'd be stares and rolled eyes about his behaviour but that was nothing. His shoulders were broad, his reputation bad and people's expectations low.

For Tamsin the gossip would be infinitely worse. He couldn't do that to her.

He'd failed Felix. Failed his men. But in this at least surely he could manage to do the right thing.

'Fireworks,' he murmured, his voice a strained whisper. He cleared his throat and released her hand, letting it slide down the wall. 'At the end of the ball we have fireworks and champagne. And a royal toast.'

He had to go. There was no chance to lose himself in Tamsin's slick, warm heat, no matter how much he craved her. Reluctantly he dragged his other hand from between her legs, felt her shudder at the movement and wished it could be different.

He let her skirts fall and stepped away, face drawing tight at the fierce pain in his groin. Desire and guilt and fury at the depth of his own need warred within him. He'd always enjoyed women but this…this was uncharted territory.

'Turn around.' The words emerged brusquely through gritted teeth. She stared up, her lips bruised to plumpness and eyes glazed, then she turned, her head bowed.

He stared at that expanse of naked back, the vulnerable line of her nape, and almost surrendered to temptation again. But a burst of green fire outside the window brought him back to the real world. To duty.

It took him a full minute to do up her dress, his hands were so uncoordinated. When it was done he moved away, wincing at each stiff-legged step as he paced to the window. He needed time before he made a public appearance. He needed to keep away from her before his resolve shattered.

'I'll have to go. I'm expected and my absence will cause speculation.'

He raised his hand to smooth his hair and caught the heady scent of her essence on his fingers. He dropped his hand, summoning every vestige of strength not to go to her when his body screamed out for completion. For Tamsin.

'Of course. I understand.' Her voice sounded flat, but then he couldn't hear clearly over his throbbing pulse and the crack of fireworks.

'Will you be all right?' Still he didn't turn around but stood silhouetted at the arched window, his back to her.

Why wouldn't he look at her?

She was the one embarrassed. He was the playboy with a reputation for loving then leaving each new mistress.

He'd known exactly what he was doing.

'I'm fine,' she murmured, wondering if the lie sounded believable. She was bereft, desperate for a look, a touch, *something*.

Tamsin shivered and slumped against the wall, hands splaying for support as she recalled how expert he'd been.

Her pulse raced out of control as she remembered his knowing, half-lidded look, watching her as he'd sucked at her breast. She squeezed her thighs together at the liquid heat between her legs. Who'd have guessed that every time he drew on her breast a taut line of fire would run down to her belly and lower, till she felt the empty ache inside?

Who'd have known she'd be so wanton as to rub herself needily against his hand? To delight in the sensation of his long fingers arrowing to her most private core?

Heat fired her cheeks at what she'd done, what she still wanted to do.

It was as if some alien woman had taken over her body. Some daring sensualist she'd never known, who acted on instincts Tamsin hadn't been aware of.

Was it remotely possible this was the real Tamsin, freed of the restraints that had ruled her life so long?

Or was this the result of a life without love or physical demonstrativeness? There'd been few cuddles growing up and no teenage kisses. With Patrick she hadn't ventured far into passion. Perhaps Alaric's caresses had unleashed a pent up longing for physical affection.

She released a shuddering breath. She'd determined to make a new start tonight, be a new woman, free of the crutches she'd used to distance herself from others. But she hadn't meant to go this far!

She hadn't thought…that was the problem.

Tamsin eyed Alaric's powerful frame, lit by a scintillating flash of red. She hadn't thought at all after he'd admitted to being jealous, to wanting her.

Had that been real? Or had it been an excuse to keep his distance because he genuinely hadn't wanted to be with her during the ball? The old Tamsin would have accepted the latter without a second's hesitation. Now she didn't know.

And this hot, heavy seduction scene? Could he have engineered it to provoke the kind of speculation he wanted? To create the illusion they were in a relationship?

But why go so far?

Yet if his desire had been genuine, and it had felt magnificently real when he'd ground himself against her, why the cold shoulder now? He'd reacted violently when she'd tried to touch him and his voice just now had been harsh.

Her lips twisted. If only she had more experience with men, with sex, she might understand!

Had he gone so far simply because she was so obviously, pantingly eager? For Alaric, was one warm female body in the dark as good as another?

The notion sickened her.

It was unfair to think it of him. Yet she remembered that first kiss and how he'd pulled up short when he'd knocked her glasses *and remembered who he was kissing*.

Tamsin bit her lip. All she knew was she wanted him to hold her and take her back to the place she'd been before he'd pulled away. She wanted him to smile and make her feel better.

Listen to her! She was a grown woman, not a child.

A knock sounded on the door and Tamsin started. Yet Alaric turned smoothly as if he'd expected it. Had this been a set-up?

He sent her a long, assessing look and her cheeks burned. Hurriedly she lifted her hands to secure her hair as best she could, then shook out her long skirts. But for the life of her she couldn't move away from the wall at her back. Her knees trembled too much.

'Enter.' Neither his voice nor his appearance gave any hint of what they'd been doing minutes before. *She'd* been the one half naked and wanting. Suddenly the fact that he'd remained fully clothed seemed suspiciously important.

Her throat closed on a knot of distress as she met his unblinking stare.

A steward entered and bowed deeply, his expression wooden. 'Your Highness. Madam.' He cleared his throat. 'I'm sorry to disturb—'

'It's all right.' Alaric's tone was clipped. 'Go on.'

Again the servant bowed. 'The guests are assembled on the terrace, Highness. The fireworks will end in five minutes.'

Alaric nodded, the picture of regal composure. 'Good. I'll be just in time for the toasts.' He turned to her and for a searing moment his gaze held hers, making her heart catapult against her ribs.

'Please accompany Dr Connors to her suite. She was overcome by the exertions of the ball. She doesn't know her way back from this part of the castle.'

The man nodded, his face betraying no emotion. Ridiculously that made Tamsin feel worse. Did Alaric make a habit of seducing women in antechambers? Given his reputation she supposed his servants were used to dealing with his cast off lovers.

A dreadful giggle rose in her throat. The joke was on them because she didn't fit the bill. She hadn't quite made it to the exalted ranks of ex-lover.

Now she probably never would.

'Dr Connors.' Alaric's bow was formal. He straightened and paused, as if waiting for her to speak.

'Your Highness.' A curtsey was beyond her. It was all she could do to stay upright, knees locked.

With a curt nod of acknowledgement he strode out the door, his bearing as rigid as a soldier on parade.

The fantasy was over.

It was time for Cinderella to leave.

At the knock on the door to his suite Alaric paused in the act of shrugging off his jacket.

Could it be her? Had she come to finish what they'd begun? His pulse rocketed, his body tensing in anticipation.

He'd been torn between visiting her now, tonight, and listening to the voice of responsibility that warned she'd been out of her depth. He'd taken advantage. He'd been so intent on seducing her he'd dismissed the need for discretion to protect her or to allow her time to think.

Yet he'd only come here to change from his uniform. He couldn't keep away after that taste of her sweet body.

Now she'd saved him the trouble!

'Come.'

It was an unpleasant shock to see his security chief enter instead. Disappointment surfaced and a disturbing premonition of bad news. The hair rose at his nape as he took in that sombre expression.

'I'm sorry to interrupt, sir, but you gave instructions about Dr Connors' phone calls. You need to hear this.'

The jacket fell from Alaric's hand to a nearby chair and he flexed his fingers. *He didn't want to hear this.*

The report on Tamsin had drawn a blank. The woman was so squeaky clean it was unbelievable. Recently Alaric had set aside his suspicion she might be connected with those trying to disrupt the government. He couldn't believe it.

After tonight he didn't *want* to believe it. He could still taste her cherry sweetness, smell the rich scent of her arousal.

He wanted to turn his back on whatever unpalatable truth awaited. But there was too much at stake.

He couldn't afford to trust his instincts when this was about far more than himself. What of the allegiance he owed Raul? If the document she'd found was genuine at the very least its public release had to be carefully managed. He couldn't fail in this as well.

'When was this call recorded?' He scrubbed a hand over his face, wearier than he'd been in months.

'Before the ball, sir. It was a while before I became aware of the contents. By then the festivities were under way and there was no time to inform you.'

'Very well.' Alaric gestured to a table, curiously unwilling to take the recording in his own hand. 'Leave it.'

His advisor looked as if he'd protest.

Between them hung the knowledge that a stable monarchy was at the core of the nation's wellbeing.

'You can go,' he ordered.

There was only a fractional hesitation. 'Yes, sir.'

The door closed and Alaric was alone. He exhaled slowly, reminding himself of his responsibilities.

Yet the imprint of Tamsin's body branded him. He could almost feel her breasts crushed against him, her hands clutching his hair as he demanded and she reciprocated with a fervour that blasted his control to smithereens. Her scent was on his clothes, his hands. His body was taut with unsated need.

No wonder it felt like betrayal when he took the CD and inserted it into the player.

Long after the recording had ended he stood, staring out into the stark blackness of the night.

Tamsin and Patrick. He knew of the other man from the investigative dossier, though it had been unclear how intimate the pair had been. Now he knew.

They'd been lovers.

His gut roiled queasily at the thought of Tamsin in the arms of another man. In his bed. Alaric's jaw ached as he ground his teeth, trying to harness the overpowering need to do something rash, something violent. It was as well the other man was out of Alaric's way, safe in England.

The way he'd spoken to her in that call! He'd dumped her then expected her to welcome him back with open arms. Alaric registered a tiny flicker of satisfaction that she'd sent him packing. She'd adopted her most glacial schoolmistress voice to get rid of him.

And still Alaric couldn't obliterate the image of her naked in a stranger's arms.

So much for his fancy that her guileless yet fervent kisses were evidence of inexperience. He shook his head. He'd fallen for that buttoned up look, been swayed into believing her prickly reserve and her cover-up clothes meant she was an innocent.

Which showed how she'd impaired his thinking!

The woman was all combustible heat, a born seductress. She'd almost blown the back off his head, just with her cries of encouragement as he'd fondled her.

Alaric planted his palms on the window sill, anchoring himself to the solid rock of the old castle. Belatedly he forced himself to confront the other implication of what he'd heard. He'd deliberately shied from it.

The document she'd found appeared authentic. The date testing proved its age.

He would be the next king of Maritz.

Pain scored his fist as he pounded the sill. His gut hollowed. It was unthinkable! The nation deserved better than him.

Bile rose in his throat and he bowed his head, knowing if he let it, the pain would engulf him. Yet even then he wouldn't be free. He was destined to be alive, whole, unscathed. The ultimate punishment for his failure.

The metallic scent of blood from his grazed fist caught his attention, forcing him to focus. His breathing thickened as he imagined breaking the news to Raul.

Damn! His cousin should be monarch, not him.

Already he was his brother's usurper. How could he oust his cousin, too?

But they had no choice. They'd both been raised to shoulder their responsibilities and face even the most unpalatable duty.

Now, tonight, he had to make arrangements. Raul had to be updated and a second date test of the document organised. He'd have to call on more experts to help prove or disprove the chronicle. The royal genealogist had cautiously advised he couldn't rule out the claim to the throne. But that wasn't good enough. They had to be *certain*.

Yet Alaric had a hollow, sinking feeling each test would only prove his succession.

Fortunately the document was under lock and key. But there was still a danger news would get out before he'd found a way to manage the transition to monarch.

His mind conjured an image of Tamsin and that journo. They'd been so intent they hadn't heard him approach.

Surely she hadn't revealed anything to the newsman. Tamsin had too much integrity. Hadn't she? Doubt sidled through his thoughts and he squashed it furiously.

But finding her with the journo was too coincidental in the circumstances. Even if she was innocent, one unguarded word could shatter the fragile situation. She was so enthusiastic about her work she might inadvertently let something slip. Alaric must ensure that didn't happen.

He shook his head. He couldn't go to her tonight and lose himself in the mindless ecstasy he craved. There were urgent plans to make.

Alaric watched fat snowflakes drift past the window and an idea began to form. The need for Tamsin still gnawed at him, a constant ache. He'd gone beyond the point of no return and abstinence was no longer possible.

He assured himself it was purely physical desire he felt. Anything more…complicated was impossible.

He had to isolate her until arrangements were in place to deal with this mess. That would take time. But wasn't time with Tamsin what he craved?

There was benefit after all in coming from a long line of robber barons and ruthless opportunists.

Kidnapping was virtually an inherited skill.

CHAPTER NINE

'GOOD morning, Tamsin.'

Her shoulders stiffened and heat crawled up her cheeks as that low voice wound its lazy way into her soul.

Her assistant's eyes widened as he looked over her shoulder then darted her a speculative glance. Castle gossip had obviously worked overtime since last night.

Tamsin steadied herself against the archive room's custom built storage units. Finally she turned. She'd been expecting a summons. Even so, facing the man who'd stripped her emotionally bare took all her willpower.

She'd spent the night awake, trying to make sense of the evening's events. For the first few hours she'd half expected Alaric to come to her once his duties were over. Despite her doubts and her pride she'd have welcomed him.

It had only been as dawn arrived she'd realised he had no intention of visiting her. She preferred not to remember her desolation then.

'Hello…' She halted, her mouth drying as that familiar indigo gaze met hers. What should she call him? It had been *Alaric* until his steward had found them together. Then they'd been *Dr Connors* and *Your Highness*. The formality had been a slap in the face, even if it had been an attempt to hide what they'd been doing.

Here he was in her domain, alone, without any secretaries or security staff. *What did he want?*

Her blush burned fiery and she saw something flicker in his eyes. Awareness? Desire? Or distaste?

Tamsin had no idea what he felt. Last night his urgency, his arousal and his words had convinced her he felt the same compulsion she did. But later doubts had crept in.

'How are you today?' His voice held only polite enquiry but she could have sworn she saw something more profound in his expression.

Or was that wishful thinking?

'Well, thank you.' Again she hesitated. Despite his slightly drawn look, she wasn't going to ask him how he was. 'Have you come to see our progress?'

Grimacing at her falsely bright tone, ignoring her staccato pulse, she gestured for him to accompany her to her small office space. She'd feel better knowing every word wasn't overheard.

'Partly.' They reached her desk and Alaric spun round, his gaze intense. 'Why? Do you want to tell me something?'

Tamsin opened her mouth then shut it, frowning.

Last night there'd been no opportunity to tell him about the dating of the manuscript. Alone with him in the antechamber all thought of the document had been blasted from her mind by Alaric and the things he made her feel.

Her gaze skittered away as she recalled what they'd done. Even now desire throbbed deep in her belly and at the apex of her thighs. That persistent current of awareness eroded her efforts to appear unaffected.

She should tell him about the test results, yet she hesitated. Tamsin believed him now when he said he didn't want the crown. For whatever reason, the idea was anathema to him. It was a shame. She'd seen him in action these past couple of weeks and he'd make a terrific king. The easy way he related to people, truly listened to them. His sharp mind and ability to get things done. His need to help.

She read his taut stillness as he awaited her response.

Should she confirm his fears when in her own mind she wasn't fully convinced? Despite Patrick's news some things in the document still needed checking.

Tamsin shrugged stiffly and tidied her desk.

'The new staff have been worth their weight in gold. We're making good headway.'

'Excellent.' He paused as if waiting. 'And the chronicle? Anything interesting in your translations?'

'No.' It wasn't lying. She hadn't uncovered any more revelations.

Alaric's silence eventually made her look up. His expression was unreadable but there was a keenness, an intensity in his scrutiny that unnerved her.

'I should have more information for you soon.'

If she didn't uncover anything to justify her niggle of uncertainty by the end of the week, two days away, she'd break the news about the UK tests.

Strange, this sense that in being cautious she protected Alaric. She'd never met anyone so obviously capable, so patently self-sufficient.

Yet she couldn't shake the feeling that beneath it all, in this one thing Alaric was vulnerable.

'Good.' He reached out and fingered the spine of a catalogue.

Tamsin watched the leisurely caress, recalling how he'd stroked *her* last night. The touch of those large hands had been so exquisite she'd thought she'd shatter if he stopped.

She shivered and suddenly she was caught in the darkening brilliance of his eyes. Heat eddied low and spread in lush, drugging waves as she read his expression. The hungry yearning he couldn't hide.

Realisation slammed into her. Her heart soared.

It was real! Not her imagination. He felt it, too.

Tamsin struggled to inhale oxygen as the air thickened. Excitement revved her pulse, making her heart pound and her head swim. She swiped damp palms down her skirt. The heat inside ignited to a flash fire as his gaze followed the movement then rose, slow and deliberate, to her breasts, her mouth. Her nipples beaded and her lips parted eagerly as if he'd touched her.

'I need to see you, in private.'

'But last night…'

'Last night I should never have started something I couldn't finish.' His mouth twisted in a tight smile that echoed the rigid expression he'd worn as he'd left her in the antechamber. 'Do you really think a few stolen minutes hard and fast against a wall would have been enough?'

Alaric's words made her head swim. Or maybe it was the graphic image that exploded inside her brain. Tamsin's mouth dried as she saw his eyes mirror her excitement and frustration.

'And afterwards…' he paused '…I couldn't come to you.' Before she could ask why he spoke again, his voice darkly persuasive, his eyes glittering. 'But I'm here now.'

Murmured voices approached from the main archive room.

'I want you, Tamsin. Now. Away from interruption.' His voice dropped to a deep resonance that brooked no refusal.

Her breathing shallowed as she teetered on the brink. Part of her was shocked by his unvarnished words. But mostly she was thrilled. Abruptly she nodded, the movement jerky.

She wanted this. The intensity of what was between them scared her, but she would not to hide from it.

She'd done with suppressing her emotions and needs. She'd always love her work but it was no longer enough. She'd be a coward to turn her back on the marvellous feelings Alaric evoked. On the chance to live and experience the passion so blatant in his heavy-lidded look.

Tamsin had no illusions. Whatever he wanted from her, whatever he offered, would be fleeting. But it was genuine. If she had no expectations, except for honesty between them, how could she be hurt?

It was the lies that hurt. The soiled feeling of being used for ulterior purposes, as Patrick had used her.

The unabashed heat in Alaric's eyes, his single-minded focus were honest and headily seductive. Tamsin swallowed hard as excitement fizzed. After a life time of celibacy, she was ready to walk on the wild side.

Alaric had made it clear he didn't believe in love. At the time she'd felt sad for him but now she realised it was a bond between them. She didn't trust herself to try what passed for love again and Alaric was immune to it.

What they shared would be simple, straightforward and satisfying.

'Fifteen minutes.' His mouth barely moved as he murmured the instructions so her approaching colleagues couldn't hear. 'In the courtyard. Your warmest clothes.'

With a searing look he spun on his heel and was gone, leaving Tamsin's heart pounding like she'd run a marathon.

Fifteen minutes. It seemed a lifetime.

Alaric stamped his feet against the cold and refrained from glancing at his watch. She'd be here. He'd read her anticipation. This was one time Tamsin wouldn't object to an ultimatum.

His prim and proper Dr Connors was eager for this too.

He paused in the act of drawing on his gloves. Since when had he thought of Tamsin as 'his'? A sixth sense warning feathered his backbone.

Alaric ignored it.

Tamsin wanted him. He wanted Tamsin. Simple.

And the fact that his intentions weren't completely straightforward?

Alaric would go quietly crazy waiting on the interminable processes to confirm the succession. There was nothing he could *do*. A move to transfer power would be premature and potentially dangerous. Yet he itched for action, to work off the tension coiling within.

With Tamsin he could at least satisfy the lust eating him. This could be his last chance to enjoy freedom before the crown settled on his head. He'd make the most of every moment.

If he became king there'd be no more spur of the moment adventures, no dangerous sports. *No escape.* He shied away from that line of thought.

Tamsin wouldn't be hurt. He'd ensure she was well satisfied.

Despite her complex, fascinating personality, she seemed easy to read. He *wanted* to believe in her. Instinct said she was honest. Yet she'd kept from him the news of the chronicle's age, confirmed last night by her ex-lover. His thoughts snagged on the other man and tension rose.

He hadn't missed her prevarication today, the way her gaze had slid away guiltily as he'd given the perfect opportunity to broach the news.

He was determined to solve the riddle that was Tamsin Connors.

Anticipation coiled in his belly. He acted for the country, but this plan promised personal satisfaction.

Alaric drew on his gloves and glanced at the leaden tint just visible on the horizon. The sooner they left the better, or the forecast snowstorm would catch them too soon. He refused to endanger Tamsin.

If he were alone he'd revel in pitting his strength against the elements. Seeking out danger was one of his few pleasures. Action for the thrill of it. For the breathless affirmation of life in a world of bleak uncertainty.

Or perhaps, he realised in a sombre flash of awareness, in the expectation that eventually his luck would run out?

A death wish?

He gazed up at the bright bowl of the sky, vivid against the mountains, and felt the sizzle of expectation in his veins as he waited for Tamsin.

No. Despite the demons that hounded him, today he could truly say that given the chance he'd choose life.

'Your Highness?'

He swung round to see one of his security staff. 'Yes?'

'I have the report you requested several hours ago. It's only cursory. We'll have more in a day or two.'

At last! Information on this tiresome Patrick who'd rung Tamsin. And on the journo who'd hung on her every word.

He caught movement from the corner of his eye.

Tamsin emerged into the courtyard in a padded anorak and thick trousers. Gone was the glamorous woman who'd entranced him last night. Yet in the sharp light of a winter's morning her beauty defied the handicap of her bulky garments. Her face glowed in the crisp air. Unmarred by heavy glasses her clean, classic bone structure drew his appreciative gaze. Her eyes shone and the lush bow of her lips reminded him of last night's heady pleasure.

Even the way she walked, an easy stride that spoke of supple limbs and natural athleticism, fired his blood.

Besides, he'd discovered at the ball he preferred she hide her luscious body from all male eyes except his.

He was rather fond now of her shapeless outfits. He enjoyed picturing the hidden curves beneath. Especially as he had every intention of stripping those garments away for his pleasure very soon.

Alaric couldn't remember any woman getting so deeply under his skin. And he hadn't even slept with her!

'Your Highness?'

He swung back to the man patiently waiting.

'Thank you.' He nodded and took the envelope. No time now to satisfy his curiosity with Tamsin approaching. He stuffed the envelope into a pocket and rezipped his all-weather jacket. 'That's all for now. If anything urgent comes up I have my mobile phone.'

The other man bowed and stepped away as Tamsin reached him. Alaric turned, reminding himself not to touch, not yet, lest his brittle control snap.

Looking down into her bright eyes he realised this felt right. *She felt right.*

He smiled. Not a deliberate ploy to entice her but because for the first time in recent memory genuine happiness flared. He'd almost forgotten how good it felt.

'Where are we going?' They were the first words Tamsin had spoken in twenty minutes.

She'd been tongue-tied by the enormity of her feelings and the potency of what she saw in Alaric's eyes. When he looked at her, his gaze smoky and possessive, tendrils of awareness curled through her, spiralling tighter. Just the graze of his gloved hand on hers as he helped her take her seat had made her breathless.

Once they were under way disbelief, delight and sheer joy had kept her silent as she watched the forest slide past. Never in her wildest dreams had she envisaged a horse-drawn sleigh ride across pristine powder snow! It was a romantic fantasy.

They threaded their way through dense forest, emerging now and then into glades where the brilliant blue sky dazzled as it shone on diamond bright snow.

'We're visiting a small hunting lodge in the mountains. The road is impassable and the only way in is by sleigh.'

It sounded thrillingly intimate.

Alaric turned from guiding the horses and bestowed a single, lingering look. Instantly, despite the chill air, heat blazed through Tamsin. Beneath the layers of heavy blankets he'd tucked around her she was burning up.

'We'll be uninterrupted there.'

'I see.' Was that her voice, husky and low?

One black eyebrow arched and a crease arrowed down his cheek as he smiled. 'I knew you would.' His rich velvet voice held a hum of anticipation that matched hers. 'I've left orders that the lodge is absolutely off limits.'

His grin worked magic, loosening the final constricting ties of doubt. Under that look Tamsin felt buoyantly alive and strong, as if she could do anything. Dare anything.

Why be nervous? They were two adults. They both wanted this. Still her heart thudded against her ribs.

So what if she was a novice? Alaric had enough experience for them both.

Whatever the next few hours held, she wouldn't regret the decision to accompany him. Being with Alaric was like the thrill she'd felt scaling that climbing wall, recognising but defying the dangerous drop below. The glow of pleasure, knowing she'd dared the risk and triumphed, had been worth the initial doubt.

How different to the hemmed in half-life she'd led! How frightening to think that just weeks ago she'd have been too nervous, too wary to take this step.

Alaric turned back to the horses and Tamsin wriggled against the seat, luxuriating in an effervescent tingle of anticipation.

In the knowledge that at the end of the journey they would finish what had begun last night.

The whoosh and slide of the sleigh and the tinkle of harness bells echoing in the pine-scented forest reminded her they were completely alone. There were no staff, no members of the public seeking Alaric's attention. No one to look askance at his choice of companion.

Companion. For a moment the word jangled a discordant note. But even the memory of his original proposition, that she accompany him as a ruse, couldn't dim Tamsin's delight.

This was now. Just the two of them. *This was real.*

The admiration in his eyes made her feel like a princess. She intended to enjoy it while it lasted.

Looking up, Tamsin noticed slate grey clouds encroaching. 'That looks like bad weather coming.'

'It's nothing to worry about.'

It was on the tip of her tongue to protest. Surely those clouds presaged snow. But it was easier to sink back and ignore them. Alaric knew this place. Perhaps she was wrong and the clouds were moving away.

Finally they arrived in a clearing, hemmed in on two sides by the mountain. Below spread more forest and in the distance a vista of Alps and valleys.

'This is your lodge?' She'd expected something tiny. She'd almost allowed herself to forget Alaric was royalty. On the re-membrance a tremor of doubt buzzed through her and she sat straighter.

'It was built by my great-great-great-grandfather Rudi as a retreat. For when he wanted to escape the court.'

She eyed the substantial building: traditional Ruvingian archi-tecture but overgrown and embellished with mullioned windows, a forest of chimneys and even a turret. 'Let me guess. He didn't want to rough it.'

Alaric laughed and delight strummed her nerves. Soon…

'Rudi enjoyed his pleasures.' Alaric's glittering look made her press her thighs close against a needy hollow ache.

'You're cold. Let's get you inside.' Deftly he flicked the reins. Ten minutes later they were in a huge stable.

'You go ahead while I see to the horses.'

'Can't I help?' She'd rather watch Alaric's easy movements as he unhitched the horses.

'No.' His eyes held hers and heat pulsed. 'Go and get warm. Make yourself at home. I won't be long, I promise.'

The lodge was unlocked and she stepped into a flagged hall. Warmth hit her as she stared up at the staircase leading down on two sides. Antlers lined the room and a vivid mural ran around the top of the walls.

Tugging off her cap and gloves she paused in the act of undoing her jacket as she followed the scenes of revellers enjoying the bounty of the forest. There were plenty of buxom maids in attendance.

Her lips turned up wryly. Maybe Alaric's ancestor had been a connoisseur of women, too.

She hung up her jacket, letting her mind skim past the idea of Alaric with other women. She unzipped her boots and left them beside the antique tiled oven that warmed the hall. Someone had prepared the place for their arrival.

'Hello?' Tamsin wandered through sitting rooms, a library, a dining room that seated twenty, a kitchen and storage room, but found no one. Yet there was enough food to feed a small army.

Curious, she walked up the staircase. Its balustrade was carved with animals: hares, deer, hounds, even a boar. The whimsy appealed. Had old Rudi possessed a smile and a laugh as fascinating as his great-great-great-grandson's?

Alaric would be here soon.

Her heart gave a great thump and began to gallop. She moved on till she reached a pair of double doors and hesitated. There was something intimate about investigating the bedrooms. But Alaric had said to make herself at home.

Turning the handle she entered. Her breath caught as she turned to take it in.

The turret room.

It was round, windows set into curved, cream walls. Velvet curtains of azure blue were pulled aside, allowing sunlight to pour across thickly cushioned window seats and a gorgeous old Turkish rug in a kaleidoscope of colours. A fireplace was set ready for the match and opposite it was the biggest four poster bed she'd seen in her life. Drapes of blue velvet were tied back to beautifully turned posts and the headboard was carved with the arms of the Ruvingian royal house.

The reminder of Alaric's status stopped her, a splinter of harsh reality in her pleasant daydream.

Prince and commoner. It was too far-fetched. Too unreal.

'I hoped I'd find you here.'

Tamsin spun round as Alaric closed the door. Its click made her jump.

'I couldn't find anyone.' Her voice emerged too high. She watched his long silent stride. Something inside her shivered and her pulse danced.

'We're the only ones here.' His lips curved up but his eyes were darkly intent.

'I see.'

She wanted this, so why had her tongue stuck to the roof of her mouth? Why did she feel suddenly nervous?

'So you want to talk now?'

He raised an eyebrow. 'Talk? What about?'

'When you came to the archives you said you wanted...'

Slowly he shook his head as he paced closer. 'I didn't mention conversation.' He stopped so near she smelled warm flesh and horse and citrus soap. She breathed deep and put out a steadying hand to the post behind her.

She was quaking but not, she registered, in fear.

'You knew that.' His gaze snared hers and her stomach dipped. 'Didn't you, Tamsin?'

She nodded. No point prevaricating. She knew exactly what he'd wanted. Why he'd invited her here.

'Would *you* like to talk?' He gestured to a couple of chairs she hadn't noticed to one side of the room.

'No.' The single syllable was all she could manage.

'What do you want, Tamsin?' He purred her name and the final thread of resistance unravelled inside her.

She lifted her face to look him in the eye. What she saw there gave her the courage to be honest.

'I want to make love with you. Now.'

CHAPTER TEN

HER words blasted away Alaric's barely formed suspicion that she was nervous.

It wasn't nerves that made her eyes widen as he crossed the room. It was excitement. Despite her initial hesitation when he kissed her, and her occasional air of other-worldliness, Tamsin was no shrinking virgin. Last night's phone call from her ex-lover had made that clear.

Alaric breathed deep as anticipation roared through him. This was exactly what he needed. A mutually satisfying interlude with a woman who knew how to give and take pleasure generously. Tamsin's passion last night left him in no doubt this would be an erotically fulfilling encounter.

He shoved to the back of his mind the knowledge that he was taking advantage. That his motives bringing her here were complex and he was keeping things from her.

But he couldn't feel guilt. Not when he looked at Tamsin and knew only one thing drove him now: the purely personal need to claim her. Make her his.

'It will be my absolute pleasure to make love to you,' he murmured, his gaze trawling her tense form and coming to rest on her parted lips.

He'd waited so long for this. Too long.

He palmed her soft cheek, noting with delight the way she tilted her head up, instinctively seeking his mouth.

But he'd learned his lesson. Kissing Tamsin would unleash a desire so combustible he'd lose control in moments. This time he'd hold back to savour every exquisite detail for as long as possible. He had no illusions that the first time would be over almost before it began.

Just as well they had leisure for a second time and a third. And more. Tamsin would be here, his, for as long as he needed her.

'Let your hair down.'

She blinked at the rough growl edging his voice but lifted her hands. Rippling swathes of dark glossy hair cascaded around her shoulders. In the bright wintry light auburn tints gleamed. So rich. So unexpected. Just like Tamsin.

He took a slippery fistful. The scent of sweet summer meadows. Skeins soft as satin slid against his lips.

He was hungry for the taste of her. Hard with wanting.

'Now your pullover.' He wanted to strip her himself but he didn't trust himself to retain control.

Next time.

No, she wouldn't have a chance to get dressed before he had her again. His groin hardened as blood pumped faster.

For an instant Tamsin hesitated then she hauled the wool over her head. As she stretched her arms high a sliver of pale skin appeared at her waist. In an instant his hands were there, slipping beneath her grey shirt.

She stilled, half out of her pullover, as he slid fingers across warm flesh that trembled under his touch.

So deliciously sensitive. Her delicate little shudder of pleasure delighted him as his hands skimmed her waist and dipped below the waistband of her trousers to explore the curve of her hips.

By the time she'd discarded the pullover he'd tunnelled beneath her shirt, up, up, till all she had to do was lift her arms again and it was gone, too.

Alaric tossed it over his shoulder as he feasted on the sight of her. Her peaches and cream complexion was flushed to a soft rose pink. He'd never known a woman to blush all over. The novelty of it tugged at something deep inside and he felt an unexpected moment of protectiveness.

His breath sawed in his throat as he traced the tell tale colour from her cheeks, past her lips, down to the base of her throat where her pulse pattered hard and fast. He stroked lower, down the upper slope of her breasts.

Her nipples puckered in welcome beneath her ivory bra. Functional, with a minimum of lacy edging and a tiny bow between her breasts, on Tamsin the plain bra looked sexier than the most revealing demi-cup or lace-up corset.

Alaric's breath grew hoarse and heavy as he slipped his hands to her breasts. Warm, perfect, full, they filled his palms as she pressed forward, her eyelids flickering closed.

Fire exploded in his belly as he held her soft bounty in his hands. Gently he caressed and her head lolled back, her neck arched invitingly.

His mouth was a hair's breadth from her scented throat when he recalled his scattered wits. No kisses. Not yet.

He dragged himself back, wincing at the shaft of discomfort in his groin.

Alaric dealt with the snap on her trousers and the zip easily, pushing the fabric down, down those long, lithe legs till at his urging she stepped out of them. Even the act of stripping her long grey and black striped socks was a sensual indulgence as he crouched before her. The intimate heat of her sex was so close. The silkiness of her calves teased as he skimmed the socks down. The seductive arch of each foot distracted as he tugged the socks free.

Low before her he was tempted to lean in and explore her feminine secrets with his lips and tongue. But he was too close to the edge to risk it.

Instead he allowed his fingertips to skim her knees and thighs as he rose, lingering for a moment at her knickers, where her heat beckoned, over her belly, breasts and up to cup her jaw.

She was sensational. All soft curves, taut lines and delicate angles. Pure female seduction. Just looking at her almost tipped him over the edge.

Eyes bright as gold stared up into his, dazzling him. The impact of her sunburst gaze thumped through his chest and showered sparks through every nerve and muscle.

'You're wearing too many clothes.' Tamsin's voice was hoarse, almost unrecognisable. He felt a kick of satisfaction low in his gut that she was as desperate as he.

'Easily remedied.' With a violent movement he dragged his shirt and sweater up and off, flinging them behind him.

Though warm, the air was cool to his burning skin. Soft palms landed on his chest, fingers splaying. Tamsin explored his pectorals, scraping her nails tantalisingly over his hard nipples, trailing her hands to his belly.

In a flash his trousers were open and he shoved them down, balancing on one leg then another as he discarded underwear, socks and trousers in record time.

Belatedly he recalled the condom in his back pocket and stooped to retrieve it. There was a box of them in the bedside table but watching Tamsin's face as she took in his naked body, he knew those few metres to the table might as well be a hundred kilometres.

Tearing the wrapper with his teeth, he deftly rolled on the protection, pleasure spiking at Tamsin's expression of shocked excitement. The way she stared he could have been a demi-god, a hero, not an earthbound man with feet of clay. His blood beat hard and fast as his hands dropped away.

He stepped forward.

Alaric loomed closer and Tamsin backed up.

She hadn't intended to. It was instinctive, an unplanned bid to escape a man who suddenly seemed dangerous in a primitive, ultra-physical way she'd never known.

The reality of Alaric the man, of what they were doing, hit her full force.

He was so big, so heavily aroused; a sliver of anxiety pierced the fog of desire. He could bend her to his will and she wouldn't be able to resist. Whatever he demanded of her he could take.

An age old female wariness sped down her backbone. It had nothing to do with his royal rank and everything to do with Alaric as a virile, dominant male.

The cool slap of the high footboard against the back of her legs brought her up short. As did his puzzled expression.

'Tamsin?' He stood where he was, only reached out one arm to her. Like the rest of him it was powerfully corded with muscle. Yet as she looked she saw his fingers tremble.

She gulped down the panic that had bubbled out of nowhere and looked into his eyes, glazed with hot desire yet questioning. This time her brain kicked into gear.

When she'd watched him roll on the condom, his eyes had eaten her up with a fierceness that thrilled and terrified her. When he'd approached she'd let fear of the unknown swamp the surge of desire.

Now she saw that despite Alaric's raw hunger, he was the same man she'd come to know these last weeks. A man who'd been honest and straight with her. Who desired her.

A man she could trust.

Maybe every woman felt that tinge of fear the first time, confronted with such unvarnished lust and the stunning reality of naked male arousal.

Her lips curved up in a wobbly smile as she realised very few women were gifted with a first lover as gorgeous as Alaric. Just looking at him made her heart throb so fast she could scarcely catch her breath.

This was what she wanted. She refused to walk away from something that felt so good, so right.

She just needed courage.

Eyes holding his, Tamsin reached around and fumbled her bra undone, letting it fall with a shake of her arms.

Alaric drew a huge breath, his chest expanding mightily. His outstretched hand curled and fell away.

Her unbound breasts felt impossibly full, the nipples hardening to aching points as his heated gaze dropped. Fire scorched a trail across her breasts and lower.

Following the direction of his gaze, Tamsin hooked her thumbs in the sides of her panties. There she hesitated as her inbuilt urge to cover herself fought the need to offer herself to Alaric. A lifetime's habit was strong, but far stronger was the magic she felt when he looked at her with such longing.

She felt desirable. Desired. Feminine. Powerful. Needy.

Without giving herself time to think she shoved her underwear down, felt the slide of fine cotton against her legs and the waft of air against her skin. All over.

'You have no idea how badly I want you.' Alaric's voice was a rough blur of words that tugged at something low in her belly. Pleasure coursed through her as his eyes sparked blue fire.

A second later he lifted her up and onto the mattress.

His hands were so large they almost spanned her waist. His sure grip reinforced the physical differences between them. Yet this time her vulnerability didn't bring fear. A delicious flutter of excitement filled her.

With one fluid, powerful movement he pushed her up the bed and sank down on her. Senses on overload, she gasped for breath, but nothing could calm the spiralling excitement that drove her on. She was hemmed in, surrounded by him and nothing had ever felt so perfect.

Arms closing round his torso, Tamsin pressed her mouth to Alaric's neck, his shoulder, tasting the spicy salt flavour of him. Sinking into the mattress, soft velvet caressed her back while her breasts, belly and legs rubbed against satiny skin, power-fully bunched muscles and coarse hair that teased every nerve ending.

He was so…male. So intriguing.

So sexy.

He moved and she swallowed a gasp of pleasure at the sensa-tion of his broad chest sliding against her breasts. Delight was a rippling wave engulfing her, surging again with each tiny move, each touch.

Driven by instinct, she'd invited this. Yet she'd been un-prepared for the stunning reality of Alaric's body against hers. Theoretical knowledge only took a girl so far.

Alaric slid a fraction and his erection pressed against her belly. Instantly the hollow ache inside intensified and her hips strained up against him.

Thankfully her body knew what it was doing. Instinct would make up for her lack of practical knowledge.

Then Alaric's mouth captured her nipple and Tamsin lost the capacity for thought as wet heat tugged at her, drawing blood-hot wires of tension through her arching body.

She needed…she needed…

'I love it that you're so hot and ready for me.' His hoarse voice was the most thrilling thing Tamsin had ever heard and the possessive splay of his hand across her feminine mound would have brought her up off the bed if she hadn't been anchored by his strong frame.

She wriggled her hips and he moved, nudging her legs apart with one solid thigh. Eagerly she complied.

'Yes. Like that,' he growled, raising his head and spearing her with a searing look of approval.

Vaguely she noticed the way Alaric's skin stretched taut over that magnificent bone structure, his mouth a grim line of tension.

His hand moved, arrowing unerringly through damp curls and folds that felt plump and hyper-sensitive. Tamsin's body jolted as long fingers slid down.

She couldn't gasp enough breath. Her chest pounded and she stretched her arms up to grab his shoulders, digging into taut, hot flesh. He said something she couldn't hear over the roaring in her ears as he looked to where his fingers stroked again, further, faster.

Tamsin bit her lip against the sob of pleasure rising in her throat. But she couldn't stop the way her body moved into his caress. Confidently, needily.

When he met her gaze again there was a feral glitter in his eyes. He looked like a marauder, a ruthless barbarian intent on plunder. As if she were the bounty he intended to take for himself.

She loved it!

Slipping her hands along those wide shoulders, she clamped her fingers behind his head, desperately burrowing through his thick hair for a good grip. Pulling down, she raised herself and plastered a raw, breathless, open-mouthed kiss on his lips.

For one fragile moment he seemed suspended above her, unmoving. Then he sank onto her again and passion erupted.

Their kiss was fervent, impatient, and his caress between her legs changed. No longer Alaric's hand but something longer, throbbing with a will of its own as he clamped his hands beneath her buttocks and tilted her hips.

'I'm sorry. I can't hold off any longer.'

Tamsin barely processed his words when he shifted and she felt heat nudge the entrance between her legs. Fire flooded her womb at the spiralling whorls of anticipation created by that blunt touch. At last!

His lips closed on hers again, inviting her to join him in pleasure as his tongue pushed greedily into her mouth. At the same time his hold on her bottom tightened and his hips plunged against hers.

One long, slow thrust stretched her body till she was taut, impaled and impossibly full. Gone was the heady passion, replaced in that instant by the first flutterings of panic. Every muscle stiffened and her eyes snapped open.

Startled ink blue irises stared back. Alaric lifted his mouth from hers and sucked in a shaky breath as he pulled away.

Surprisingly, the sensation of his withdrawal instantly distressed her and she clamped her knees against his hips. She didn't want him gone! She just didn't want the scary feeling that he was too big for her. That despite their desire, this wasn't going to work.

'Alaric?' Tamsin didn't care that the word wobbled or that he could hear the entreaty in her voice. Pride had no place here. 'Please.' She didn't know what she expected him to do. She only knew she couldn't bear it to end like this.

A gusty sigh riffled her hair and his head dropped between his bunched shoulders. Tendons stood out on his neck and arms and inside she felt a pulse where the tip of his erection moved.

Response shivered through her at that tiny, impossibly erotic movement. Involuntarily she twitched, circling her hips and his breath stopped.

In answer he withdrew a fraction then slowly pushed forward. This time it didn't feel quite so scary. Or maybe that was his warm breath blowing on her nipple, teasing the aroused bud and distracting her from the slide of his body away then back again.

The next time he eased forward her hips lifted to meet him and he sank a fraction further. But before she had time to register the sensations he was gone again, pulling away and leaving her frustratingly empty.

The fourth time he began to move she anticipated him, arching upwards simultaneously, then gasping as a fiery spark of pleasure flared at the point of friction. Her breath hitched and instantly he stilled, his breathing harsh and uneven.

Tamsin waited but he didn't move. What now? Had he decided this wasn't going to work? Her hands fisted at his shoulders and she bit her lip against the protest that hovered on her tongue.

Then she saw the pulse at the base of Alaric's neck, thudding out of control. He was waiting for her. Trying to accommodate her fear, her discomfort. The rigidity of his body, the way his broad chest heaved like overworked bellows told their own story of the toll this took.

Suddenly this wasn't just about her. Tamsin felt ashamed by her self-absorption.

Tentatively she slipped her hands down his body, feeling muscles flinch at her light caress. Daringly she reached out and smoothed her palms over his hips, down to his taut, rounded buttocks that felt so good under her increasingly needy touch. She wanted to explore him all over, she realised with a shock.

A spasm shook him as she tightened her hold and pulled him towards her. For an instant he resisted then allowed himself to be tugged closer, inside. Even further than before. This time instead of panic, Tamsin felt a niggle of a strange new sensation. A gnawing need for more. When he withdrew she followed. When she urged him close he slid even deeper and a shaky sigh of pleasure escaped her lips.

Gradually, a fraction at a time, their movements became rhythmic and fluid. Tamsin hated each withdrawal and welcomed each thrust, even when it seemed he plunged impossibly deep. Yet even that felt right. More than right. Fantastic.

Now she revelled in the way he drove so far within her.

Alaric's head lifted and his gaze locked with hers. It felt absurdly as if he touched a part of her no medical scan would ever identify. As if he caressed her very soul with his eyes, his body, his tenderness.

Tamsin's breath sucked out at the heat glazing Alaric's eyes and the reflection there of her own overwhelming need.

Lightning flickered as electricity jolted through her body. His tempo increased, her body tightened, achingly close to some unseen goal. A shudder raked him, raked her, and their rhythm rocked out of control into a fierce pounding beat that brought the world tumbling around them.

A gasping scream rent the air as Tamsin fell into pleasure. Everything swam around her except dark blue eyes, fixed on hers in the maelstrom of exquisite delight. Then, with a hoarse shout, Alaric followed her and she drew him close with trembling arms and an overflowing heart.

CHAPTER ELEVEN

A VIRGIN.

Alaric shook his head as if to dislodge the knowledge that weighted him. How had he convinced himself Tamsin was experienced?

He doused his head under the basin's cold tap but that didn't obliterate the voice of his conscience. He'd seduced a virgin. Deliberately set her up to fall into his bed.

He grimaced. He'd shown little consideration for her inexperience as he'd hammered her untried body.

It was no excuse that the feel of her virginal body tight around him had been the ultimate aphrodisiac.

Experienced as he was he had no defence against the pleasure she offered so unstintingly.

Would he have held back if he'd suspected the truth?

Nothing on earth would have held him back. He was as bad as that old roué Rudi, the ancestor who'd designed the place to keep his scandalous liaisons from prying eyes. Alaric's shoulders tightened. No, he was worse. The women Rudi had bedded had reputedly been experienced. Even his father had kept that rule.

Hell! This was a new take on *noblesse oblige*.

Alaric raised his eyes to the bathroom mirror, expecting, as ever, to see his sins marked on his face. But as usual he was the same. Unblemished. Outwardly whole. As if the darkness within were a figment of his imagination.

What right had *he*, of all men, to take her innocence? She deserved a man who could give her more.

Familiar pain lanced his chest, a physical manifestation of his guilt. The ghosts stirred and he waited for the inevitable chill to engulf him.

Yet there was only the remembered heat of Tamsin's sweet body. The warmth of her eyes, looking up as if he'd done something heroic rather than ravish her virginity. And around his heart was an unfamiliar glow.

Alaric shook his head again, splattering the mirror and his shoulders with icy droplets. This was no time for flights of fancy. He grabbed a towel and roughly dried his hair. With a final accusing glare at the mirror he left.

'You were gone a long time.'

He stopped mid-stride. He'd thought Tamsin would be asleep. Or was that his conscience hoping she'd be too exhausted to confront him?

His skin tightened as he looked up to find her propped against pillows, her hair a sensuous tangle of silk on pale shoulders. A flush coloured her cheeks and her lips were plump and enticing after those bruising kisses.

Alaric's belly went into freefall. His penis throbbed into life and he wished he'd thought to take his clothes with him into the bathroom.

Colour intensified in her cheeks as her gaze skated down. His arousal grew, as if eager for her attention.

'You're…ready again?' Her voice faltered and he winced, imagining her nerves.

'Don't worry.' He paced to the foot of the bed where his clothes lay scattered. 'I'm not going to pounce on you.'

'You're not?' He imagined a thread of disappointment in her tone and gritted his teeth. He looked for any excuse to have her again, even pretending she was eager for more.

'Of course not. You're a virgin and—'

'Was.' The flush intensified, spreading over her throat and down to where she clamped a snowy sheet against her breasts. Alaric's gaze lingered on the way they rose and fell. 'What's that got to do with anything?'

'Sorry?' He'd lost the thread of the conversation.

'The fact that I was a virgin. What's that got to do with not having sex again?'

He liked the way she said 'having sex' with a slight hesitancy. It reminded him of her innocently incendiary kisses and the initially faltering yet devastating way she'd taken him into her body.

He scooped up some clothing. Damn. It was her shirt. Where was his?

'Didn't you like it?' Now she sounded frosty. Good. They could do with reducing the temperature around here.

He grabbed something else off the floor. Her trousers, still warm from her body. Another reminder of the speed of their coupling. He should be ashamed. It was sheer luck she'd climaxed. Once he'd buried himself fully he'd been incapable of holding back to ensure her pleasure.

'Alaric? You didn't like it?'

He gritted his teeth. Thinking about what they'd done spun him to the edge of control. 'Men don't perform when they're not enjoying themselves.'

'Then why not again?'

He didn't meet her eyes. Coward that he was he turned to scan the room for his trousers.

'Wasn't once enough?' Surely his unskilled efforts didn't merit a repeat. 'Besides, you'll be sore. You're not used to sex.' The words were brutal but it was all he could do to keep talking when he wanted to vault into that bed, tug her close and take her again. The battle against his selfish, baser self was all consuming.

'I'm not sore.'

'You will be.'

'So you're an expert on virgins?'

'Of course not! I'm no expert on innocence.' He spun round, his temper flaring under the goad of her lashing words. *Do you really think I'd have brought you here if I'd known the truth about you? This wouldn't have happened!'*

A half-smile stiffened on her lips and the bright flare of gold in her eyes dimmed. Too late he realised she'd been teasing, inadvertently zeroing in on his guilty conscience.

He raked a hand through his hair and breathed deep. His brain wasn't working and the words shooting from his mouth were all wrong. He couldn't think straight. Not with her sitting there all demure invitation, tempting him.

He'd thought to kill two birds with one stone. Keep Tamsin where she couldn't spill any headline news and sate his hunger. Suddenly, though, this had become something else altogether. The stakes, and his own culpability, had grown enormously.

There was a flurry of movement as she clambered out of bed, dragging a coverlet. Her chin was set belligerently but he couldn't read her face. She kept her expressive eyes downcast as she walked the length of the bed.

Automatically he backed away, knowing if she got too close he'd do something reprehensible, like grab her and plant kisses all over her petal soft skin.

At his movement she stopped so abruptly she seemed to shudder to a halt. Close up her mouth looked pinched tight, her face drawn.

He wanted to ease her hurt, tease her into smiling, but his light-hearted seduction skills had deserted him the moment he'd taken her in his arms.

His hands fisted as he watched her bend to retrieve some clothing. It was only as she rose that he caught the glitter of moisture at the corners of her averted eyes.

'Tamsin?' He stepped near and she stiffened. Pain scraped his heart. 'Don't cry. Please.'

'Don't be absurd. I'm not crying.' She sniffed and turned away, the bedclothes twisting around her. 'You've made it clear this afternoon was a monumental disappointment. If you don't mind I'd like to get dressed. Alone. I'll return to the castle as soon as possible.'

She shuffled away, hampered by the long trail of material which slid down to reveal the voluptuous curve of her spine.

'You've got it wrong!' He closed the space between them till he could smell the scent of her skin and the sunshine in her hair. Close enough to see her bare flesh prickle with cold. Or distress.

'Don't!' She breathed deep, her back to him. 'Please don't. I understand. I may be naïve but I'm not dumb. You wanted it to look like we were having an affair. To fool those other women. So you brought me here and…' Her averted head dropped low, revealing the vulnerable arch of her nape.

'I misunderstood.' Her voice was a whisper now and he had to crane to hear. 'I thought…you know what I thought. And when you said you didn't want to talk…'

Her head jerked up and around and she pinioned him with a furious amber stare.

'No! It's your fault as much as mine. You *know* what you implied. You let me think…' She bit her lip and swallowed hard. 'You didn't say anything *then* about only wanting experienced women!'

'Because it's not true.'

'So it's just me.' She blinked and turned away. 'I see. Well, I'm sorry I don't come up to your *royal* standards.' The wobble in her voice gouged a hole through his chest.

'I didn't mean that.' He planted a hand on her shoulder but she shrugged it off and moved to the head of the bed. 'Tamsin! You don't understand.'

'Leave me alone, Alaric. I was stupid ever to imagine you'd be attracted to a woman like me. I got carried away with the fairy tale, that's all. It must happen to you all the time. Women with stars in their eyes.'

She dropped her clothes on the bed in front of her and bent to step into her panties but the coverlet got in the way. With an exclamation of impatience she thrust it aside, letting it slide to the floor.

Frustration filled him. Self-contempt and annoyance at finding himself on the defensive. Plus a sexual hunger even greater than before. *One taste hadn't been enough.*

He reached for her again.

'Does it *feel* like I'm not attracted?' With his hands on her hips he jerked her back so his arousal pressed blatantly against her buttocks. He almost groaned at how right that felt.

The breath hissed from her lungs as he slid his palms over her belly and ground his hips in a slow rotation that left him light-headed.

'I want you, Tamsin. I brought you here with the express intention of getting you into my bed.' He slipped one hand down to the moist heat between her thighs and felt her shudder as he homed in on that most sensitive of spots.

'Or not. Anywhere would do. The sleigh, the barn, the kitchen. I don't care. But I've been trying, unsuccessfully, to keep my distance because I realised too late how I've taken advantage. I'm responsible—'

'You're not responsible for me.' Her defiance was belied by her throaty pleasure as her lower body moved a fraction against his stroking fingers. Her responsiveness cracked his resolve further and he slid himself provocatively against her cushioning curves.

'I'm responsible for taking your innocence.'

'You're talking antiquated rubbish. It's my business when I choose to lose my virginity.'

'That doesn't diminish my culpability.'

'Oh!' With a violent jerk Tamsin freed herself and swung to face him. Before he could prevent her she snatched up the coverlet and hid all that firm, glorious flesh. 'You're infuriating! Do you always take the world on your shoulders?'

Alaric watched passion animate her features and felt desire cloud his brain. 'I knew what I was doing. You didn't.'

She rolled her eyes. 'You know, women even have the vote these days. We're capable of making decisions about who we want to make love to.'

Make love. It hit him with a jolt that for the first time the euphemism seemed more apt than 'having sex'.

Ridiculous. What they'd shared was carnal pleasure at its most raw. Pleasure so complete he could no longer resist its pull. Love didn't enter into it.

'All right. Who do you want to make love to?' Alaric loomed towards her. *His conscience could go hang.*

Tamsin shuffled back, eyes widening as she realised she was trapped against the bed.

'I want to go back to the castle.'

'No, you don't. You want to climb on that mattress and let me show you the things we didn't have time for earlier.' Heat sizzled under his skin just watching her shocked delight as she processed his words. The furtive way her eyes darted to the bed. 'I want it too.'

She tilted her chin defiantly and her grip tightened on the bedspread. 'It didn't sound like it a minute ago. Are you sure?'

'Totally.'

'Why?'

Why? The question flummoxed him. Couldn't she feel the erotic charge leaping between them? Didn't she understand what they'd shared had been remarkable, despite its brevity? So wondrous, so perfect no one in their right mind could walk away from it. He speared a hand through his hair in frustration. *Why did women always want to talk?*

The belligerent jut of her finely honed jaw said she wasn't going to make this easy.

'Because I've wanted you so long,' he murmured, finally giving himself up to the truth. 'Since I walked into the library and saw your sexy leg swinging above my head. Since I discovered a woman who challenges and intrigues and piques my curiosity. Who's passionate about something as complex as translating ancient books and as simple as a waltz. Who's not overawed by my title. Who's not charmed by wealth and prestige and isn't afraid to tell me what she thinks.'

'This isn't about duping those other women?' She gnawed on her lip and hurt shaded her fine eyes.

Alaric's mouth thinned and he silently cursed the fact he'd used that excuse to keep her close. If he'd known how unsure she was about her own desirability he'd never have done it. It had taken him too long to understand that her professional confidence hid deep vulnerability.

'It's got nothing to do with anyone but us.'

He lifted a hand and stroked the hair from her face, revelling in the way she swayed infinitesimally towards him. 'You're the most naturally sexy woman. Yet you hide your sensuality from everyone but me.' He smiled and slid a hand down her throat to where her pulse thrummed.

'Do you know what a turn on it is, being the only one in on your secret? Seeing your buttoned up shirts and long skirts, your sensible shoes and no-nonsense bun? Knowing that beneath is a siren who makes my pulse race with just one demure glance from those brilliant eyes?'

'I…' She shook her head as if words failed her.

He smoothed his index finger down her brow. 'Even that tiny frown you have when you're concentrating gets me. And the way you pout your lips over a knotty problem.' He breathed deep, trying to slow his escalating heartbeat.

'Every time I visit the archives and find you poring over papers I want to slam the door shut. I want to take you there, against the storage units. Or on that massive desk. You wouldn't believe how often I've imagined it.'

Colour flared in Tamsin's pale face and her mouth softened. Alaric bent his head, letting his breath feather her temple, torturing himself with the scent of her.

'You've imagined it too. I can see it in your face.'

For the first time Tamsin was bereft of speech. She just stood, staring up at him in mute appeal.

Unfamiliar sensations stirred. Something deep inside swelled, filling the tattered remnants of his soul.

'It's all right,' he murmured, wondering if he was reassuring himself as well as her. 'I'll make it all right.' He let his hand drop. 'But only if you want.'

Silence thundered in the air, pulsing like a living thing as their eyes meshed. Something unfamiliar twisted in his chest as he waited for her response. Something more than desire. Something far stronger.

'I want you too, Alaric.'

Relief speared him. She was his. For now.

That's all he wanted. He ignored the half-formed idea that there was more than simple sex between them.

Making love…

No. Emotional connections were too dangerous.

But sex…sex he could handle. Sex they would both enjoy. A final fling before he faced the burdens of the crown. Desperation edged his movements as he wrenched the coverlet from her slack hold. Rosy nipples like proud dusky buds pouted just for him.

He reached out to the bedside table and yanked open the drawer, unerringly finding one of the packets he needed.

'This time,' he promised with a taut smile, 'we're going to take things slow.'

Hours later Tamsin lay, limbs deliciously weighted, so exhausted she felt like she floated on a cloud above the huge four poster bed. The shift and rustle of logs burning in the grate was the only sound. Never had she felt so languid, yet so alert to each sensation. The tickle of hair across her shoulders as she burrowed beneath the covers, the awareness of her body. Especially those parts where Alaric had devoted such lingering attention.

She squeezed her thighs together, conscious of the achy, empty feeling just *there*. Not sore. More *aware*.

Her lips curved dreamily. It wasn't merely what they'd done together. Warmth like honeyed chocolate flowed through her as she remembered Alaric's words.

She wouldn't be human, wouldn't be female if she wasn't thrilled by the thought of him secretly desiring her, even though she couldn't compete outwardly with the glamorous sophisticates who were his usual companions.

He enjoyed her body as much as she enjoyed his.

For long moments she distracted herself remembering his powerful limbs, the curve and dip of his back and taut buttocks, the heavy muscle of his chest. She'd explored his body till he'd pinioned her to the bed with a growl that had awoken every sated nerve. She blushed all over recalling what he'd done then. How she'd delighted in it. So much that she'd cried his name as she'd shuddered in ecstasy.

After Patrick she'd wondered if she'd ever trust a man enough for intimacy. She'd assumed her first time with a man might be clumsy, uncomfortable and nerve-racking.

Instead she felt…treasured. Appreciated. Set free.

The fire in Alaric's eyes had incinerated the doubts and insecurities that had hemmed her in for so long. As if it was right to give in to the passions that simmered below the surface. To trust in herself and him.

He saw beyond her clothes and her job. He was attracted to *her*. He wasn't put off by the fact that she spoke her mind. He even liked her enthusiasm for her work! The news that he'd been intrigued by her right from the start made them seem like equals, despite the disparity in their social positions and experience.

This was true sharing. Something she'd never had.

Bemused, she snuggled into the pillows. If it wasn't for the proof of her exhausted body she'd think it a dream, too good to be true.

Forcefully she reminded herself this wouldn't last.

He was royalty. A tiny chill pierced her glow. He might even be *king*.

Tamsin pulled the bedclothes close as a disturbing thought surfaced. Could that be at the root of her nebulous doubts about Tomas's chronicle? It was the right date. Yet she had doubts.

Doubts or hopes? Selfish hopes that the chronicle was somehow wrong. That Alaric wasn't king.

Because if he became king there was even less chance he'd be interested in plain Tamsin Connors.

Her breath seized on a guilty gasp. Is that why she hadn't told him about the dating? The idea went against every professional principle. Yet deep in her heart a seed of disquiet grew.

Was it so wrong to wait a little to tell him about that? Enjoy this precious interlude before reality intruded?

This…relationship would end soon enough. Her mind shied from the idea of returning to her normal life without Alaric. But he'd given her a wonderful, precious gift. Honest passion and caring, shared unstintingly.

Nothing could ever take that away.

'Ah, Sleeping Beauty awakes.' That deep, rich voice slid like rippling silk right through her insides. Her breath caught at its beauty.

Slowly she rolled over. Backlit by the fire's glow Alaric's long frame was mouth-wateringly athletic in just a pair of black trousers. What was it about a bare male chest, tousled dark hair and a smile that drove sexy creases down his lean cheeks? Tamsin's breath sighed out in a whoosh.

Ink blue eyes met hers and heat trickled in her belly.

'What have you got there?' Her voice was husky and his smile widened. Every doubt fled as its warmth filled her.

He lifted his hand and a splash of fluid gold ran through his fingers. 'Here.' He sauntered to the bed and held up a silken robe.

She reached but he didn't release it, just stood, holding it by the shoulders, wearing a smile of secret challenge. Her gaze flicked to Alaric's bare chest. He had no qualms about nudity, but he was the most magnificent male. Whereas she…she was used to covering up.

His eyes beckoned.

'There's something I want to show you.' When he looked at her that way she felt she could walk across hot coals and feel nothing but the pleasure of his smile.

Shimmying to the edge of the bed she slid out, holding the covers as long as possible. It was stupid to feel shy after what they'd done together. Yet it was only the fact that his eyes remained fixed on her face that gave her courage to step from the bed and slip into the seductively soft silk.

'Excellent.' Why she should feel such pleasure at his approval she didn't want to consider. He smoothed the garment across her flushed skin, wrapping the sides closed across her breasts and stomach, tying the belt and caressing her unashamedly through the sensuous silk.

Her heart beat fast, lodging up near her throat as she sagged into his solid heat. She was exhausted, yet with a touch he overturned every sensible thought. She trembled, eager for his caresses. For more of his loving.

'Come and look.' He ushered her to the window then stood behind her. His arms wrapped around her waist, his body warmed her back and she sank against him.

The sky was dark and the vista almost obliterated by wafts of white. 'A snowstorm?'

His jaw scraped her hair as he nodded. 'We're not going anywhere today.'

Heat blazed and she grinned. Their idyll wasn't over. Yet she tried to be sensible. 'Won't your staff worry? Don't you have appointments?'

'Nothing that can't be delayed. They know we're safe. I texted them before we crossed that last ridge down into this valley. All we can do is wait.'

Tamsin tried to feel regret for Alaric's predicament, cut off from the meetings and important people he dealt with daily. But she couldn't repress a shiver of anticipation.

Before she could guess his intention, he hoisted her into his arms and carried her across the room. No other man had held her like this and she marvelled at the way she fitted so naturally in his embrace.

'We'll have to rough it here,' he murmured.

'Rough it?' The place was pure luxury.

Alaric shouldered open a door into a massive bathroom. The sound of running water made her turn. Set in an arched alcove, lit by flickering candles and topped by a mural of Venus bathing, was the largest bath she'd ever seen. Subtly scented steam curled above it.

On a table nearby were crystal flutes, an ice bucket cradling a foil topped bottle and a plate of plump fresh raspberries and peaches. He must have had the out of season fruit flown in.

'There's only one bath,' Alaric replied. 'I'm afraid we'll have to share.' His eyes gleamed and his roguish smile thrilled as he lowered her, inch by provocative inch to the floor. His hands warmed her hips as she swayed.

Tamsin blinked, overcome by emotion. By the devastating pleasure of this over the top seduction scene. *He'd done this for her.* His darkening gaze invited her to enjoy it all, and him, to the full.

Guilt lanced Tamsin. She should tell him about the chronicle. But with guilt came a renewed sense of urgency. This would be over soon. She knew a bitter-sweet yearning to hoard every precious moment. She'd tell him when they returned to the castle. When the fantasy ended.

She'd never felt so cherished. Invited to share his laughter as well as the passion that lurked in the curve of his lips, his hooded eyes and his tight, possessive grip.

'Thank you, Alaric.' Her voice was hoarse as she stared at this man who'd given her so much. Physical pleasure, but more too. Something that made her feel strong and special.

She stretched up on tiptoe and pressed her unsteady lips to his. Instantly he gathered her close, arms wrapping tightly around her, kissing her with tender persuasion.

Alaric didn't believe in love or commitment. Yet it would be so easy to fall for him. Totally foolish, definitely dangerous, but, oh, so easy.

CHAPTER TWELVE

'No, NOT like that, keep your palm flat.'

Alaric wrapped his hand round Tamsin's, holding it steady while the mare snuffled a chunk of carrot. Tamsin's gurgle of laughter echoed through the stable. He felt it as he stood behind her, his other arm pinning her close.

The horse whickered and mouthed Tamsin's palm. She crooned to it, rubbing her hand along its nose.

Alaric's belly clenched in response to her tone. It was like the one she used when they were naked and he discovered a new erogenous zone on her supple, gorgeous body.

He loved listening to Tamsin, he realised. Whether the soft gasps and cries of delight as they found ecstasy together, or the quiet, serious way she discussed other matters. Or her passion when she talked about books and dead languages and preserving the past. He even liked the schoolmistress voice she used to counter his teasing.

His groin stirred and he tugged her nearer, taking her weight. He was turned on by a woman whose eyes shone with delight over the size of his library!

This was new territory.

Normally his interest in a woman was skin deep. But these past few days with Tamsin he'd discovered a deeper pleasure, sharing her delight, not just with intimacy, but with the world around her.

He'd known joy unfettered by the cold shadows of the past. He even slept soundly, devoid of dreams.

Was it any wonder he didn't want her out of his sight? It was selfish, but the sunshine she brought to his soul was worth ignoring the responsibilities it would be his duty to shoulder soon. Already discreet arrangements were under way to ensure the crown's smooth transition if necessary.

Just a little longer…

A disturbing memory surfaced of Felix talking excitedly about finding the one right woman. *But his brother had made the mistake of believing in love.*

Alaric would never make that error.

'Why are you shaking your head? Aren't I touching it right?'

Alaric rubbed his chin against her hair. 'You *always* touch just right. It's one of your talents.'

Tamsin was a natural sensualist who loved giving and receiving pleasure. Her tentative forays into pleasing him reduced him to a slavering wreck. Imagine when she became expert at seducing a man!

A splinter of dismay punctured his self-satisfaction at the notion of Tamsin sharing herself with another.

Alaric's jaw tensed.

He wouldn't let it happen.

Not yet. Not for a long time. He wouldn't relinquish her until this liaison had run its course.

His left hand crept towards the apex of her thighs.

Her hand clamped his wrist and instantly he felt ashamed. Only an hour ago they'd finally emerged from bed. His attempts to restrain himself, allowing her time to recuperate from their lovemaking, kept failing abysmally. He needed to be more considerate. Until a few days ago she'd never been with a man.

His chest expanded on a rough breath of satisfaction. He couldn't help it. He tried to feel guilty for stealing her virginity but now all he experienced was pleasure knowing he was her first, her only.

It must be the novelty that made him feel he never wanted to let her go.

'Not in front of the horses,' she whispered as he nudged her ponytail aside and kissed her neck.

'You think they'll be offended?' He smiled against her fragrant skin, pulling her back from the stall.

'I…' The word disintegrated in a sigh of delight that stoked his ego.

'You've never been naked in front of a horse?' he teased as he laved her skin.

'I've never been near a horse.' She tilted her head to allow him better access.

'Tragic,' he murmured. 'So much to make up for. Horses, sledding, caviar, breakfast in bed. So many firsts.' He punctuated each word with a tiny bite to her neck and was rewarded by tremors of response that racked her body. He gathered her close. 'What were your parents thinking to deprive you so?'

Did he imagine a stiffening of her slender form?

'I was a very fortunate child. You can't call me deprived.'

No? Alaric thought of how she hid her bright, strong personality behind a dowdy façade. It wasn't a deliberate ploy, he knew now, but part of who she was. He recalled the way her eyes clouded when she'd thought she'd disappointed him. There was a strong streak of self-doubt in his lover and Alaric wished he knew why. With her intelligence and drive it was a wonder she wasn't over-confident.

'Ah.' He nuzzled her hair. 'So you were a pampered miss who got everything her way. All the latest toys on demand?'

She shook her head. 'My parents didn't believe in store bought toys. I amused myself. But I had access to books and solitude to read. I had a secure home and time to dream.'

Alaric's hands stilled in the act of slipping up her ribcage. 'Secure' didn't sound like 'happy'. 'Solitude' had a lonely ring. A familiar ring. His father had ensured Alaric and Felix grew up in impeccable isolation. But at least Alaric had had a brother to look up to.

'What did you dream about, Tamsin?' He cupped her soft breasts and felt her sink against him. 'A prince in a far-away castle?'

'Sometimes,' she whispered.

'Did he have dark hair and blue eyes and his very own sleigh?'

She twisted in his arms. A moment later her arms twined around his neck.

'Of course!' Her eyes gleamed and her lips curved in a gentle smile that tugged at something deep inside.

'What else did you dream about?'

Tamsin shrugged and her gaze dropped. 'I don't know. Adventure. Going out with friends. The usual.'

Alaric thought of the dossier at the castle. It described a girl without siblings or close friends, whose much older parents had busy careers. A girl living a solitary life.

Did she realise how much her words revealed about her loneliness? Something swelled in his chest. Something like pain or regret.

'I think we can organise some adventure.' He tipped her chin and looked into her now guarded eyes. 'We could climb the base of the cliff behind the lodge if it's not too icy.'

Tamsin's eyes lit with golden sparks. Her smile made him feel like royalty in a way he never had before.

'I'd love that! Thank you. When can we go?'

He grinned. He'd *known* she had an adventurous streak. How easy it was to make her happy!

It surprised him how much he wanted her to be happy.

Alaric lifted his hand and pulled her ponytail loose so he could feel her heavy tresses on his hands. He needed this constant connection. To touch and taste, as if he feared she'd vanish if he didn't hold her.

'Another hour to let the sun melt any fresh ice.'

'That gives us time.' Her hands slid down, trailing fire. She yanked his shirt loose and slipped her palms up his torso, flesh against sizzling flesh. His body hardened.

Alaric loved that she was a quick learner.

'Time for what?' His voice was husky as desire twisted in his belly.

'Another first.' Now her smile was mischievous and he felt its impact in some unnamed part of him. 'I've never made love in a stable.'

Heart pounding, Alaric slipped his arms around her and lifted her into his embrace. It felt right. Satisfying.

He turned and strode towards the clean hay in the far corner. 'Allow me to remedy that right now.'

* * *

It was the noise that woke Tamsin. A cry so raw and anguished it made her blood congeal in atavistic terror.

Startled, she lay, breathing deep, wondering what had shattered her slumber. Moonlight streamed through the windows and behind the fire screen embers glowed.

Instinctively she moved closer to Alaric. For the past three days there'd barely been a moment when they weren't touching, even in sleep.

Amazing how she missed that contact.

As she rolled over she realised he was burning up, his skin feverish and damp with sweat.

Tamsin touched his shoulder. It was rigid as if every sinew dragged tight. She leaned close and heard his breathing, sharp and shallow. Her hand slid across his muscled chest that rose and fell in an unnatural rhythm.

'Alaric?'

No response. Did she imagine his breathing was laboured? Desperately she tried to recall everything she'd read about asthma and restricted airways.

'Alaric!' She shook him, alarmed at how her hands slipped on his fever-slickened flesh. 'Alaric. Wake up!' She shook his shoulders.

Restlessly his head turned back and forth. He mumbled something. But try as she might she couldn't wake him.

Fear spiked. They were out of phone range and she couldn't summon help if his condition worsened. Tamsin bit her lip. It wouldn't come to that.

First she had to get his temperature down.

She slid back the covers ready to fetch a damp flannel when another cry rent the air. Her blood froze at the wordless horror of that shout. It tapered into a wail of such grief every hair stood on end.

There was a convulsion of movement. The covers were flung wide and Alaric's hard frame landed on hers with such force it knocked the air from her lungs.

'No!' Huge hands gripped her shoulders. 'You can't!' He choked on the words, his head sinking to her breast.

It took a moment to realise the dampness she felt there wasn't sweat but tears. A sob shook his big body and Tamsin reached up, cradling him close.

'Sh, Alaric.' His distress frightened her, evoking fierce protective instincts. She felt his pain as if it shafted through her body. 'It's all right, darling, do you hear me?' Tamsin squeezed as tight as she could while his shoulders heaved and hot tears smeared between them.

She hated feeling so useless.

She hated that he hurt so badly.

'It's OK. It'll be OK,' she crooned, rocking him as best she could. 'My darling. Everything's all right.'

Gradually, as she murmured endearments, the rigidity seeped from his body and his breathing evened a little.

'Tamsin?'

Still she rocked him, her arms clamped tight. 'It's all right. It was just a dream.'

For long moments he lay still in her arms, then without warning he rolled off her, leaving her bereft.

'Alaric? Are you all right?'

He raised his forearm over his face. In the pallid light she saw his mouth crimp into a stern line as he fought whatever demons plagued him.

Instinctively she moved closer, tugging the discarded bedding to his waist and nestling her head on his chest, one arm wrapped protectively across him. He'd always seemed so strong and confident, so casually in command.

Her distress at his pain was a sharp ache. Was this what happened when you connected with another person? When you shared your true self as well as your body?

'I'm sorry.' His voice was slurred. 'You shouldn't have to witness that.' His breath shuddered out. 'I didn't mean to frighten you.'

For answer she snuggled closer, lifting her leg to anchor his thighs, as if by surrounding him she could blot out his nightmare.

'Don't worry. Everything's fine now.'

'Fine?' The word cracked like a gunshot. 'It'll never be fine.' He tore his arm from his face and she saw his fist pound the other side of the bed. But behind her his arm curved tight, holding her close.

'Did I hurt you?' His voice was a deep rumble. He stared at the top of the four poster bed, as if unwilling to face her. 'Tamsin, are you OK?'

'Of course I'm OK.'

'No questions?' he asked after a minute. 'Surely that enquiring mind of yours wants answers?' His mouth was a grim line in the half-dark.

A month ago his expression would have deterred Tamsin. But now she knew the tender, caring man behind the royal title and the rogue's reputation. She sensed his deep hurt.

She stretched up. Her breasts slid over his chest but she managed to ignore the inevitable tremor of awareness. She leaned over him till her hair curtained their faces in darkness. Holding his jaw in her hands she planted a whisper-light kiss on his lips.

He tasted of salt and heat and suffering.

His mouth was warm beneath hers as she repeated the action, allowing all she felt for him loose in that simple caress. Feelings she hadn't censored.

When she lifted her head one large palm covered the back of her skull and urged her down for another kiss. One so piercingly sweet she ached with the beauty of it. His other arm roped around her hips, drawing her in as if to ensure she wouldn't escape.

As if she wanted to go anywhere!

Never had they kissed like this: a sharing of the soul, not the body. Emotion escalated, filling every lonely part of her. She clung, wanting to explain how she felt but not having the words. Letting her body say what she couldn't.

From nowhere tears welled and spilled unheeded.

'Tamsin?' His thumb stroked her cheek, blurring the hot trail. 'Don't cry. Not over me.'

Too late. She was in too deep. Asking her not to care was like asking her to set fire to a library. Impossible.

Fervently she pressed her lips to his, blotting out whatever he was going to say. He kissed her till she sank into languorous pleasure. Finally he pulled back.

In the dark she felt his gaze. With a sigh he settled her on his chest and wrapped her close. Beneath her ear his heartbeat thrummed steadily.

'I owe you an explanation.' His voice was husky.

'You don't owe me anything. It was just a nightmare.'

'I was selfish, sleeping with you. What if I'd hurt you? I should have let you sleep alone.'

'It's you I'm worried about.' She hesitated, trying to summon an even tone and force away the chill that invaded at the idea of sleeping alone. 'You have these dreams often?'

His silence answered for him.

'You're afraid you might lash out in your sleep?'

'It's too dangerous. I risked your safety.'

'I told you, Alaric, I'm—'

'OK. So you say. But you don't know.' His words tailed off and the desolation she heard cut to her heart. 'Everything I touch turns to ashes. *Everyone.*'

Tamsin froze at the profound despair in his voice.

'Tell me.' She cuddled closer, her mind whirring while she tried to sound cool and detached.

'Talking about it will help?' Sarcasm threaded his voice. She ignored it, guessing he fought deep-seated pain any way he could.

'Bottling it up is no solution.' Look at the way she'd turned inwards, isolating herself rather than take the risk of being rejected. 'Whatever the problem, it will fester if you don't face it.'

'Now you're calling me a coward.' There was a huff of amusement in his voice that made her smile sadly. Alaric was excellent at using humour and his killer charm to deflect attention from the inner man.

How had she not seen it before?

'What have you got to fear? Unless you think I'll do a kiss and tell interview?'

'I can't imagine anything less likely.' He stroked her hair and Tamsin's tension eased a little. She had his trust at least. That was a start.

Silence fell.

'It's not about me,' he said eventually. 'It's the people I failed. That's who I dream of.' He sounded so stern, so judgemental, not like the Alaric she knew.

'I can't imagine you letting anyone down.'

His laugh was bitter. 'Don't you believe it. I was an unruly kid, always in trouble, a constant disappointment to my father. I heard often enough it was lucky I was just a second son. I didn't have what it took to rule.'

Tamsin bit her tongue rather than blurt out that his father sounded like a brute. A man who hadn't loved his wife, or, it seemed, his child. The more she heard the more she disliked.

'Then he'd be surprised to see Ruvingia flourishing now.'

Alaric said nothing. She sensed the reference to his father had been a distraction.

'Alaric? Tell me about your dreams.'

His chest rose beneath her like a wave cresting to shore. Tamsin clung grimly, willing him to share the source of his grief. It ate at him, destroying his peace.

At last he complied. 'I see them all die,' he whispered, 'and I can't save them.'

Tamsin's blood chilled at his haunted tone. 'Tell me.'

'So you can absolve me?' But his scepticism held anguish. Finally when she didn't answer he explained.

As a career army officer he'd jumped at the chance a few years ago to put his skills to good use, volunteering as a peacekeeper overseas. No sooner had he signed on than his whole unit had followed him.

They were posted near an isolated village, protecting a wide area from insurgents. Short bouts of dangerous activity were interspersed with long quiet periods which allowed time to get to know the locals. One little fatherless boy in particular had hung around, fascinated by the foreigners and especially Alaric. From his tone it was clear Alaric had been fond of him too.

When a report came of trouble in an outlying zone Alaric responded immediately, taking men to investigate.

'It was a ruse. But by the time we got there and discovered that it was too late.' They'd returned to their base to discover the village had been attacked. Both soldiers and civilians had been wounded and some had died, the little boy among them.

'He died in my arms.' Alaric's voice was hoarse. 'I couldn't save him.' A sigh racked his body. 'There were too many I couldn't save.'

'There's nothing you could have done.' Her heart broke at the pain ravaging him.

'No?' Glittering eyes clashed with hers. 'I was the officer in charge. If I hadn't split my men the village would have been safe. If I hadn't responded so quickly to an unconfirmed report—'

Tamsin cupped his jaw in her hand. 'You don't know what would have happened. Maybe the attack there would have been worse. You did your best.'

'You don't understand. I was there to protect them and *I failed*. I failed my men too. They were only there because of me. Some didn't survive. Others still bear the scars.' He halted, swallowing. 'Except me. I came home without a scratch.'

Tamsin's heart clenched at the guilt and self-loathing in his voice. She remembered Peter, his livid scar and how he'd talked of Alaric's sense of responsibility. Now it made terrible sense.

'Far better if I'd died too.'

'Don't say that!' Her fist clenched on his chest.

For a moment Alaric let himself enjoy the pleasure of her innocent belief in him. It was novel to have anyone so vehemently on his side.

The whole truth would rip the scales from her eyes. Part of him wanted to keep her in ignorance.

But he didn't deserve her charity.

'I came back to Ruvingia.' He'd been at a loose end, unable to settle, finding it hard to carry out the most routine official duties whilst memories of the deaths plagued him. 'I spent my time amusing myself. Fast cars, parties, women. Lots of women.' Sex had at least brought the oblivion of exhaustion, allowing him to sleep.

'My older brother, Felix, welcomed me.' His gut twisted, remembering Felix's patience with his wayward and tormented younger sibling. 'He was full of plans, even talking of marriage, but I wasn't interested. I was too wrapped up in my own troubles to listen.'

Some days it had been almost too hard to see Felix, so successful, capable and grounded. The epitome of what Alaric had aspired to be but not achieved.

Felix wouldn't have let those he was responsible for die. Felix would have found a way to save them.

'Alaric?'

'There was a girl,' he said, eager now to get this over. 'A beautiful girl. I first noticed her at a function when I saw Felix watching her.' He hefted a breath into tight lungs. 'Two days later she was in my bed.' Another of the stream of women he'd used to lose himself for a while.

Tamsin's body stiffened. Grimly he ploughed on, knowing by the time he'd finished she'd never want to look at him again. He ignored the shaft of pain that caused.

'I didn't love her. I never pretended to. And she… I think my reputation appealed. She wanted the thrill of being with someone notorious.' He grimaced. 'It was mutually satisfying. Till Felix discovered us and I found out she was the woman he'd already fallen for. The one he'd wanted to marry after a proper courtship.'

Tamsin gasped. 'You didn't know?'

'I knew he planned to marry but I assumed it would be an arranged marriage. He hadn't mentioned a name and frankly I wasn't interested.' Alaric paused, forcing out the truth. 'But I knew he was attracted to Diana. Most men were.'

Again he wondered if his pleasure in winning her had been fuelled in part by the need to best Felix. To prove that in this one thing, the ability to get any woman he wanted, Alaric was superior.

Could he have been so shallow? So jealous? What did that say about him?

He'd never before thought himself envious of Felix. But now he couldn't banish telling doubts about his motives.

'Felix was furious when he found out. I'd never seen him like it.' Alaric remembered not only his anger, but his pain. The disillusionment of finding out the woman he'd put on a pedestal had sullied herself with his scapegrace brother. 'He accused us of betraying him.' That memory alone crucified Alaric. Felix was the only person with whom he'd been close. The only person who'd ever really cared.

'And Diana?'

'She was angry she'd made such an error. She hadn't realised he intended marriage. She didn't love him but she liked the notion of being a princess.'

'So what happened?'

Typically, Tamsin was intelligent enough to sense there was more. He let his arm tighten round her soft body, knowing it would probably be for the last time.

'Felix changed. He became short-tempered, not just with me, but everyone. He grew erratic, increasingly unreliable and he began drinking heavily.' The memory of that time, and his inability to stop his brother's slide into depression, chilled Alaric.

'One day I found him climbing into my sports car, determined to drive himself to a function. He reeked of whisky.'

'Oh, Alaric.' Tamsin's palm flattened on his chest and he covered it with his own.

'I couldn't stop him but I couldn't let him go. I jumped in just as he accelerated out of the courtyard.' He drew a deep breath, letting the familiar, corrosive pain claim him. 'We argued.' And each word of Felix's accusations was branded in Alaric's memory, reinforcing every doubt he'd ever harboured about himself.

'Felix lost control on a hairpin bend and I grabbed the steering wheel. We didn't make it around the next curve. We went into the embankment.' His breath grew choppy and sweat prickled his skin. 'I'd buckled my seat belt and the airbag saved me. Felix wasn't wearing his belt. He died instantly.'

Alaric forced himself to relinquish his hold on Tamsin, knowing she'd move away now.

* * *

Tamsin held her breath, shocked at his story. Stunned by the blankness in Alaric's voice. How much he'd suffered! He'd hidden it all behind that charming mask.

It was obvious he'd loved his brother. Given the little she knew, perhaps Felix was the only person who'd ever cared for Alaric.

'I'm so sorry.' The words were pathetically little.

'So am I. Every day. But that doesn't change the fact I'm to blame.'

'Don't say that!'

'If I hadn't seduced Diana, none of it would have happened. If I'd stopped him—'

'If Diana had loved him back, nothing you did could have caused a rift between them.'

There was silence for a moment as if Alaric considered the idea for the first time. Then he shook his head.

'I should have been more careful, less eager to get her into my bed.'

Tamsin couldn't argue with that. 'Your brother blamed you because he was disappointed. It wasn't your fault he loved someone who didn't return his feelings.'

'But he didn't need me undermining him. He deserved my loyalty. I should have been there to help him. Protect him from himself when he turned to drink. I couldn't even do that. *I failed him when he needed me.*' His voice hollowed and Tamsin's throat ached as she stifled tears at his pain.

From the first she'd noticed his tendency to set high standards for himself. Look at the way he'd talked about *taking her virginity.*

Did that overblown sense of responsibility come from being told constantly by his father that his best wasn't good enough? She sensed the weight Alaric bore didn't stem solely from tragic recent events, but from unhealed scars he'd carried a long time.

It didn't surprise her that he wasn't thinking clearly. He'd had one shock piled on another.

Alaric's bitter laughter shredded the silence. 'And here I am, about to take the crown. To do my duty and promise to serve and *protect*! How can I be sure I won't fail again?'

Tamsin's heart broke at his pain and self-doubt. He truly didn't see how capable and competent he was.

No wonder he spent his time dallying with socialites and risking his neck in extreme sports. No wonder he never wanted to be still. He was running from this trauma.

Fury rose in her that those closest to him hadn't seen this. That they hadn't helped him.

Her mind boggled at the weight of guilt he bore. How did he function, much less put on that devil-may-care air? He believed he'd failed his duty to his comrades and his brother. That he was to blame.

That explained why he was appalled at becoming responsible for a nation. And why he didn't want to get close to anyone. He felt himself unworthy. She'd bet, apart from his brother, his comrades were the closest he'd come to a family.

Tamsin breathed out a huff of relief that she hadn't told him the chronicle's date had been verified. Wild horses wouldn't drag that from her now.

'Oh, darling.' She pressed closer, kissing his chin, neck and face. 'You have to forgive yourself. Believe me, you're a victim too.'

He shook his head. 'Tell that to men who came home scarred. Or the mother of an innocent boy who died.'

Tamsin framed his face with her palms. His pain tore at her and she couldn't bear it. 'Your ego is out of control if you think you caused all that! Your brother would be horrified to know you blamed yourself. Do you really think he'd want that? You're a good man, Alaric. I'd trust you with my life.'

'Sweet Tamsin.' He raised a hand and brushed a furious tear from her cheek. 'Don't waste your tears on me.'

'I'll cry if I want to.' He was so stubborn! So eager to shoulder guilt.

Yet his loyalty and honour were part of what made him the man she cared for. *The man she loved.*

Knowledge sideswiped her with a force that left her speechless. Somehow, without her realising, he'd changed from fantasy prince to the man she loved.

Her heart gave a massive jerk and thundered out of control. Her hands shook against his lean cheeks.

She'd thought she risked her pride in coming here, only to discover she'd risked much more.

She'd given her heart to Alaric.

A man with no thought of long term relationships. Who distrusted love. Yet for now even that couldn't dim the incandescent glow filling her.

'We can talk about this later. Now you need sleep.'

'I'll move to another room.'

'Don't even think about it! I'll just follow you.' She slid down into the bed. 'Shut your eyes and rest. I'll stay awake. You won't hurt me.'

'I could get used to you trying to dominate me,' he murmured in a pale imitation of his usual teasing. 'I'm too tired to resist.'

His breath was warm on her skin, his hand splayed possessively at her waist as he tucked her close. But there was nothing sexual about the way they lay. This was about comfort and peace and love.

Even if he didn't believe in it, Tamsin hoped Alaric felt the love drenching her skin, filling her heart, wrapping itself around him.

Later, she knew, her predicament in falling for this man would devastate her. But for now it filled her with a peace she'd never known.

CHAPTER THIRTEEN

THE pink flush of dawn lit the sky as Tamsin crept downstairs. Though Alaric had slept for hours she didn't want to wake him.

She shivered and pulled the silk wrap tighter as she reached the ground floor. The lingering warmth from the central heating made the chill bearable.

Yet nothing dispelled the cold squeezing her heart. How could she even begin to help Alaric?

Or herself. Her situation was impossible.

She was in love.

With Prince Alaric of Ruvingia.

A man with no history of commitment. A troubled man who scorned the notion of falling in love. A man so far beyond her sphere any idea of a relationship was laughable.

Alaric was used to the best in everything. Could he ever settle for someone as ordinary as her? It was ridiculous to hope, but she couldn't stop herself.

Would he ever tie himself to a woman? Especially a woman who wasn't witty or glamorous or well born?

She'd come here knowing she was a short term diversion. At first the bright promise of his offer had been enough. Now she realised she'd been dragged out of her depth.

She loved him.

Tamsin hugged the bitter-sweet knowledge to herself, alternately thrilled and horrified.

Yet as she'd lain, overwhelmed by the realities she faced, part of her brain had pondered the one useful thing she could do: prove once and for all if Tomas's chronicle was legitimate. Lately she'd harboured doubts. Were they well founded or, as she'd begun to suspect, an excuse not to break the news that would take Alaric even further from her?

She thrust open the library door, flicked on the light and headed for the desk. She worked best with pen and paper. Perhaps if she listed her concerns she'd get them straight in her head.

She'd happily give up the kudos of rewriting history with her find if it meant bringing Alaric peace of mind.

He was more important than any professional coup or the chance to rub Patrick's nose in her success. Nothing mattered more than his peace and happiness.

How much had altered these past months!

Despite her selfish fear about the yawning void it would open between them, Tamsin couldn't help regretting that he didn't want the crown. The respect and admiration between Alaric and his people was tangible even if he didn't see it. He'd make an excellent monarch with his dedication to duty and practicality. If only he could see beyond his pain.

She opened a drawer and found a notepad. She withdrew it then paused, an envelope catching her eye.

Tamsin Connors. It was addressed to her?

Her brow puckered as she reached for it. No stamp. No address. Just her name. What did it mean? A trickle of sensation slid down her spine.

'Tamsin!'

Startled, she turned to find Alaric filling the doorway, his face pale and set. Her gaze traversed his perfect, muscular torso and a familiar weakness hit her knees. He wore only jeans, zipped but not buttoned.

No man had a right to look so magnificent! Her pulse gave a queer little leap and hurried on.

'What are you doing?' The hoarse edge to his voice reminded her of his revelations last night. She moved towards him then stopped, uncertain.

'I came to find pen and paper. I had an idea about the chronicle. I wanted—'

'Come back to bed.' He held out a hand, his eyes boring into hers as if to force her to obey. Despite his outstretched hand it wasn't an invitation. It was an order.

'What's wrong?' The room hummed with tension.

'Nothing. I just want you with me. This can wait.' He smiled, but it didn't reach his eyes.

'I'll be up soon,' she assured him. 'I only want to jot some points. Besides, I found this.' She looked at the envelope, frowning as she read her name again.

Before she realised what he intended, Alaric had crossed the room. He stood before her, his palm open as if inviting her to pass the envelope over.

'Leave that. It's not important.' His clipped tone surprised her and she stiffened.

Tamsin looked from those blazing indigo eyes and the stark lines accentuating the stern set of Alaric's mouth to the envelope in her hand. A frisson of foreboding rippled through her. Suddenly the envelope didn't seem quite so innocuous. She wanted to drop it on the desk but her fingers locked tight.

'Why don't you want me to open it?'

Silence. He moved close but didn't touch her. That tiny distance made her feel colder than the chilly dawn air.

'Because it's not for you. It's about you.'

For what seemed an age Tamsin stood, unmoving, staring blankly at her printed name. About her?

Realisation, when it came, rocked her onto her heels.

'You mean an investigation? *Of me?*' For the first time she noticed the date under her name. The day they'd left the castle. Alaric must have brought it with him.

Her head jerked up and their eyes met. His were blank.

Tamsin's heart tripped. She'd grown used to the other Alaric. Warm, generous and fun loving. Caring. She'd almost forgotten the cool control he could summon at will.

'Yes,' he said at last. 'I had you investigated.'

Something squeezed around her lungs and it took a few moments to catch her breath. 'What's in it?'

'I don't know. I haven't read it.'

'Do you have dossiers on every employee?'

It must be a routine security check. But why was it done so recently rather than before she'd come to Ruvingia?

'Not like that.'

Tamsin's heart plummeted. She slipped her finger under the flap and drew out the papers.

Alaric didn't move a muscle. His eerie stillness only increased her fear.

The first page puzzled her. It was about the journalist at the ball. It was only when she turned the page and read a note that there was no evidence of previous contact between him and Tamsin that she understood.

The paper fluttered to the floor.

Other pages were about her and Patrick. Heat rose in Tamsin's cheeks as she recognised office gossip about them. How could Alaric have ordered someone to pry into her life?

'Why didn't you ask, if you wanted to know about the men in my life?' Her mouth twisted bitterly.

Alaric was the only man in her life! Somehow, now, the idea didn't thrill her so much.

'Do you normally vet prospective lovers?'

Alaric shook his head. 'It's not like that.'

'How did you know about Patrick anyway? I didn't mention him to anyone here.' She turned to the last page. What she found turned her heart to a solid lump of ice.

'You had my phone tapped!' She could barely believe it. 'Surely that's not legal, even if you are the prince!'

'It is, if it's a matter of state security.'

'State security! I'm a curator, not a spy!'

'You turned up out of the blue—'

'You invited me here, remember?'

'At a volatile time,' he said as if she hadn't interrupted. 'There's no king. Parliament is in recess till after the coronation, which by law can't take place for several months. It's a time ripe for factions building on past dissension to try toppling the democracy.'

He looked utterly implacable and something inside Tamsin shrivelled. Gone was her tender, vulnerable lover.

'Suddenly you appear, claiming to have proof that I, not Crown Prince Raul, am the legitimate heir. Can you imagine how catastrophic it might be if that news reached the wrong people before we had time to prepare?'

Tamsin stepped behind the desk, needing space to clear her head. Her eyes widened as she saw Alaric's severe expression. The tiny voice that cried this was all a mistake fell silent under the impact of his stare.

'You thought I lied about what I found?' The edges of the room spun as she grappled with the depths of his distrust.

'I acted in the interests of my country.' His tone was stiff, as if he was unused to being challenged.

'You thought that and *still* you took me to bed?'

No, Tamsin. That's why he took you to bed! To distract you, keep you from doing any more damage.

Neutralise the threat. Wasn't that what they called it?

She braced herself against the desk as pain gutted her and she doubled up. Blood roared in her ears like a deafening tide. In a series of snapshots, Tamsin recalled so many tell tale moments.

Her carefully monitored access to the chronicle.

The presence, wherever she went, of staff, no doubt reporting her movements.

Alaric asking her to be his companion, just the day after she'd told him about the chronicle. It had been a ruse, not to keep women away, but to keep an eye on her!

Alaric's fury at the ball when he'd found her with that journalist. He'd lied. He wasn't jealous, just angry she might have revealed something. Or maybe, she thought of what she'd read, Alaric suspected them of being in cahoots.

Pain blurred her vision and cramped her breathing. Her breath sawed in aching lungs as she fought to stay upright.

A hand reached for her and she jerked away.

'Don't touch me! Don't…' She drew an uneven breath. 'I can't bear it.'

To think she'd felt guilty, not telling him immediately about the test results, agonising over whether she could find something to prove or disprove the document once and for all. *And all the time he'd known!*

Her own small omission was nothing compared to his elaborate machinations!

'Tamsin. Have you heard a word I've said?'

'I don't want to hear!' She stumbled to the window, arms wrapped tight around her middle.

'Bringing me here was a ploy, wasn't it?' She stared dry eyed across the snow as cold facts solidified in her shocked brain. 'No wonder the pantry was well stocked. You planned to keep me here, out of harm's way.'

Bitterness scalded her throat. He'd succeeded. For days she'd delighted in the mirage Alaric had created. She'd barely given a thought to her work.

He'd been so sure of her. Had it been a lark, or an unpalatable duty, seducing her?

Tamsin's breath hissed as another piece of the picture slotted into place. The man at the sleigh, handing Alaric an envelope before they left. Alaric's dismissal of her concerns about a change in weather.

'You knew heavy snow was forecast.' She didn't turn. She couldn't face him. Not when the knowledge of her naivety filled her and every breath lanced pain. 'Didn't you? You wanted me cut off here.'

'I knew,' he answered at last, his words dropping like stones into an endless icy pool.

No apology. No regret.

She squeezed her eyes shut. *What they'd shared meant nothing.* Nothing to him but expediency.

It must have galled him to go to such lengths. No wonder he'd been disappointed the first time in that big bed. She hadn't even possessed the skills to please him.

Had he closed his eyes when they'd made love—no, when they'd had sex—and thought of another woman? Someone gorgeous and alluring?

How had she thought, even for one moment, that she'd snared the interest of Alaric, Prince of Ruvingia? Tamsin cringed inside but she kept her spine straight.

'You're an excellent actor.' She ignored the tremor in her voice and stared at the gorgeous alpine vista. 'You had me convinced. Congratulations.'

'Tamsin, it wasn't like that. Not all of it. To start with, yes, I wondered about you. About the way you hid behind that spinster look. About the odds of you finding such a document so conveniently.'

'It wasn't convenient!' She'd spent long hours working in the archives. And all the time he'd thought she'd lied.

'But later it wasn't about the papers, Tamsin.' His voice was nearer, as if he'd followed her to the window. 'It was about how you made me feel. And how you felt.'

'How I felt?' Her fury boiled over and she swung round. 'Are you saying I *asked* you to dupe me? That I *invited* you to make a fool of me?' As she spoke the final, fragile shell of happiness round her heart crumbled.

She'd believed. She'd actually believed in him! How many times before she finally learned her lesson? Was she so imbued with romantic fantasy that she was doomed to fall again and again for men's lies?

Even as she thought it she realised that wasn't possible. She'd survived Patrick's deception but this was far worse. She'd fallen in love with Alaric.

Now she hated him too.

'I'll tell you how this feels, *Your Highness*. It feels like hell! There was no excuse for what you did. None!'

'Tamsin, you have to listen. That's not really why I brought you here.'

She backed away from his outstretched hand as if it were poisoned.

'Not really?' Her voice dripped sarcasm. 'So the phone tap wasn't real? And the goons patrolling the grounds to make sure I didn't meet anyone in secret?' She flung an accusatory hand towards the papers on the floor. 'And the investigator's report—I suppose that was make-believe?'

Did she imagine he stiffened as each accusation lashed like a whip? Or that his face paled beneath its tan?

No! She could afford no sympathy for this man. Already it felt as if she bled from an unseen wound. The sort of injury that would never heal.

'You know what hurts most?' She stood rigidly straight. 'That you discovered how Patrick used me and decided to try the same tactic yourself. And that I fell for it.'

His brow puckered in a marvellous show of apparent innocence. 'I don't follow you.'

'Your report didn't detail that juicy titbit?' She'd skimmed the text, unable to take in every word. 'I don't believe you.' She sucked air to her lungs.

'Patrick set out to make me fall for him. He conned me into helping him *manage his workload* till I found him passing off my work as his. Using it to get a promotion at my expense. When he got it he dumped me and took up with a sexy blonde who knew how to please a man.' She almost gagged, remembering Patrick's satisfaction as he'd said that.

'And now you, you…' She blinked dry, scratchy eyes. 'I can't believe I fell for it again. That I actually *believed* you were attracted to me.'

She couldn't go on. Bile rose in her throat and her stomach churned queasily. Being sick in front of Alaric would be the final humiliation.

Tamsin stumbled to the door, thrusting aside his hand, ignoring his call for her to stop as pain, nausea and despair took hold.

The cold seeped into Alaric's bones as he stood, staring at the library's empty fireplace. It wasn't the chill air that froze his half-dressed body. It was the memory of Tamsin's distress. *The pain he had caused.*

Guilt flexed its claws, raking his belly. Lacerating the peace he'd discovered these past days with Tamsin.

Seeing her anguish, hearing her desperate attempt to keep her voice steady, Alaric had wanted to gather her close and comfort her. Force her to accept his embrace. Accustomed as he was to causing pain, he couldn't bear this.

Letting her leave had been the ultimate test of endurance when every instinct roared for him to go to her.

Yet he had to give her time alone. Enough to calm a little so she'd listen.

She felt betrayed by him.

He turned to pace, unable to remain inactive. If only he'd known her history with the Englishman! How much more damage had Alaric done to her bruised self-esteem?

She thought he'd used her for his own ends too.

But it hadn't been like that.

Yes, he'd been selfish. He'd seduced an innocent. But his motives, though not pure, hadn't been as despicable as the Englishman's. Her work had been a catalyst for intimacy. Yet it had also provided a convenient excuse. How much easier to explain away his fascination with a drably dressed bookworm than admit she intrigued him? That he wanted her in ways he'd never wanted anyone? Ways that had as much to do with emotions as with sexual gratification?

Air punched from his lungs as an unseen blow pummelled his solar plexus.

Emotions.

He'd spent so long distancing himself from intimacy except the sort he found in the beds of accommodating women. It was a shock to realise how much he felt for Tamsin. How much he *cared.* He'd thought it impossible, but it was true.

Instantly fear rose. Its familiar, hoary hand clenched his heart and iced his blood. No matter how he fought he couldn't blot out the voice in his soul.

He tainted everyone he touched.

He should never have allowed himself near Tamsin, so bright and generous and trusting.

His darkness spread like a miasma, infecting everyone he cared for. Now it had soiled that brief bright moment of delight. It had engulfed Tamsin too. He'd let her down.

But how to look into her bright eyes and listen to her soft, serious tones and not give in to temptation? For all his inner darkness, he was a man, not a machine. Resisting her innocent sweetness, her tart asperity and her zest for living had been impossible.

He'd craved an end to the darkness and he'd got that from her. No wonder he'd been insatiable, unable to bear her out of his sight. Before her his smiles and banter had carefully masked bleak emptiness. She'd filled that void with light and warmth.

Alaric recalled her soft murmurings as she'd listened to his story. Instead of shunning him when she'd heard what he'd done she'd called him 'darling' as naturally as if it might even be true. The sound of it had lodged somewhere near his heart and he'd cherished it.

He'd be damned if he'd give that up.

Twenty minutes since he'd let her walk away. A sensitive man might wait longer before confronting her. But his need was too urgent. He strode from the room.

The turret bedroom was empty. Alaric refused to think of it as *their* room, though the hint of her scent and the sight of rumpled sheets hit him in the chest like a ton of bricks. Setting his jaw, he searched the other rooms. Empty.

Fear ratcheted up in his belly.

It was only as he paused by a window that he realised where she'd gone. Her tracks led to the cliff where he'd given her a climbing lesson.

His heart almost failed as he remembered telling her that was the quickest way to the castle. It was an easy climb if you were experienced, but for a novice…

He'd hurt her so badly she'd rather face the mountain than him?

Alaric was no stranger to anguish but as he raced downstairs his torment was worse than anything he'd known.

If anything happened to her…

The cold numbed Tamsin's hands as she trudged through the snow. She'd forgotten her gloves in her haste but she wouldn't return for them. Not yet. Not till she'd found the strength to face Alaric without crumbling in a heap.

The nausea had eased a little but the pain was so raw, so sharp, she could barely breathe.

She shoved her hands in her anorak pockets and averted her eyes from the place where he'd taught her to climb. He'd been so tender and patient.

A sham!

Quickening her step she passed the small cliff and came to the base of a steep mountain slope. She'd have no trouble retracing her steps but for now she wanted solitude.

If she could she'd run away and never face him again.

The thought made her stumble to a halt.

She'd run across Europe rather than face Patrick. She'd spent years hiding herself rather than risk the chance of rejection. She'd thought there was strength in independence. But she hadn't been independent. She'd been a coward.

If she were truly the new, independent woman she'd been so proud of the night of the ball, she'd face Alaric.

She was furious and hurt by how he'd used her. But almost as bad was knowing she'd made the same mistake again. Fooled twice by manipulative men. Only this time her mistake was irredeemable. She'd fallen for Alaric, heart and soul. Despite his ruthless actions he was so much more than the flawed man he thought himself.

Something, an awareness, made her turn. An hour ago the sight of Alaric chasing her through the snow would have thrilled her, a precursor to some new lovers' game.

Now it was despair she felt, for even knowing how he'd used her, her heart leapt at the sight of him. Her blood roared in her ears. Would she always react to him like this?

'Run!' He was so near she saw his eyes blaze fire.

For a moment she saw stark fear in those glittering depths, then his hands closed on her and she was running, stumbling, carried by the force of his charging body. He kept her on her feet, urging her, tugging her at an impossible speed through the snow.

It was only as he spoke again that she realised the whispering roar wasn't her blood. She saw his lips move but the sound was obliterated by the thunder of tonnes of snow and rock falling off the mountain.

Avalanche! She read his lips but it was his urgent hands, his grim expression, that gave her strength to run.

Ahead a curve in the line of the mountain promised safety. They couldn't possibly make it. Then with a tremendous shove at her back Alaric propelled her forward.

She sprawled, hands over head as snow and scree dropped around her. The thud of the avalanche reverberated through the valley, snapping her teeth together. But the fall here on the periphery of the slide was relatively light.

Finally it was over. Gingerly she moved, burrowing her way up, grateful for the sight of sky above. She dragged in a deep breath scented with pine and ice and adrenaline.

Without Alaric she would have been buried under the massive fall. She turned to thank him.

To find only a huge tumbled mass of ice and boulders.

CHAPTER FOURTEEN

'THE prince is being released from hospital.' Tamsin's colleague gave her a sidelong glance. 'He'll be back at the castle soon.'

'That's excellent news.' Tamsin pinned on the cool, professional smile she'd perfected. It concealed the fluttery reaction in her stomach at the mention of her employer, her ex-lover. The man she dreamt of every night. 'I didn't think he'd be out so soon.'

After fracturing his collarbone, a leg and an arm, as well as sustaining concussion, the pundits had said Alaric would be under medical supervision far longer.

'Apparently the doctors didn't want to release him but he refused to stay any longer.'

Tamsin nodded, remembering Alaric's determination and strength. He had so little regard for himself he'd probably ignored medical warnings. A twinge of worry stabbed her. Would he be all right?

She still got chills thinking of those long minutes as she'd scrabbled beneath the debris to the seemingly lifeless form she'd finally found. Her heart had plunged into freefall as she'd searched for a pulse.

In that moment it didn't matter how he'd used her, how he'd cold-bloodedly taken her into his bed. All that mattered was that she loved him and he might die.

It had felt like *her* life blood oozing across the snow.

The metallic taste of fear filled her mouth as memory consumed her. Her helplessness, till she'd found Alaric's mobile phone and, miracle of miracles, discovered it still functioned. She'd felt only a desperate satisfaction that, despite what he'd led her to believe, there was perfect phone reception. Within twenty minutes medical staff had arrived by helicopter.

'Perhaps he'll visit the archives to see how we're getting on.' No missing her colleague's arch tone of enquiry. Not surprising given Alaric's previous impromptu visits.

But he'd only come because he didn't trust her.

Had he fretted all those weeks in hospital, wondering if she'd talked of what she'd found? The surveillance seemed to have stopped. She'd lost the claustrophobic sense of being watched.

'I suspect the prince has more important things to do.'

Even she had heard the speculation about Crown Prince Raul's delay in finalising his coronation, and how much time he spent closeted with his injured cousin. No doubt they were organising for Alaric to be crowned when he recovered.

He'd make an excellent monarch. Stoically she ignored the fact that his coronation would hammer the final nail in the coffin of her wishful dreams. Dreams that even his actions hadn't quite managed to stifle.

Tamsin looked at her watch. 'Time to pack up, don't you think?' She ignored her companion's curious look. For well over a month she'd faced down blatant interest about her relationship with Alaric.

Only when she was alone in the room did she slump in her chair, her heart pounding at the thought of Alaric here, in the castle again.

His pain still haunted her. Her heart ached for him and all he'd been through. Once she'd believed she could help him. As if *she*...

She bit her lip. She'd done with fantasy.

These past weeks had been a hell of worry about Alaric and constant scrutiny from the curious. Yet she'd endured. She'd put up with the gossip and completed the initial period of her contract, determined to fulfil her obligation.

Did her resolve stretch to seeing him again?

Tamsin shot to her feet, too edgy to sit. They'd find someone to replace her when she didn't renew her contract. Patrick perhaps. Strangely she felt no qualms about the idea of him here in what had been her territory.

She wouldn't return to Britain. But there'd been that offer last year of a job in Berlin, and a hint about work in Rome. She'd delayed following up either opportunity. Her lips twisted as she realised it was because in her heart she wanted to be close to Alaric.

Pathetic! There was nothing to stay for. The sooner she moved on the better. Starting with a weekend in Berlin or Rome. Either would do.

Would it be easier to heal a broken heart in new surroundings?

Out of nowhere pain surged, cramping her body and stealing the air from her lungs. It took a full minute to catch her breath and move again.

Tamsin refused to acknowledge the fear that nothing would heal what ailed her. She felt a terrible certainty that the love she still felt for Alaric, despite everything, would never be 'healed'.

'The answer is still no.' Alaric hobbled across the hospital room. He set his mouth against the pain when he moved too fast. 'I won't do it. That's final.'

'Do you think I liked the idea of an arranged marriage, either?' Raul sounded weary. They'd been over this time and again. 'It's your duty, Alaric. If you accept the crown then you accept the responsibilities that go with it.'

'Don't talk to me of duty!' Alaric's clenched fist connected with the wall but he barely felt the impact. 'I don't want this, any of it. I'm only accepting the crown because, like you, I've been brought up to do my duty.'

Strange how things had changed since the accident. His fear of failure had dimmed. He no longer got that sick feeling in his belly at the thought of ruling the nation. He could face the idea of leadership again with equanimity, though being monarch wasn't his choice.

In hospital he'd had plenty of time to think. To his surprise he'd realised how much he'd enjoyed the work he'd begun in Ruvingia. It had been satisfying solving problems and organising innovative community renewal. He'd like to follow through the improvements they'd begun in his own principality.

But as king he couldn't be so hands on. His life would be all protocol and diplomacy.

At least he knew now he could face what was required of him.

What had changed? Even the nightmares had receded a little. Because he'd broken the curse of good luck that had seen him emerge unscathed from tragedy? Because he'd shattered his body and almost lost his life, proving his mortality? No, it couldn't be that simple.

He'd been overwhelmed by the genuine distress of his people after the accident. The number of communities and groups who'd sent representatives had stunned him. They'd wished him well, and, as he recovered, sought his renewed input to their projects.

Yet Alaric knew the real change had come from his brief glimpse of happiness. The peace and sense of connection he'd felt in his short time with Tamsin. Surely that's what had hauled him back from the brink of self-destruction, giving him hope for the first time in years.

Six months ago he'd have embraced death with equanimity. But lying in hospital as doctors fussed over him; Alaric had discovered he wanted to live so badly he could taste the need.

He *had* to live, to see Tamsin and set things right.

The night he'd shared his past with her had cracked something wide open inside him. Not just his guilt and fear. But a lifetime of barriers. Barriers that had kept him cut off from love, preventing him building a real relationship.

'Alaric.' His cousin's voice yanked him from his reverie. He turned and met Raul's sympathetic look. 'I know this is hard on you.'

'Hard on us both.' Raul had been raised to be king. It was a measure of his integrity that he'd taken so well the stunning news that Alaric should be monarch. The final testing and double checking of Tamsin's document and other contemporary sources had proven her right. Alaric was destined to be king, not Raul.

Raul shrugged. 'There's no way out of the wedding. You think I haven't double checked? It's a binding agreement. The Crown Prince of Maritz is betrothed to marry the Princess of Ardissia. No negotiation.'

'Even though we don't know where she is?' If Alaric had his way they'd never locate her.

'We will soon. And when we do…' Raul shrugged.

'A royal wedding.' A loveless marriage. Surely the only sort he wanted or deserved. Yet his blood froze.

He remembered Tamsin's smile, felt the radiant warmth it brought his blighted soul. He heard her soft cries of delight as he pleasured her, smelled her fresh summer scent.

She hadn't come near him since the accident. She *hated* him for what he'd done to her.

His chances of persuading her to forgive him were slim.

But to marry another woman…

Alaric stiffened, realising there was only one way forward. It would be perhaps the most difficult thing he'd ever done, but he had no choice.

'I *beg* your pardon?' Tamsin couldn't believe her ears.

'None of the documents held in safekeeping can be released without His Highness's permission.' The secretary sounded uncomfortable.

'But it's *my* passport!' Tamsin shot to her feet, the phone pressed to her ear, then drew a calming breath. 'There must be a misunderstanding. The passport was held for safekeeping only.'

'You're planning to travel?'

Tamsin frowned. She shouldn't have to report her plans. But maybe it would stir this bureaucrat into action.

'I fly to Rome this weekend.' An overnight trip to discuss a possible job. She told herself she'd be enthusiastic about it once she got to the sunny south. 'So when can I collect it?'

Another pause. 'I'll have to get back to you on that. The prince gave specific instructions…'

A chill fingered its way down Tamsin's spine. *Alaric's* instructions? Impossible! He couldn't want her here.

Yet he'd manipulated her before. Was it possible he was doing it again? Fury sparked. She would *not* be a pawn in his games again.

The secretary was talking when she dropped the phone into its cradle.

Fifteen minutes later Tamsin entered the royal antechamber. Ironically she'd made it through security easily. Chancing to meet the servant who'd come to fetch Alaric the night of the ball, she'd asked for directions, letting him believe Alaric had sent for her.

As she entered the room a man, busy at a desk, looked up.

'The prince is not receiving visitors.'

Tamsin's eyes narrowed as she recognised his voice. The secretary who'd stonewalled her on the phone.

'This can't wait.' She kept walking.

'Wait!' His eyes flicked to the double doors on the other side of the room. 'If you take a seat I'll check the prince's schedule.'

Her pace quickened. She was sure now that Alaric was in the next room. Tamsin wasn't about to be fobbed off. Whatever was going on she'd get to the bottom of it. Now.

'Thank you. But I'll make my own appointment.'

From the corner of her eye she saw him scramble to his feet, but he was too late. She wrenched open the door and catapulted through it, her heart pounding as adrenaline surged. She'd hoped to avoid confronting Alaric again, yet part of her longed to see him one last time.

Two steps into the room she stumbled to a halt, eyes widening at the tableau before her. Alaric was there but so were many others, all formally dressed and wearing sober expressions. There was a sprinkling of uniforms, clerical robes and a few judges in old-fashioned costumes.

In the centre sat Alaric, one arm in a sling, writing at a vast desk. He put his pen down and looked up.

Lightning blasted her senses as his piercing eyes met hers down the length of the chamber. Her body quivered with the impact of that look.

Tamsin swayed and shut her eyes, aghast at her weakness. She had to get away from him once and for all. Going to Rome was the right thing.

A hand grabbed her elbow. 'My apologies for the intrusion, Highness.' The hand tugged and Tamsin opened her eyes.

The secretary's words had made everyone present turn to look. Silence reigned for a moment and despite crawling embarrassment she stood straight, facing the curiosity of the gathered VIPs.

What had she stumbled into?

'It's all right.' Alaric's voice drew her gaze to where he sat, so handsome in dress uniform. 'Dr Connors is my welcome guest.' Did she imagine his voice deepened seductively?

No! There was nothing between them. There never had been. She had to remember that.

'Of course, Your Highness.' The man released her, bowed and melted away.

Silently Alaric gestured her to a chair and she went to it gratefully. Yet she didn't sit. By now she knew she'd interrupted something important. The judges stepped forward with deep bows and signed the document Alaric passed to them. Then several others, all with a slow formality that proclaimed this a significant occasion.

Finally Alaric stood. Tamsin's heart clenched as he limped from his chair. He was pale, his face pared down. She wanted to smooth her palm across his face, trace the high slant of his cheekbone and reassure herself he was all right. Her hands trembled with the force of what she felt.

The day of the accident she'd stayed as close as she could, scared to let him out of her sight till finally the doctors pronounced him out of danger. Since then she hadn't seen him, knowing it was better that way. Yet she'd scoured the news reports for updates on his recovery.

He must have come here straight from the hospital.

Anyone else seeing his straight backed stance would think him fully recovered. But to Tamsin's eyes there was a stiffness around his neck and shoulders and a tension in his jaw that betrayed pain.

What was so important he'd left the hospital for it? Couldn't anyone else see he needed rest?

Impotent anger surged. It was no use telling herself he didn't need her sympathy. She couldn't squash her feelings.

Alaric turned to the man beside him. A tall, handsome man with familiar features. Alaric said something she couldn't hear and bent his head in a bow. But before he could complete the action the other man spoke sharply and put a hand on Alaric's shoulder.

Alaric raised his head and for a moment Tamsin saw something flash between the two. Wordless understanding. Then Alaric spoke, making his companion laugh and reach to shake his hand vigorously.

There was a burst of applause and cheers in Ruvingian that Tamsin wished she understood. The two men turned to face their audience, accepting the accolade with an ease that spoke of long practice.

She watched Alaric avidly. This might be the last time she saw him and she wanted to imprint every detail. The way he smiled. The light in his eyes as he nodded at something his companion said. Familiar hunger swamped her. It was like watching a feast through a window and knowing though you were starving you couldn't reach out and eat.

Instead she tasted the ashes of hopeless dreams on her tongue.

At a word from Alaric, the crowd began to leave. They were too well bred to stare, but she felt their surreptitious glances. Heat gathered in her cheeks but she stood her ground. She wasn't into hiding any more.

Last to leave was the tall man who'd stood with Alaric. He too was in his early thirties. He wore his hand-tailored suit with an easy elegance that might have made her stare if she hadn't been so conscious of Alaric behind her.

'Dr Connors.' The stranger lifted her hand to his lips in a courtly gesture that would stop most feminine hearts. Over his shoulder she caught Alaric's sharp stare and fire sparked in her veins.

'It's a pleasure to meet you. I'm Alaric's kinsman, Raul.'

Tamsin blinked and focused on the man who she now saw bore a striking resemblance to Alaric. Jade green eyes instead of indigo and a leaner build, but the same angled cheekbones, strong jaw and lush dark hair. The same indefinable air of power and authority.

'Your Highness.'

He smiled, unfazed by the tension emanating from his cousin's rigid form. Tamsin could feel it from where she was but Prince Raul merely released her hand slowly. 'I'll look forward to our next meeting.'

Then he was gone. She was alone with Alaric.

CHAPTER FIFTEEN

'HELLO, Tamsin. It's good to see you.'

Alaric's voice was low and smooth, evoking memories of heady passion and soft endearments. In that moment her indignation bled away, replaced by longing and regret.

'Hello, Alaric.' Her voice was breathless, as if she'd run across the castle compound and up four flights of stairs instead of being escorted in a state of the art lift.

Silence fell as their eyes locked. Tamsin wanted to look away but couldn't, mesmerised by something in his gaze she'd never seen.

Despite the sling and a slight limp as he walked towards her, Alaric was a formidable figure: handsome, virile and powerful. Tamsin's nerves stretched taut as she fought not to respond to his nearness. Yet her stomach filled with butterflies and her knees trembled.

If only she couldn't remember so clearly the bliss she'd found in his arms.

But seeing him at the centre of that gathering, easily dominating the proceedings, had reinforced everything she'd told herself the last six weeks or so. That they belonged to different worlds.

'What was that, just now?' Jerkily she gestured to the desk where so many people had come forward to sign that large parchment. 'Some sort of ceremony?'

'Royal business,' he said, watching her so intently it seemed he noted every move, every expression. Was he wondering how he'd brought himself to make love to her?

Heat rushed into her cheeks. When he didn't explain further, Tamsin understood. His silence reinforced that she had no business enquiring into matters of state. The gulf between them was unbreachable.

He seemed taller, looming over her, making her feel vulnerable. His eyes were darker. They looked almost black. Try as she might she couldn't read his shuttered expression.

He stepped near and instantly her nerve ends tingled in awareness. Automatically she inched back a step, then, realising what she was doing, planted her feet.

'How are you, Alaric?'

'As you see.' His lips twisted ruefully. 'I survived.'

'Will you recover fully?' She gestured to his stiff leg.

'I'm told so.'

Her heart thudded in relief and she clasped her hands, unable to tear her gaze from those unfathomable eyes.

'It's my fault you were injured—'

'Don't even *think* of apologising!' The words shot out like bullets. He leaned towards her, his eyebrows lowering like storm clouds over flashing eyes.

'I'm the one who's sorry.' His mouth flattened. 'I tried earlier, at the lodge, but you wouldn't accept my apologies.'

Tamsin frowned. She couldn't remember that. But the scene was a blur of misery and grief.

He shifted as if it pained him to stand. 'I had no business seducing you. You are a guest in my country, an employee.'

Tamsin didn't know why her heart shrivelled at his reminder of their relative stations. It was true yet for a bright brief period it hadn't seemed to matter. That had been an illusion. Part of his seduction technique.

'I should never have—'

'Please!' She couldn't bear him to go on, enumerating everything that had happened between them. She'd relived every moment these past weeks and it brought no solace, just aching regret like a cold lump of lead in her chest.

'Don't go on. I accept your apology.' She turned to face the glowing fire in the ornate fireplace rather than meet his intense gaze. 'You believed you were protecting your country.'

It had taken her a long time but finally she'd seen a little of his perspective. A perspective reinforced by the scene she'd just witnessed. He had responsibilities for a nation that weighed heavily.

Tamsin understood his motives but that didn't excuse his tactics. She cringed at the thought of others listening to her conversation with Patrick. And as for Alaric letting her think he really cared, really desired her...

'You're very forgiving.'

She avoided his eyes. 'I've had time to consider.'

'But there's no excuse for—'

'No, but I don't want to discuss it.' Pain clawed at her. She didn't want to revisit the details. Like how he'd bedded her as part of his scheme. Or how she'd given her heart to him.

At least he didn't know that. How much more sorry for her he'd be if he knew she'd fallen in love.

Listening to his mellow baritone was delicious torture. Being here with him was what she'd dreamed of and yet it was dangerous.

She wanted what she could never have. She'd fallen for an illusion, believing in a relationship that could never be. Pain seeped from her cracked heart.

'You saved me the trouble of coming for you.'

At his words her head jerked round. Alaric had intended to come for her? For a foolish instant hope quivered in her heart, only to be dashed by harsh reality. No doubt he'd planned to deliver his apology and suggest she leave, rather than stay and embarrass them both.

'I've come for my passport.' The words came out full of strident challenge.

Did she imagine a stiffening of his tall frame?

'You want to leave?' He frowned.

'Yes!' How could he even ask it? 'But I need my passport and I'm told I need your permission to get it.'

'What if I asked you to stay?' His eyes probed, laser bright.

'No!' Her response was instantaneous. He couldn't be so cruel as to expect her to remain. Seeing him, always from a distance, would be unbearably painful.

A sound broke across her thoughts and she looked up. Alaric's mouth had twisted up at one side.

Surely he wasn't laughing at her?

Indignation and fury warred with hurt. A voice inside protested Alaric would never be so deliberately cruel. He wasn't callous like Patrick.

But she knew to her cost men *were* cruel.

She spun on her foot and marched to the door. She'd get a lawyer to retrieve her passport.

Tamsin was reaching for the door handle when something shot over her shoulder. A hand slammed onto the door, holding it shut. Alaric's arm stretched in front of her and her skin prickled at how close he stood. His heat was like a blaze at her back.

'No!' The single syllable cracked like a gunshot. 'You're not leaving. Not like this.'

Alaric's chest ached as he forced himself to drag in oxygen. His pulse thundered, pumping adrenaline through his body. The sight of Tamsin storming out of his life had been impossible to bear.

'I refuse to stay and be the butt of your humour.'

He stared at her glossy hair, her slim shoulders and lithe body and felt heat punch his belly. She thought he'd laughed at her?

'Tamsin, no. It's not like that.' It had been more a grimace of pain than anything else. Pain that slashed bone deep. 'If I was laughing it was at myself.'

'I don't understand.' She didn't move a muscle, but neither did she try to wrestle the door open.

'I told Raul I was going to ask you to stay. I was just remembering his response.'

'You talked to your cousin about me?'

She turned, looking up with wide amber-gilt eyes that melted his bones. He shuddered with the effort of controlling the emotions threatening to unravel inside.

'He thought I'd have no trouble persuading you. Then, as soon as I suggested it, you instantly objected.' Objected! *She'd turned ashen. As if she couldn't think of anything worse than being with him.*

Fear petrified him, as strong as in that soul-wrenching moment when he'd seen her in the path of the avalanche.

What if he couldn't persuade her? Had he hurt her so much he'd destroyed his last tentative hope?

He refused to countenance the thought.

'I don't understand.' She blinked and looked away, as if she couldn't bear to look at him. He didn't blame her.

His self-control splintered. He lifted his hand, stroking knuckles down her velvet cheek. His fingers hummed as a sensation like electricity sparked beneath his skin. She gulped and a tiny fragment of hope glowed in the darkness of his heart.

'I don't want you to leave. I won't allow it.' He cupped her chin and lifted her face till she had no option but to meet his gaze. The jolt of connection as their eyes clashed shook him to the core.

'You have no right to talk about allowing.' The belligerent set of her jaw spoke both of pain and strength. His heart twisted as he recognised one of the things that drew him to her was her indomitable spirit.

'No. I have no right.' The pain of these past weeks returned full force. 'But I'm too selfish to give up. *I'll make you stay.* Whether I have to persuade you or seduce you or imprison you in the highest tower.' Her lips parted in shock. The urge to kiss her soft mouth was almost more than he could bear.

'You're crazy.' She stepped away, only to back into the door. Alaric paced forward till a hair's breadth separated them. Tamsin drew a strained breath and the sensation of her breasts brushing against him made him groan. It had been so long since he'd held her. Too long since he'd kissed her.

'No!' She held him at bay.

She didn't want him after what he'd done.

'Tamsin, I…' He hesitated, groping for words to express unfamiliar feelings. Feelings he hadn't believed in before her.

'Let me go, Alaric.' She looked away, blinking. 'I don't know what new game this is but I've had enough.'

'Sh, darling, I know.' Gently he brushed a strand of hair off her face, his heart twisting as she flinched from his touch. But he couldn't resist tracing the line of her throat down to the pulse hammering at her collarbone.

'It's not a game. It's gone far beyond that. Once, in my complacency, I planned to seduce you.' Pain wrapped gnarled fingers around his heart as he read her anguish.

'I told myself it was for the benefit of the nation I kept you close, kept you with me, even kidnapped you.' He drew a breath that racked his body. 'But from the start I lied, not just to *you* but to myself. I plotted to get you into my bed *because I wanted you*. I needed you as I've never needed anyone. I couldn't stop thinking about you. Not your chronicle and your news about the throne, but you.'

He tunnelled his good hand through her hair, revelling in its silk caress and the warmth of her close to him. For the first time since the accident he felt *complete*.

'You don't know how I've missed you.' His voice was a hoarse groan and her eyes riveted to his. He was drowning in warm, amber depths.

'I fell for you, Tamsin. That's why I kidnapped you. The rest was an excuse.' She shook her head but he pressed on. 'At first you were a problem with your unwanted news. But you were a conundrum, too, a woman I couldn't get out of my head. You intrigued me. I've never met anyone like you.'

'Because I'm a misfit, is that it?' Her eyes shimmered, overbright.

'You? A misfit? The way you charmed ambassadors and aristocrats and commoners alike at the ball? The way you bonded with those teenagers at the community centre? I hear you've kept visiting and they love it. And your staff in the archives have nothing but admiration and liking for you.'

'You've been spying on me again?'

'No!' It had gone against the grain the first time. He'd never do that again. 'Their permanent employer wants them back and they petitioned my staff to remain. While you stay they want to.'

He watched her eyes widen. She genuinely had no idea how special she was with her talents, her intellect and above all her passion.

'I used every excuse I could think of to keep you with me, Tamsin. But the truth is I did it all because I wanted you.' Even though he didn't deserve her, he was too selfish to let her go.

'I still want you. I need you.' Saying it aloud for the first time Alaric was stunned by the force of his emotions. Emotions he'd never thought to experience. Emotions strong enough to obliterate a lifetime's cynicism.

She shook her head so vigorously her hair came down to swirl like a dark cloud around her. He wanted to bury his face in it, inhale her sweet scent and lose himself.

But her pain, like a razor wire fence between them, held him back.

'I'm a novelty. A change from your sophisticated women.' Bitterness laced her voice. 'You don't need me.'

'You *are* different.' He reached for her hand and planted it over his chest, pressing it to his pounding heart. 'For the first time in so long I *feel,* Tamsin. It scared the life out of me. That's why I kept telling myself it wasn't real.'

'No!' Her shout startled them both. 'Please, don't. This isn't real. You feel guilty, that's all.'

Alaric looked into Tamsin's taut features, searching for a softening, some proof she cared. But there was nothing, only pain. The tiny flame of hope flickered perilously and his chest hollowed.

Had he lost his one chance of happiness?

'I love you.' He swallowed and it was like every broken dream scored his throat. He'd never thought it possible to feel so much and it scared him as nothing ever had.

'I realised that as I lay in hospital and replayed every mistake I'd made. That's why I signed myself out early, to come and tell you. *I love you.*'

She stood like a statue, her brow furrowed and her mouth a tight line.

He'd never felt like this, never told any other woman he loved her.

He'd expected a better response!

Alaric was tempted to kiss her into compliance. He could win her body. Yet he wanted her mind too. Her heart.

'You don't believe me?'

'I…don't know. It seems so unlikely.' She looked so dazed his heart squeezed in sympathy. Or was that fear?

'Then believe this. That scene you walked in on? I wanted it over before I came to you today.' His lips twisted, thinking how Tamsin always managed to turn his plans on their head. 'The reason for all the witnesses was because I wanted there to be no question about my actions.' He drew a slow breath and squeezed her hand. 'I just signed away my claim to the throne of Maritz. Raul will be king after all.'

'You did *what*? Oh, Alaric! You'd make a wonderful king. You mightn't be able to see it but I can. And I'm not the only one. The—'

He silenced her with a finger on her lips, telling himself soon he'd feel their soft caress with his mouth.

'It's all right, Tamsin. I didn't do it because I feared to take the throne.' That was well and truly behind him, though it warmed him to have her as such a passionate advocate. Hope flared again and excitement sizzled in his bloodstream.

'I discovered the king is obligated to marry a princess from Ardissia. I'd have to take on the throne and a ready-made wife. When it came to the crunch I couldn't do it. I'd accept the king-ship and all its responsibilities but I can't marry another woman. Not when I love you.'

'*You did that for me?* You hardly know me!'

'I know you, Tamsin. I know the real you.'

He'd never known a lovelier woman.

He looked down into her stunned face. Her hair was loose around her shoulders. Her intelligent eyes were bright, her skin glowed and the delicate curve of her cheek made him want to stroke her till she purred. She wore a fitted russet suit he'd never seen before. It skimmed her curves in a way that made his hormones rev into high gear.

'You've bought new clothes.' He frowned. He wasn't sure he wanted her looking good for anyone but him.

'You really abdicated?' She cut across him, staring as if she'd never seen him before. 'But that's...'

Her lips curved in a tremulous smile that snared his heart all over again and sent heat scudding through every tense muscle. 'I can't believe you gave up a crown for me.'

'In the end it wasn't the crown I objected to.' He hauled her close with one arm, his pulse racing. 'It was the bride. I prefer to choose my own.'

Cool palms slid around his neck as she pressed close, her eyes a blaze of molten gold. It was like staring into the sun. Surely she couldn't look at him like that and not...

He took his courage in his hands.

'Tamsin, could you forget the past and start again?'

For what seemed an age she stood silent. He held his breath.

'I don't want to forget,' she murmured. 'You've given me so much.' Her smile warmed every corner of his soul and his pulse tripped into overdrive.

'Tamsin.' His voice was so husky he had to clear his throat. 'Could you live with a man who's made mistakes? Who still has to learn to how to settle down? A man with a scandalous reputation?' He lifted her palm to his lips. 'A man who has occasional nightmares about the past?'

'I could.' She looked so solemn, as if making a vow. 'If you're *sure*?'

The doubt in her eyes made him vow to prove to her, daily, how much she meant to him. 'Never more so, my love.'

'A scandalous reputation sounds intriguing.' Her expression grew tender. 'And as for nightmares...they'll pass with time and help.'

She leaned up on tiptoe, her mouth brushing his in the lightest of kisses.

'I love you, Alaric. I fell for you the night we met. I still can't believe—'

He slanted his mouth over hers, relief and triumph and love overwhelming him.

She was his! He'd silence the last of her doubts. He'd devote his life to making her happy.

Much later, when the flare of passion threatened to roar out of control, Alaric stepped away.

'What are you doing? Alaric! Your leg!'

Ignoring the pain he finally managed to settle on his good knee. He held her hand tight in his, their fingers threaded together.

'I'm proposing. I want to do this right.'

'Oh.'

She looked stunned. He'd finally found a way to silence her. But she confounded him by dropping to the floor in front of him.

'Yes,' she said, her voice breathless.

'I haven't asked you yet.' He couldn't prevent the grin that split his face. Joy welled in an unstoppable flood.

'I'm saving time. You have to get off that knee.'

'In that case…' He pulled her off balance as he toppled back onto the thick carpet. She sprawled over him and his unruly body stirred.

'Alaric!' Tamsin gasped as he pulled her down hard over his groin. 'We can't. We shouldn't. You're just out of hospital!'

'We can. We will.' He kissed her soft lips and sighed his pleasure. 'You can spend your life reforming me.'

'Never. I love you just the way you are.'

She kissed him and Alaric silently gave thanks. In Tamsin he'd found the one perfect woman to make his life complete. He'd found love.

EPILOGUE

THE Gothic cathedral glowed as afternoon sunlight poured through the stained-glass windows. The scent of candles mingled with expensive perfumes and the fragrance of fresh flowers that were massed everywhere.

It was like a dream, walking down the aisle, the focus of every look. The place was crowded. Aristocracy from all around Europe, diplomats and community leaders, plus members of the public who'd been lucky enough to win a ballot to attend. But among them Tamsin spotted familiar faces: her colleagues, friends from the youth centre, Alaric's old comrades, smiling as they nodded encouragingly. Even her parents, looking proud and slightly bewildered.

But she'd barely been able to tear her gaze from the man who watched her every step with an intensity that sent heat and excitement spiralling through her.

Alaric. Tall, proud and handsome in his uniform.

His cousin Raul had stood beside him, stunningly good looking with his killer smile and black as night hair. Yet Tamsin had barely spared him a glance, her whole being focused on the man she was to marry.

Seeing the love in Alaric's eyes had made it all real as nothing else had. The luxuriously embroidered crimson velvet gown and its long train had felt unfamiliar and daunting as it trailed impressively behind her. The weight of the delicate beaten gold diadem had made her nervous, as had the filigree collar of gold and rubies circling her throat.

When she'd entered the cathedral to the triumphant blare of trumpets and swelling organ music she'd felt like an impostor, a little girl pretending to be a princess.

But from the moment Alaric's gaze had locked with hers joy had sung in her heart and the world had righted itself.

This was so right she almost cried with happiness.

Now, with the ceremony over, they faced the congregation. Alaric stood behind her and in defiance of all protocol wrapped his arms around her, pulling her close.

'Tamsin?' Pleasure skated through her at the intimate purr of his voice saying her name.

'Yes?' She struggled to focus on the smiling throng and not Alaric's hot breath feathering her neck.

'No regrets?'

'Never!' She twisted round in his arms to see his indigo eyes dark with love. Neither heard the jubilant roar of the crowd as she kissed him full on the mouth and he responded emphatically.

Afterwards everyone present attested Prince Alaric and his bride had broken tradition and married for love.

THE INCORRIGIBLE PLAYBOY

EMMA DARCY

CHAPTER ONE

THIRTY.

The big three zero.

If ever there was a birthday to inspire the determination to make a change in her life, this was it.

Elizabeth Flippence assessed her reflection in the mirror with a mixture of hope and anxiety. She'd had her long brown hair cut to just below her ears and layered so that it fluffed out around her face in wild waves with bangs across her forehead. It was a much more modern look and softer, more feminine, but she wasn't sure she should have let the hairdresser talk her into the vibrant auburn colour.

It was certainly striking. Which was probably what she needed for Michael Finn to really notice her today— notice her as a woman instead of taking her for granted as his superefficient personal assistant. She desperately wanted their relationship to shift from its consistently platonic level. Two years was long enough to pine for a man who seemed fixated on not mixing business with pleasure.

Which was ridiculous. They were so well suited to each other. Surely Michael knew that in his heart. It couldn't be more obvious. Her frustration over this stand-off situation had been simmering for months, and Elizabeth had decided that today was the day she was going to try smashing down his guard. This make-over should at least capture his attention.

And the hairdresser was right about the auburn tones making her dark brown eyes look brighter. The new hairstyle also seemed to put her rather long nose in better proportion with the rest of her face. It highlighted her slanted cheekbones in a strangely exotic way and even her slightly wide full-lipped mouth looked more right somehow.

Anyway, it was done now and she fiercely hoped it would promote the desired result. When Michael commented on her changed appearance, she would tell him it was her birthday present to herself and maybe…please, please, please…he would suggest celebrating the occasion by taking her out to lunch, or better still, dinner.

She didn't want to be his Girl Friday anymore. She wanted to be his every day and every night girl. If that didn't start happening… Elizabeth took a long deep breath as she faced the unavoidable truth. Thirty really was the deadline for a woman to give serious consideration to finding a life partner if she wanted to have a family of her own. Michael Finn was her choice but if he didn't respond to her differently today, she'd probably be wasting her time to hope for any change from him in the near future. Which meant she would have to move on, try to meet someone else.

She quickly banished the downer thought. It was imperative to be positive today. Smile and the whole world smiled back at you, she told herself. It was one of Lucy's principles and it certainly worked for her sister, who invariably carved a blithe path through life, using her smile to get her out of trouble. A lot was forgiven with Lucy's smile.

Elizabeth practised her own as she left the bathroom. She was just slipping her mobile phone into her handbag, ready to leave for work when it played her signature call tune. Quickly flipping it open she lifted it to her ear, anticipating the caller would be Lucy, who had spent the weekend with friends at Port Douglas. Her sister's voice instantly bubbled forth.

'Hi, Ellie! Happy birthday! I hope you're wearing the clothes I bought for you.'

'Thanks, Lucy, and yes, I am.'

'Good! Every woman should look bold and beautiful on their thirtieth birthday.'

Elizabeth laughed. The beautiful butterfly blouse, basically in glorious shades of blue and green but with the wings outlined in brown and enclosing a vivid pattern in red and sea-green and yellow and lime, was definitely eye-catching, especially teamed with the sea-green pencil skirt. The outfit was a far cry from her usual style in clothes, but under Lucy's vehement persuasion, she had let herself be seduced by the gorgeous colours.

'I've had my hair cut, too. And dyed auburn.'

'Wow! Can't wait to see that! I'll be back in Cairns later this morning. I'll drop in at your office for a peek. Got to go now.'

The connection clicked off before Elizabeth could say, 'No, don't!'

It was probably silly but she felt uncomfortable about Lucy visiting her at work and had always deterred her from doing it. Because of Michael. As much as she loved her ditzy younger sister, there was no escaping the fact that men seemed irresistibly drawn to her. Her relationships never lasted long. Nothing with Lucy lasted long. There was always another man, another job, another place to go.

For several moments Elizabeth dithered over calling her sister back, not wanting this day to be spoiled by a possible distraction from herself. Yet, didn't she need to test Michael's feelings for her? He should value her worth above Lucy's honeybee attraction. Besides, he might not even see her sister drop in. The door between her office and his was usually closed.

She didn't feel right about putting Lucy off this morning. It was her birthday and her sister was happy and excited about seeing her. They only had each other. Their mother had died of cancer when they were still in their teens, and their father, who had since settled in Mt Isa with another woman, wouldn't even remember her birthday. He never had.

In any event, Michael would have to meet Lucy sooner or later if the closer involvement Elizabeth was aiming for came to pass. Accepting this inevitability, she picked up her handbag, slid the mobile phone into its compartment and headed off to work.

The month of August was a pleasant one in Far North Queensland, not too hot to walk the five blocks from the apartment she and Lucy shared to The Esplanade, where the head office of Finn's Fisheries was located. Usually she drove her little car, leaving it in the space allocated for her in the underground car park of her boss's building, but she didn't want to be tied to driving it home today. Much better to be free to do anything.

The thought brought another smile to her face as she strolled along. Michael really was the perfect man for her. Finn's Fisheries was a huge franchise with outlets all around Australia. They not only stocked every possible piece of fishing gear—a lot of it imported—but the kind of clothing that went with it: wetsuits, swimming costumes, shorts, T-shirts, hats. The range of merchandise was fantastic and Michael dealt with all of it. She loved how he never missed a beat, always on top of everything. It was how she liked to be herself. Together they made a great team. He often said so himself.

If he would just see they should take the next step, Elizabeth was sure they could team up for life and make it a very happy one, sharing everything. He was thirty-five. It was time for both of them to start building a far more personal partnership. She couldn't believe Michael wanted to remain a bachelor forever.

In the two years she'd known him his relationships with other women had never lasted long, but Elizabeth reasoned it was because he was a workaholic. It would be different with her. She understood him.

Despite all this positive thinking, her heart fluttered nervously as she entered her office. The door to Michael's was open, which meant he was already in, organising the business of the day. It was Monday, the beginning of a new week. The beginning of something new between them, too, Elizabeth fiercely hoped as she took a deep breath to calm herself and walked purposefully to the opened door.

He was seated at his desk, pen in hand, ticking off

items on a sheet of paper, his concentration so total he didn't sense her presence. For a few moments Elizabeth simply gazed at him, loving the clean-cut perfection of the man; the thick black hair kept short so it was never untidy, the straight black eyebrows that gave slashing emphasis to the keen intelligence of his silver-grey eyes. The straight nose, firm mouth and squarish jaw all combined to complete the look of the alpha male he was.

As always he wore a top quality white shirt that showed off his flawless olive skin and undoubtedly he would be wearing classy black trousers—his customary work uniform. His black shoes would be shiny and... he was just perfect.

Elizabeth swallowed hard to clear her throat and willed him to give her the kind of attention she craved.

'Good morning, Michael.'

'Good morn—' His gaze lifted, his eyes widening in shock. His mouth was left slightly agape, his voice momentarily choked by the unexpected sight of an Elizabeth who was not the same as usual.

She held her breath. This was the moment when the only-business attitude towards her had to snap. A host of butterflies invaded her stomach. *Smile*, her mind wildly dictated. *Show him the warmth in your heart, the desire heating up your blood.*

She smiled and suddenly he grinned, the silver eyes sparkling with very male appreciation.

'Wow!' he breathed, and her skin tingled with pleasure.

'Great hair! Fabulous outfit, too!' he enthused. 'You've done wonders with yourself, Elizabeth. Does this mean there's some new guy in your life?'

The high that had soared from his first words came crashing down. Associating her makeover with another man meant the distance he kept between them was not about to be crossed. Although…maybe he was tempted. Maybe he was just checking if the coast was clear for him to step in.

She rallied, quickly saying, 'No. I've been unattached for a while. I just felt like a change.'

'Super change!' he warmly approved.

That was better. Warmth was good. Elizabeth instantly delivered the planned hint for him to make his move.

'I'm glad you like it. The clothes are a gift from my sister. It's my birthday. She insisted I had to look bold and beautiful today.'

He laughed. 'Well, you certainly do. And we should celebrate your birthday, too. How about lunch at The Mariners Bar? We can make time for it if we get through this inventory this morning.'

Hope soared again. A lunch for two at one of the most expensive restaurants in Cairns, overlooking the marina full of million-dollar yachts…her heart sang with joy. 'That would be lovely. Thank you, Michael.'

'Book us a table. One o'clock should see us clear.' He picked up a sheaf of papers, holding it out to her. 'In the meantime, if you could check this lot…'

'Of course.'

Business as usual, but there was a rainbow at the end of it today. Elizabeth could barely stop her feet from dancing over to his desk to collect the work that had to be done first.

'Bold and beautiful,' Michael repeated, grinning at

her as he handed over the papers. 'Your sister must have a lot of pizzazz.'

It killed the song in her heart. He was supposed to be showing more interest in her, not wondering about Lucy. She shouldn't have mentioned her sister. But there was no taking it back, so she had to live with it.

'Yes, she has, but she's terribly ditzy with it. Nothing seems to stay in her head long enough to put any order into her life.' It was the truth and she wanted Michael to know it. The thought of Lucy being attractive to him in any way was unbearable.

'Not like you,' he said appreciatively.

She shrugged. 'Chalk and cheese. A bit like you and your brother.'

The words tripped off her tongue before Elizabeth could catch them back. The anxiety about Lucy had caused her control to slip. It wasn't appropriate for her to make any comment about her boss's brother. Normally she would keep her mouth firmly shut about him, despite the heartburn Harry Finn invariably gave her with his playboy patter. She hated it when he came into the office. Absolutely hated it.

Michael leaned back in his chair, his mouth tilted in a musing little smile. 'Working behind a desk is definitely not Harry's thing, but I think you might have the wrong impression of him, Elizabeth.'

'I'm sorry.' She grimaced an apology. 'I didn't mean to...to...'

Now she was lost for words!

'It's okay.' Michael waved off her angst. 'I know he seems very casual about everything but his mind is as sharp as a razor blade and he has his thumb on everything to do with his side of the business.'

Charter boats for deep-sea fishing, dive-boats for tourists wanting to explore the Great Barrier Reef, overseeing the resort they'd built on one of the islands— it was playboy stuff compared to what Michael did. Elizabeth's opinion of Harry Finn didn't shift one iota.

'I'll try to see him in that light in the future,' she clipped out.

Michael laughed. Elizabeth's toes curled. He was so charismatically handsome when he laughed. 'I guess he's been ruffling your feathers with his flirting. Don't let it get to you. He's like that with every woman. It's just a bit of fun.'

Oh, sure! Great *fun*! For Harry Finn.

Elizabeth hated it.

However, she managed to paste a smile on her face. 'I'll keep that in mind,' she said. 'Must get to work now. And I'll book our table at The Mariners Bar.'

'Do that.' Another grin. 'We can discuss brothers and sisters over lunch.'

No way, Elizabeth thought as she walked briskly to her own office, firmly closing the door behind her to ensure that Michael didn't see Lucy when she dropped in. She didn't want her sister sparking any interest in his mind. Nor did she want Harry Finn intruding on any part of this special lunch date. This precious time together had to be about moving closer to each other on a really personal plane. All her hopes for a future with Michael Finn were pinned on it.

CHAPTER TWO

TEN thirty-seven.

Elizabeth frowned at the clock on her desk. The arrangement with the coffee shop on the ground floor was for coffee and muffins to be delivered at ten-thirty—black expresso and a chocolate muffin for Michael, cappuccino and a strawberry and white chocolate muffin for her. She skipped breakfast to have this treat and her empty stomach was rumbling for it. It was unusual for the delivery to be late. Michael hated unpunctuality and the shop tenants were well aware of his requirements.

A knock on her door had her scuttling out of her chair to open it, facilitating entry as fast as possible. 'You're late,' she said chidingly, before realising the tray of coffee and muffins was being carried by Harry Finn.

Vivid blue eyes twinkled at her. 'Short delay while they made coffee for me, too,' he said unapologetically.

'Fine! You can explain that to Michael,' she bit out, forcing her gritted teeth open to get the words out.

'Oh, I will, dear Elizabeth. Never would I leave a blemish on your sterling record of getting everything right for him,' he rolled out in the provocative tone that made her want to hit him. She was not given to violence but Harry Finn invariably stirred something explosive in her.

'And may I say you look stunning this morning. Absolutely stunning!' he rattled on as he stepped into her office, eyeing her up and down, his gaze pausing where the butterfly wings on her blouse framed her breasts, making her nipples stiffen into bullets. She wished they could be fired at him. His white T-shirt with tropical fish emblazoned on it wouldn't look so sexy on him if there were black holes through it to his all-too-manly chest.

'The hair is spectacular, not to mention—'

'I'd rather you didn't mention,' she cut him off, closing the door and waving him towards Michael's office. 'Your brother is waiting.'

He grinned his devil-may-care grin. 'Won't kill him to wait a bit longer.'

She crossed her arms in exasperated impatience with him as he strolled over to set the tray down on her desk, then hitched himself onto the edge of it, ignoring any reason for haste. The white shorts he wore emphasised his long, tanned, muscular legs. One of them he dangled at her, teasing her need for proper behaviour.

'A moth turning into a butterfly doesn't happen every day,' he happily remarked. 'I want to enjoy the glory of it.'

Elizabeth rolled her eyes. She was not going to stand for this. A moth! She had never been a moth! She had simply chosen to be on the conservative side with her appearance to exemplify a serious career person, not someone who could ever be considered flighty like her sister.

'The coffee will be getting cold,' she stated in her chilliest voice.

'Love the sea-green skirt,' he raved on. 'Matches the colour of the water near the reef. Fits you very neatly, too. Like a second skin. In fact, it's inspiring a fantasy of you as a mermaid.' He grinned. Evilly. 'I bet you'd swish your tail at me.'

'Only in dismissal,' she shot at him, pushing her feet to walk to the desk and deal with the coffee herself since Harry was not inclined to oblige. It meant she had to go close to him, which she usually avoided because the man was so overwhelmingly male, in-your-face male, that her female hormones seemed to get in a tizzy around him. It was extremely irritating.

He wasn't as classically handsome as Michael. He was more raffishly handsome—his longish black curly hair flopping around his face, crow's-feet at the corners of his eyes from being out in the weather, a slightly crooked nose from having it broken at some point in his probably misspent youth, and a mouth that was all-too-frequently quirked with amusement. At her. As it was now.

'Have you ever wondered why you're so uptight with me, Elizabeth?' he tossed out.

'No. I don't give you that much space in my mind,' she answered, deliberately ignoring him as she removed her coffee and muffin from the tray.

'Ouch!' he said as though she'd hurt him, then laughed to show she hadn't. 'If I ever get too big for my boots, I know where to come to be whipped back into shape.'

She gave him a quelling look. 'You've come to see Michael. Just follow me into his office.'

The devil danced in his eyes. 'Only if you swish your tail at me.'

She glared back. 'Stop playing with me. I'm not going there with you. Not ever,' she added emphatically.

He was totally unabashed. 'All work, no play—got to say you're safe with Mickey on that score.'

Safe? The word niggled at Elizabeth's mind as she carried the tray to Michael's door. Why was Harry so sure she was safe with his brother? She didn't want to be safe. She wanted to be desired so much, there would be no distance left between them.

Harry bounded past her, opened the door and commanded his brother's attention. 'Hi, Mickey! I held up the coffee train to have one made for myself. Have a few things to discuss with you. Here's Elizabeth with it now.'

'No problem,' Michael answered, smiling at her as she sailed in with the tray.

She hugged the smile to her heart. Michael was the man of true gold. Harry was all glitter. And she hated him calling his brother Mickey. It was rotten, schoolboy stuff—Mickey Finn—linking him to a spiked drink, and totally inappropriate for the position he now held. No dignity in it at all. No respect.

'Thanks, Elizabeth,' Michael said warmly as she unloaded the tray, setting out the two coffees and muffin on his desk. 'Table booked?'

'Yes.'

'What table?' Harry asked, instantly putting her on edge again.

'It's Elizabeth's birthday. I'm taking her out to lunch.'

'A...ha!'

Her spine crawled at the wealth of significance she heard in Harry's voice. If he was about to make fun of the situation... She picked up the emptied tray and swung around to shoot him a killing look.

He lifted his hand in a salute, pretending to plead for a truce between them but his eyes glittered with mocking amusement. 'Happy birthday, dear Elizabeth.'

'Thank you,' she grated out, and swiftly left the two men together for their discussions, closing the door to give them absolute privacy and herself protection from *that man*.

It was difficult to concentrate on work. She tried, but the clock kept ticking on—eleven o'clock, eleven-thirty, twelve. Lucy hadn't dropped in and Harry was still with Michael. Anything could have happened with Lucy. It frequently did. She might not make it into the office at all, which would be a relief, no chance of a meeting with Michael. Harry was the main problem. She wouldn't put it past him to invite himself to her birthday lunch. If he did, would Michael put him off?

He had to.

No way could a romantic mood develop between them if Harry was present. He would spoil everything.

A knock on her door cut off her inner angst. Elizabeth looked up to see the door opening and Lucy's head poking around it.

'Okay to come in?'

Her stomach cramped with nervous tension at the late visit but it was impossible to say anything but 'Yes.'

Lucy bounced in, exuding effervescence as she always did. Today she was dressed in a white broderie anglaise outfit: a little frilly skirt that barely reached midthigh, an off-the-shoulder peasant blouse, a wide tan belt slung around her hips, lots of wooden beads dangling from her neck, wooden bangles travelling up one forearm and tan sandals that were strapped up to mid-calf. Her long blond hair was piled up on top of her head with loose strands escaping everywhere. She looked like a trendy model who could put anything together and look good.

'Ooh...I *love* the hair, Ellie,' she cooed, hitching herself onto the edge of Elizabeth's desk, just as Harry had, which instantly provoked the thought they would make a good pair.

'It's very sexy,' Lucy raved on. 'Gives you that just-out-of-bed tumbled look and the colour really, really suits you. It complements the clothes I picked out for you brilliantly. I have to say you look absolutely marvellous.' Her lovely sherry-brown eyes twinkled with delight. 'Now tell me you *feel* marvellous, too.'

Lucy's smile was so infectious, she had to smile back. 'I'm glad I made the change. How was your weekend?'

'Oh, so-so.' She waved her hand airily then pulled a woeful grimace. 'But I've had the most terrible morning.'

Out of the corner of her eye Elizabeth caught the opening of the door to Michael's office. Tension whipped along her nerves. Was it Harry coming out or both men?

Lucy rattled out her list of woes, her hands making a host of dramatic gestures. 'A body was buried in the wrong plot and I had to deal with that. Then a call came in that someone was interfering with a grave. I had to go out to the cemetery and investigate, but that wasn't too bad. It was only a bereaved husband digging a hole on top of the grave to put in potting soil so he could plant his wife's favourite rose. Nice, really. The worst thing was a dog running amok in the memorial garden and knocking off some of the angels' heads. I had to collect them, load them into the van, and now I have to find someone who can stick them back on again. You wouldn't believe how heavy those angels' heads are.'

'Angels' heads…' It was Michael's voice, sounding totally stunned.

It jerked Lucy's attention to him. 'Oh, wow!' she said, looking Michael up and down, totally uninhibited about showing how impressed she was with him.

Elizabeth closed her eyes and sucked in a deep breath.

'Are you Ellie's boss?' The question popped out with barely a pause.

Elizabeth opened her eyes again to see Michael shaking his head as though bringing himself out of a daze, and Harry behind his shoulder, looking straight at her with a sharp intensity in his bedroom blue eyes she had never seen before. It gave her the weird feeling he was tunnelling into her mind. She quickly dropped her gaze.

'Yes. Yes, I am,' Michael finally answered. 'And you are?'

'Lucy Flippence. Ellie's sister. I work in cemetery administration so I often have to deal with angels.'

'I see,' he said, looking at Lucy as though she was a heavenly apparition.

She hopped off her perch on the desk and crossed the

floor to him with her hand extended. 'Pleased to meet you. Okay if I call you Michael?'

'Delighted,' he said, taking her hand and holding on to it as he slowly turned to make the last introduction. 'This is my brother, Harry.'

Elizabeth fiercely willed Lucy to find Harry more attractive. No such luck! Her hand was left in Michael's snug grasp. She raised her other in blithe greeting. 'Hi, Harry!' It was tossed at him in a kind of bubbly dismissal, which meant in Lucy's mind he didn't really count.

'Charmed,' Harry purred at her.

It floated right over her head, no impact at all.

Elizabeth's heart sank like a stone.

Lucy was intent on engaging Michael and he was obviously enthralled with her.

'I don't know if you know but it's Ellie's birthday today and I thought I'd treat her to a really nice lunch somewhere. You won't mind if I take her off and she's a bit late back, will you, Michael?' she said appealingly.

There was a terrible inevitability about what happened next.

'Actually, I'd decided to do the same myself. Lunch at The Mariners Bar.'

'Oh, wow! The Mariners Bar! What a lovely boss you are to take Ellie there!'

'Why don't you join us? It will be a better celebration of her birthday if you do.'

'I'll come, as well. Make a party of it,' Harry put in, instantly supporting the idea.

'I only booked a table for two,' Elizabeth couldn't help saying, even though knowing it was a futile attempt to change what wouldn't be changed now. Her secret dream was already down the drain.

'No problem. I'm sure the maître d' will make room for us,' Michael said, oozing confidence as he smiled at Lucy. 'We'd be delighted to have the pleasure of your company.'

'Well, a foursome should be more fun, don't you think, Ellie?'

The appealing glance over her shoulder forced Elizabeth to smile and say, 'Certainly no awkward silences with you, Lucy.'

She laughed. 'That's settled, then. Thank you for asking me, Michael. And it's good of you to join in the party, too, Harry.'

The death knell to a happy birthday, Elizabeth thought. Not only would she have to watch Michael being fascinated by her sister, she'd also have to put up with Harry getting under her skin all the time. She slid him a vexed look. His mouth quirked at her, seemingly with more irony than amusement, but that probably didn't mean anything. No doubt he was anticipating having heaps of *fun* at her expense.

This lunch was going to be the lunch from hell.

Elizabeth didn't know how she was going to get through it without throwing in the towel, having hysterics and drowning herself in the marina.

CHAPTER THREE

ELIZABETH knew she'd be paired with Harry for the stroll along the boardwalk to the marina, and she was. There was no point in trying to fight for Michael's company. His preference for Lucy to be at his side had been made so clear, pride dictated that the arrangement be accepted with as much dignified grace as she could muster.

The two of them walked ahead and it was sickening watching the connection between them flourishing. Lucy, of course, was never short of a word, and Michael was lapping up every one of them, enjoying her bubbly personality. It wouldn't last, Elizabeth told herself, but that was no consolation. The damage was done. Lucy had achieved in one minute flat what she had been unable to draw from Michael in two years. Even if he turned to her later on, she would never be able to forget that.

The boardwalk ran along the water's edge of the park adjoining The Esplanade, and she tried to distract herself with the people they passed; couples lounging under the shade of trees, children making use of the play areas set up for them, boys scaling the rock-climb. It was a relief that Harry was leaving her to her silence for a while. It was difficult to cope with him at the best of times, and this was the worst.

She could have chosen to tell Lucy about her secret passion for her boss. That would have warned her off although she wouldn't have understood it. It simply wasn't in Lucy to pine for a man who didn't respond to her as she wanted him to respond. She probably would have looked aghast and said, 'Throw him away, Ellie. He's not that into you if you've waited this long for him to make a move.'

That truth was staring her in the face right now.

And it hurt.

It hurt so badly, she had to keep blinking back the tears that threatened to well into her eyes. Her chest was so tight she could hardly breathe. She'd been a fool to hope, a fool to think today might be the day. It was never going to happen for her.

'Ellie…'

It was a jolt to her wounded heart, hearing Harry speak her childhood name in a low, caressing tone.

'I like it,' he went on. 'Much better than Elizabeth. It conjures up a more carefree person, softer, more accessible.'

Her spine stiffened. He was doing it again, digging at her. She shot him a hard, mocking look. 'Don't get carried away by it. Lucy simply couldn't say Elizabeth when she was little. She calls me Ellie out of habit.'

'And affection, I think.' There was a look of kindness in his eyes that screwed up her stomach as he added, 'She doesn't know she's hurting you, does she?'

Her mind jammed in disbelief over Harry's insightful comment. 'What do you mean?'

He grimaced at her prevarication. 'Give it up, Ellie. You're not Mickey's type. I could have told you so but you wouldn't have believed me.'

Humiliation burned through her. Her cheeks flamed with it. She tore her gaze from the certain knowledge in Harry Finn's and stared at his brother's back—the back Michael had turned on her to be with her sister. How had Harry known what she'd yearned for? Had Michael known, too? She couldn't bear this. She would have to resign from her job, find another.

'Don't worry,' Harry said soothingly. 'You can keep on working for him if you want to. Mickey doesn't have a clue. He's always had tunnel vision—sets his mind on something and nothing else exists.'

Relief reduced some of the heat. Nevertheless, it was still intensely disturbing that Harry was somehow reading her mind. Or was he guessing, picking up clues from her reactions? She hadn't admitted anything. He couldn't really *know*, could he?

'On the other hand, it would be much better if you did resign,' he went on. 'It's never good to keep being reminded of failure. And no need to go job-hunting. You can come and work for me.'

Work for him? Never in a million years! It spurred her into tackling him head-on, her eyes blazing with the fire of battle. 'Let me tell you, Harry Finn, I have never failed at any work Michael has given me and working for you has no appeal whatsoever.'

He grinned at her. 'Think of the pleasure of saying what you think of me at every turn instead of having to keep yourself bottled up around Mickey.'

'I am not bottled up,' she declared vehemently.

He sighed. 'Why not be honest instead of playing the pretend-game? Your fantasy of having Mickey fall at your feet is never going to come true. Face it. Give it up. Look at me as the best tonic for lovesickness you could have. Balls of fire come out of you the moment I'm around.'

'That's because you're so annoying!'

Her voice had risen to a passionate outburst, loud enough to attract Michael's and Lucy's attention, breaking their absorption in each other. They paused in their walk, turning around with eyebrows raised.

'It's okay,' Elizabeth quickly assured them. 'Harry was just being Harry.'

'Be nice to Elizabeth, Harry,' Michael chided. 'It's her birthday.'

'I *am* being nice,' he protested.

'Try harder,' Michael advised, dismissing the distraction to continue his tête-à-tête with Lucy.

'Right!' Harry muttered. 'We need some control here, Ellie, if you want to pretend there's nothing wrong in your world.'

'The only thing wrong in my world is you,' she muttered back fiercely. 'And don't call me Ellie.'

'Elizabeth reigns,' he said in mock resignation.

She bit her lips, determined not to rise to any more of his baits.

They walked on for a while before he started again.

'This won't do,' he said decisively. 'We'll be at the restaurant soon. If you sit there in glum silence, I'll get the blame for it and that's not fair. It's not my fault that Mickey's attracted to your sister. Your best move is to start flirting with me. Who knows? He might suddenly get jealous.'

This suggestion stirred a flicker of hope. Maybe...

The shared laughter from the couple in front of them dashed the hope before it could take wing. Nevertheless, Harry did have a valid point. If she didn't pretend to be having a good time, even Michael and Lucy would realise this birthday treat was no treat at all for her. She had to *look* happy even though she couldn't *be* happy.

She sighed and slid him a weighing look. 'You know it won't mean anything if I flirt with you.'

'Not a thing!' he readily agreed.

'It's just for the sake of making a cheerful party.'

'Of course.'

'It's obvious that you're a dyed-in-the-wool playboy, and normally I wouldn't have anything to do with you, Harry, but since I'm stuck with you on this occasion, I'll play along for once.'

'Good thinking! Though I take exception to the play-boy tag. I do know how to play, which I consider an important part of living—something I suspect you do too little of—but that's not all I am.'

'Whatever...' She shrugged off any argument about his personality. Arguing would only get her all heated again and she needed to be calm, in control of herself. Harry was right about that.

They'd walked past the yacht club and were on the path to the cocktail bar adjoining the restaurant when Harry made his next move.

'Hey, Mickey!' he called out. 'I'll buy the girls cock-tails while you see the maître d' about our table.'

'Okay' was tossed back at him, his attention reverting to Lucy with barely a pause.

'No doubt about it, he's besotted,' Harry dryly commented. 'How old are you today, Elizabeth?'

'Thirty,' she answered on a defeated sigh. No point in hiding it.

'Ah! The big three zero. Time to make a change.'

Precisely what she had thought. And still had to think now that Michael had proved his disinterest in her personally.

'Go with me on this,' Harry urged.

'Go with you on what?'

'Something I was discussing with Mickey this morning. I'll bring it up again after lunch. Just don't dismiss it out of hand. It would be the perfect change for you.'

'You couldn't possibly know what's perfect for me, Harry,' she said sceptically.

He cocked a teasing eyebrow. 'I might just be a better judge on that than you think I am.'

She shook her head, her eyes mocking this particular belief in himself.

He grinned. 'Wait and see.'

She wasn't about to push him on it. Harry enjoyed being tantalising. Elizabeth had found her best course was simply to show complete disinterest. In this case, she couldn't care less what he had in mind. All she cared about was getting through lunch without showing how miserable she was.

Michael left them at the cocktail bar, striding swiftly into the restaurant to speak to the maître d', obviously in a hurry to get back to Lucy. Harry led them to a set of two-seater lounges with a low table in between and saw them settled with her and Lucy facing each other.

'Now, let me select cocktails for you both,' he said, the vivid blue eyes twinkling confidence in his choices. 'A Margarita for you, Elizabeth.'

It surprised her that he'd actually picked her favourite. 'Why that one?' she asked, curious about his correct guessing.

He grinned. 'Because you're the salt of the earth and I revere you for it.'

She rolled her eyes. The day Harry Finn showed any reverence for her was yet to dawn. He was just making a link to the salt-encrusted rim of the glass that was always used for a Margarita cocktail.

'You're right on both counts,' Lucy happily volunteered. 'Ellie loves Margaritas and she *is* the salt of the earth. I don't know what I'd do without her. She's always been my anchor.'

'An anchor,' Harry repeated musingly. 'I think that's what's been missing from my life.'

'An anchor would only weigh you down, Harry,' Elizabeth put in dryly. 'It would feel like an albatross around your neck.'

'Some chains I wouldn't mind wearing.'

'Try gold.'

He laughed.

'Do you two always spar like this?' Lucy asked, eyeing them speculatively.

'Sparks invariably fly,' Harry claimed.

It was on the tip of her tongue to say she invariably hosed them down, remembering just in time that flirting was the order of this afternoon, so she gave him an arch look and said, 'I would have to admit that being with Harry is somewhat invigorating.'

Lucy laughed and clapped her hands. 'Oh, I love it! What a great lunch we'll all have together!' Her eyes sparkled at Harry. 'What cocktail will you choose for me?'

'For the sunshine girl… A Piña Colada.'

She clapped her hands again. 'Well done, Harry. That's *my* favourite.'

'At your service.' He twirled his hand in a salute to them both and headed off to the bar.

Lucy was beside herself with delight. 'He's just what you need, Ellie. Loads of fun. You've been carrying responsibility for so long, it's well past time you let loose and had a wild flutter for once. Be a butterfly instead of a worker bee.'

At least she didn't say *moth*, Elizabeth thought wryly.

'I might just do that,' she drawled, encouraging the idea there was a connection between her and Harry.

'Go for it,' Lucy urged, bouncing forward on her seat in excitement. 'I'm going for Michael. He's an absolute dreamboat. I'm so glad I wasn't held up any longer at the cemetery. I might have missed out on meeting him. Why didn't you tell me your boss was gorgeous?'

'I've always thought him a bit cold,' she said carefully.

Lucy threw up her hands in exasperation at her sister's lack of discernment. 'Believe me. The guy is hot! He makes me sizzle.'

Elizabeth shrugged. 'I guess it's a matter of chemistry. Harry is the hot one for me.' It wasn't entirely a lie. He frequently raised her temperature...with anger or annoyance.

Lucy heaved a happy sigh. 'Brothers and sisters... wouldn't it be great if we ended up together...all happy families.'

Elizabeth's mind reeled from even considering such a prospect. 'I think that's a huge leap into the future. Let's just take one day at a time.'

'Oh, you're always so sensible, Ellie.'

'Which is something I value very highly in your sister,' Michael declared, picking up on Lucy's words and smiling warmly at Elizabeth as he returned, but he seated himself beside Lucy, who instantly switched on a brilliant smile for him, fulsomely agreeing, 'Oh, I do, too. But I also want Ellie to have fun.'

'Which is where I come in,' Harry said, also catching Lucy's words as he came back. His eyes danced wicked mischief at Elizabeth. 'Starting with cocktails. The bartender will bring them over. Here are the peanuts and pretzels.'

He placed a bowl of them on the table and settled himself beside Elizabeth, too closely for her comfort. She wanted to shift away and somehow Harry knew it, instantly throwing her a challenging look that made her sit still and suffer his male animal impact. If she was really attracted to him, she would welcome it. Playing this pretend-game was not going to be easy, but she had to now in front of Lucy.

Her sister turned her smile to Harry. 'What cocktail did you order for Michael?'

'A Manhattan. Mickey is highly civilised. He actually forgets about sunshine until it sparkles over him.'

Lucy laughed. 'And yourself?'

'Ah, the open sea is my business. I'm a salty man so I share Elizabeth's taste for Margaritas.'

'The open sea?' Lucy queried.

'Harry looks after the tourist side of Finn's Fisheries,' Michael answered. 'I take care of buying in the stock for all our franchises.'

'Ah!' Lucy nodded, understanding why Harry was dressed the way he was and how very different the brothers were.

Why she was attracted to Michael and not Harry was beyond Elizabeth's understanding. Sunshine and sea should go together. They both had frivolous natures. It wasn't fair that sexual chemistry had struck in the wrong place. Why couldn't it strike sensibly?

The bartender arrived with their cocktails.

Harry handed her the Margarita and clicked his glass against hers. 'Happy Birthday, Elizabeth,' he said warmly, making her squirm inside even as she forced a smile and thanked him.

The others followed suit with their glasses and well-wishing.

Elizabeth settled back against the cushions and sipped her cocktail, silently brooding over the totally non-sensible ironies of life. Was there any reward for being *sensible*? The old saying that *good things come to those who wait* was not proving true for her.

She wondered how long was the life of a butterfly.

Probably very short.

But it might be sweet if she could bring herself to be a butterfly—just cut loose from all her safety nets and fly wild for a while, thinking of nothing but having a good time. She should take a vacation, get right away from whatever was developing between Michael and Lucy, try drowning her misery with mindless pleasures.

The Margarita was good. And it packed quite a punch. Maybe if she stopped being sensible and had two or three of them, her mind would get fuzzy enough to put this whole situation at an emotional distance, let her float through lunch...like a butterfly.

CHAPTER FOUR

ELIZABETH stared blankly at the luncheon menu. Food. She had to choose something. Her head was swimming from two Margaritas in quick succession. Bad idea, thinking alcohol could fix anything. It didn't help at all.

'I bet I know what you're going to order, Ellie,' Lucy said with a confident grin.

'What?' Any suggestion was welcome.

'The chilli mud crab.'

Chilli. Not today. Her stomach was in too fragile a state.

'Actually, I can't see that on the menu,' Michael said, glancing quizzically at Lucy.

'Oh, I didn't really look. I just assumed,' she quickly defended. No way would she admit that her dyslexia made reading menus difficult. 'What have you decided on, Michael?'

Lucy would undoubtedly choose the same. She was so adept at hiding her disability, hardly anyone ever guessed she had a problem.

'How about sharing a seafood platter for two with me, Elizabeth?' Harry said, leaning closer to point out the platter's contents on the menu. 'You get crab on it, as well as all the other goodies and we can nibble away on everything as we please.'

'Harry will eat the lion's share,' Michael warned.

Yes, Elizabeth thought, relieved to have such ready help, making it easier for her lack of appetite to go unnoticed.

Harry instantly raised a hand for solemn vowing. 'I swear I'll give you first choice of each titbit.'

'Okay, that's a done deal,' she said, closing the menu and slanting her food-rescuer a grateful smile.

'Sealed with a kiss,' he said, bright blue eyes twinkling wickedly as he leaned closer still and pecked her on the cheek.

Her teeth grated together as heat bloomed from the intimate skin contact. The *flirting* agreement flew right out of her mind. His ability to discomfort her on any spot whatsoever had her snapping, 'You can keep that mouth of yours for eating, Harry.'

He gave her his evil grin as he retorted, 'Elizabeth, I live for the day when I'll eat you all up.'

'That'll be doomsday,' she slung back.

'With the gates of heaven opening for me,' Harry retaliated, his grin widening.

Lucy's laughter reminded her just in time that flirting shouldn't have too sharp an edge, so she swallowed her *hell* comment, heaved a long-suffering sigh and shook her head at Harry. 'You are incorrigible.'

'A man has to do what a man has to do,' he archly declared, sending Lucy off into more peals of laughter.

Elizabeth declined asking what he meant.

Nevertheless, as the birthday luncheon progressed, she schooled herself to respond lightly to Harry's banter, pretending to be amused by it, making a show of enjoying his company. At least he was very persistent in claiming her attention, forcefully distracting her from Lucy's and Michael's stomach-curdling absorption in each other, and he did eat the lion's share of the seafood platter without trying to push her into trying more than she could manage.

It was weird finding herself grateful to have Harry at her side, but just this once she actually did. Without him she would feel wretchedly alone, facing the worst scenario of lost hopes. How she was going to cope, hiding her feelings from both Lucy and Michael in the days to come, she didn't know. She hoped they would go off somewhere together after this luncheon, give her some space, release her from the tension of keeping up a happy pretence that everything was fine.

A waiter cleared the table and offered them the sweets menu. Elizabeth decided on the selection of sorbets since they should just slide down her throat without any effort. As soon as the orders were given, Harry leaned an elbow on the table and pointed a finger at his brother, claiming his attention.

'Mickey, I have the solution to my problem with the resort.'

'You have to clear that guy out, Harry,' came the quick advice. 'Once you confront him you can't leave him there. The potential for damage...'

'I know, I know. But it's best to confront him with his replacement. We walk in and turf him out. No argument. A done deal.'

'Agreed, but you don't have a ready replacement yet and the longer he stays...'

'Elizabeth. She's the perfect person for the management job—completely trustworthy, meticulous at checking everything, capable of handling everything you've thrown at her, Mickey.'

Confusion over this brother-to-brother business conversation instantly cleared. *This* was what Harry had intended to bring up after lunch—the perfect change for her. Except it wasn't perfect. Working for him would drive her bats.

'Elizabeth is my PA,' Michael protested.

'I'm in more need of her than you are right now. Lend her to me for a month. That will give me time to interview other people.'

'A month...' Michael frowned over the inconvenience to himself.

A month...

That was a tempting time frame—manageable if Harry wasn't around her all the time. The resort wasn't his only area of interest and responsibility. A month away from Michael and Lucy was a very attractive proposition.

'On the other hand, once Elizabeth gets her teeth into the job, she might want to stay on,' Harry said provocatively.

No way—not with him getting under her skin at any given moment!

Michael glowered at him. 'You're not stealing my PA.'

'Her choice, Mickey.' Harry turned to her. 'What do you say, Elizabeth? Will you help me out for a month... stay on the island and get the resort running as it should be run? My about-to-be ex-manager has been cooking the books, skimming off a lot of stuff to line his own pockets. You'll need to do a complete inventory and change the suppliers who've been doing private deals with him. It would be a whole new challenge for you, one that...'

'Now hold on a moment,' Michael growled. 'It's up to me to ask Elizabeth if she'll do it, not you, Harry.'

'Okay. Ask her.'

Yes was screaming through her mind. It offered an immediate escape from the situation with Michael and Lucy; no need to explain why she wanted to go away; a whole month of freedom from having to see or talk to either of them; a job that demanded her complete attention, keeping miserable thoughts at bay. These critical benefits made the irritation of having to deal with Harry relatively insignificant. Her heart was not engaged with him. Her head could sort out his effect on her, one way or another.

Michael heaved an exasperated sigh, realising he'd been pushed into a corner by his brother. 'It's true. You would be helping us out if you'd agree to step in and do what needs to be done at the resort,' he conceded, giving Elizabeth an earnest look. 'I have every confidence in your ability to handle the situation. Every confidence in your integrity, too. I hate losing you for a month...'

You've just lost me forever, Elizabeth thought.

'...but I guess someone from the clerical staff can fill in for a while....'

'Andrew. Andrew Cook,' she suggested.

He frowned. 'Too stodgy. No initiative.'

'Absolutely reliable in doing whatever task he's set,' she argued, rather bitchily, liking the fact that Michael found him stodgy. He'd obviously found her stodgy, too, in the female stakes.

'I take it that's a yes to coming to the island with me,' Harry slid in, grinning from ear to ear.

She shot him a quelling look. 'I'm up for the challenge of fixing the management problems, nothing else, Harry.'

'Brilliant!'

He purred the word, making her skin prickle. It instantly gave her the unsettling feeling she might have bitten off more than she could chew with Harry Finn. But he wouldn't be at her side all the time on the island. Going was still better than staying at home.

'That's it, then,' Michael said with a resigned air.

'A whole month! I'll miss you, Ellie,' Lucy said wistfully.

'The time will pass quickly enough,' Elizabeth assured her—*particularly with Michael dancing attendance.*

The waiter arrived with the sweets they'd ordered.

'We need to get moving on this,' Harry muttered as he dug into his chocolate mud cake.

'As soon as possible,' Michael agreed.

'Today,' Harry decided, checking his Rolex watch. 'It's only three o'clock now. We could be over on the island by four-thirty. Have him helicoptered out by six. We leave here when we've finished our sweets, hop on the boat...'

'It is Elizabeth's birthday, Harry,' Michael reminded him. 'She might have other plans for today.'

'No, I'm good to go,' she said, recklessly seizing the

chance to be relieved of staying in Michael's and Lucy's company any longer.

'What about clothes and toiletries and stuff?' Lucy put in. 'You're going for a month, Ellie.'

'You can pack for her, Lucy,' Harry said decisively. 'Mickey can take you home, wait while you do it, take Elizabeth's bags and arrange their shipping to the island.'

'No problem,' Michael said, smiling at Lucy like a wolf invited into her home to gobble her up.

Lucy happily agreed with the plan, her eyes sizzling with sexual promises as she smiled back at her new lover-to-be.

Elizabeth shovelled the sorbet down her throat. The faster she got out of here, the better.

'Ready?' Harry asked the moment she put her spoon down.

'Ready,' she answered emphatically, grabbing her handbag and rising to her feet, wanting to run but knowing she had to discipline herself to suffer goodbyes.

Lucy wrapped her in a big hug, mischievously saying, 'Have a lovely time with Harry, Ellie.'

'I will,' she replied through gritted teeth. Denials of that idea would not only be a total waste of time, but also prolong this whole wretched togetherness.

Michael kissed her cheek, wryly murmuring, 'I'll miss you.'

I won't miss you, Elizabeth thought fiercely, barely managing to force a smile. 'Thank you for my birthday lunch, Michael.'

'Pleasure,' he replied, his gaze sliding to Lucy.

'We're off,' Harry said, seizing Elizabeth's hand and pulling her with him.

His hand was strong and hot, wrapping firmly around her fingers, shooting warmth up her arm, but she didn't care if heat travelled to her brain and fried it right now. He was acting fast, taking her to the freedom she needed, and she was grateful for that. Once they were outside, he led her straight to the long wharf where rows of million-dollar yachts were docked on either side.

'Where's your boat?' she asked.

'Right at the end. No shuffling around. A quick, easy getaway. Full throttle to the island.'

'Good!'

He slid her one of his devilish grins. 'I must say I admire your decisiveness.'

She gave him a baleful look. 'Save your chatting up for some other woman, Harry. I played your game in front of Michael and Lucy because it suited me to do it, and I accepted your job offer because that suited me, too. As far as I'm concerned, there's work to be done and I'll do it. I don't expect to have *a lovely time* with you.'

His eyes held hers with a blast of discomforting intensity. 'No, not right now,' he drawled. 'Having had your expectations comprehensively dashed, I daresay you'll be a sourpuss for some time to come. But the island is a lovely place and I hope it will work some magic on you.'

A sourpuss...

The shock of that description halted her feet. She stared back at the blazing blue eyes, hating the knowledge she saw in them, knowledge of her hopes and the humiliation of seeing Michael respond to her sister as he had never—would never—respond to her. She couldn't wipe away Harry's perception of the situation, couldn't deny the truth, but was that any reason to be sour on him? He'd been her saviour today.

'I'm sorry,' she blurted out. 'I haven't thanked you.'

His sexy mouth moved into an ironic tilt. 'No thanks necessary, Elizabeth.'

His voice was soft, deep, and somehow it made her heart turn over.

She shook her head. 'That's not true, Harry. You were very effective in covering up my...my difficulties with how things went down today. I am grateful to you for rescuing me every time I hit a brick wall.'

'You'll bounce back, Elizabeth. Look on tomorrow as the first day of a new life—a butterfly breaking free of its confining cocoon and finding a world of sunshine. Come on—' he started walking down the wharf again, tugging her along with him '—we're on our way there now.'

The first day of a new life...

Of course, that was how it had to be.

There was no point in looking back, mourning over foolish dreams that were never going to come true. She had to put Michael behind her. Lucy would still be there along the track, her episode with Michael gone and forgotten, flitting along in her usual ditzy way. Her sister would always be her sister. It was she who had to start a different journey and being sour about it was just going to hold her back from getting somewhere good.

Harry helped her onto a large, deep-sea fishing

yacht, which undoubtedly had powerful motors to get them to their destination fast. 'Do you get seasick, Elizabeth?' he asked as he released the mooring rope. 'There are pills in the cabin you can take for it.'

'No, I'll be fine,' she assured him.

'I need you to be in top form when we arrive.'

'What do you consider top form?' She needed to know, get it right.

He jumped on board, grinning at her as he stored the rope correctly. 'Your usual self. Totally in charge of everything around you and projecting that haughty confidence you do so well.'

'Haughty?' she queried, not liking that description of herself, either.

'You're brilliant at it. Subject me to it every time.'

Only because Harry was Harry. It was her defence against him.

'I want you to give our target a dose of it when we confront him. No chatter. Just freeze him off.'

'No problem,' she stated categorically.

He straightened up and headed for the ladder to the bridge, tapping her cheek in passing, his eyes twinkling as he said, 'That's my girl!'

She barely stopped her hand from clapping her cheek to rid it of his electric touch. She clenched it into a fist and swiftly decided there would have to be some rules made about this short-term job on the island—like no touching from Harry. No kissing on the cheek, either. He was altogether too cavalier about taking liberties with her.

She was his stand-in manager, *not his girl*!

She was never going to be *his girl*.

One Finn brother had taken a bite out of her life. She was not about to give Harry the chance to take another. A month was a month. That was it with the Finns. She was thirty years old. When she'd completed this escape phase, some serious steps would have to be planned to make the best of the rest of her life.

She needed to find herself a serious man to share all that could be shared.

There was no hope of that happening with a playboy like Harry.

'Think you can make us both a sobering coffee while I fire up the engines?' he tossed back at her from the ladder.

'Sure! Though I'm not the least bit intoxicated, Harry.' She'd sobered up over lunch.

He grinned at her. 'I am. A straight black would be good. Join me on the bridge when you've made it.'

'Okay.'

She wanted to be fully briefed on the situation she was walking into, and Harry certainly needed to be fully in command of himself before they reached the island. Not that she'd noticed any lack of command. In fact, he'd been quite masterful in manipulating Michael into complying with what he wanted. She would have to watch that particular skill of his and not fall victim to any manipulation that would end up with her in the playboy's bed!

CHAPTER FIVE

EXHILARATION bubbled through Harry's brain. Who would have thought when today had started out that he would be riding towards the end of it on this glorious high? Here he was on the open sea, carving through the waves, the problem with his thieving manager solved, and the deliciously challenging Elizabeth at his beck and call for at least a month.

Her brick wall against him was still in place, but that blind obsession of hers with Mickey was gone. Lovely, lovely Lucy had done the job, blitzing his brother right in front of her sister's eyes. And at the most opportune moment! So easy to step in and take advantage of Elizabeth's disillusioned state.

She'd found herself trapped in a situation where pride had forced her to side with him, undoubtedly kicking and screaming about it in her mind, but totally unable to disguise the fact that she reacted to him physically. Always had. She could deny it as much as she liked but sexual chemistry didn't lie, and now that Mickey was out of the picture, cultivating the instinctive attraction she couldn't quite control was going to be the most enjoyable task Harry had set himself for some time.

Ellie Flippence…

That's who she needed to be, not stiff-necked Elizabeth. Though she did have a lovely long neck. He'd often fantasised bending that swanlike column with a trail of hot kisses, melting the rest of her, too. She had beautiful lush breasts and the gorgeous butterfly wings on her blouse showed them off a treat.

This morning he'd wanted to reach out and touch them, cup them, kiss them. He'd find the right time and place for that now. The moment would come when she'd give in to good old healthy lust, and Harry intended to make it so good she'd forget all about her shattered Mickey dreams and revel in the pleasure he'd give her.

But business came first.

He definitely needed to sober up, not give away the game before Elizabeth was ready for it.

Just as well she'd worn sandals, Elizabeth thought as she moved around the galley, steadying herself to the sway of the yacht as it headed out to sea. High heels would have been disastrous in this environment. Clearly there were tricks to keeping everything safe on board. She found a drink holder attached to a sling which made transporting coffee to the bridge relatively easy, and mugs with lids like the takeaway variety used by coffee shops. There was no risk of slopping it onto her good clothes which had to last her until her luggage arrived.

A scene flashed into her mind of Lucy in their apartment, with Michael advising her on what to choose for her sister's island wear—an intimate little scene that made Elizabeth gnash her teeth. She had to stop thinking of *them* together, think about what was ahead of her instead.

Finn Island was at the high end of the tourist industry—exclusive to only twenty couples at a time, people who could pay thousands of dollars for a minimum three-day stay. She had never been there, since it was way beyond her pocket. However, the Cairns office did have a video of it, showing its attractions and facilities, so she had some idea of how it operated.

There were twenty luxury villas, a tennis court, a gym with a pampering centre offering all sorts of massages. The administration centre, boutique, restaurant and bar faced the main beach and were spread around a landscaped area with lush tropical plants and clusters of palm trees, plus a swimming pool and spa. Apart from this artfully designed section, most of the island was covered with rainforest. A creek running from the central hill provided delightful waterfalls and rock pools, and walking tracks had been made to these natural beauty spots.

Dive-boats for exploring the Great Barrier Reef were readily available, as were yachts for deep-sea fishing and small motorboats for reaching the other beaches at the various inlets around the shoreline. All in all, Finn Island provided the perfect tropical getaway…if you were rolling in money.

Guests who could afford it would obviously be demanding, expecting the best for what they were paying. Elizabeth hoped there would be no hiccups to the island's excellent reputation for providing it while she was in charge. She knew supply boats called regularly. However, how the staff operated was a mystery to her and the need for that information was foremost in her mind as she climbed the ladder to the bridge.

She sat down in the chair beside Harry's before handing him his coffee. 'Black, as requested,' she said, forcing a smile to disprove his *sourpuss* description and holding on to a fierce determination not to be prickly in his presence.

'Thanks.' He smiled back. 'We'll be there in about forty minutes.'

'I know the general layout of the resort, but I know nothing about the staff, Harry. Or how everything runs.'

'You'll learn fast enough,' he assured her. 'Basically you have three undermanagers. Sarah Pickard is the head housekeeper. She handles the cleaning staff. Her husband, Jack, is the head maintenance man, who has his own team of helpers. The head chef, Daniel Marven, runs everything to do with the restaurant. He also keeps a check on the bar and will tell you what needs to be ordered in.' He made a wry grimace. 'The guy you are going to replace was overordering and reselling elsewhere, not to mention a few other perks he was working.'

'His name?'

'Sean Cassidy. Not important for you to remember. He'll be gone within an hour of our arrival. I'll call up a helicopter to take him off.'

'Are you going to prosecute?'

He shook his head. 'Bad publicity. Besides, it wasn't major criminal stuff.'

'How did you find out he was crooked?'

'Our sommelier in Cairns remarked to me that our island guests drank an inordinate amount of wine and spirits. Surprisingly inordinate, despite the fact that we run an open bar. It rang warning bells. When Sean had his mainland leave this past weekend, I did a thorough check of all supplies and usage, and bingo! No doubt he was robbing us and has been doing it for some considerable time.'

'Will he know you were checking on him?'

'He knows I was there but I didn't tip my hand to anyone. Mickey and I still had to decide what to do about it. Any disruption is not good for business.' He flashed a grin at her. 'Which is where you come in. No disruption.'

She nodded. 'I'll do my best to make it appear a smooth transition, but I'll need some help to begin with.'

'No problem. I'll be your guide for the first few days, until you've familiarised yourself with how everything runs.'

A few days in close contact with Harry had to be tolerated. The groundwork for this management job had to be laid if she was to carry it through successfully. It was the measure of closeness she had to watch. If he started taking liberties with her person...somehow she had to deal with that if and when it happened.

'I'll get on top of it all as soon as I can,' she said with strong resolution.

Harry chuckled, his vivid blue eyes dancing with teasing knowledge as he slowly drawled, 'I'm sure you will, Elizabeth. Can't get rid of me fast enough, can you?'

She felt heat rushing up her neck and turned her face away, looking out to sea, hating how he could read her mind and provoke this reaction in her. 'I'm sure you have to keep a check on other things besides the resort,' she said flatly.

'True. Though I am aware that I'm throwing you into a position you haven't held before. I'll spend a few days with you, then drop in from time to time in case you have any problems that I can resolve.'

She wished she could say, *Don't. I'll call you if I need your help.* But he was her boss now and what he was laying out was reasonable. Problems could arise that she didn't even recognise because of her inexperience. 'Do you have accommodation kept especially for you on the island?' she asked, worrying about how *close* he was going to be to her.

'No. I'm happy sleeping aboard this yacht. The Pickards have their own private villa as they are the only ones on the staff, apart from the manager, who actually live on the island full-time. The rest work on a rotation basis—ten days here, four days on the mainland—and they're accommodated in a series of motel-like structures.'

'Is that where I'll be staying?'

He shook his head. 'You'll have your own private quarters in the administration building.'

Where Harry could make private visits.

Elizabeth grimaced at that thought. She was getting paranoid about the man. He could not get her into bed with him unless she allowed it. All she had to do was keep him at a sensible distance. It was only for a month and he wouldn't be there all the time.

'Don't be worrying about clothes for tomorrow,' he suddenly tossed at her. 'I'll get Sarah to issue you with the island uniform.'

'What's the island uniform?' she queried, not having seen that on the video.

'This…' He indicated his T-shirt and shorts and pointed to the emblem just below his left shoulder—a stitched line of waves in blue over which *Finn Island* was written in a small flowing multicoloured script to match the multicoloured fish across his chest.

She hadn't noticed the emblem before, distracted by the way the T-shirt clung to Harry's very male physique. 'I hadn't realised. Of course, you came from there this morning.'

So much had happened today, her state of hopeful eagerness this morning felt as though it had been wiped out a million years ago. Another life ago.

'Makes it easier for the guests to know who's staff and who's not,' Harry explained, adding with one of his devilish grins, 'That won't take care of your undies, though.'

He was probably having a fantasy of her naked beneath her outer clothes.

'I'll manage,' she said through gritted teeth.

He laughed. 'You can probably pick up a bikini from the boutique. Sarah can provide you with a hair-dryer and a toothbrush. Don't know about make-up.'

'I have some in my handbag.'

'No worries then.'

Only you, she thought.

Yet when they arrived on the island and confronted Sean Cassidy in his administration office, the playboy image Elizabeth had of Harry Finn in her mind was severely dented. Right in front of her eyes his easygoing attitude disappeared, replaced by a formidable air of authority. There was no semblance of light banter in his voice as he set about firing the crooked manager with ruthless efficiency.

Sean Cassidy had risen from the chair behind his office desk to greet his visitors, a smile on his face that didn't quite reach his eyes, which skated over Elizabeth and settled warily on Harry. He was a tall, lean man, dark-haired, dark-eyed, and the unheralded appearance of his boss clearly caused some tension in him.

'You're out, Sean,' Harry shot at him before the manager could say a word. 'Move away from the desk. Don't touch anything in this office. A helicopter will be arriving shortly to fly you to the mainland. Go and collect all your personal effects from your apartment. You won't be coming back.'

'What the hell…' the guy started to expostulate.

Harry cut him off. 'You know why. I have evidence of all your skimming activities. Providing you go quietly, I won't hand you over to the police at this time. If you know what's good for you, Sean, you'll stay quiet. Any bad-mouthing of the Finn family and its business operations will have consequences you won't like. Do you understand me?'

The threat had a steely edge to it that would have intimidated anyone. Sean Cassidy sucked in his breath, swallowed whatever defensive words he might have spoken and nodded. He looked shell-shocked.

'Let's go then.' Harry waved commandingly to a door in the rear wall of the office. 'I'll accompany you into the apartment to ensure you don't take anything that doesn't belong to you.'

As the man started to move as directed, Harry turned to Elizabeth, his blue eyes ice-hard, not a vestige of a twinkle in them. 'Take over the desk, Elizabeth. You're now in charge of this office.'

She nodded, her mouth too dry to speak. Her heart was beating faster than normal. The air felt charged with electricity. She was still stunned by the strike-anyone-dead energy that had emanated from Harry. In her two years of working for Michael, she had never witnessed anything like it coming from him, and she had always thought he was the stronger brother.

It wasn't until Harry had followed Sean into the apartment and closed the door that she could bring herself to actually move her feet. The desk was large and L-shaped with a computer workstation on one side. She sat in the chair that was now hers, grateful for its firm support. Witnessing the formidable side of Harry Finn had shaken her. The man was lethal, and she suddenly felt very vulnerable to whatever he might turn on her, now that she was locked into this situation with him.

That nerve-quivering blast of forcefulness... A shiver ran down her spine. Though surely he would never *force* a woman. *He wouldn't have to*, came the instant answer in her head. He was so innately sexy he could make her feel hot and bothered with just a teasing look. But he needed her here for business so maybe he would refrain from pushing anything sexual with her. Teasing was just teasing. Hopefully she could keep a level head with that.

Having cleared her mind enough to concentrate on business, Elizabeth took stock of the other office furnishings—filing cabinets, a couple of chairs for visitors, a coffee table with brochures fanned out on top of it, framed photographs of celebrities who had stayed here hanging on the walls.

On the larger section of the desk, which faced the entrance doors to administration, was a telephone attached to an intercom system with numbers for all the villas, the staff quarters and the restaurant. Beside it was a notepad and pen for writing notes or messages. On the top page were two reminders which had been ticked. *Chocs to 8. Gin to 14.* Obviously she had to deal with all requests from guests as well as handle bookings and coordinate the staff for whatever was needed.

Directly in front of her was a spreadsheet, detailing the occupancy of the villas this week—arrivals and departures. Three couples had left this morning. Their villas were vacant until another three couples arrived tomorrow. One of them was only staying three days, the other two for five. Most of the bookings were for five, only a few for a whole week. She would have to have her wits about her, coordinating the turnovers, personalising the welcomes and the farewells, memorising the names of all the guests. Wealthy people always expected that courtesy and respect.

She was matching names to the occupants of each villa when she heard the distinctive sound of a helicopter coming in. The door behind her opened and Harry led Sean, who was loaded up with luggage, out of the apartment, waving him to go ahead, pausing at the desk long enough to say, 'Hold the fort, Elizabeth. I'll be back in twenty minutes.'

He didn't wait for a reply, intent on escorting Sean to the helipad, wherever that was. The glass entrance doors to the office opened automatically for ease of access and Harry caught up with Sean as he made his exit. There was no verbal exchange between them. The ex-manager was going quietly.

Elizabeth watched Harry until he moved out of sight. Her heart was hammering again. Experiencing a completely different side of Harry Finn to the flirtatious tease she was used to was having a highly disturbing impact on her. It was impossible now to dismiss him as a lightweight playboy. The man had real substance, impressively strong substance, powerful substance, and it was playing havoc with her prejudice against him.

Michael had said this morning that Harry's mind was as sharp as a razor blade and he had his thumb on everything to do with his side of the business. That description could no longer be doubted. She'd had evidence enough today of how accurately he could read her thoughts—something she would have to guard against more carefully in the future—and she would never again underestimate how capable he was of being master of any situation.

His attraction was all the stronger for it. Dangerously so.

Nevertheless, that still didn't make him good relationship material.

He was a dyed-in-the-wool flirt with women.

And that wasn't just her judgment. Michael had said so.

Regardless of what Harry Finn made her feel, she was not going to have anything to do with him apart from the business of managing this resort for a month. He could flirt his head off with her but she would stand absolutely firm on that ground.

He was not what she wanted in her life.

She had to look for someone steady, solid, totally committed to her and the family they would have together.

Not like her father.

And not like Harry, who probably treated women as though they were a carousel of lollipops to be plucked out and tasted until another looked tastier.

CHAPTER SIX

WHEN Harry returned he was accompanied by a middle-aged woman with whom he appeared to be on very friendly terms. They were smiling at each other as they entered the office. She had short, curly dark hair, liberally streaked with grey, a very attractive face set in cheerful lines and merry hazel eyes that invited people to enjoy life with her. Of average height, her trim figure declared her fit to tackle anything, and she exuded positive vibes at Elizabeth as Harry introduced her.

'Sarah Pickard, Elizabeth.'

'Hi! Welcome to Finn Island,' the woman chimed in.

'Thank you.' Elizabeth smiled back as she rose from the desk to offer her hand at this first meeting. 'I'll have to learn a lot very fast and I'll appreciate any help and advice you can give me, Sarah.'

She laughed and gave Elizabeth's hand a quick squeeze. 'No problem. I'm only ever a call away. Harry tells me you've been Mickey's PA. I'm sure you'll fit in here very quickly.'

Mickey? The familiar use of Harry's name for his brother struck her as odd.

'Go into the apartment with Sarah, look around, see what you need,' Harry instructed. 'I'll man the desk.'

'Okay. Thank you,' Elizabeth replied, gesturing to Sarah to lead the way.

It was a basic one-bedroom apartment, spotlessly clean and pleasantly furnished with cane furniture, cushions brightly patterned in tropical designs. The floor was tiled and an airconditioner kept the rooms cool. The kitchenette was small, and its only equipment appeared to be an electric kettle, a toaster and a microwave oven.

'You won't need that for much,' Sarah explained. 'Meals will be brought to you from the restaurant. Just tick what you want on each menu. You'll find tea, coffee and sugar in the cupboard above the sink, milk and cold drinks in the bar fridge.'

Elizabeth nodded, thinking the gourmet meals provided here were a wonderful perk—no shopping for food, no cooking and no cleaning up afterwards.

'The bed linen was changed this morning so everything's fresh for you apart from these towels.' Which she'd collected from the bathroom as she'd showed Elizabeth the facilities. 'I'll send clean ones over for you. Plus a hair-dryer and toothbrush. Harry said he'd whipped you off Mickey with no time to pack anything.'

Again the familiar name usage. Elizabeth frowned quizzically. 'He's always been Michael to me. I've only heard Harry calling him Mickey. And now you.'

She laughed. 'I've known those two since they were teenagers. Jack and I looked after their parents' place in those days. I guess I was like a second mother to them. Never had kids of my own. Good boys, both of them. You couldn't be connected to better men, Elizabeth, as employers or people.'

It was a high recommendation, though probably a biased one, given Sarah's obvious fondness for them. 'They're very different,' she commented, wanting to hear more.

'Mickey's more like his dad, a seriously driven achiever. It's in his genes, I reckon. Harry's nature is more like his mum's. She had a very sunny disposition, radiating a joy in life that infected everyone around her. It was a wicked shame when...' She heaved a deep sigh. 'Well, I guess we never know the day or the hour, but I tell you, those boys are a credit to their parents. Losing them both when they did, they could have run off the rails, plenty of money to spend, but they took on the business and pushed forward. And they looked after everyone who could have been hurt by the loss. Like me and Jack.'

She paused, grimaced. 'Here I am running off at the mouth but you know Mickey. Harry said you've been working closely with him for two years.'

'Yes, I have.'

'You'll find Harry good to work for, too. Just a different nature, that's all.'

Sunny...like his mother...like Lucy. Was that why Michael was so attracted to Lucy? But why wasn't Harry? Why did he have to plague her with his endlessly provocative attention?

'I'll only be here for a month, Sarah. I'm the fill-in until Harry finds a replacement for Sean.'

'Whatever...' She waved airily. Obviously it was not something that weighed on her mind. 'I'll send over sets of the island uniform with the towels etc. Do you want short shorts, Bermuda length or three-quarters?'

'Bermuda length,' Elizabeth decided, thinking that would look more dignified for her position as manager.

'Harry thought a bikini…?'

'No. I'll wash my undies out tonight. I'll be fine, thanks, Sarah.'

She grinned. 'I love your butterfly blouse. It's just the kind of thing Harry's mum used to wear.'

Lucy's choice, Elizabeth thought. 'I'll gladly change it for tropical fish,' she said. The butterfly blouse represented failure with Michael and trouble with Harry, since he saw it as sexy. 'I'll be more comfortable here in the island uniform.'

'Well, it is easy. You don't have to think about what clothes to put on. I'll be off now. You might want to freshen up before rejoining Harry in the office.'

'Yes, I do. Thanks, Sarah.'

She was relieved to have such a good ally in the head housekeeper. It would surely make this job easier. Sarah's long association with the Finn family meant that she could be absolutely trusted, too.

What she'd said about *the two boys* lingered in Elizabeth's mind as she made use of the bathroom facilities. The plane crash that had taken the lives of Franklyn and Yvette Finn had been frontline news about ten years ago, soon after her own mother had died. She hadn't known the people so it had meant nothing personal to her at the time, yet it must have been a traumatic period for Michael and Harry, both young men, possibly still at university, having fun, believing there was plenty of time to work out what they wanted to do with their lives. It *was* admirable that they'd taken on their father's business empire instead of selling up and shedding all responsibility.

But it still didn't make Harry good relationship material. She could respect him for what he'd done. He might be very *solid* in that sense. However, that did not mean he had any staying power where women were concerned.

For the next hour she had to sit beside him at the computer workstation in the office while he went through the Finn Island website, showing her how bookings were made over the internet and their dates subsequently slotted into the island calendar. He explained how to work out all the schedules that had to be kept and Elizabeth had no trouble grasping what she had to do.

However, being so close to Harry—virtually shoulder to shoulder—did make concentration more difficult than it should have been. With their brief encounters in the Cairns office, she'd always managed to keep her distance from him, hating how he could exude a male sexiness that made her acutely conscious of being a woman whose needs weren't being answered. Now, having barely any space between them made her senses hyperalert to almost everything about him.

Her nose kept being invaded by his smell—a sharp tanginess like a sea breeze somehow mixed with an earthy animal scent. His strong, muscular forearms were a very masculine contrast to her more slender, softly rounded ones and she couldn't help noticing his long dexterous fingers as he worked the computer mouse—fingers that fascinated her into flights of erotic fantasy. He didn't touch her, not even accidentally, but she was wound up inside, expecting him to, silently schooling herself not to react as though his touch was like a hot iron scorching her skin.

She had to learn how to behave naturally around him. Whenever he glanced at her to check if she understood what he was explaining, the vivid blue eyes seemed to be tunnelling into her mind and she had to force herself to hold his gaze as she assured him everything was clear to her. Then he smiled approval which made her stupid stomach contract. He was an extremely disturbing man even when he wasn't teasing or flirting and she didn't want him to be. Hopefully his wretchedly unsettling effect on her would gradually fade away over the next few days.

People started strolling by on the path outside, heading towards the bar for predinner drinks. Harry named them as they passed. Of course he had been here over this past weekend, but it was impressive that he could identify every guest on the island and tell her where they came from, as well as how they'd come by their wealth. Elizabeth tried to commit most of what he said to memory but it was a struggle—too many of them, too quickly.

'You'll soon have them down pat,' Harry said confidently. 'I told Daniel we'd be eating in the restaurant tonight. I'll drill you on everyone at the other tables while we dine, then introduce you around before they leave.'

'That would help a lot,' she said gratefully.

'Hope you can find some more appetite than you had for lunch. Daniel will be miffed if you don't do justice to his gourmet creations.'

He knew she'd been too upset to eat much lunch but tonight she wouldn't have to watch Michael and Lucy gobbling up each other and she wanted to stop Harry from poking any further at the still-raw place in her heart. 'Actually I'm rather hungry. Must be the sea air,' she answered airily, resolving to eat everything put in front of her and show appreciation of it, regardless of how she *felt*.

His eyes glittered satisfaction. 'Remarkable what a sea change will do.'

Well, it won't extend to sharing your bed, she silently promised him as she rolled her chair back from the desk and stood up. 'Speaking of change, I'll go and swap these clothes for the island uniform before we go to the restaurant.'

Two young women on Sarah's staff—Maddie and Kate—had brought everything she needed while Harry had been teaching her the ins and outs of the website. The way they'd looked at Harry—telegraphing they thought he was *hot*—had made her wonder if he played musical beds on the island.

'Good idea!' He eyed her up and down in that lingering way that made her skin prickle. 'We wouldn't want our lady guests going pea-green with envy at how gorgeous you look in that outfit,' he drawled. 'Nor would we want their guys seeing you as more desirable than their partners.'

'Oh, really!' she huffed, crossing her arms defensively.

'Just telling you how it is, dear Elizabeth.'

'Don't *dear* me!' she snapped, still very much on edge from having to weather the sexual pitfalls of his proximity and wanting to cut off his flirting routine.

His eyebrows arched provocatively. 'What? I can't express how I feel about you?'

One of her hands sliced out in negative dismissal. 'I don't want to hear it.'

'Wrong time, wrong man, but that doesn't make it any less true.'

She rolled her eyes in disbelief. 'Let's keep to business, Harry.'

'Okay.' He gestured at the door to the apartment. 'Go and change. It will be a start to fitting in with me instead of Mickey.'

She felt purpose underlying those words, spine-crawling purpose as she turned her back on him and walked quickly from the office into the apartment, closing the door very firmly behind her.

It caused her to work up some steely purpose of her own. She would do her best to fit in on the island but fitting in with Harry on any personal basis had to stop. It had been a purely defensive move, going along with him today, using him as a shield to hide her distress. From now on she should take control of whatever happened between them. Her mind was very clear on that. She certainly didn't want to invite any sexual complications with him, which would only mess her around more than she was already messed up by the situation with Michael and Lucy.

It was a relief to shed the clothes that had fed her hopes this morning. She had a quick shower to wash away the misery of the day and give herself the sense of making a fresh start. It felt liberating donning the island uniform. This was the end of maintaining the professional image of an executive PA, at least for the next

month. The casual, carefree look of shorts and T-shirt
was suddenly very welcome to her.

It seemed she'd been carrying a heavy weight of responsibility for many years, ever since her mother had
fallen ill with terminal cancer and her father had deserted them. The need to hold everything together for
herself and Lucy had been driving her for a long time.
Somehow it didn't matter so much anymore. She was
on an island, away from the life she had known up until
now, all by herself…except for Harry, who'd be gone as
soon as she was on top of the job.

That was her main priority now—demonstrating to
Harry that his guidance was no longer needed. Once
she was free of his presence, this place might very well
work some magic for her—time out of time to find herself again—no hanging on to what Michael thought or
felt about her, no worrying about Lucy, just Elizabeth.

CHAPTER SEVEN

HARRY watched her come out of the apartment, all bright-eyed and bushy-tailed, determined to get on with the job and do it well. He admired her strength of character, her refusal to be utterly crushed by disillusionment. On the other hand, he had kept her mind very occupied these past few hours and would continue to do so until they parted for the night. That would be crunch time for her, when she was lying in bed, alone in the darkness. It would all be about Mickey and Lucy then.

He was strongly tempted to give her something else to think about—something she couldn't dismiss as easily as she had in the past, writing him off as of no account. He didn't like it. He never had liked it. Tonight might be too soon to pounce but...what the hell! She was never going to be *ready* for him. Her mind-set against getting personally involved with him was so fixed, perhaps physically shaking her out of it was the best way to go.

If he set the scene right...

An idea came to him. A private word to the chef before dinner, concentrate on business over the meal, wait until the guests had drifted off to their villas or the bar, then spring the surprise.

He grinned at her as he rose from the office chair. 'Time to see if the stars are burning bright tonight.'

She shook her head at him. 'It's not dark enough yet.' Her tone denied any interest in an activity which probably smacked of romance to her.

'Well, we can watch for them to appear from our table in the restaurant. You are allowed to enjoy the ambience of this island, Elizabeth.'

He could see her consciously relaxing, working up a smile. 'I will, Harry. I'm glad I have the opportunity to do so.'

'Good! I want you to be happy here.'

Happy...

Why not? Elizabeth thought. She should let everything else float out of her mind and embrace this experience—tropical night, stars burning bright, glorious food, lots of interesting people to meet. All she had to do was ignore Harry's insidious effect on her, and with the ready distraction of the guests around them, surely that could be kept at bay.

He led her out of the office, locked the doors and handed her the key, which made her feel secure about any unwanted attention coming from him later on in the evening. As soon as they entered the spacious, open-air restaurant, he was called over to a table where two couples were very happy with their day of diving near the reef, happy that Harry had arranged such a marvellous experience for them.

Elizabeth was introduced as the new manager. It was easy to smile at these people, easy to smile at all the other guests when other introductions were made throughout the evening. They were all having a great time and their mood was infectious, and however they'd filled in their day, the evening meal certainly topped it off.

Every course was superb. Elizabeth really enjoyed the food and complimented the chef on it, praising the attentiveness of the waiters, too. Daniel Marven definitely ran a high-class restaurant. Elizabeth couldn't see any problem arising on this front during her management month, and she was sure Sarah and Jack Pickard handled their roles just as efficiently. This could very well be a *happy* position for her.

'You have a great set-up here, Harry,' she complimented him over coffee. 'The guests are so clearly enjoying themselves.'

He leaned back in his chair, smiling at her. 'You've handled everything extremely well, Elizabeth.'

His voice was like a soft purr that somehow seemed to curl around her, adding more heat to the warmth of his smile. All evening it had been strictly business, with Harry coaching her in her managerial role, and she'd relaxed enough to actually feel comfortable with him. She was caught off guard by the switch to personal appreciation that felt as though he was physically caressing her.

Her pulse quickened. Her toes scrunched up in her sandals. He wasn't really *doing* anything, she fiercely told herself. It hadn't even been a flirtatious remark. Reacting like this was off the wall.

'Thank you,' she said quickly, fighting off the unwelcome feelings.

'No. Thank *you*,' he replied just as quickly, the smile gone, respect shining in his eyes. 'Coming in cold, taking over from Sean...you're picking up on everything much faster than I expected. This morning I had a problem. Tonight…' He spread his hands in an awed gesture. 'You're a wonder, Elizabeth.'

She floundered for a moment, his warmth and respect tearing at her heart—the heart she had given to Michael, who didn't want it. She made an ironic grimace. 'Your brother trained me to pick up on everything.'

He returned the grimace. 'Of course. Mickey would. But I'm glad you're here with me.'

And she was glad to have this getaway.

That was the bottom line.

She forced herself to relax again. Today was almost over. She'd made it through without falling apart.

As the last couple rose from their table to leave the restaurant they called out goodnights to Harry and Elizabeth, which, of course, they reciprocated. 'Colin and Jayne Melville from Goulburn,' Elizabeth murmured, shooting a triumphant grin at Harry. 'I've got them all sorted now.'

He laughed, the blue eyes twinkling pleasure in her. 'I knew you'd meet the challenge.'

Her heart did a flip-flop. The man was sinfully attractive, actually more so when he wasn't doing his playboy *flirting* stuff. Tonight he hadn't strayed into any irritating dalliance with her, focusing entirely on easing her into this new job. He'd been exceptionally good at it, too, charming the guests into talking about themselves, giving information for Elizabeth to memorise. They enjoyed chatting with him. Of course, in their eyes Harry Finn was an equal. He had the money, the looks and the self-assurance that came with both those assets.

'One more thing to do before we part for the night,' he said, standing up and moving to draw back her chair.

'What's that?' she asked, pushing herself up from the table, feeling it had been a very long day already.

'A little ceremony from the staff to welcome you,' he answered. 'It's been set up down on the deck.' He nodded towards the bar where many of the guests had gathered for a nightcap. It was directly across from the restaurant, the walkway down to the pool deck dividing the two entertainment areas. 'More private than here.'

Elizabeth had no qualms about accompanying Harry to wherever the welcome ceremony was going to be held. It was a nice gesture from the staff and gave her the opportunity to meet more of them.

There were actually two decks. The first one surrounded the swimming pool. It was strewn with sun-lounges, tables with folded-up umbrellas, and a couple of day beds flanking it. Steps led down to a lower deck, which had a large spa to one side.

A table for two was set up just in front of more steps that led straight onto the beach; white tablecloth, an ice bucket containing a bottle of champagne, two flute glasses, two bread plates with cake forks beside them. *A table for two*, in what was so obviously a romantic setting, close to the sound of waves lapping on the beach and under a sky full of stars.

Elizabeth jolted to a halt. Her pulse jumped into an erratic beat. This looked too much like a playboy setting. Was Harry about to turn into a wolf now that business was over for the day? She shot him a hard, suspicious look.

'I don't see any staff.'

'Waiting for me to get you settled,' he said, moving ahead to hold out one of the chairs for her.

Was it true? Surely he wouldn't lie when the lie could be so quickly disproved. It was okay, she told herself, taking a deep breath and letting it out slowly as she forced her feet forward and sat where Harry had directed. He lifted the bottle of champagne out of the ice bucket, popped the cork and filled the flute glasses before sitting down himself.

'A celebratory drink,' he said, smiling at her as he raised his glass, expecting her to do the same.

She did, though his smile did nothing to calm her down. Quite the opposite.

'To a new start,' he added, clicking her glass with his.

'A new start,' she echoed, hoping the staff would hurry up and appear. Her nerves were twitching. Her heart was thumping. There was too much intimacy about being alone with Harry out here, and the control she was trying to hold on to was frayed by having had to deal with too many difficult situations.

Harry's eyes caressed her with admiration as he complimented her again. 'You've been brilliant today, Elizabeth.'

For some stupid reason, tears pricked her eyes. She managed a half smile of acknowledgment and quickly sipped the champagne, needing it to loosen up the sudden lump in her throat. The day had been overloaded with tensions but it was almost over. All she had to do was hold herself together a little bit longer.

'Ah! Here it comes!' Harry said happily, looking up towards the restaurant.

Elizabeth blinked hard, set her glass down, mentally gathered herself to deal with the welcome ceremony, then turned her head to see…

Not a group of staff members.

Only one person walking down the steps.

It was Daniel Marven, carrying a cake on a platter.

She looked for others to come streaming down behind him but no one did. He proceeded to the table alone, placing the platter in front of her.

'Enjoy,' he said, smiling at her.

Happy Birthday Elizabeth was written across the chocolate icing on top of the cake. She stared at it, barely finding voice enough to say, 'Thank you.'

'Good work, Daniel,' Harry said, and the chef took off, leaving the two of them together.

A dam of tightly held emotion burst inside Elizabeth. Her birthday. Her thirtieth birthday. She'd so much wanted it to be…not how it had turned out. Tears spurted into her eyes, welling over and streaming down her cheeks. Impossible to stop them. Her heart was not strong enough to absorb any more stress. It felt as though it was breaking.

Strong hands lifted her out of her chair. Strong arms engulfed her, clamping her to a strong chest. Her head was gently pressed onto a strong shoulder. There was no resistance in her. None at all. She was as weak as a baby—a baby who had been born thirty years ago and didn't know what life had in store for her. Still didn't. And she was too much at sea to think about it…think about anything.

CHAPTER EIGHT

HARRY had not anticipated having a weeping Elizabeth in his arms. The birthday cake surprise had been planned to give her pleasure and undermine her resistance to a friendly goodnight kiss, which could have easily escalated into something more, sparking up the chemistry that she'd always been so determined to deny. He didn't feel right about taking advantage of *this* situation.

What had caused such deep distress? Was it the reminder that she had turned thirty today? Single women could be rather touchy about reaching that age goalpost, particularly if they weren't in a relationship and wanted to be. Was it the lost chance with Mickey catching up with her at the end of the day?

It was so damnably frustrating. He'd finally got her to himself. She felt good in his arms—all woman—soft, warm and curvy. Smelled good, too. He rubbed his cheek over her hair, breathing in the scent of her—a fruity shampoo and an enticing trace of exotic perfume. He patted her back, trying to impart comfort, and felt relieved when the weeping started trailing off, interrupted by deep, heaving breaths that made him very aware of the lush fullness of her breasts. He wanted to pick her up, carry her over to the nearest day bed and blow her mind with wild, passionate sex.

The emotional storm eventually came to a shuddering halt but she remained leaning on him, her head resting on his shoulder, her body still, limp, spent of all energy. His hands wanted to wander, travelling down the very female curve of her spine to her even more female bottom—the bottom that swished provocatively every time she'd turned away from him. His fingers itched to curl around it, press her body into a more intimate fit with his, stir the same desire in her that was heating up his blood, arousing the beast.

He couldn't stop himself from hardening, didn't want to anyway. Let her feel what she did to him. Let her know she was desirable even as a limp, tear-soaked rag doll. It might jolt her out of whatever sea of misery she was swimming in. Life was for living, not wallowing in a trough of depression.

Elizabeth didn't care that it was Harry holding her. It was simply nice to be held in such a secure comforting way, propping her up when she was down, not asking anything of her, just being another body emanating warmth that took the chill of loneliness from her bones.

She wished she had someone who would always be there for her like this, someone strong who would never let her down. She'd wanted to believe it would be Michael, but it wasn't. And Harry...oh hell! She could feel him getting hard! No matter that she'd been weeping all over him. He still had sex on his mind.

A flood of embarrassment poured heat into her face as she jerked her head up from his shoulder. She'd been hanging on to him like a limpet. It took a moment to unglue her hands from his back and try shoving them up his chest to make some space between them.

'Sorry...sorry,' she gabbled, frantically looking up to beg his understanding that she hadn't been passively inviting *anything*!

'Sorry for what?' he mocked, his eyes glittering a hard challenge at her.

'I didn't mean to...to use you like that.'

'You needed to...just like I need to do this.'

He whipped up a hand to hold her chin. Elizabeth didn't have time to protest, nor time to take any action to stop his mouth from swooping on hers. The impact shocked her. It was not a gentle seductive kiss. It was a full-on sensual assault, his lips working over hers, forcing them open with the strong thrust of his tongue that instantly swept over her palate, causing her whole mouth to tingle as though it had been charged with electricity.

Instinctively she used her own tongue to fight the invasion of his, angry at his bold aggression. Whether he took this as encouragement or not, she didn't know, but his hand moved to the back of her head, fingers thrusting into her hair, holding her so there was no escape from his marauding mouth. His tongue was teasing, goading, enticing hers to tangle erotically with it, resulting in an explosion of sensation that tore any sensible thoughts out of her mind.

The whole physicality of the moment was totally overwhelming. She didn't care that he pressed her lower body so closely to his that his erection furrowed her stomach. Some primitive part of her revelled in it, revelled in the hot hard wall of his chest squashing her breasts. She was swamped by a tidal wave of chaotic need to feel everything more and more intensely. Her own hands raked down his beautifully muscled back and curled around his taut male butt, exulting in the sense of taking this incredibly sexy man as hers.

It was wildly exciting, intoxicating—one avid kiss merging into another and another, inciting a fever of passion that possessed her with such power she completely lost herself in it, craving the fierce climactic union they were driving towards, the desire for it sweeping through her like a firestorm, all-consuming.

The mouth engaging hers suddenly broke the primal connection. 'Yes...' hissed into her ear—a sound of exultant triumph. Then the intimate body contact was shifted. Her legs were hoisted up and she was being carried with heart-pounding speed, cool air wafting over her hot face, reducing the fever of urgently demanding desire.

She was tumbled onto a bed and Harry—Harry!—was leaping onto it to join her there. Her eyes were wide-open now. Her mind crashed into working gear. This was one of the day beds on the deck. She'd wanted the sex that Harry was intent on having with her. Her body was still quivering at a peak of need for it. But it was madness to go on with it—madness to muddy up what should be a clean break away from everything, starting what would inevitably be a messy affair going nowhere and interfering with carrying through this management job.

He flung one strongly muscled thigh over hers and started lifting her T-shirt as he lowered his head to start kissing her again. She'd lain inert with shock at finding herself so complicit in stirring this situation. It had to be stopped. Now! Already his hand was on her breast, fingers moving under the cup of her bra, tweaking her nipple, and for a moment she was paralysed by a rebellious wish to feel more of his touch. She stared at his mouth coming closer and closer, her mind screaming that another kiss would tip her over into Harry's world.

Did she want that?

Did she?

Losing control of everything?

A flash of fear whipped her hand up to Harry's mouth, covering it just before it made contact with hers. His eyebrows beetled down in a puzzled frown.

'Stop!' she croaked.

He jerked his head back from her halting hand, his frown deepening as he shot a disbelieving 'What?' at her.

She swallowed hard to give her voice more strength. 'I don't want you to take this any further, Harry.'

'Why not?' he demanded. 'You want it as much as I do.'

She wrenched his hand away from her breast and pulled the T-shirt down. 'A momentary madness,' she excused.

'Rubbish! It's been simmering between us for years,' he insisted vehemently. 'It just came to a head and it's damned dishonest of you to back off now.'

Anger stirred. She hadn't really consented to this. He'd started it when she was at her weakest, taking advantage of her vulnerable state. 'I don't care what you

call it, I don't choose to go on with it,' she said fiercely
and attempted to roll away from him.

He scooped her back to face him, his eyes blazing
furious frustration. 'What is the matter with you? We
want each other. It's only natural to…'

'Let me go, Harry. This isn't right for me.'

'Not right?' he repeated incredulously. 'It sure as
hell felt right until you suddenly decided it wasn't, but
I'm not into forcing any woman to have sex with me.'
He threw up the arm that had halted her rejection of
any more togetherness. 'If you hadn't responded as you
did…'

'I didn't mean to,' she yelled at him, her face flam-
ing at the truth he was flinging at her.

'Oh, yes you did! Just for once you let that steel-
trap mind of yours open enough for your instincts to
take over and it was dynamite between us. Is that what
scares you, Elizabeth?'

She hated how he could always hit the nail on the
head with her. Yes, it scared her but she wasn't going to
admit it. She glared resentment at him. 'I figure you're
dynamite to a lot of women, Harry, and I don't care to
be left in little pieces when you move on to your next
piece of fluff.'

His hand sliced the air in savage dismissal of her
argument. 'I don't think of you as *fluff*! Do you imagine I'd give this management job to someone I thought
of as *fluff*?'

'I'm not saying you didn't believe I could do the
work. But having a bit of sex on the side was on the
plate, too, wasn't it?' she hurled back at him. 'And now
you're peeved because I've decided not to cooperate.'

He rolled his head in exasperation. 'Peeved does not describe what I feel right now, Elizabeth.'

There was a mountain of feeling brooding behind those words and Elizabeth instantly felt threatened by it. She scrambled off the day bed, swinging around on her feet to face down any follow-up from Harry. He hadn't moved. He lay sprawled across the bed with his head propped up on his hand, his eyes searing hers with blistering accusation.

'You're shutting the gate on living life to the full,' he said bitingly. 'I don't want your cooperation, Elizabeth. I want your surrender to what we could have together.'

'That's not the life I want,' she retorted decisively.

'You're chasing dreams instead of taking on what's real.'

'*My* choice.'

'One I can't respect,' he mocked.

'I won't stay here unless you do, Harry.'

'Oh, I will on the surface, Elizabeth. You need have no fear of any unwelcomed advances from me. It will be strictly business tomorrow and any other day I'm here.'

She should have felt relieved, but there was an aching heaviness in her stomach, a drag of physical disappointment that was not about to be easily shifted. 'In that case I'll stay,' she said flatly. Where else could she go and not be faced with Michael and Lucy? One thing she could certainly say for Harry—he had the knack of blotting them out for a while.

'Your call.' His mouth took on an ironic twist as he added, 'And do feel free to call on me if you decide to change your mind and explore a different kind of life to the one you've planned so rigidly.'

She took a deep breath to ease the tightness in her chest and said, 'Well, I'm glad we have that sorted.'

'Yes, you're a regular sorting machine, Elizabeth, everything slotted into its proper place,' he drawled as he rolled off the other side of the day bed and faced her across it. 'One day you might find there's pleasure in improper activities.'

'Not today,' she said through gritted teeth, determined not to be taunted into doing anything reckless and stupid.

'No, not today,' he agreed mockingly. 'I take it you're about to say goodnight?'

'Yes.'

'I'll fetch your cake. I wouldn't want you to go without comfort food in the lonely darkness of the night.'

The cake.

She had completely forgotten it.

Wanted to forget it now but she couldn't, not with the chef having made it especially for her. She would have to eat some of it, too, show appreciation.

Harry strode down the steps to the table that had been set for them. At his orders. She was sure of that. Hoping to sweeten her up to the point where he would slide into making a move on her. Her stomach curdled at how easy she had made it for him, and how quickly she had been caught up in the dynamic sexuality he could put out at will.

Her thighs were aquiver from having been in such intimate contact with him and her breasts were still in a state of arousal. He had excited her—almost to the point of no return—and he could probably do it again if she let him. Would he keep his word—strictly business from now on unless she gave him the green light?

He picked up the cake platter. Elizabeth realised she hadn't even moved from where she'd scrambled off the day bed. If Harry saw her still standing beside it he might think she regretted her decision. She jerked into walking, rounding the bed and heading up towards the administration office.

Harry had given her the door key after he had locked up before dinner. She dug it out of her shorts pocket, anxious to have the door open and be standing right there, ready to receive the cake from him so he had no reason to come in with it. Being alone with him in any enclosed space right now would severely stretch nerves that were already wildly agitated at having to be face to face with him, just for a few moments.

It surprised her to see guests laughing and chatting in the open bar lounge as she passed by. It had seemed so *private* on the lower decks. What if any of these people had strolled down to the beach while she and Harry... It didn't bear thinking about. Reckless, shameless...her face flamed at how very nearly she had succumbed to almost a *public* sex act.

Anger simmered as she unlocked the door, opened it and turned to take the cake platter from Harry, who had virtually caught up with her. 'Did you realise there were still people up and about when you swept me off to that bed?' she demanded accusingly.

'So what?' He arched his eyebrows at her as though she was mad.

'Oh, you don't care about anything, do you?' she

cried in exasperation and tried to snatch the platter from him.

He held on to it, forcing her to meet his gaze, a blast of hot resentment burning over her own. 'On the contrary, I care about a lot of things, Elizabeth. As to your quite unnecessary embarrassment at the thought of being observed in flagrante, this happens to be a tropical island where people drop their inhibitions and feel free to have sex wherever and whenever they want it. Using that bed under the stars for some natural pleasure in the privacy of the night would not offend anyone.'

'I'm not a guest. I'm staff,' she argued furiously.

His chin jutted with arrogant authority. 'This island is mine. I can make any rules I like for whomever I like.'

'I live by my own rules, Harry,' she flared at him. 'Now let me have the cake and let's say goodnight.'

He released the platter and stepped back, nodding mockingly as he said, 'Goodnight, Elizabeth.'

Then he strode away, back towards the beach, not giving her the chance to say another word.

She was so wound up it took several seconds for her to realise the threat of him was gone—not that he'd been threatening her. It was just how she felt with him, as though in constant danger of having her *rules* undermined or blown apart.

She quickly took the platter to the office desk, set it down and returned to lock the door, telling herself she was now safe for the night. Tomorrow...well, she would deal with tomorrow when it came.

She carried the untouched cake into the apartment, shutting herself into her own private domain. In a violent reaction to the whole stressful day, she found a knife and cut the *Happy Birthday* writing off the icing. It had been a rotten birthday. No happiness at all. She'd suffered a devastating let-down from Michael, as well as what felt like a betrayal from Lucy and persecution from Harry.

Tomorrow had to be better.

She only had to put up with Harry tomorrow.

And while that might not be a piece of cake, she would stomach it somehow.

No way was she going to break up again anywhere near Harry Finn!

CHAPTER NINE

HARRY clenched his hands into fists as he strode back down to the lower deck. The urge to fight was still coursing through him. He'd barely reined it in to bid Elizabeth a fairly civilised goodnight. He certainly didn't *feel* civilised.

Okay, he'd jumped the gun with her but she'd been right there with him. Not one other woman he'd been with had ever pulled back when both of them were fired up to have sex. Being rejected like that was an absolute first, though he probably should have been prepared for it. Elizabeth Flippence had made an art form of rejecting him over the past two years.

What were her damned rules? No mixing business with pleasure? She would have mixed it with Mickey so that didn't wash. Did she have to have a wedding ring on her finger before she'd have sex? Where was she coming from to have that kind of attitude in this day and age? A thirty-year-old virgin? Harry didn't believe it. Not with her looks.

Clearly he needed to know more about her, form another plan of attack because she was *not* going to get away from him. He didn't understand why she dug so deeply under his skin, what made her so compellingly desirable, but the buzz was there and he couldn't get rid of it. What caused him even more frustration was *knowing* she felt the same buzz around him.

It was a maddening situation.

He lifted the bottle of champagne out of the ice bucket, stepped over to the edge of the deck and poured the remaining contents onto the sand. The only thing worse than flat champagne was the flat aftermath of flattened desire. He popped the emptied bottle back in the bucket and started the long walk down the beach to the wharf where his yacht was docked.

He thought of his own birthday—thirty-three last month. Mickey had thrown him a party. They always did that for each other because their parents had and neither of them could quite let go of that golden past, though they had sold the marvellous family property on the hill overlooking Cairns because it wasn't the same—couldn't be—without their mother and father there.

He remembered the great tennis parties and pool parties his mother had organised. His and Mickey's school friends had loved coming to their place—always so much fun to be had. The fishing trips with his father had been great, too. He'd had the best childhood, best teen years, a really happy life until that black day when his father's plane went down.

This resort had still been on the drawing board then. His father had been excited about building it, showing him and Mickey the plans, talking about how he would market it. After the funeral Harry had wanted this project, wanted to be physically busy, creating something, bringing his father's vision to reality. He'd lived here, worked here until it was done, organising everything for it to be a successful enterprise.

Mickey had thrown himself into managing the franchises, needing to be busy, too, both of them wanting to feel their parents would be proud of them. It had seemed the best way to handle their grief, filling the huge hole of loss with hard absorbing work. Neither of them had been interested in managing girlfriends during that dark period, not wanting any emotional demands on them from people who had no understanding of what was driving them. The occasional night out, some casual sex…that had been enough.

Over the years neither he nor Mickey had fallen into any deep and meaningful relationships. Somehow there was always something missing, something that didn't gel, something that put them off. Occasionally they chatted about their various failures to really connect with one woman or another. It always came back to how happy their parents had been together, complementing each other, and ultimately that was what they wanted in a life partner. In the meantime they floated, docking for a while with whatever woman they felt attracted to.

Harry wondered if Lucy would last with Mickey, then chewed over his own problem of even getting a start with Elizabeth.

Why was giving in to a perfectly natural attraction such a problem to her? Why not pursue it, find out if it could lead to a really satisfying relationship? Was she so hung up on her unrequited love for Mickey that she didn't want to admit that something else could be better?

Whatever…he'd get to the bottom of her resistance and smash it, one way or another.

By the next morning Harry had cooled down enough to realise he should give Elizabeth more time to come to terms with the changes in her life. He had rushed her last night. Today he would be very *civilised*. Though not necessarily according to *her* rules.

He had breakfast on the yacht, suspecting that Elizabeth would avoid having breakfast with him in the restaurant. Undoubtedly Miss Efficiency had set her bedside alarm clock for an early hour to be up and about before any of the guests, opening the office and at her desk, ready to deal with anything that came her way. She would certainly have used the convenience of a call to the restaurant to have her breakfast delivered.

As expected, she was at her desk when Harry strolled into the administration office. He beamed a warmly approving smile at her and put a bright lilt in his voice. 'Good morning, Elizabeth.'

It forced her attention away from the computer. She pasted a tight smile on her face and returned his greeting. Her big brown eyes had no shine. They were guarded, watchful. Harry knew her brick wall was up and there would be no easy door through it. The urge to at least put a chink in her defensive armour was irresistible.

He hitched himself onto the corner of the desk, viewing her with curious interest. 'Are you a virgin, Elizabeth?'

That livened up her face, her eyes widening in incredulity and shooting sparks of outrage as she completely lost control of her voice, shrilling, 'What?' at him.

'It's a simple question,' Harry said reasonably. 'Are you a virgin, yes or no?'

'You have no right to ask me that!' she spluttered.

He shrugged. 'Why is it a problem?'

Anger shot to the surface. 'It's none of your business!'

'I guess the answer is yes since you're so sensitive about it,' he tossed at her affably.

'I am *not* sensitive about it!'

'Looks that way to me.'

She glared at him, and if her eyes had been knives they would have stabbed him in a million painful places. Harry found it wonderfully exhilarating. He'd definitely got under her skin again, regardless of how firmly she had decided to keep him out.

Her jaw tightened and he knew she was gritting her teeth as she struggled to bring herself under control. Finally she gnashed out the words 'It's just none of your business, Harry. It is totally irrelevant to this job and I'll thank you to remember that.'

'Bravo!' he said admiringly.

It confused her. 'Bravo what?'

He grinned at her. 'The rule book rules. Almost forgot it there for a moment, didn't you?'

She huffed to release some of the tension he'd raised, viewing him balefully. 'I'd appreciate it if *you* didn't forget it.'

'I do apologise for the transgression.' He made a wry grimace. 'Curiosity slipped through my usual sense of discretion. However, it does give me a better understanding of you now that I know you're a virgin. Head stuffed with romantic dreams…'

'I am *not* a virgin!' tripped out of her mouth before she could stop the wave of exasperation he'd whipped up.

He arched his eyebrows in surprise. 'You're not?'

She closed her eyes. Her mouth shut into a tight thin line. Quite clearly she hated herself for biting at his bait. Harry revelled in her discomfort. Serve her right for the discomfort she'd given him last night. And it was great to have that problem box ticked off. No virginity barrier.

Another big huff. Her eyes opened into hard, piercing slits. Shards of ice came off her tongue. 'Can we please get down to work now?'

'Jumping to it,' he said obligingly, hitching himself off the desk and rounding it to view the computer screen. 'Any bookings come in this morning?'

'Yes.' She swung her chair around to face the computer and started working the mouse. 'I think I've dealt with them correctly. If you'll check what I've done...?'

For the next half hour Harry kept strictly to business, giving Elizabeth no reason to complain about his behaviour. She had a good understanding of what was required of administration. Supply issues still had to be addressed but that could wait until later. She was so uptight he decided to give her a break, let her relax for a while.

'Before the heat of the day sets in, I'm going to call Jack Pickard to take you around the resort, show you the practical aspects of how it runs. You need to be familiar with all of it,' he said, reaching for the telephone. 'I'll stand in for you here.'

'Okay,' she answered levelly, but the relief he sensed coming from her told him exactly what she was thinking.

Escape.

Escape from the pressure of having to keep deny-ing what was undeniable…the constant sizzle of sexual chemistry between them.

Harry told himself he could wait.

Sooner or later it would come to a head and boil over.

Then he would have her.

Elizabeth took an instant liking to Jack Pickard. She probably would have liked anyone who took her away from Harry this morning but Sarah's husband was a chirpy kind of guy, nattering cheerfully about the is-land and his maintenance job—easy, relaxing company. He was short and wiry and his weather-beaten face had deep crow's-feet at the corners of his eyes from smiling a lot. His hair looked wiry, too, a mass of unruly curls going an iron-grey.

'Show you one of the vacant villas first.' He grinned at her. 'Before the new guests fly in this morning.'

'Do they all come by helicopter?' Elizabeth asked.

'Uh-uh. Most come by motor launch. We meet them at the jetty and drive them around to administration. Those that fly in land on the back beach and take the wooden walkway that leads here.'

Wooden walkways led everywhere, with flights of steps wherever they were needed. The one they took to the vacant villa ran through rainforest, the lovely green canopy of foliage above it shading them from the direct heat of the sun. On either side of them were masses of tropical vegetation—palms, vines, bamboo, hibiscus, native flowers.

The villa was situated on a hillside overlooking the

bay leading into the main beach. Its front porch had a lovely view and the breeze wafting in from the sea made it a very inviting place to sit in the deckchairs provided. Jack opened a sliding glass door and gestured for her to step inside.

The structure was split-level. Elizabeth entered a spacious living room—a comfortable lounge setting with coffee table facing a television set and CD player, a writing desk and chair, a counter along one wall containing a sink and a bar fridge. Above the counter were cupboards containing a selection of glasses for every kind of drink, bottles of spirits, plus tea and coffee-making facilities, a jar of home-made cookies and a selection of crackers to go with the cheese platter in the fridge, which also held a box of Belgian chocolates, fruit juice, beer, champagne, wine and plenty of drink mixers.

Up a few steps from the living area was a mezzanine bedroom containing a huge king-size bed, lots of pillows, plenty of cupboard space, bedside tables with lamps in the shape of dolphins. All the decor had a sea-and-beach theme, most of the furnishings in white and turquoise, knick-knacky things constructed from driftwood and coral and shells. White walls and polished floorboards completed the clean, airy look.

'There's an extensive library of books, CDs and games in the bar-lounge adjacent to the restaurant,' Jack told her. 'Guests can help themselves to whatever they like. You, too, Elizabeth.'

She smiled at him. 'That's good to know.'

Should fill in some lonely hours, she thought, once Harry was gone and she could get him out of her mind.

That *virgin* question still had her seething, as though *that* was the only possible reason for not getting her pants off for him. In hindsight, she probably should have said she was, put him right off his game. On the other hand, he might have fancied himself as teacher, giving her a first experience in sex. It was impossible to pin down anything with Harry. He could slide this way or that way at the blink of an eye. Which made him so infuriating and frustrating and...

Elizabeth clamped down on those feelings, forcing herself to focus on what she was seeing here. The bathroom was positively decadent, a shower for two, a spa bath, the walls tiled in a wavy white with turquoise feature tiles and turquoise towels. The long vanity bench held two wash basins and a pretty collection of shells. Everything in the villa was clearly designed to give guests pleasure.

'This is all fantastic,' she commented to Jack.

He nodded agreement. 'Sarah and I reckon Harry did a great job of it.'

'Harry? Surely he had an interior decorator fitting out the villas.'

'Oh, he had a professional finding the stuff he wanted, but how the villas are all decked out was his idea. His dad had an architect design how they're built. It was his vision in the first place, but after he died, Harry took on the whole project and saw it through to completion. Did a great job of marketing it, too.'

This information did not fit her view of Harry Finn as a playboy. It was disconcerting until she remembered that admirable work and talent had no relevance to how he dealt with women.

She and Jack moved on. He showed her the gym, which contained most of the popular work-out equipment, introducing her to staff she hadn't met yet. A large shed near the beach where the helicopter landed contained a desalination plant that ultimately provided fresh water for the resort. The power generator was also housed there.

'This beach faces west,' Jack said, pointing to the hill above it. 'Up there are the two pavilion villas, both of them occupied today so I can't show them to you. Their porches lead out to infinity pools that catch the sunset. Feels like there's just you and the water and the sky. They weren't on the original plan. Harry's idea to build them, make them really special.'

Elizabeth nodded. 'I noticed it cost more to stay in them.'

Jack grinned. 'Honeymoon paradise.'

As they continued the tour, chatting as they went along, Elizabeth realised her escort was extremely well skilled—electrician, plumber, carpenter, gardener—capable of turning his hand to any maintenance work.

She couldn't help remarking, 'How come you never started a business of your own, Jack? You're so well qualified.'

He grinned. 'Hated all the paperwork the government expects you to do. Reckon I got a plum job with Harry's dad, maintaining the property he had overlooking Cairns. Free cottage, good pay, all the fun of creating and being in a beautiful environment. Got the same deal here on the island with Harry. We've got a good life, Sarah and me. Can't think of anything better.'

'Then you're very lucky,' she said warmly.

'That we are.'

A contented man, Elizabeth thought, wondering if she would ever reach the same state of contentment. Not today. And not here with Harry waiting for her back at the office. It was awful to think of how tempted she had been last night to just let herself be swept up in physical sensation. It had been a long time—almost three years since her last semiserious relationship ended—but that was no reason to engage in casual sex.

She'd never been into bed-hopping. Trying guys out on a purely physical basis did not appeal to her. She needed to feel really connected to the person before taking the next step to absolute intimacy. If Harry considered that attitude a headful of romantic dreams it was because it didn't suit his playboy mentality. Bending her principles for him was not on, though she had to admit he was the sexiest man she had ever met, which made everything wretchedly difficult when she was alone with him.

Just one hour in the office this morning had been exhausting, having to use so much energy blocking out his physical impact on her. Of course, last night's wild interlude had made her even more sexually aware of him. She'd been out of her mind to let him go so far with her. Now she had to cope with that memory in his eyes as well as the memories he'd stamped on her consciousness.

On the walk back to administration, Jack started talking about Harry again, how good he had been at all sports in his teens—that was easy to imagine—and what a pity it was that the untimely death of his parents had caused him to drop them. 'Could have been a champion on any playing field,' was Jack's opinion.

Elizabeth could think of one sport Harry hadn't given up.

He was a champion flirt.

She hoped he wouldn't exercise that particular skill while she had to be with him for the rest of the day. So long as he kept to business, she should be reasonably okay. Nevertheless, it was impossible to stop her nerves twitching in agitation when Jack left her at the office door and Harry swung his chair around from the computer and smiled at her.

'Enjoy the tour?'

She smiled back, deciding to show appreciation of all he'd done here. 'You have created quite an extraordinary resort, Harry. I can't think of anything that could make it better.'

'If you do, let me know. I aim for perfection.'

Would he be the perfect lover?

Elizabeth was shocked at how that thought had slid right past her guard against *the playboy*. She hurled it out of her mind as she hitched herself onto the corner of the desk just as he had this morning, casually asking, 'Anything come in that I should know about?'

'Mickey called. He's putting the suitcase your sister packed for you on the helicopter bringing the guests today.' He gave her a quirky smile. 'Should save you from having to wash out your undies tonight.'

'That's good,' she said equably, determined not to be baited into being prickly.

'Lucy says if she's missed anything you need, send

her an email,' Harry went on. 'She'll bring it with her when she comes here with Mickey this weekend.'

Elizabeth sat in frozen suspension.

Her heart stopped.

Her lungs seized up.

Her mind stayed plugged on one horribly chilling thought.

Lucy…coming with Michael…to her island escape from them.

No escape at all!

CHAPTER TEN

Harry saw her eyes glaze. She sat completely still. He knew this was a crunch moment. He waited, silently speculating on how she would react to the bombshell when she snapped out of the shock wave.

Would pride dictate that she welcome Mickey and her sister onto the island, keeping up the pretence that seeing them together did not hurt her?

Mickey was totally unaware that Elizabeth was hung up on him. So was Lucy. Neither of them would be looking for signs of hurt. It was quite possible to get through this visit, leaving them none the wiser, especially if Elizabeth was willing to let him be the man *she* was interested in. Which had to bring them several steps closer, Harry thought, willing her to choose that path.

Alternatively, since her escape from Mickey and Lucy had just been scuttled, the island no longer represented a safe refuge for her. And Harry knew he'd gone too far too fast last night, which was certainly ruffling her feathers. She might throw in this job, walk down to the back beach, wait for the helicopter to come in and fly out on it, take a trip somewhere else, not caring what anyone thought—wipe her hands of all of them.

Except she couldn't quite.

Lucy was her sister.

Lucy depended on her to be her anchor and Elizabeth took responsibility seriously. She wasn't the type to cut free. Not completely. But she might want to for a while.

Harry needed to stop her from walking out on him. Having her here on the island was his best chance with her. It gave him time to keep challenging her, wear down her resistance, make her realise they could have something good together.

Elizabeth felt totally numb. It had been such a struggle, holding herself together in front of Michael and Lucy yesterday, a struggle coping with what Harry made her feel, a struggle learning how to manage this resort as fast as she could. Now the whole reason for so much effort, the whole reason for being here was slipping away from her.

She couldn't bear to play out yesterday's scenario with Michael and Lucy again this weekend. It was too much pretence, too much pressure, too much every-thing with Harry hanging around, ready to take ad-vantage of any weak moment, and she'd be tempted to use him again as a buffer. It was all horribly wrong and the worst part was she was trapped here—trapped by her own deceit.

If she walked out on the job after pretending to like being with Harry, how could she ever explain that to Lucy? It wouldn't make sense. Telling her the truth wasn't fair. It would cut into whatever happiness she was finding with Michael, tarnish it because it was causing her sister unhappiness, which Elizabeth knew

Lucy would never knowingly do. Underneath all her ditziness was a very caring heart.

Having taken a deep breath and slowly released it to get her lungs working again and feed some much-needed oxygen into the hopeless morass in her brain, she squared her shoulders and looked directly at Harry Finn—her rescuer and tormentor. There was no devilish twinkle in the blue eyes. They were observing her with sharp attention, alert to any give-away signs of what she was thinking and feeling.

He had demonstrated yesterday how perceptive he was, and remembering how accurately he had read the situation, Elizabeth felt a strong stab of resentment that he hadn't acted to protect her this time.

'You could have dissuaded your brother from coming, Harry,' she said accusingly.

'How?' he challenged. 'By saying you don't want him here? Mickey wants to see if you're managing okay. Both of them do.' His mouth lifted in an ironic tilt. 'I did spring the job on you, Elizabeth.'

'You could have said all the villas were taken—no ready accommodation for them,' she argued.

He shrugged. 'I'm not in the habit of telling lies. Besides, Mickey has a motor-cruiser. They'll be arriving in it and could just as easily sleep in it. A head count of guests at dinner would have told him we have two villas vacant this weekend and he might have confronted me about it, raising questions. Would you have liked to answer them?'

She grimaced, accepting there was no way out of this and there was no point in protesting the arrangements already made. 'Which villa did you put them in?' she asked flatly.

'Mickey requested a pavilion villa if available. Since one of them is vacant from Friday afternoon to Sunday afternoon, I've obliged him.'

A pavilion villa...honeymoon paradise!

She turned her head away, evading Harry's watchful gaze. Flashing through her mind were images of Michael and Lucy enjoying an intimate weekend—making love on the king-size bed, cooling off in the infinity pool, drinking champagne as they watched the sunset. It was sickening. She couldn't help thinking, *It should have been me with Michael. Me, not Lucy.*

For two years she had been dreaming of having just such a romantic weekend with him. Why couldn't he have found her as wildly attractive as he obviously found Lucy? Harry had no problem in seeing her as sexy. He would have whizzed her off to bed in no time flat. Almost had last night.

'They're not coming in until Saturday morning,' Harry said quietly. 'It will only be for one night, Elizabeth.'

As though that made it better, she thought savagely. Lucy would be parading her happiness with Michael from the moment she landed to the moment she waved goodbye, and during that two-day span it was going to be one hell of an uphill battle to keep pretending happiness with Harry.

Unless...

A wicked idea slid into her mind.

It grew, sprouting a whole range of seductive thoughts,

becoming a plan that promised a way to get through this weekend reasonably intact.

Harry would view it as a night of fun and games, the playboy triumphant. He wouldn't care about what she was using him for since he'd get what he wanted. And *she* wouldn't be hurt by it because she was the one directing the play, the one in control of what was to happen.

She could set aside her principles, be a butterfly flying free for one night. Maybe it was what she needed to do, use it as a catharsis, releasing all the emotional mess in her mind and heart and wallowing in purely physical sensation. Harry had proved last night he could drive up her excitement meter. Why not experience how far he could take it?

If it was good…if it was great…she could face Lucy and Michael without the horribly hollow sense of missing out on everything, especially since she would have already had what they were going to have and where they were going to have it. That part of it should kill off any sense of jealousy and envy, which were horribly negative feelings that she didn't want to have towards her sister. Lucy was Lucy. It wasn't her fault that Michael was totally smitten by her, and Elizabeth was not going to let *their* connection affect the close relationship she'd always had with her sister.

But she needed help from Harry to make all this stick.

His expert playboy help, smashing her mind with so much pleasure it took away the pain.

If he didn't cooperate with her plan… But he would,

wouldn't he? He wanted her to *surrender* herself to him and that was what she'd be doing.

She threw a quick glance at him. He was leaning back in the chair, apparently relaxed as he waited for her to respond to the situation. However, his gaze instantly caught hers, sharply searching for what was in her mind. There was no point in taking any evasive action. She had decided on what she wanted from him. Her own eyes watched his very keenly as she put the question which would start a new situation rolling.

'Do you still want to have sex with me, Harry?'

His eyebrows shot up in surprise. There was no instant *yes*. Elizabeth's heart pounded nervously as she waited for his reply, watching his eyes narrow speculatively. He was obviously digesting what this change from her meant.

'That's been a constant for me over quite a long time, Elizabeth,' he said slowly. 'I think the more pertinent question is do you finally realise that you want to have sex with me?'

'Yes, I do,' she answered unequivocally. 'But only if certain conditions are met.'

It had to be her plan or nothing.

His head tilted to one side. He was not rushing to accommodate her. His eyes watched her with an even higher level of intensity. Elizabeth held his gaze defiantly, determined not to budge from this stance. After a long nerve-racking silence, he casually waved a hand in an invitational gesture.

'Spell out the conditions.'

Elizabeth took a deep breath, fiercely willing him to fall in with what she wanted. 'The pavilion villa is empty on Friday night. I want it to be there. And then. The rest of this week we just keep to business.'

It took every ounce of Harry's control not to react violently, to absorb this slug to his guts and remain seated, appearing to be considering what all his instincts were savagely railing against. This wasn't about him and the chemistry between them. It was about Mickey and Lucy. In some dark twisted place in her mind, she probably wanted to pretend he was his brother, having it off in the same romantic setting where Mickey was about to take her sister.

No way would he be used as a freaking substitute!

It was a bitter blow to his ego that she should ask it of him. It showed how little she cared about what he thought, what he felt. He had encouraged her to use him as a blind to hide her angst over Mickey yesterday but to use him this far…it was brutal and he hated her for corrupting what they could have had together.

Hate…

He'd never felt that towards anyone. Why did she get to him so strongly? It was crazy. He should wipe her off his slate right now, find some other woman who thought he was worth having, who'd be sweetly giving, at least for a while.

Except…damn it! He still wanted the ungettable Elizabeth Flippence!

Have her and be done with it, he thought savagely.

He could use her scenario his way, add his own conditions, make her so hyped up with sexual awareness, Mickey would be blotted right out of her mind and he'd be *the man*—the only man she'd be conscious of all through the night.

She was patiently waiting for his agreement, her eyes boring into his, boldly challenging his desire for her. He sensed that some essential part of her had clicked off. She'd moved beyond caring what he said or did. The equation was simple. He either went with her plan or that was the end of anything personal ever happening between them.

'Okay,' he said calmly. 'I'll make arrangements for us to occupy the pavilion villa on Friday night.'

She nodded, the expression in her eyes changing to a knowing mockery. She had labelled him a playboy on quite a few occasions so he knew what she was thinking—a night of sex would always be amenable to him, regardless of why it was offered.

He decided to live up to her idea of him.

'As long as you'll fit in with some conditions I have in mind,' he said with a quirky little smile.

That shot some tension through her. 'Like what?' she asked sharply.

'Like not saying no to anything I want to do.'

She frowned. 'I won't do kinky stuff, Harry.'

'I'm not into sado-masochism, domination or bondage,' he assured her. 'But I don't particularly care for clinical intimacy, either. A bit of sexy fun is more to my liking.'

'What do you consider sexy fun?' she asked suspiciously.

He grinned. 'How about you wear that butterfly blouse again, without a bra underneath? Be *wicked* for me.'

Hot colour raced up her neck and scorched her

cheeks. Harry didn't care if she connected the butterfly blouse to her Mickey fantasy. He'd had a few fantasies about it himself.

'And team it with a bikini bottom with side strings
that I can undo with a flick of the fingers,' he added.
'Some bright colour that goes with your butterfly. I'm
sure you'll be able to find one in the boutique.'

She rolled her eyes. 'I didn't realise you needed provocative clothes to turn you on, Harry.'

He shrugged. 'I don't. I'd simply like you to look
and be accessible for once. I've been hitting a brick
wall with you for two years. *Accessible* has a lot of appeal to me.'

Her cheeks heated up again, making her eyes look
glittery. 'Do you have anything else in mind?' she
clipped out.

He waved an airy hand. 'Let me think about it. You
have rather sprung this on me. If I'm only to ever get
one night with Elizabeth Flippence…' He cocked an
eyebrow at her. 'That is the plan, isn't it?'

'Yes' hissed out between her teeth.

'Then I want it to be a night to remember. Something
extra special. The most sensual trip of a lifetime. I need
to let my imagination work on it for a while.'

'Fine!' she snapped, and hopped off the desk, adopt-
ing a brisk and businesslike air. 'You have three and
a half days for your imagination to flourish. Since we
have the essentials settled, let's get on with resort management.'

He could almost hear the steel click in her mind. In
his experience of women, Elizabeth Flippence was defi-

nitely something else. But she would soften for him on Friday night. He'd make damned sure she did!

He rose from the chair. 'I've brought up the file on all our suppliers on the computer. Go through it. Write down any questions you have and I'll be back later to answer them. Okay?'

'Okay.'

Her relief that he was leaving her to work alone was palpable.

He strode quickly out of the office, needing time apart from her, too. He was still churned up inside. A work-out in the gym should rid him of the violent energy that was currently coursing through him.

Three and a half days...

He wondered if he'd feel free of this mad obsession with Elizabeth Flippence after Friday night. He really was beginning to hate how much she got to him. Probably she hated how he got to her, too.

Was having sex the answer to settling everything?

Impossible to know beforehand.

Afterwards...

That should tell him whether to persist with trying to form a relationship with this infuriating woman or let her go. It all hung on one night and—by God!—he was going to make the most of it!

CHAPTER ELEVEN

ELIZABETH found herself rebelling against any regret over her decision to take Harry Finn as her lover for one night. It might be stupidly reckless of her to have sex with him. There would probably be consequences she wouldn't like but she refused to care about what could happen next. Just for once she would be totally irresponsible, except for the important issue of birth control, which was impossible to ignore.

She tackled Harry on that point as soon as he returned to the office. 'I'm not on the pill,' she stated bluntly. 'Will you take care of contraception on Friday night?'

'No problem,' he blithely replied. 'And incidentally, I've thought of another condition.'

Elizabeth tensed. If it was too outlandish…

'When we're in the villa, I want to call you Ellie.'

She was startled into asking, 'Why?'

He shrugged. 'A childhood name, conjuring up the age of innocence. I like that idea.'

'I'm not innocent, Harry.' Surely he couldn't still be thinking she was a virgin.

'Nevertheless, it's what I want. Okay?'

She shook her head over his whimsy but...what did it matter? 'If it pleases you,' she said carelessly.

'It *will* please me,' he asserted, then smiled at her. 'I also want to please you. If you think of anything you'd particularly enjoy on the night, let me know. Your wish is my command.'

'I prefer to leave everything in your very capable hands, Harry,' she said dryly, not wanting to think too much about it.

But she did over the next couple of days. And nights. It was weird how completely distracted she was from thinking about Michael and Lucy. The now-certain prospect of having sex with Harry made her more physically aware of him than ever, and the anticipation of it was zinging through her almost continually.

He didn't come up with any more conditions, didn't raise the subject at all, keeping their time together on a strictly business basis, as she had requested. Somehow that contributed to a sense of secretive intimacy, knowing what they were going to do when Friday night came but not mentioning it.

She found a red string bikini in the boutique and bought it, deciding it suited the occasion since she was acting like a scarlet woman, taking a lover she didn't love. Oddly enough she felt no guilt about doing it. Somehow it represented the kind of freedom she probably wouldn't feel with someone she did love. There were no dreams to be smashed, no expectations of sharing a life together. It was just a night of sexy fun with Harry Finn.

On Friday morning, Harry announced he had business in Port Douglas and would be gone for most of the day. He printed a notice that the office would be closed at 6:00 p.m. today and stuck it on the door. 'Go on up to the villa then,' he instructed. 'I'll be there. Don't want to miss the sunset,' he added with a smile that sparkled with anticipation.

'I'll bring a bottle of champagne from the bar,' she said, remembering how she had envisaged the scene with Michael and Lucy.

'No need. I'll have one ready to open.'

'What about food? Shall I order…?'

He shook his head. 'I have that organised, as well. You only have to bring yourself, Elizabeth.' He raised his hand in a farewell salute. 'Bye for now. Have a nice day.'

'You, too,' she replied, smiling back at him.

It was a genuine smile, not the slightest bit forced. Not having to keep her guard up against him all the time had made her more relaxed in his company. She had nothing to guard against since she was giving in to what he wanted from her. And if she was completely honest with herself, she wanted it, too.

He was a sexy man.

He made her feel sexy.

She was looking forward to having this experience with Harry tonight. She probably would have hated herself if she'd been seduced into it, but the sense of empowerment that came with having decided on it herself made all the difference.

Nevertheless, when six o'clock came and she was on her way to the pavilion villa, her nerves started getting very jumpy. She had never had an assignation like this before. It was totally out of character for her. But there was no turning back from it, she told herself fiercely. Everything was in place to take this step, and take it she would.

Harry was standing by the infinity pool, looking out to sea. He wore only a pair of board shorts, printed with white sailing ships on a blue background. She paused on the last step leading to the open deck, her heart skittering at the sight of so much naked masculinity—broad shoulders tapering to lean hips, bronze skin gleaming over taut, well-defined muscles. He had the perfect male physique and it tugged on some deeply primitive female chord in Elizabeth.

It was okay to feel attracted to him, she told herself.

It was natural.

On the physical level.

As though sensing her presence he swung around, his gaze instantly targeting her, piercing blue eyes raking her from head to toe, making her hotly conscious that she was still in the island uniform. She quickly held up the carry bag holding the clothes he'd requested and gabbled an explanation.

'I've just finished at the office, Harry. I thought I'd take a shower here.'

He nodded. 'Make it fast. The sun is already low in the sky.'

The glass doors to the villa were open. The layout inside was similar to the one Jack had shown her. She headed straight for the bathroom, anxious not to be found wanting in keeping to her side of their deal. One minute to turn on the shower taps and strip off her clothes, two minutes under the refreshing beat of the water, one minute to towel herself dry, one minute to pull on the red bikini bottom and put on the butterfly blouse, fastening only one button to keep it more or less together.

Accessible was what he'd asked for. He couldn't say she wasn't delivering it. The shape of her braless breasts and the darker colour of her areolae were certainly visible through the sheer fabric, and her nipples were already stiffening, poking at the butterfly wings. She hoped he had the champagne ready. Carrying this much accessibility off with any air of confidence required some alcoholic fortification.

It was only on her exit from the bathroom that Elizabeth caught a waft of nose-teasing scent coming from the mezzanine level. She looked up to where the king-size bed was waiting for intimate activity. Candles—from small to large—lit a path to it. A long sniff identified their fragrance as frangipani, the flower most reminiscent of tropical nights.

Harry must have set them up. Had he bought them in Port Douglas today? Why go to the trouble? This was not a night of romance. Did he want her to imagine it was? And why should he want that? She didn't understand. But it was…nice of him to do it.

She was smiling over what she had decided was playboy fun as she walked out onto the deck. 'Do you treat all your women to scented candles?' she asked.

He was about to pop the cork of a bottle of champagne. He paused to give her a very long, all-encompassing look that made her extremely conscious of every female part of her body. 'No. I simply associate the scent of flowers with butterflies, Ellie. An innocent pleasure,' he said softly.

His use of her childhood name instantly reminded her of how he'd linked it to an age of innocence. She wished she knew what was going on in his mind. It seemed to be off on some quirky journey tonight.

He popped the cork and reached for one of the flute glasses sitting on the low table that served the sun-lounges. A plate of lush fresh strawberries was placed beside the ice bucket that awaited the opened bottle. As he poured the champagne, Elizabeth saw that a couple of crushed strawberries lay in the bottom of the glass, making it a very sensual drink.

'Enjoy,' he said as he passed it to her, his smile inviting her to share all sorts of pleasure with him.

'Thank you, Harry,' she said appreciatively, grateful that he wasn't grabbing at her *accessibility* or doing anything off-putting.

He waved her to one of the sun-lounges. 'Relax. Looks like being a spectacular sunset.'

She sat on the lounge, not quite ready to put herself on display by stretching out on it. Harry poured champagne for himself, then clicked her glass with his. 'To our first night together,' he said, smiling as he dropped onto the adjacent lounge, propped himself against the backrest, lifted his long legs onto the cushioned base and gazed out to a sea that was shimmering like polished crystal.

It released Elizabeth's inhibitions about doing the same. This villa certainly had a prime position for viewing the sunset. The subtle colour changes in the sky would challenge any artist—impossible to capture on canvas, she thought. It truly was lovely, just watching it and sipping strawberry-flavoured champagne.

'Have you ever been to Broome?' Harry asked.

'No.' Broome was right across the country on the coast of Western Australia. She knew it was world famous for its pearls but she'd never had any reason to go there. 'Why do you ask?'

'Sunset there is amazing. People drive down on the beach, set up their barbecues, bring eskies loaded with cold drinks, play music, sit back and enjoy Mother Nature's display for them. They completely tune out from news of the world and just live in the moment.'

He rolled the words out in a low, almost spellbinding tone that was soothing, like a physical caress that eased the last threads of tension in Elizabeth's body.

'We don't do enough of it…living in the moment,' he went on in the same seductive murmur. 'Let's try to do that tonight, Ellie. No yesterdays…no tomorrows… just each moment as it comes.'

'Yes,' she agreed, happy with the idea.

They sipped their champagne in silence for a while, watching the sun slowly disappear below the horizon.

'My parents used to do this…have a sundowner together at the end of the day,' Harry said, slanting her a reminiscent little smile. 'What about yours, Ellie? Do they have a special time to themselves?'

She shook her head. 'My mother died of cancer when I was nineteen. I haven't seen my father since the funeral. He's a miner and living with some other woman in Mt Isa. It was never much of a marriage. Mum more or less brought Lucy and me up by herself.'

Harry frowned at her. 'Your father doesn't care about you?'

She grimaced. 'I think we were responsibilities he

didn't really want. Mostly when he came home on leave from the mine, he'd get drunk and we'd stay out of his way.'

'What about when your mother became ill?'

'He came home less. Didn't want to be faced with what was happening to Mum. He said it was up to me and Lucy to take care of her.'

'That must have been hard,' Harry said sympathetically.

'Yes. Though it was a special time, too. Like you said…living in the moment…because the last moment could come at any time so every good moment was precious.'

'At least you knew that,' he murmured, nodding understandingly before throwing her a wry little smile. 'Mickey and I…we didn't realise how precious those good moments were until after our parents were gone.'

'I guess that kind of sudden death is harder to come to terms with,' she said thoughtfully.

'I don't know. We didn't have to see them suffer.' He shook his head. 'You were only nineteen. How did you manage?'

'I was at business college so I could be home quite a lot. Lucy dropped out of school to look after Mum when I couldn't be there.'

'Did she pick up her education again at a later date?'

'No.' Impossible to explain that school had never been easy for Lucy. She didn't like people knowing about her dyslexia. 'She didn't want to, didn't need it to get work.'

'But without qualifications…'

'Lucy is adept at winning her way into jobs.'

'While you're the one with the steady career. That's why she calls you her anchor.'

Elizabeth heaved a sigh. 'This is a weird conversation to be having when we're supposed to be enjoying a night of sexy fun, Harry.'

'Oh, I don't know. I'd call this an intimate conversation. We have all night to get to physical intimacy. We've been on the fringes of each other's worlds for two years. I think I know Elizabeth fairly well—' he rolled his head towards her, giving her his quirky smile '—but I want to get to know Ellie tonight.'

'That's yesterday, Harry. My childhood,' she pointed out. 'It's not living in the moment.'

The blue eyes gathered the piercing intensity that always gave her discomfort. 'Ellie is inside you right now,' he said softly. 'She's the foundation of the woman you are. She directs your life.'

'That's ridiculous!' she protested.

'Is it? You're the older child, the one who helped your mother, the one who protected your sister, the one who carried the responsibility of arranging everything when your mother was ill, when she died, the one who wants a man in her life who will never do to her what her father did to her mother, to his children.'

He was digging at her again—digging, digging, digging! In a burst of frustration, Elizabeth swung her legs off the lounge, sat up straight and glared at him. 'I did not come up here to be psychoanalysed, Harry.'

He swung his legs down to the deck in a more leisurely fashion, his eyes holding hers in glittering challenge. 'No, you didn't. Ellie wanted to break out of the Elizabeth cocoon and fly free for once, didn't she?'

She hated how he could connect everything up and be so damned right about everything! It made her feel naked in far more than the physical sense. In a purely defensive action, she snatched the bottle of champagne from the ice bucket, intending to refill her glass.

Harry took it from her. 'Allow me.'

She did, letting him pour the champagne, though it made her feel he was taking control away from her, which wasn't how she'd planned to have this encounter with Harry. 'Do you probe into the lives of all your one-night stands?' she asked waspishly.

He cocked an eyebrow at her. 'What makes you think my life consists of a series of one-night stands?'

'The way you flirt. Michael said you flirt with every woman. It isn't just me.'

'Flirting can be fun. It can be enjoyable to both parties. In a way it's a search for that magic click which will lead to bed, but that doesn't happen very often. When it has, I can't recall one instance when it only lasted for one night. You've assumed something about me that isn't true, Ellie.'

'Well, this is only going to be for one night,' she insisted, needing to regain the control that seemed to be sliding out of her grip.

'Why?'

'Because...' She floundered, not wanting to say the whole idea had erupted from the fact his brother was going to be here with her sister and she hadn't really looked beyond that painful circumstance. 'I just don't want to get heavily involved with you, Harry,' she said evasively, wishing he would simply accept what she'd offered him.

'Why not? You think I'll let you down?'

Yes was on the tip of her tongue but he didn't give her time to say it.

'Did I let you down when you needed to cover up your distress over Mickey attaching himself to your sister? Did I let you down when you needed an escape from them? Have I let you down in fulfilling your requests this week, meeting what you wanted? Haven't I shown I care about how you feel, Ellie?'

She couldn't deny any of that, yet... 'It...it fitted into your own agenda,' she blurted out.

'Which is?' He bored in.

Her head was spinning from the pressure he was subjecting her to with all his questions. She had to seize on the one point she was certain of, drive it home. She set her glass on the table, stood up, challenging him to get on with what he'd been aiming for all along.

'Having me like this! *Accessible!*' She threw the words at him. 'So why don't you stop talking and take what you want with me?'

Anger burned through Harry. He'd tried to reach out to her, tried to find a special meeting ground with her. She just kept closing her mind, shutting the door on him, keeping him out. He set his glass down, rose to his feet and hurled her confrontation right back in her face.

'You want to be treated like a piece of meat instead of a woman I care about? Fine! Just stand there and let me oblige!'

CHAPTER TWELVE

HARRY saw her eyes dilate with shock.

He didn't care.

She'd invited him to take her without caring and his level of frustration with her was so high, turning away from following through on her invitation was beyond him. His hands lifted and cupped the breasts they'd wanted to cup in Mickey's office days ago. He fanned her rock-hard nipples with his thumbs. The soft sheer fabric of the butterfly blouse gave a sensual sexiness to feeling her like this, causing a rush of hot blood to his loins.

He wanted her.

He'd been burning up for her all week.

Her eyes refocused on his, still slightly glazed but clearing as she sucked in a deep breath.

Yes, look at me! he thought savagely. *Know it's me and not Mickey!*

He undid the button holding her blouse together and spread the edges apart, wanting to feel the naked lushness of her breasts against his chest. His arms slid around her waist, scooping her into firm contact with him. It felt good. It felt great.

'Harry…' It was a husky gasp.

He didn't want to hear anything she had to say. His name on her lips shot a soaring wave of triumph through him—*his* name, not Mickey's—and he was hell-bent on keeping it stamped on her consciousness. His mouth crashed onto hers, intent on a blitzkrieg invasion that would blast any possible thought of his brother from entering her head.

To his surprise her tongue started duelling with his and a wild elation burst through his brain when her hands clutched his head, not to tear them apart but to hold them together, her fingers kneading his scalp, her mouth working to meet and escalate the passion surging through him.

He pressed one hand into the sexy pit of her back, forcing her body into contact with his erection as he pulled the bikini string at her hip apart, changed hands to do the same with the other, whipped the scrap of fabric from between her legs. The lovely female curves of her naked bottom were sensual dynamite, igniting his need for her to the brink of explosion.

He tore his hands off them to sweep the blouse from her shoulders and pull it off her arms. It broke her hold on his head, broke the marauding madness of their kissing, but it had to be done. She was fully naked now, totally *accessible* to anything he wanted with her.

He bent and scooped her off her feet, holding her crushed to his chest as he strode from the deck, into the villa, up the steps to the mezzanine level. He tumbled her onto the king-size bed, snatched up the contraceptive sheath he'd laid ready on the bedside table, discarded his board shorts in double-quick time, pulled on the sheath and leapt onto the bed, rolling her straight into his embrace, not allowing any sense of separation to strike any doubts about what they were doing in her mind.

Their mouths locked again, driving passion to fever pitch. Her body was arching into his, explicitly needful. He barely controlled the urge to zero in to the ultimate intimacy with her. Only the bitter recollection of her *one night* insistence forced him to a different course of action. If this was all there was to be between them he'd satisfy every desire she'd ever stirred in him—eat her all up so he could spit her out afterwards, not be left fantasising over what he could have done.

He wrenched his mouth from hers, trailed hotly possessive kisses down her lovely long neck, tasted the tantalising hollow at the base of her throat, slid lower to feast on her sensational breasts, swirling his tongue around her provocative nipples, sucking on them, devouring them, taking his fill of her luscious femininity, revelling in the little moans vibrating from her throat, the twist of her fingers tangling with his hair.

He reached down to part the soft folds of her sex, his own fingers sliding, searching, finding the excited wetness that gave him easy entry to stroke the excitement to a much-higher level. She cried out, her body arching again, her need growing in intensity. He moved lower, determined on driving her crazy for him.

He spread the folds apart to expose the tight bud of her clitoris and licked it, slowly teasing at first, then faster, faster until she was writhing, screaming for him, begging, her legs encircling him, feet beating a drum of wild wanting. He surged up to take the ultimate plunge, but the savage need inside him demanded a last absolute surrender from her.

Her head was thrashing from side to side. He held it still. 'Look at me!' he commanded.

She blinked and looked but there was no real focus in her eyes.

'Say my name!'

'What?' It was a gasp of confusion.

'Say my name!'

'Har...ry...' It was a weak waver of sound.

'Say it again!'

'Harry, Harry, Harry...' she cried hysterically. 'Please...'

'You want me?'

'Ye-s-s-s.' She beat at his shoulders with tightly clenched fists. 'I'll kill you if you don't...'

He silenced her with a deep, thrusting kiss as he propelled his flesh into hers. When he lifted his head, the animal groan of satisfaction from her throat rang jubilant bells in his ears. She clutched his buttocks, trying to goad him into a fast rhythm, but he wanted the excitement to build and build, not explode all at once. He started slowly, revelling in her eagerness for him, the convulsive little spasms that told him she was totally engaged in feeling him—*him*, not Mickey.

He felt her creaming around him and couldn't keep controlling the rampantly growing need of his own body. It overtook his mind, oblivious to everything but the physical scream to reach climax, releasing the fierce tension raging through every muscle of his body. It pumped from him in a glorious burst of ecstatic satisfaction, and with all tension draining away, he rolled onto his side, pulling her with him, wanting to hang on to the sense of intimate togetherness as long as he could.

She didn't attempt any move away from him. Maybe she was drained of all energy, too. Whatever...she left her legs entwined with his, their bodies pressed close, her head tucked under his chin. He stroked her hair, enjoying the soft silky texture of it, thinking he still had the freedom to touch. He wondered how she was going to act for the rest of the night. Would Ellie emerge and see him for the man he was, or would Elizabeth stick to her guns?

He couldn't call it.

He told himself he didn't care.

At least he had the satisfaction of making her want him with every fibre of her being, if only for one night.

Elizabeth didn't want to move. It felt unbelievably good, cuddled up with Harry, having her hair stroked. Her mind drifted to her childhood, sitting on her mother's lap, head resting just like this while her hair was stroked lovingly. No one else had ever done it. She'd always been the one to comfort Lucy, not the other way around. It was weird, feeling comforted by Harry but...she didn't want to move.

She liked being naked with him, too, the warm flesh contact, the sense of his male strength holding her safe. It was so nice and peaceful after the storm of incredible sensation. Having sex with Harry...her mind was still blown by it...just totally unimaginable before experiencing it. She'd never tipped so utterly out of control, never been taken to such peaks of exquisite pleasure-pain, and the sheer ecstasy of floating in the aftermath of one climax after another…well, that had certainly set the bar for how fantastic sex with the right man could be.

Though she hadn't thought Harry was the right man in any other respect…or…might he be?

Maybe she had been a bit too quick to judge, misreading his character. Or maybe she was just being influenced by how *right* he was in bed for her. Most probably he was the best action man on that front for every woman he took to bed. Just because this had been special to her didn't make it special to him. But she was still glad she'd had this with Harry.

'Are you okay?' he murmured caringly.

She sighed contentedly. 'Very okay, thank you.'

'Then let's go take a shower. Once we're done there we can get in the pool and cool off.'

She *was* hot and sticky. 'Good idea,' she said.

The shower was more than big enough for two and Elizabeth was in no hurry using it this time. She enjoyed soaping Harry's great body, touching him intimately, letting him do the same to her.

'Having fun?'

The wry note in his voice made her look up. There was no amusement twinkling in the vivid blue eyes. The mocking glint in them dried up the pleasure she had been feeling, sending a chill through her as she remembered her taunt about having a night of sexy fun, rejecting having any deeper involvement with him, virtually dismissing him as a person of no account in her life. He'd been so angry—*shockingly* angry. She'd forgotten that, her mind swamped by so much else.

Instinctively she reached up to touch his cheek in an

apologetic appeal. 'I was taking pleasure in you, Harry. I thought you were taking pleasure in me.'

For a moment his mouth took on an ironic twist. Then he bent his head and kissed her, a long sensual kiss that swallowed up any worry about him still being angry with her.

Finishing off in the infinity pool was another sensual pleasure, the water like cool silk caressing her skin. 'Just stay there,' Harry instructed as he heaved himself out. 'I'll light the torches to keep the insects away and bring out the oysters with some chilled wine.'

'Oysters!' She laughed. 'I don't think I need an aphrodisiac, Harry.'

He stopped. His shoulders squared and she saw his back muscles tense. He half turned to face her, a cutting look in his eyes that ripped through the amusement in hers. 'I'm not into playboy tricks, Elizabeth. I simply remembered you liked them at your birthday lunch.'

That coldly spoken *Elizabeth* slapped her with the realisation that she was offending him every time she painted him as a playboy. Perhaps even insulting him. He'd told her straight out that the label was wrong in his eyes. Had she been doing him an injustice all this time? What hard evidence did she actually have that he used women lightly? None!

There was a sitting shelf at one end of the pool, and she settled on it, still enjoying the soft ripple of the water around her dangling legs as she thought back over the two years Harry had been dipping into her life while she'd been working for his brother. When he'd first walked into her office he'd emanated a megawatt attraction that had put her in such a tizzy physically she had instantly mistrusted and disliked his power to do that to her.

She'd reasoned that a man with so much personal magnetism was very likely to stray from any relationship since other women would always be eyeing him over, wanting a chance with him, especially when he was both wealthy and sexy. Determined not to go anywhere near that playing field, she had kept a rigid guard against his insidious assaults on her armour.

Now it felt as though she had prejudiced herself against a man who might well be worth knowing in a deeper sense than she had ever believed possible. Could he actually fulfil everything she had been looking for? His brother had definitely been more the type of character that appealed to her—solid, responsible—not dangerous like Harry. Yet Michael had not seen what he wanted in her. And was Harry really dangerous, or was that a false perception on her part?

She watched him emerge from the villa and stroll across the deck towards her, carrying a platter of oysters, a bottle of wine and two fresh glasses. He'd tucked a white towel around his waist. The sky had darkened and the flickering light of the torches he'd lit at the corners of the deck was not bright enough for her to see the expression in his eyes. Was he still angry with her?

'Shall I get out?' she asked.

'Not if you don't want to,' he answered with a careless shrug. 'I can serve you just as easily there.'

'The water's lovely.'

'Then stay.'

He set the platter on the deck, sat on the edge of the

pool and proceeded to open the bottle of wine and fill the glasses.

'I do like oysters, Harry. Thank you for remembering,' she said, hoping to erase the *aphrodisiac* remark.

He handed her the glass of white wine with a droll little smile. 'I remembered your sister saying you loved chilli mud crab, too. I know a restaurant in Port Douglas that specialises in that dish so I had it cooked for you and it's waiting in the microwave to be heated up when you want it.'

She stared at him, horribly shamed by his caring and generosity when she had treated him so meanly, using him as a distraction, even to going to bed with him in this villa because of Michael bringing Lucy here.

'I'm sorry,' she blurted out.

He frowned. 'Sorry about what?'

'My whole attitude towards you. It's been uncaring and bitchy and…and soured by things that you weren't even a part of. I haven't been fair to you, Harry. I've never been fair to you and I don't know why you're being so nice to me because I don't deserve it.' Tears suddenly welled into her eyes and she quickly tried to smear them away with the back of her hand. 'I'm sorry. I'm all messed up and I can't help myself.'

'It's okay,' he said soothingly. 'Just take a few deep breaths and let it all go. Life is a bitch sometimes. The trick is to get past the bad bits. I've been trying to help you do that, Ellie.'

Ellie… The soft caring way her childhood name rolled off his tongue brought another spurt of tears to her eyes and screwed her up inside, stirring up the craven wish for someone to take care of her. She'd been taking care of herself and Lucy for so long, she needed someone to simply be there for her. But she couldn't expect Harry to keep doing that. She didn't know how far his kindness would stretch. What she could do was bask in it for a little while.

It took quite a few deep breaths to bring herself under control enough to manage a smile at him. 'Thank you for helping me.'

'You do deserve to have nice things done for you,' he said seriously. 'Everyone does. It makes the world a happier place. My mother taught me that. She was brilliant at it.'

She sipped the wine he had poured for her, remembering Sarah Pickard's description of Yvette Finn—*a sunny nature, radiating a joy in life that infected everyone around her.* 'Sarah said you're like your mother,' she remarked, starting to reappraise the man in a completely different light to how she had previously perceived him.

He gave a wry shake of his head. 'A hard act to follow, but I try.'

'Tell me about her,' she said impulsively, wanting to understand where Harry was coming from.

He made an indecisive gesture. 'Where to start?'

'Start with how your father met her,' she encouraged.

He laughed. 'In hospital. He'd broken his leg and Mum was the only nurse who wouldn't let him be grumpy.'

'She was an ordinary common nurse?' It surprised her, having imagined that Franklyn Finn would have married some beautiful accomplished socialite.

Harry shook his head. 'I don't think anyone would

have said she was ordinary. All the patients loved her, my father included. He always considered himself extremely privileged that she learned to love him back. It took him quite some time to win her.'

'She didn't like him at first?'

'It wasn't that. She wasn't sure about how she would fit into his life. Dad was a seriously driven guy. In the end, she made up a set of rules for how their marriage could work and he had to promise to keep to them.'

'Did he?'

'Never wavered from them. She was the light of his life and he was never going to let that light go out.' He grimaced. 'In a way, I guess it was a kind fate that they died together. They were so tied to each other.'

It must have been a wonderful marriage, Elizabeth thought, wishing she could have one like it. Her own mother hadn't known much happiness in hers and the end of her life had certainly not been kind, though she and Lucy had done their best to ease the pain of it. 'I always thought Lucy could have made a great nurse,' she murmured, remembering how good she had been at cheering up their mother.

'She could have become one if she'd wanted to,' Harry remarked.

'No' slipped out before she could stop it.

'Why not? She could have gone back to school….'

'Lucy was never good at exams,' she prevaricated. Her dyslexia made it impossible for her to pass them. She was smart enough to pick up anything as an apprentice and she had a great memory, but examinations that required reading and writing within a set time simply couldn't be done. 'I don't think she had the head for study after Mum died,' she added to put him off pursuing the point. 'She was only seventeen and she took it hard, Harry.'

'Understandable,' he said sympathetically.

She sipped some more of the wine and eyed the platter of oysters. 'I think I'm ready to eat now.'

He laughed. 'Help yourself.'

'I'll get out first.'

Harry quickly rose to his feet, grabbing a towel to dry her off and wrap around her. She didn't try to take it from him and didn't protest his action when he finished up tucking it around her waist, leaving her breasts bare. 'They're too beautiful to cover up,' he said with a smile.

'I'm glad you think so,' she said a little shyly.

Exhilaration zinged through Harry. She'd dropped all the barriers. There was no rejection in her eyes, no guard up against him. And it remained like that for the rest of the evening, no bitchy barbs slung at him, no hiding what she thought or felt about anything, no shutting him out.

She might not have forgotten all about Mickey but she had definitely put his brother aside and was actively taking pleasure in finding connections with him—connections beyond the purely physical. The sexual chemistry was still there, of course, simmering between them, heightened by their newly intimate knowledge of each other, but Harry was encouraged to believe this could actually be the beginning of a relationship that might become very special.

He wasn't driven to carry her off to bed in a fury of frustration a second time. She happily walked with him and they both indulged in slow, sensual lovemaking—a sweet pleasuring of each other that was intensely satisfying to Harry. No way was this going to be a one-night stand. He wouldn't accept that. Elizabeth Flippence had opened up to him and he liked it too much to let her slip away from him.

Tomorrow he would see if her attachment to Mickey had been broken.

He wanted it broken.

It had to be broken.

CHAPTER THIRTEEN

A WOMAN I care about...

Those words spoken last night kept running through Elizabeth's mind all morning, keeping any anxiety over coming face to face with Michael and Lucy again at bay. She added up all the caring from Harry and realised no other man in her life had done as much for her—helping, comforting, pleasuring, answering her needs.

It couldn't be just about having sex with her.

There had been genuine concern in his eyes when he'd asked, 'Are you going to be okay today?' before leaving her at the office door after their night at the pavilion villa.

She'd assured him that she would be and he'd added, 'I'll be on hand.'

Ready to run interference if she needed it, as he had last Monday.

It felt really good to have him caring about her—someone she could depend on to get her through this weekend without too much heartache. Oddly enough, she wasn't feeling any heartache at all over Michael wanting Lucy, although seeing them together again might strain her current sense of being able to set them at an emotional distance.

Harry was to meet them at the jetty and transport them to the administration centre. Elizabeth felt reasonably confident about handling their queries about how well she was coping with management responsibilities. Lucy, of course, would angle for a private conversation with her, but she didn't think that would trouble her too much. She no longer felt so shattered over her lost dreams.

A few guests dropped into the office to check on arrangements they'd made for diving expeditions. There were inquiries about bookings to be answered. A couple of beach picnics had to be sorted out with the chef. Sarah Pickard came by, ostensibly to put in an order for new towels, but her eyes shone with lively curiosity about this new development between Harry and his stand-in manager.

Probably all the staff on the island knew about it by now since the villa had to be cleaned this morning, ready for Michael and Lucy. Elizabeth had decided it didn't matter but she certainly wasn't going to talk about her private life to anyone.

'Harry said it's your sister coming with Mickey today,' Sarah remarked.

'Yes,' Elizabeth answered briefly.

'That's nice.'

Elizabeth smiled. 'Yes, it is.'

'When did they meet?'

'Lucy came into the Cairns office to see me and they clicked. Simple as that,' she said airily.

'And Harry, of course, met you when he went to see Mickey.'

'Yes.'

Realising that Elizabeth was not about to be chatty, Sarah backed off, only tossing out the comment, 'Well, it's all very interesting,' as she left the office.

It wasn't interesting so much as complicated, Elizabeth thought. She didn't know if these connections were likely to lead anywhere good for either Lucy or herself. Two brothers who were close, two sisters who were close, the work situation—if things started going wrong, there could be a nasty ripple effect.

She remembered Lucy's blithe comment when Harry had been ordering their cocktails last Monday— *wouldn't it be great if we ended up together...all happy families!* Possibly it could be great if it worked out like that but Elizabeth wasn't counting on it. It was far too early to think the possibility was high.

Lucy slid out of relationships almost as fast as she started them.

As for herself and Harry, she couldn't even call it a relationship yet. All she could really say for certain was that her stance against him had been substantially shifted. And he was fantastic in bed!

It was almost midday when he called from the jetty to say Mickey's motor-launch was about to dock. Her nerves instantly started jangling, mocking any idea that she could breeze through this meeting with no angst at all. She fiercely told herself the important thing was to keep her composure, regardless of what she was feeling.

Lucy was hugging Michael's arm when Harry led them into the office—the woman in possession and obviously loving having this man in tow. Her skin was glowing, her eyes were shining and the smile on her face beamed brilliant happiness. Elizabeth's heart contracted at this evidence that her sister was over-the-moon in love.

'This island is fabulous, Ellie,' she cried. 'What a great place to work!'

'Tropical paradise,' Elizabeth responded, pasting a smile on her face and moving from behind the desk to greet them appropriately.

Lucy released Michael's arm to rush forward and give her a hug. 'Are you loving it?' she asked, her eyes bright with curiosity about the situation, which, of course, included Harry.

'Not too much, I hope,' Michael semigrowled in the background.

'It's been quite a change,' she said dryly, flicking him a sharply assessing look.

Somehow he was more handsome than ever, his face relaxed in a friendly way, his very male physique shown off in casual clothes—smartly tailored shorts in a blue-and-grey check teamed with a royal blue sports shirt. He still had the impact of an alpha man scoring ten out of ten, but she wasn't feeling it so personally anymore. He belonged to her sister now.

'A good one, I hope,' Harry slid in, drawing her attention to him.

Another alpha man—no doubt about it now—and the memory of last night's intimacy caused a wave of warm pleasure to roll through her. The piercing blue eyes were digging at her again, but she didn't resent it this time. He *cared* about what she was feeling.

'Yes,' she answered with a smile, wanting to allay his concern for her.

'Now, Harry, poaching my PA is not on,' Michael shot at him.

'Like I said before, Mickey—*her choice*,' he replied with an affable shrug.

'Okay, while you two guys argue over my brilliant sister, I want her to show me her living quarters,' Lucy put in quickly. 'You can mind the office, can't you, Harry?'

'Go right ahead,' he said agreeably.

'Come on, Ellie,' she urged, nodding to the door at the back of the office. 'Michael said your apartment was right here. I want to see everything. And while I'm at it, may I say you look great in the island uniform?'

Elizabeth laughed. 'Not as spectacular as you this morning.'

Lucy wore cheeky little navy denim shorts with a red-and-purple halter top, big red hoop earrings, red trainers on her feet and a purple scrunchie holding up her long blond hair in a ponytail.

'Am I over-the-top?' she asked.

Elizabeth shook her head. 'You can carry off anything, Lucy.'

'I wish…' she replied with a wry grimace as Elizabeth ushered her into the apartment and closed the door on the two men in the office.

Elizabeth eyed her quizzically, sensing something was weighing on her sister's mind. 'Is that a general wish or…?'

'Oh, nothing really,' came the airy reply, her hands gesturing dismissively as her gaze swung around the living room. 'This is lovely, Ellie. Show me the bedroom and bathroom.'

She stopped at the queen-size bed, her sherry-brown eyes twinkling mischief at Elizabeth. 'Have you shared this with Harry yet?'

'Actually, no.' Wanting to divert any further personal probing, she retaliated with, 'Do you want to tell me what's going on with Michael?'

She threw up her hands. 'Everything is happening! I swear to you, Ellie, I've never been this mad about a guy. I'm in love like you wouldn't believe, and while it's incredibly wonderful, it's also scary, you know?'

'In what way scary?'

She flopped onto the bed, put her hands behind her head and stared at the ceiling. 'Michael is smart. I mean *really* smart, isn't he?'

'Yes.'

'So what happens when he finds out that my brain wasn't wired right and I'm a dummy when it comes to reading and writing? So far I've been winging it as I usually do, but this is far more intense than it's been with other guys, and he's bound to start noticing I'm a bit weird about some things.' She rolled her head to look straight at Elizabeth, a yearning appeal in her eyes. 'You've worked for him for two years. Will it put him off me if I tell him I'm dyslexic?'

Having experienced how exacting he was about everything to do with work, Elizabeth could only answer, 'I honestly don't know, Lucy. Does it feel as though he's in love with you?'

'Well, definitely in lust.' Her forehead puckered. 'I can't be sure that's love, but I really want it to be, Ellie. More than I've wanted anything. I want him to care so much about having me, it won't matter that I'm flawed.'

Elizabeth sat on the bed beside her and smoothed the worried furrows from her brow. 'It shouldn't matter if he loves you. And stop thinking of yourself as a dummy, Lucy. You're very smart, and you have so many talents...any man would be lucky to have you in his life.'

She heaved a rueful sigh. 'Well, I don't want him to know yet. I couldn't bear it if...' Her eyes shot a pleading look at Elizabeth. 'You haven't told Harry, have you?'

'No. And I won't.'

'I need more time. To give it a chance, you know?'

'Yes, I know.'

'I've been running off at the mouth about me. What about you and Harry?'

Elizabeth shrugged. 'Same thing. More time needed.'

'But you do like him.'

'Yes.' The hostility towards him had completely dissipated last night, as had the steaming vexation and resentment he had so frequently stirred. As it was now, there was nothing not to like.

Lucy propped herself on her elbow, an earnest expression on her face. 'Promise me you won't go off him if things don't work out between me and Michael.'

She hadn't expected Lucy, who had always seemed to be a live-in-the-moment person, to look ahead and see complications arising from the situation. It took her by surprise. Before she could consider the promise, Lucy rattled on.

'Harry could be the right guy for you. Let's face it... he's gorgeous and sexy and wealthy and obviously keen to have you in his corner. You could be great together and I don't want *me* to be the reason for you not having a future with him. I'd be happy to see you happy with him, Ellie, regardless of what happens between me and Michael.'

Deeply touched by her sister's caring, she couldn't help replying, 'But being so madly in love with Michael, you'll be hurt if he walks away from you.' Just as *she* had been on Monday—totally shattered and never wanting to see him again.

'Oh, I'll muddle along like I always do,' Lucy retorted with a wry grimace. 'I'm good at putting things behind me. I've had a lot of practice at it.' She reached out, took Elizabeth's hand and squeezed it reassuringly. 'You mustn't worry about me. Go for what you want. You deserve a good life, Ellie.'

'So do you.'

'Well, maybe we'll both achieve it. Who knows? I just want to clear the deck for you and Harry. Now tell me you're okay with that.'

Elizabeth heaved a sigh to relieve the heavy emotional fullness in her chest and finally said, 'I'm okay if you're okay.' She squeezed her sister's hand back. 'Whatever happens with either of us, we'll always have each other, Lucy.'

'Absolutely!' she agreed, the earnestness breaking into a wide grin. 'Now let's go get our men!' She bounced off the bed and twirled around in a happy dance. 'Let's have a fabulous weekend, following our hearts' desire and not thinking about tomorrow.' She paused in the doorway to the living room to give Elizabeth a wise look. 'You never know when something might strike us dead so we do what we want to do. Right?'

'Right!' Elizabeth echoed, suddenly wondering how much of Lucy's attitudes and behaviour stemmed from their mother's early death and the suffering that had preceded it. She'd only been seventeen. Would Michael wrap her in the loving security blanket she needed? It was simply impossible to know at this point.

When she and Lucy emerged from the apartment, the two men were still standing where they'd left them in the office. Michael's attention instantly swivelled away from Harry, his face lighting up with pleasure at seeing her sister again. He held out his arms in a welcome-back gesture and Lucy waltzed straight into them, laughing up at him as she curled her arms around his neck.

'All done here?' he asked indulgently.

'Yes. But I want all four of us to lunch together in the restaurant.'

He threw a quick appeal to his brother. 'That can be arranged?'

'Leave it with me,' Harry said, not exactly committing to the idea. 'Why don't you take Lucy across to the restaurant, order a bottle of wine, and we'll join you when we've cleared the way?'

'See you soon,' Lucy tossed at Elizabeth as Michael scooped her away with him.

Which left her alone with Harry.

She'd been watching Michael very intently, wishing she could see into his mind and heart, knowing now that he could hurt Lucy very badly if lust didn't turn into love. This wasn't another flash-in-the-pan attraction for her—easy come, easy go.

Was he *the right man* for her sister?

A little while ago she had believed he was the perfect

match for herself. It was hard to get her head around transferring that sense of *rightness* to the connection between Michael and Lucy, but at least it didn't hurt anymore. She felt no jealousy. No envy. Just a rather horrid sense that fate was playing a capricious trick in seeding attractions with the potential to mess up their lives.

Harry clenched his hands in instinctive fighting mode. Throughout the whole encounter with Mickey and Lucy, Elizabeth's attention had been trained on them. She hadn't looked to him for any help. Even now with them gone, her focus was inward, probably measuring her feelings and unwilling to reveal them.

Was she still obsessed with Mickey?

He needed to know.

'Elizabeth…' he said more tersely than he'd meant to.

Her gaze flicked up to his. He saw no pain in her eyes. It was more a look of curious assessment. *Of him.* Was she comparing what she'd felt for Mickey with how she now felt about him? Last night's intimacy had to have had some impact on her. She'd responded to him very positively.

'If you'd rather not have lunch with them…' he started, willing to make up some excuse for her to avoid spending more time in their company if she found it intolerable.

'No, it's fine,' she cut in. 'If it's okay with you for me to vacate the office for the lunch hour.'

'You're sure?' he asked, wanting absolute confirmation that she was free of any angst over her sister's connection with his brother.

A whimsical smile softened her expression as she

walked towards him. To his surprise and delight, when she reached him she slid her hands up his chest and linked them around the back of his neck. 'Lucy said to go get our men and right now you're my man, Harry. I hope you're happy about that,' she said in a soft seductive lilt.

Was it true?

He fiercely didn't want it to be on the rebound.

He wrapped his arms around her and pulled her into full body contact with him. No resistance. In fact, she rubbed herself teasingly against him, stirring an instant erection. Her eyes blazed with a boldness he'd never seen in them and he sensed a determination in her to take life by the scruff of the neck and give it a good shake.

Whatever... Her dream about Mickey was gone and she was choosing to have him. He kissed her and she kissed him right back, no hesitation, no inhibitions—a full-blooded response that made it extremely difficult to rein in the desire she'd fired up. It was the wrong time to race her off to bed. Mickey and Lucy were waiting for them in the restaurant and he wouldn't put it past Lucy to come looking for them if they didn't appear within a reasonable time.

Besides, the promise was certainly there that last night was not going to be the one-night stand Elizabeth had dictated.

He could wait.

He was satisfied that he'd won.

Elizabeth Flippence was now *his* woman.

CHAPTER FOURTEEN

ELIZABETH woke up on Sunday morning and was instantly aware of the man lying in the bed he hadn't shared with her before last night—the sound of his breathing, the warmth emanating from his naked body, the memories of intense pleasure in their lovemaking. Harry Finn...

She rolled onto her back to look at him, a smile twitching at her lips. He was still asleep. Her gaze wandered over every part of him that was not covered by the bed sheet—the strongly muscled shoulders and arms, the ruggedly masculine face with its slightly crooked nose, the black curls flopping over his forehead, the five o'clock shadow on his jaw. *Her man*, she thought, at least for the time being.

It felt slightly weird but definitely liberating to have thrown out her rule book on how life should be led, diving straight into the deep end with Harry and not caring if it was a big mistake. Lucy's comment yesterday—*you never know when something might strike us dead so we do what we want to do*—had made it seem stupid to deny herself what Harry could give her out of fear that she'd made a rash choice and this lovely time with him probably wouldn't last.

So what if it didn't!

She was thirty years old. Why not experience all the pleasure she could with this man? When—*if*—it ended, at least she would have had the most marvellous sex any woman could have.

She wondered if Lucy was feeling the same about Michael. Was he as good a lover as his brother? Did being *in love* make it better? It was far too soon to say she was in love with Harry but he was much—*nicer*—than she had ever thought he could be, not like a superficial playboy at all. He really did care about her feelings.

His eyes suddenly flicked open, instantly catching her looking at him. 'Hi!' he said, his mouth curving into a happy smile.

She smiled back. 'Hi to you, too!'

'How long have you been awake?'

She reached out and ran a finger down his nose. 'Long enough to wonder how this got broken.'

He laughed and rolled onto his side, propping himself up on his elbow, answering her good-humouredly. 'Rugby tackle. It made a bloody mess of my nose but I stopped the other guy from scoring a try and we won the game.'

'Sport,' she said, mentally correcting her former prejudice that had decided the injury had come out of a misspent youth. 'Jack Pickard told me you'd been good at all sports in your teens. He reckoned you could have been a champion on any playing field.'

He cocked an eyebrow at her. 'You were asking him about me?'

'No. I was being told about you. But I am asking

now. Tell me about those years, Harry. What were your proudest moments in sport?'

He was happy to talk about them, basking in her interest. For two years she had rejected knowing more about him, always projecting the attitude that he wasn't worth knowing. That glacier of disinterest had definitely thawed over the past two days.

'Did you ever dream of competing in the Olympic Games? Or representing Australia in rugby or cricket?' she asked.

He shook his head. 'I simply enjoyed sport. I never aimed to make a career out of it. Mickey and I wanted to join Dad in the business. He used to talk to us about what he was doing, what he was planning. It was creative, challenging, exciting....' He grinned. 'And you made your own rules, no toeing a line drawn for you by sport officialdom.'

'You were lucky to have a father like that, Harry.'

Not like hers.

He saw it in her eyes, heard it in the tinge of sad envy in her voice. He remembered what she had told him about her own father and realised how cautious she would be about her relationships with men, judging them on character before allowing them into her life. Playboy—womaniser—that would be a firm no-no regardless of physical attraction. No doubt she would instantly back off from anyone showing a bent towards drinking too much alcohol, as well.

A very strong-minded woman.

Her sister's anchor.

She'd been a challenge to him and he hadn't looked

any further than winning her over, having her like this, but he found himself wanting to prove she was safe with him. He was not one of the bad guys.

'I'm going to be the same kind of father to my children,' he said firmly.

It raised her eyebrows. 'You see a future with a family in it?'

'Yes, I do. Don't you?'

She looked uncertain. 'I don't know anymore. I feel a bit adrift at the moment, Harry.'

She had probably dreamed of it with Mickey and that dream was gone. He understood her sense of being adrift. He didn't know how deep it went until much later in the day.

Lunch with Lucy and Michael again before they headed back to the mainland. Elizabeth felt no stress about joining them. She wanted to observe how well they were responding to each other, watch for any pricks in their bubble of happiness. It troubled her that Lucy saw her dyslexia as a possible breaking point. She wished she could have given her sister an assurance that it wouldn't be.

It was a problem, no denying it. She suspected it played a big part in Lucy's flightiness, why relationships and jobs never lasted long. It wasn't a happy position—being thought defective. If Michael ever did think it and rejected her sister on that basis, Elizabeth knew she would hate him for it.

As soon as they were all seated in the restaurant and handed menus with the limited list of four starters, four mains and four sweets, Elizabeth mused over all of them out loud so Lucy could make her choice without having to say she'd have the same as someone else. Often in restaurants a waiter listed Specials which made a selection easy, but that wasn't the case here.

Lucy grinned at her, eyes sparkling gratitude, and it was obvious that nothing had changed between her and Michael. They still looked besotted with each other, and the meal progressed in a very congenial atmosphere.

Until they were sitting over coffee at the end of it.

'Any prospects for the position of manager here, Harry?' Michael asked.

He shrugged. 'A few résumés have come in. I haven't called for any interviews yet. Elizabeth may want to stay on now that she's on top of the job.'

'Elizabeth is mine!' Michael shot at him with a vexed look.

'No!' tripped straight out of her mouth.

The vexed look was instantly transferred to her. 'Don't tell me Harry has seduced you into staying here.'

'No, I won't be staying here beyond the month he needs to find someone suitable.'

As beautiful as the island was, it was a getaway, too isolated from a normal social life for her to stay on indefinitely, too far away from Lucy, too. Besides, if the affair with Harry ran cold, she'd feel trapped here.

'So you come back to me,' Michael insisted.

She shook her head. 'I'm sorry, Michael, but I don't want to do that, either.'

Being his PA wasn't a straightforward work situation anymore. The personal connections that had started this week—him and Lucy, herself and Harry—made it too emotionally complicated for her to feel comfortable about working closely with him.

'Why not?' he persisted.

She was acutely aware of Lucy listening and needed to dissuade her sister from thinking it was because of her. 'Being here this week made me realise I want a change. Try something different. I'd appreciate it if you'd take this as my notice, Michael.'

He wasn't happy. He glared at his brother. 'Goddammit, Harry! If it wasn't for you...'

'Hey!' Harry held up his hands defensively. 'I'm not getting her, either.'

'Please...' Elizabeth quickly broke in, feeling the rise of tension around the table. 'I don't want to cause trouble. I just want to take a different direction with my life.'

'But you're brilliant as my PA,' Michael argued, still annoyed at being put out.

'I'm sorry. You'll just have to find someone else.'

She wasn't about to budge from this stance. It felt right to divorce herself from both the Finn men as far as work was concerned. Whatever developed in a personal sense had to be something apart from professional ties, not tangled up with how she earned her income.

'Why not try out Lucy as your PA?' Harry suggested to Michael with an airy wave of his hand. 'She's probably as brilliant as her sister.'

Lucy looked aghast, panic in her eyes.

'It's not her kind of thing,' Elizabeth said firmly.

Michael frowned and turned to her sister. 'You do work in administration, Lucy,' he remarked quizzically.

'I'm the front person who deals with people, Michael,' she rushed out. 'I don't do the desk work. I'm good at helping people, understanding what they want, helping them to decide...there's quite a bit of that in cemetery administration. And I like it,' she added for good measure, pleading for him to drop the issue.

He grimaced, accepting that Lucy was no easy solution to his problem.

She reached out and touched his hand, desperate to restore his good humour with her. 'I'm sorry I can't fill Ellie's place.'

The grimace tilted up into a soothing smile. 'I shouldn't have expected it. You are a people person and I like that, Lucy. I wouldn't want to change it.'

Elizabeth saw relief pouring through the smile beamed back at him. Another hurdle safely jumped, she thought. Yet hiding the dyslexia from Michael couldn't go on forever and there was one thing she needed from him before the situation could get horribly messed up.

'I hope you'll give me a good reference, Michael.'

He sighed and turned a rueful smile to her. 'It will be in the mail tomorrow. I hate losing you but I wish you well, Elizabeth.'

'Thank you.'

Harry didn't like Elizabeth's decision any more than Mickey did. She was cutting ties with them, closing doors, and he didn't know her reasons for it. This morning he could have sworn she was over her emotional fixation on his brother but if that was true, why give up her job with him? It was a top-line position and on the salary front Harry doubted she could better it.

He had offered her an alternative but she wasn't taking up that option. It was understandable that staying on the island long-term would not suit her. She and her sister lived together and were obviously close—family who really counted as family, like him and Mickey. Apart from that, if she wanted to rejoin the social swing, Cairns was the place to do it.

He didn't like this thought, either. It meant she didn't see much of a future with him, which raised the question in his mind—how much of a future did he want with her?

She touched places in him that no other woman had, but did he do the same to her? More time together should sort that out, but there was one thing he needed to know right now because it was twisting up his gut.

Was she still using him to fight off her feelings for Mickey?

Elizabeth silently fretted over whether she had spoken her mind too soon, aware that her announcements had upset the happy mood around the table. Although Michael had accepted her decision on the surface, it was obvious from the stony glances he threw at Harry that he blamed his brother for it and was barely holding in his frustration over the situation. Her nerves picked up tension emanating from Harry. Lucy kept looking anxiously at her. No one chose to eat any of the petit fours that accompanied coffee.

As soon as Elizabeth had finished her cappuccino, Lucy pushed back her chair and rose to her feet. 'I'm off to the ladies' room. Will you come with me, Ellie?' Her eyes begged agreement.

'Of course,' she said, immediately rising to join her sister.

The barrage started the moment they were closeted in the ladies' room. 'Why are you leaving your great job with Michael? He's not happy about it.'

Elizabeth shook her head. 'It's not my mission in life to keep Michael happy,' she said dryly.

'But you always said you loved that job.'

'I did, but it's high pressure, Lucy. I didn't realise how much it demanded of me until I came out here. I don't want to be constantly on my toes anymore. I want to look for something else—more relaxed, less stressful.'

'Then it's not because of me and him?' she said worriedly.

'No,' Elizabeth lied. 'I'm sorry Michael is unhappy about it but I don't think he'll take it out on you, Lucy. If he does, he's not the man for you.'

She heaved a sigh. 'You're right. Okay. It's completely fair for you to look for something else. He's just got to lump being put out by it.'

'You can play nurse and soothe his frustration,' Elizabeth said with a smile.

Lucy laughed.

It eased the tension on that front.

However, Michael's displeasure with her decision made the farewells after lunch somewhat strained. Elizabeth hoped that Lucy's company would be bright enough to move his annoyance aside. She hadn't meant to spoil their day.

Harry followed her into the administration office, obviously intent on pursuing the issue of her leaving his

employ, as well, although he shouldn't have any griev-
ance with her. She had only ever agreed to the month
needed for him to find another manager.

Wanting to clear that deck, she swung around to face
him, quickly saying, 'I won't stay on, Harry. I didn't
promise to.'

His grim expression surprised her. The laser-blue
eyes were so hard and piercing, her heart jumped into
a gallop. The air between them seemed to gather an intensity that played havoc with her nerves.

'Why did you throw in your job with Mickey?' he
shot at her.

'I explained why,' she said defensively.

'You waffled to whitewash the true reason,' he accused. 'Tell me, Elizabeth.'

He had no right to delve into her private reading of
a highly personal situation for herself and her sister. It
was not his business. It was the involvement with his
brother that was the problem and she was not about to
spell that out.

'I'm sorry you thought it was waffle.' She shrugged.
'I don't know what else to say.'

His mouth thinned in frustration. He shook his head
at her refusal to open up to him. 'I knew you were using
me on Friday night,' he stated bitingly. 'That whole
scenario at the pavilion villa was more about Michael
and Lucy than being with me. I want to know if what
you've done with me since then and what you decided
today was also driven by your feelings for my brother.'

Her face flamed with shame at how she had used him
and her mind jammed with shock that he could believe
she was still doing it. 'No!' she cried, forcing her feet

forward to go to him, her eyes pleading forgiveness for her brutal lack of caring for *his* feelings. 'I don't even think of Michael anymore, not with any wanting in my mind or heart,' she said vehemently. 'I haven't been using you, Harry. Even on Friday night I was confused about why I was doing what I did with you.'

She reached him and laid her hands on his chest, meeting his scouring gaze with open honesty. 'Since then, I swear I've enjoyed every minute with you, wanting to know the person you are, liking what I'm learning about you. Please don't think any of it was related to your brother.'

He frowned, not yet appeased by her outcry. 'Then why not work for Mickey?'

She grimaced at his persistence. 'Maybe I just don't want to be reminded of how silly I was. A break is better, Harry.' She slid her hands up around his neck and pressed her body to his, craving the wild warmth and excitement of his desire again. 'Can we forget about Michael now? Please?'

His eyes still scoured hers for the truth. His hands gripped her waist hard as though he was in two minds whether to pull her closer or push her away. 'He's my brother,' he said gruffly.

And Lucy was her sister, whom Michael could hurt very badly.

'Does that mean I *have* to work for him or I'll lose any interest you have in me, Harry?'

Again his brow beetled down. 'That's not the point.'

'Good! Because as much as I want what you and I are having together, I won't let any man dictate how I lead my life.'

That was a core truth.

She wanted a partner in life, not a lord and master.

Harry believed her. There was a strength in this woman that had always challenged him. As much as it had frustrated him in the past, he admired the way she made a decision and stuck to it. A warrior woman, he thought wryly, one who would fight tooth and nail for what she believed was right.

Yet she was vulnerable to the womanly needs that he'd tapped into. The wanting for him was in the soft giving of her body appealing to his, the hand-lock at the back of his neck, the slight pouting of her mouth waiting for a kiss that would blow everything else away. The challenge in her eyes burned into his brain. She was his for the taking, not Mickey's, and the compulsion to take her forced him to set all reservations aside.

He kissed her.

She kissed him back.

And Harry revelled in the sense that this was a true beginning of a relationship that promised to be more *right* than any he had known.

CHAPTER FIFTEEN

ELIZABETH managed the administration office on her own throughout her second week on Finn Island. She didn't feel lonely. There were daily meetings with Sarah and Jack Pickard and Daniel Marven. Apart from them, many of the guests dropped by to chat about what they'd done or what they planned to do while they were here. Quite a few were much-travelled tourists from other countries, who couldn't resist comparing this place to other getaways they had enjoyed, always favourably, which Elizabeth thought was a feather in Harry's cap.

He'd carried through his vision for this resort with an attention to detail that was every bit as meticulous as Michael's in his side of the business. In that respect he was just as solid as his brother. In fact, he really had none of the characteristics of a playboy who cared little for anything except indulging himself with passing pleasures.

He called her each day to check on how she was doing and they had quite long conversations that always left her smiling. Contact with him didn't make her tense anymore. They discussed many things with an ease that she thoroughly enjoyed. Even the flirtatious remarks that she'd once hated, once left her steaming with anger, now made her laugh and spread a delicious warmth through her body.

It continually amazed her how much her life had changed in such a short amount of time. Giving up the Michael dream that had been gnawing at her for so long and giving in to the attraction Harry had always exerted on her…it was as though a whole lot of inner conflict had been lifted from her. She had set aside worries about the future, letting herself be a happy butterfly. When serious issues had to be faced, she would face them. But that wasn't yet.

Emails from Lucy were full of dizzy pleasure with her love affair with Michael. According to her sister, he was everything wonderful. Still early days, Elizabeth thought, but hoped the relationship would become what both of them were looking for to complement their lives. And who knew…maybe Harry might turn out to be the right partner for her?

He returned to the island on Saturday morning, strolling into the office, a wide grin on his face, eyes sparkling with pleasure at seeing her again. Her heart jumped. Her feet jumped. She was out of her chair, wanting to skip around the desk and hurl herself at him, driven by a wild eagerness to revel in all the sexual excitement his physical presence instantly aroused in her. Only a sense of decorum held her back. Or rather a very basic female instinct to have him demonstrate his desire for her first.

Her smile, however, was an open invitation to take up where he'd left off last weekend. 'Hi!' she said in a breathy rush.

He strode forward, dumped the attaché case he was

carrying on the desk and swept her into his embrace. 'Can't wait another minute,' he said and kissed her with a hunger that ignited the same hunger in her.

It was great to feel so wanted.

What made the physical sizzle between them even better was the respect he subsequently showed for her opinion. He'd brought the résumés of the most likely prospects for the position of manager with him and wanted her input on them before deciding on interviews. This sharing on a business level made Elizabeth feel like a real partner, not just for sharing a bed.

They talked about the possibilities for most of the day, weighing up the pros and cons, deciding on who would best deal with the situation. There seemed to be a wonderful, vibrant harmony flowing between them, making their lovemaking that night extra special. It wasn't until Harry chose to query her choices that the pleasurable flow was broken.

They were lying face to face, their legs still intimately locked together. Harry softly stroked the feathery bangs off her forehead, looking deeply into her eyes. 'I'd really like you to stay on here, Ellie,' he said. 'It's not too late to change your mind.'

Her chest instantly grew tight. It was difficult to resist the seductive pressure of his words when she wanted to cling onto the sweet sense of everything being perfect. 'I can't, Harry,' she blurted out.

He frowned at her quick reply. 'You've been happy here this past week. I've heard it in your voice every time I've called. And today you've been so relaxed, confident. Why not reconsider?'

'It's better that you get someone else,' she argued.

'But I like feeling you're part of my world, Ellie. It's been great this week, sharing it with you.'

She sucked in a deep breath, needing to hold firm against the persuasive pull of a future that might mean sharing his world forever. It was too soon to know, her mind screamed, too soon to commit to the possibility. She reached up and stroked his cheek, her eyes pleading for understanding.

'I'm not rejecting you, Harry. I just need to be where Lucy is. Being on this island in a permanent position is too far away.'

He heaved a sigh, his mouth turning into a wry grimace. 'You have to be there for her.'

'Yes.'

'Well, I guess I'll just have to invade your world in Cairns.'

She relaxed at his acceptance of her decision, smiling as she said, 'I hope you do.'

Harry told himself to be content with her apparent willingness to continue their relationship once she was back in Cairns. Separating herself from both Mickey and himself professionally had niggled at him. She'd been so elusive in the past, he wasn't absolutely confident that he'd won her over into moving forward with him.

They'd certainly gone beyond a one-night stand and he no longer thought this was a rebound situation. The connection between them was too good to doubt it. Still, the fact that she was severing the work connection… Harry shook it out of his mind. There was no point in letting it throw a cold shadow over the warmth of their intimacy tonight.

He had her where he wanted her.

It was enough for now.

The call-tune on his mobile phone woke him to the dim light of dawn.

Elizabeth stirred, as well, asking, 'Who'd be wanting to contact you at this hour?'

'Don't know,' he muttered, hoping it wasn't bad trouble of some sort as he rolled out of bed and retrieved the mobile from his shorts pocket. He quickly flipped it open, held it up to his ear and spoke a terse, 'Yes?'

'Harry Finn?' asked a male voice he didn't recognise.

'Yes. Who's speaking?'

'This is Constable Colin Parker. I'm calling from the Cairns Base Hospital. I'm sorry to say your brother, Michael Finn, was involved in a serious car accident earlier this morning....'

Harry's heart stopped. Shock and fear jammed his mind for a moment, fear spearing through to force out the words, 'How serious?'

'Your brother and two teenagers are in intensive care. I can't say exactly what injuries were sustained but I'm told they are extensive. Two other teenagers...'

'He's not dead.' Relief poured through Harry. Although there was no guarantee Mickey would pull through, at least he had a chance, not like their parents.

'Who?' Elizabeth cried, alarmed by what she'd heard.

It instantly recalled the high probability that Lucy had been with Mickey—a Saturday night—out on the town. 'Was my brother alone in his car?'

Elizabeth clapped her hands to her face, her eyes wide with horror, a gasp of shock leaving her mouth open.

'Yes, he was. No passengers.'

'Lucy wasn't with him,' he swiftly assured her. 'Thank you for letting me know, Constable. I'll get to the hospital as soon as I can.'

He grabbed his clothes and headed straight for the bathroom, his mind racing over which would be the fastest way to the mainland. Calling for a helicopter, getting the pilot out of bed and to the airfield—no, he couldn't bear waiting around. Best to take the yacht back to Cairns at full throttle, be on the move. He could easily summon a car to meet him at the marina, drive him straight to the hospital, no time wasted.

You hang on, Mickey, he fiercely willed his brother.

Elizabeth had wrapped a robe around her and was pacing the bedroom floor when he emerged from the bathroom. 'How bad is it?' she shot at him, anguish in her eyes.

It made Harry think she still cared a hell of a lot for his brother, which put another savage twist in his heart.

Her hands lifted in urgent plea. 'Lucy will want to know.'

Anguish for her sister or herself? He shook his head. He didn't have time to sort this out. 'He's in intensive care. That's all the cop could tell me,' he answered. 'I have to go now, Elizabeth. Will you hold on here until... until...' He couldn't bring himself to voice whatever was going to happen.

'Of course I will,' she cried. 'I'll do anything you want me to do. Just call me. I'll stand by as long as you need me.'

Yes, Harry thought. *The one who had always carried the load. Always would. The anchor.*

He walked over to her, scooped her into a tight embrace, needing a brief blast of warmth to take some of the chill out of his bones. He rubbed his cheek over her silky hair and kissed the top of her head. 'Thank you. I'll be in touch,' he murmured, then set her aside to go to his brother.

Elizabeth was not going to leave him any day soon. Mickey might.

Elizabeth's heart bled for him as she watched him make a fast exit from her apartment. To have his parents killed in an accident and now to have his brother on the danger list from another accident…it was a wickedly unkind twist of fate.

When she had thought Lucy could be involved, too… The huge relief at hearing she wasn't made her feel guilty for being spared what Harry was going through—totally gutted with fear and anxiety. It was no empty promise that she would do anything to help. If she had the power to make everything better for him, she would. He was a good man.

So was Michael.

And Lucy would want to know that the man she loved was in hospital, possibly fighting for his life.

Where was her sister? Why hadn't she been with Michael? Had there been a bust-up between them? Questions fired through Elizabeth's mind as she used her mobile phone to make contact with her. The call tone went on for a long nerve-tearing time before it was finally cut off by Lucy's voice, sounding groggy with sleep.

Of course, it was still very early in the morning—

Sunday morning—but time didn't matter. 'Wake up, Lucy!' she said sharply. 'There's been an accident.'

'What? Is that you, Ellie?'

'Yes. Michael was injured in a car accident early this morning. He was badly hurt.'

'Michael…oh, no…no…' It was a wail of anguished protest. 'Oh, God! It's my fault!'

'How is it your fault?'

'I ate something at dinner last night that upset me. He brought me home. I was vomiting and had dreadful diarrhoea. He left me to find an all-night pharmacy, get me some medicine. I was so drained I must have drifted off to sleep. He should have come back but he's not here and… Oh, God! He went out for me, Ellie!'

'Stop that, Lucy! You didn't cause the accident and getting hysterical won't help Michael,' she said vehemently, needing to cut off the futile guilt trip. 'I take it everything was still good between you last night?'

'Yes…yes…he was so caring when I was sick. Oh, Ellie! I'll die if I lose him.'

'Then you'd better do whatever you can to make him want to live. Are you still sick? Can you get to the hospital? He's in an intensive care unit.'

'I'll get there.' Gritty determination was in her voice, hysteria gone.

'Harry was with me on the island. He's on his way. Be kind to him, Lucy. Remember he and Michael lost their parents in an accident. I have to stay here. Harry's counting on me to take care of business but I think he'll need someone there, too.'

'I understand. You love him but you can't be with him.'

Love? That was typical Lucy. Elizabeth cared about

the man and she certainly loved aspects of him, but she mentally shied from putting a boots-and-all love tag on her feelings for Harry. However, right at this moment it was easier to just let her sister think what she wanted to think.

'I need to know what's happening, Lucy. Please… will you keep me informed?'

'Sure! I'll call you with news as soon as I have it. Moving now. Over and out. Okay?'

'Okay.'

Elizabeth took a long deep breath, trying to settle some of her inner agitation. There was no more she could do about the situation, yet the need for some kind of action was twitching through her nerves. The office didn't have to be opened for hours yet. It was too early for anyone on the island to require her for anything.

She showered and dressed, then walked down to the beach, dropping onto a deckchair to simply sit and watch the sunrise, wanting to feel some peace with a world that had just changed again. Nature kept rolling on, regardless of what happened to human beings. While it could be ugly, too—cyclones, floods, droughts—this morning it had a beautiful tranquillity that soothed the turmoil in her soul.

The sea was a glittering expanse of shimmering wavelets. The sky slowly turned into a pastel panorama of pinks and lemons. The sun crept up over the horizon, shooting beams of light into the tinted clouds. It was a lovely dawning of a new day—another day that she was *alive*.

Life was precious.

More than ever Elizabeth felt a pressing need to make the most of it.

This past week with Harry had been good.

She'd felt happy with him.

Love was a big step from there but her mind and heart were opening up to the chance that Harry Finn might be the man who could and would share her life in all the ways she'd dreamed of.

CHAPTER SIXTEEN

ELIZABETH was on tenterhooks all morning waiting for news of Michael. She thought it would be Lucy who called, but it was Harry, instantly assuring her that his brother's injuries were not life-threatening as they had feared.

'He was hit on the driver's side, right arm and hip fractured, broken ribs, lacerations to the face, a lot of bruising, concussion. The doctors were worried that a broken rib had punctured his liver but that's been cleared and bones will mend.' His sigh transmitted a mountain of relief. 'He's going to be incapacitated for quite a while, but there should be no lasting damage.'

'That's good news, Harry,' Elizabeth said, her own relief pouring into her voice.

'Lucy's here. I've left her sitting beside Mickey, holding his left hand. She's certainly a surprise, your sister.'

'What do you mean?'

'He's not a pretty picture—face cut, bruised and swollen. I didn't think it was a good idea, her going in to see him. Thought she'd have hysterics or faint at the sight of him. She gave me an earbashing on how much she cared about Mickey and she was no wimp when it came to facing anyone who was suffering anything.'

Elizabeth smiled, imagining the scene. 'I told you she was good with Mum.'

'Looks like she'll be good with Mickey, too. Like Mum was with Dad. He'll need cheering up in the days to come, that's for sure. He's sedated right now. Haven't spoken to him, only to the doctors, who assure me he's out of the woods.'

'That's the important thing, Harry. Whatever the future brings, he does have a future.'

'Thank God!'

'How did the accident happen? Lucy said he'd left her to find an all-night pharmacy...'

'Drunken teenagers in a stolen car running a red light. They just slammed into him. All four of them are here in the hospital, undoubtedly ruing their stupid joy ride. I can't say I'm feeling any sympathy for them.'

Harsh words, but justified, Elizabeth thought. Nevertheless, concern for him made her ask, 'Are you okay, Harry? I know shock can hit hard and have lingering after-effects.'

He heaved another big sigh, releasing tension this time. 'I'll be fine. Got to step in for Mickey. I'll have to run the Cairns office until he can pick up the reins again. I can delegate the running of the tourist side for a while, but Mickey has always kept a very personal control of the franchises. There's no one I can hand it to.'

'I know,' she murmured understandingly, realising that his mind was racing, trying to foresee problems he had to deal with.

'I'll set up interviews with the two people we selected for the management position on the island, hopefully this week, then send the one I think is most appropriate out to you. If you'll train whomever I choose…'

'No problem,' she assured him. 'I'll get Sarah and Jack and Daniel to come on board for that, as well. We'll handle it for you, Harry. Don't worry about it. You'll have enough on your plate taking over from Michael. Just keep me informed on what's happening.'

'Will do. And thanks for…' He paused a moment, his voice gathering a husky note as he added, 'for being you, Elizabeth.'

The emotional comment brought a lump to her throat. It had been a stressful morning and she teetered on the edge of weeping now that the practicalities of the situation had been sorted out. She knew intuitively that Harry was close to breaking up, too, having held himself together to face the worst.

Having swallowed hard to clear her throat, she softly said, 'Don't be too alone in this, Harry. Anything you need to share…you can talk to me any time. Okay?'

Another pause, longer this time, making her wonder if she had stepped too far, assuming an intimacy he didn't feel with her when they weren't in bed together.

'Though I'm not into phone sex,' she blurted out.

He cracked up. Peal after peal of laughter sent her brain into a tizzy. She had no idea what it meant—a release from tension, amusement at her prudish restriction?

'Oh, Ellie! I love you,' he bubbled forth. 'I really, truly do.'

She was stunned into silence. Was this a genuine declaration or was he funning her?

'And it will kill me if you don't love me back,' he went on, slightly more soberly.

How was she to reply to that? 'Umm... Well, don't die any time soon, Harry.'

'I won't. I have too much to live for. And so do you, Ellie,' he said with conviction. 'Bye for now.'

Elizabeth didn't know what to think. In the end she decided Harry's *loving* her was simply an impulsive reaction to her helping him at a time of crisis. It was more comfortable putting it in that box than believing he was serious, because she didn't want to feel pressured about loving him back. As much as she liked him—maybe loved him—she wasn't ready to lay her heart completely on the line. It was too...*hasty*.

Harry knew he'd jumped the gun with the *love* words. They'd spilled out of him before he realised what he was saying, no consideration given to how they'd be received or interpreted and, worst of all, he couldn't *see* Elizabeth's reaction to them.

He'd spoken the truth. He knew that without any doubt now. The instinctive attraction had always been there and he'd never been able to give up on it, despite her constantly blocking it, preferring to see his brother as the more desirable man. But they were *right* together, *right* for each other. He felt it in his bones. Though he suspected she wasn't quite ready to hear or accept it.

Having given her word, she would still stand by him during this crisis. But until he was actually with her again, he'd steer clear of pouring out personal feelings. He wasn't absolutely sure that her emotions had been detached from his brother. Having sex with him—liking it, wanting it—that was certainly answering a need in her, but whether he'd won through to her heart was not certain at this point.

Patience, Harry, he cautioned himself.

Elizabeth Flippence was the woman worth keeping.

He had to convince her he was the man worth keeping.

Every day following Michael's accident, Elizabeth found herself literally hanging on calls from Cairns. She cared about Michael's progress—of course, she did—yet she grew impatient when Lucy went on endlessly about every little detail and her sympathy was sorely stretched at times. She really wanted to hear from Harry, not her sister.

Her heart always jumped when his voice came over the line and her body flooded with warm pleasure. Not once did he mention *loving* her, and despite thinking she didn't want to hear it, weirdly enough she actually did, although she was happy to simply chat with him and it felt really good to help him with problems he was encountering in Michael's office.

His confidence in her, his respect for her opinion, his desire for her input on everything, did touch her heart. Very deeply. None of her previous relationships with men had reached this level of sharing. She loved it. When he told her he was bringing his chosen candidate for manager over to the island himself at the weekend, she was thrilled at the prospect of being with him again, if only for a few hours.

He instructed her to hold a villa aside for herself from Saturday to the following Friday as the new man-

ager would be taking over the apartment and she would
probably need a week to ensure he was on top of the job.
His name was David Markey and he was only twenty-
eight, but he'd had experience as assistant manager at
a resort on Kangaroo Island, which was down below
Adelaide off the coast of South Australia. According to
his résumé, he was keen to take up a position in a more
tropical climate. Elizabeth had thought him a good possibility and she was glad he had interviewed well, leading Harry to choose him.

They were to arrive by helicopter on Saturday morning and the moment Elizabeth heard the distinctive noise
of the rotors, her pulse started racing. She'd barely slept
the night before, thinking of Harry and how it might be
with him this time. It was difficult to contain the nervous excitement buzzing through her but somehow she
had to keep it in check while she handled the business
side of this visit.

Professionalism insisted that she couldn't run down
to the back beach, waving madly like a child as the helicopter landed and flinging herself at Harry the moment
he stepped out of it. Waiting in the office for the men
to enter it was the right and sensible thing to do—the
Elizabeth thing, she thought wryly, not the Lucy thing.
But Harry was counting on her to be sensible and help-
ful. This was not *butterfly* time.

She'd asked Jack to meet the helicopter, introducing himself to David Markey as well as giving any
help needed with luggage. While she waited, she forced
herself to check through items laid out on her desk in
preparation for making the job transition as easy as
possible for David—a list of the current guests and the

villas they occupied with a notation of activities some of them had booked today, contact numbers for the chef and the Pickards, a list of staff names under headings of housekeeping, maintenance and restaurant. It was all there waiting...waiting....

Harry led the others into the office. His vivid blue eyes connected with hers with such riveting intensity, Elizabeth was pinned to her chair while her heart rocketed around her chest. She stared back, feeling as though he was wrapping a magnetic field around her entire being, claiming her as his, tugging her towards him.

She stood. Her thighs were quivering, but her legs moved as though drawn by strings, drawn by the power of an attraction that had become totally irresistible. His smile bathed her in tingling pleasure. She was so consumed by sheer awe at the strength of feelings shooting through her, the man moving in beside Harry didn't register on her radar until her attention was directed to him.

Harry lifted his hand in an introductory wave, inclining his head towards the slightly shorter man. 'David Markey, Elizabeth.'

'Good to meet you,' the newcomer promptly said, stepping forward and extending his hand.

Elizabeth met it with her own hand, belatedly smiling a welcome. 'Likewise, David. I hope you'll be very happy working here on Finn Island.'

He was a clean-cut, good-looking young man—short brown hair, bright brown eyes with a ready smile to charm, a typical front man in the hospitality industry. 'I'm very glad to have the chance,' he said enthusiastically.

Jack had manoeuvred around the two men, wheeling two suitcases towards the door into the manager's apartment. Harry gestured towards him as he spoke to David. 'If you'll just follow Jack, he'll show you your living quarters and answer any questions you might have about them. I want a private word with Elizabeth.'

'Of course. Thank you,' was the ready reply, and taking the privacy hint, he closed the apartment door after himself.

The brief business with David had given Elizabeth enough distraction to recover from the initial impact of Harry's presence. Having regained some control of herself, she turned to him with a sympathetic smile. 'Tough week?'

'Mmm…' His eyes twinkled teasingly as he spread his arms in appeal. 'I think I need a hug.'

Her heart started racing again as she laughed and moved straight into his embrace, eager for the physical contact she had craved all week.

He hugged her tightly to him, rubbing his cheek against her hair, breathing in deeply and releasing a long, shuddering sigh before murmuring, 'There is nothing like a warm living body to make you feel better. I have so much wanted you with me this week, Ellie.'

'I wished I could have been there for you, too, Harry.'

'Can't be in two places at once,' he said wryly, tugging her head back so they were face to face. 'I'll stay here overnight if that's okay with you.'

'I was hoping you would,' she answered, openly showing that she welcomed every intimacy with him.

Desire blazed into his eyes. He lifted a hand and ran a feather-light finger over her lips. 'If I start kissing you I won't want to stop and there's no time for it now.

When Jack comes out I'll leave you with David. Sarah wants me to lunch with them, hear all the news about Mickey firsthand. You should lunch with David in the restaurant, introduce him to the guests. I'll catch up with the two of you afterwards, find out how he's doing and hopefully get you to myself for a while.'

Assured they would be together later in the afternoon, Elizabeth didn't mind seeing Harry go off with Jack, happy with the plan of action he'd laid out. She knew how fond Sarah was of both the Finn brothers, and it was nice of Harry to answer the housekeeper's concern about Michael. It was also appropriate for her to introduce David to the guests since she was known to them, having been the resident manager all week.

Over lunch, David proved to have a very pleasant manner with the guests and the restaurant staff. Elizabeth quite enjoyed his company herself. He readily answered her questions about his experience on Kangaroo Island and was keen to question her experience at this resort, garnering as much knowledge as he could as quickly as he could.

It occurred to her that it might not take a week to fill him in on everything and make sure he understood the whole working process of the island. He wasn't coming in cold to the job as she had. He was already a professional in this field. It might only take a few days and then she could get back to Cairns.

To Lucy…

To Harry…

To real life again…

Although the island *getaway* hadn't really been a getaway for her. She'd been well and truly faced with real life here—forced to accept the reality of Michael's connection with Lucy, having her misconceptions about Harry ripped apart, learning that an attraction based on sexual chemistry could gather many more levels, given the chance.

Her time here had been one of intense emotional turmoil, yet coming now to the end of it, she was ready to move forward, wanting to move forward, hopefully with Harry, who had become a very vital part of her world. No denying that. Though she was not going to spin rosy dreams about him, as she had with Michael. She would do the realistic thing and live in the moment with Harry.

The moment could not come fast enough today.

She accompanied David back to the office after lunch and they settled in front of the computer workstation to go through the booking system. It took an act of will for Elizabeth to concentrate on it. Anticipation was like a fever in her blood. She kept glancing at the wall clock, wondering how long Harry would stay with Jack and Sarah, aching for him to leave them and come for her.

It had just turned two o'clock when he entered the office, filling it with an electric energy that zapped through every nerve in Elizabeth's body.

'How's it going?' he asked.

'Fine!' Elizabeth managed to clip out.

'Fine!' echoed David.

'Well, I need to have a meeting with Elizabeth now,' Harry said, exuding the alpha male authority that had so surprised her when he'd sacked Sean Cassidy. 'After we leave, you can close the office, David. It doesn't need to be reopened until five o'clock. Take the time to settle in or stroll around, familiarising yourself with the island's attractions. We'll have dinner together this evening.' His arm beckoned commandingly. 'Elizabeth...'

'See you later, David,' she threw at him as she rose from her chair, her heart pounding with excitement at the prospect of spending at least three hours with Harry.

That gave her a lot of moments to live in...to the full.

CHAPTER SEVENTEEN

As soon as they left the office, Harry caught her hand, his long fingers intertwining with hers, gripping possessively, shooting an instant wave of tingling heat up her arm. 'Which villa is yours?' he asked.

'Number one. It's the closest to the office in case I'm needed.'

He smiled at her, his eyes twinkling admiration and approval. 'Standing by,' he said warmly.

'I don't think I'll have to stand by for long, Harry. David's very quick on the uptake.'

He nodded. 'A case of been there, done that. Do you like him?'

'Yes. I think he'll manage very well. He's at ease with the guests, too, eager to please.'

'Good!'

'I doubt he'll need me for more than a few days. When I'm satisfied he's on top of everything I'll come back to Cairns and help you in the office.' She threw him an anxious look, suddenly thinking she might have assumed too much. 'If you want me to.'

He grinned happily. 'I was going to ask if you would. Just to tide us over until Mickey can take control again. Andrew—the guy you suggested could fill in for you—

is floundering like a fish out of water under the pressure of too much responsibility. Not his bag at all. Mickey had already directed an agency to find a better replacement for you, but had yet to set up interviews.'

'I'll stay until that can be sorted out,' she promised.

'You wouldn't walk out on anyone at a bad time, would you, Ellie?'

His eyes caressed her as though she was someone very special and her heart fluttered with happiness. 'Not if I could help,' she answered, knowing intuitively that Harry wouldn't, either. He was a caring man who had looked after the people who could have been hurt by Franklyn Finn's sudden death. He hadn't walked away. Not like her father, she thought.

She didn't mind him calling her Ellie anymore. Every time he used that name she heard affection in it, and Harry's affection had become very addictive.

They mounted the steps to the villa's deck. He paused by the railing, his gaze sweeping around the bay below. 'I don't know how Mickey can stand being closed up in an office day after day.'

'He likes running the franchises,' Elizabeth pointed out. 'And since you say he has tunnel vision, I guess that's all he sees when he's there.'

'Mmm…lucky for me! I don't think I could have handled it. I'll be glad when he's back in the driving seat.' His gaze swung to target hers, the blue eyes gathering the intensity that always made her feel he was digging into her mind. 'What about you, Ellie? Have you thought of what you want to do when everything's on course again?'

She shook her head. 'I'm just taking one day at a time.'

'May I make a suggestion?'

'I'm not going to work full-time for you, Harry,' she said quickly, hoping he wouldn't try to persuade her to take up that option again. She had fallen in love with him, and while working together might be great for a while, if he lost his desire for her...

'I wasn't about to ask you to,' he said, drawing her into his embrace.

'What then?' she asked, relieved by this assurance and sliding her hands up his chest, over his shoulders and around his neck, inviting a kiss, wanting him to make love to her, craving intimate contact.

His mouth quirked teasingly. He lifted a hand and gently stroked her cheek, looking deeply into her eyes. 'I don't want you working for me, Ellie. I want you living with me. I'm suggesting that you think about marrying me. We could start a family, make a home together and hopefully live happily ever after. How does that sound?'

She was totally stunned. No way had she anticipated a marriage proposal! Her heart slammed around her chest. She stared at Harry, utterly speechless, barely able to believe what he'd just said.

The shock dilating her eyes told Harry he'd jumped the gun again. This time he didn't care. He wanted her thinking about it, wanted her knowing that he was serious about sharing his future with her. She was *the one* he'd been looking for, *the one* who would complement his life in all the ways that mattered to him. He couldn't bear her having any doubts about where she stood with him.

He had no doubts. This past week had clinched it for him. His brother was no longer a gut-tearing factor in their relationship. That had become clear in all the conversations they'd had. Caring for Mickey had not been at the heart of them. Her focus had been on him—his thoughts, his concerns, his feelings.

He wanted to banish her sense of being adrift, wanted to become *her* anchor, just as she had become his. She might not yet be ready to commit herself to marriage but he saw no harm in laying it on the line. Her mind was clearly rocked at the moment but he didn't sense any negative vibrations coming from her.

'Think about it, Ellie,' he softly commanded, then kissed her.

Elizabeth didn't want to think. She wanted to feel all that Harry made her feel. She threw herself into the kiss, hungry for the wild rush of passion between them—the passion that swept away everything else but the fierce need for each other. It surged through her bloodstream. Her body ached for him, yearned for him, silently but intensely communicating more than she could say.

Harry didn't push for any verbal answer from her. He swept her into the villa and they tore off their clothes, reaching for each other, desire at fever pitch, falling onto the bed, moving urgently to come together. She grasped him with her hands, her legs. He kissed her as the strong shaft of his flesh slid into the pulsating passage that exultantly welcomed their joining. The sheer bliss of it spread through her entire body.

Her mind sang his name…Harry, Harry, Harry….

They rode the waves of pleasure together, driving up the intensity of feeling, instinctively intent on making it more sensational than it had ever been because it was more than physical this time. Much more. Her heart was beating with love for this man, bursting with it as they both climaxed, tipping them over into a world that was uniquely theirs, an intimate sharing that Elizabeth now knew with absolute certainty she would never find with any other man.

It was only a few weeks since she had dreamed of having this with Michael. It seemed weird that in such a short time Harry had so completely supplanted his brother in every sense, but he had. And this was *real*, not a fantasy. She hugged him to her, wanting this *reality* to go on forever.

She thought of Lucy.

Did her sister feel as deeply as this with Michael?

She heaved a sigh, knowing that whatever happened in that relationship was beyond her control.

Harry planted a warm kiss on her forehead. 'Is that a sigh of satisfaction?' he murmured.

'I do love you, Harry,' she said, opening up to him. 'It may seem like an incredible turnaround, but it's true.'

He eased away enough to prop himself up on his elbow and look into her eyes. A smile slowly curved his mouth. 'I love you, too. We're right for each other, Ellie. I know you'll stand by me in all the years to come and I hope you know I'll stand by you.'

'Yes…yes, I do,' she said with certainty.

'So…will you marry me?'

She wanted to.

Lucy would want her to, regardless of what happened with her and Michael. She'd told her so, saying quite vehemently that she didn't want to be the reason for Elizabeth not to have a future with Harry.

Her long hesitation prompted him to ask, 'What reservation do you have in your mind?'

'Will you be kind to Lucy if she and Michael break up?'

It was important to her. She couldn't brush that possibility aside as though it wouldn't count in the future.

He frowned, obviously puzzled that she should be concerned about this. 'Of course I will, Ellie. She's your sister.'

'And Michael's your brother,' she reminded him. 'We could have divided loyalties, Harry.'

'We'll work it out,' he said without hesitation. 'I know Mickey would never interfere with what makes me happy and I bet Lucy would hate feeling she was any kind of block to your having a happy life with me. Am I right about that?'

'Yes,' she conceded, remembering how accurately Harry could read people.

'Then we don't have a problem,' he argued. 'They might not end up together but that won't break our family ties, Ellie. They will both wish us well.'

Yes, she could believe that. It shouldn't be too much of a problem.

'Ellie, we only have one life to live,' Harry pressed on, the intensity back in his eyes. 'We've found each other. Let's not waste time we could have together. You never know when it will be taken away from us.'

Like it had been with his parents.

Like what had almost happened to Michael.

'You're right,' she said, all doubts blown away. 'We should get married. Start having a family. I'm thirty, you know.'

His face broke into a wide grin. 'Yes, I know. And it was the best birthday of all because it brought you to me.'

She laughed, her eyes happily teasing. 'Not very willingly.'

'It was only a matter of time,' he said with arrogant smugness.

She heaved a contented sigh before challenging him one last time, her eyes dancing flirtatiously. 'Well, you're not going to waste any of it, are you? I have to be back at the office…'

His mouth silenced hers.

Her body revelled in having this man.

Her mind was at peace.

She loved Harry Finn and he loved her.

Whatever future they had together they would make the most of it, always being there for each other. That was how it should be and it was going to happen. She and Harry would make it happen because they both wanted it. Everything felt right.

It *was* right.

* * * * *

POSTSCRIPT

Dear Reader,

You have just read Harry's and Elizabeth's story. Michael and Lucy are two entirely different people. While part of their story intersects with this one—their first meeting, the romantic weekend on Finn Island, Michael's car accident—these situations will be related from their points of view in my next book, along with the highs and lows experienced by both of them in their journey towards finding out if they are right for each other. Lust is not love, and passion can turn cold when expectations are not met, when deeply set needs are not answered. The added complications of brothers and sisters can throw shadows, as well, as you've seen in this book. I hope you'll look forward to following the lives of these people. I hope you'll feel for them and want them to end up happily together.

With love always,
Emma Darcy

THE SHEIKH'S SON

KRISTI GOLD

To Bob . . . for giving me a quiet place to finish this book, and for showing me that new beginnings do happen when least expected.

One

If a woman wanted a trip to paradise, the gorgeous guy seated at the bar could be just the ticket. And Piper McAdams was more than ready to board that pleasure train.

For the past twenty minutes, she'd been sitting at a corner table in the Chicago hotel lounge, nursing a cosmopolitan while shamelessly studying the stranger's assets, at least those she could readily see in the dim light. He wore an expensive silk navy suit, a pricey watch on his wrist and his good looks like a badge of honor. His dark brown hair seemed as if it had been intentionally cut in a reckless—albeit sexy—style, but it definitely complemented the slight shading of whiskers framing his mouth. And those dimples. She'd spotted them the first time he smiled. Nothing better than prominent dimples on a man, except maybe...

The questionable thought vaulted into Piper's brain like a bullet, prompting her to close her eyes and rub her temples as if she had a tremendous headache. She chalked up the reaction to her long-standing membership in the Unintentional Celibacy Club. She wasn't necessarily a prude, only picky. She certainly wasn't opposed to taking sex out for a spin before saying, "I do," in the context of a committed relationship. She simply hadn't found the right man, though not from the lack of trying. But never, ever in twenty-six years had she considered ending her sexual drought with a complete stranger...until tonight.

The sound of laughter drew her gaze back to said stranger, where the pretty blond bartender leaned toward him, exposing enough cleavage to rival the Grand Canyon. Oddly, he continued to focus on Blondie's face, until his attention drifted in Piper's direction.

The moment Piper met his gaze and he grinned, she immediately glanced back to search for a bathroom or another blonde but didn't find either one. When she regarded him again and found his focus still leveled on her, she started fiddling with her cell phone, pretending to read a nonexistent text.

Great. Just great. He'd caught her staring like a schoolgirl, and she'd just provided a big boost to his ego. He wouldn't be interested in her, a nondescript, ridiculously average brunette, when he had a tall, well-endowed bombshell at his disposal. He could probably have any willing woman within a thousand-mile radius, and she wouldn't be even a blip on his masculine radar. She took the mirror out of her purse and did a quick check anyway, making sure her bangs were smooth and her mascara hadn't gone askew beneath her eyes.

And going to any trouble for a man like him was simply ridiculous. History had taught her that she more or less attracted guys who found her good breeding and trust fund extremely appealing. Nope, Mr. Hunky Stranger would never give her a second look....

"Are you waiting for someone?"

Piper's heart lurched at the sound of his voice. A very deep, and very British, voice. After she'd recovered enough to sneak a peek, her pulse started to sprint again as she came up close and personal with his incredible eyes. Eyes that were just this shade of brown and remarkably as clear as polished topaz. "Actually, no, I'm not waiting for anyone," she finally managed to say in a tone that sounded as if she was playing the frog to his prince, not the other way around.

He rested his hand on the back of the opposing chair, a gold signet ring containing a single ruby circling his little finger. "Would you mind if I join you?"

Mind? Did birds molt? "Be my guest."

After setting his drink on the table, he draped his overcoat on the back of the chair, sat and leaned back as if nothing out of the ordinary had occurred. Then again, this was probably the norm for him—picking up someone in a bar. For Piper, not so much.

"I'm surprised you're not keeping company with a man," he said. "You are much too beautiful to spend Saturday night all alone."

She was surprised she hadn't fainted from the impact of his fully formed grin, the sexy half-moon crescent in his chin and the compliment. "Actually, I just left a cocktail party a little while ago."

He studied her curiously. "In the hotel?"

She took a quick sip of her drink and nearly tipped

the glass over when she set it down. "Yes. A party in honor of some obscenely rich sheikh from some obscure country. I faked a headache and left before I had to endure meeting him. That's probably a good thing, since for the life of me, I can't remember his name."

"Prince Mehdi?"

"That's it."

"I happened to have left there a few moments ago myself."

Lovely, Piper. Open mouth, insert stiletto. "Do you know the prince?"

"I've known him for a very long time. Since birth, actually." He topped off the comment with another slow smile.

She swallowed around her mortification while wishing for a giant crevice to open up and swallow her whole. "I'm sorry for insulting your friend. I just have an aversion to overly wealthy men. I've never found one who isn't completely consumed with a sense of entitlement."

He rimmed his finger around the edge of the clear glass. "Actually, some would say he's a rather nice fellow."

She highly doubted that. "Is that your opinion?"

"Yes. Of the three Mehdi brothers, he is probably the most grounded. Definitely the best looking of the whole lot."

When Piper suddenly realized she'd abandoned her manners, she held out her hand. "I'm Piper McAdams, and you are?"

"Charmed to meet you," he said as he accepted the handshake, and then slid his thumb over her wrist before letting her go.

She shivered slightly but recovered quickly. "Well, Mr. Charmed, do you have a first name?"

"A.J."

"No last name?"

"I'd like to preserve a little mystery for the time being. Besides, last names should not be important between friends."

Clearly he was hiding something, but her suspicious nature couldn't compete with her attraction to this mysterious stranger. "We're not exactly friends."

"I hope to remedy that before night's end."

Piper hoped she could survive sitting across from him without going into a feminine free fall. She crossed one leg over the other beneath the table and tugged at the hem of her cocktail dress. "What do you do for a living, A.J.?"

He loosened his tie before lacing his fingers together atop the table. "I am the personal pilot for a rich and somewhat notorious family. They prefer to maintain their privacy."

A pretty flyboy. Unbelievable. "That must be a huge responsibility."

"You have no idea," he said before clearing his throat. "What do you do for a living, Ms. McAdams?"

Nothing she cared to be doing. "Please, call me Piper. Let's just say I serve as a goodwill ambassador for clients associated with my grandfather's company. It requires quite a bit of travel and patience."

He inclined his head and studied her face as if searching for secrets. "McAdams is a Scottish name, and the hint of auburn in your hair and beautiful blue eyes could indicate that lineage. Yet your skin isn't fair."

She touched her cheek as if she had no idea she even

owned any skin. "My great-grandparents were Colombian on my mother's side. My father's family is Scottish through and through. I suppose you could say I'm a perfect mix of both cultures."

"Colombian and Scottish. A very attractive combination. Do you tan in the summer?"

A sudden image of sitting with him on a beach—sans swimwear—assaulted her. "I do when I find the time to actually go to the beach. I'm not home that often."

"And where is home?" he asked.

"South Carolina. Charleston, actually." She refused to reveal that she currently resided in the guesthouse behind her grandparents' Greek Revival mansion.

He hesitated a moment as if mulling over the information. "Yet you have no Southern accent."

"It disappeared when I attended an all-female boarding school on the East Coast."

He leaned forward with obvious interest. "Really? I attended military academy in England."

That certainly explained his accent. "How long were you there?"

His expression turned suddenly serious. "A bloody lot longer than I should have been."

She suspected a story existed behind his obvious disdain. "An all-male academy, I take it."

"Unfortunately, yes. However, the campus was situated not far from a parochial school populated with curious females. We were more than happy to answer that curiosity."

No real surprise there. "Did you lead the panty raids?"

His smile reappeared as bright as the illuminated beer sign over the bar. "I confess I attempted to raid a few panties in my youth, and received several slaps for my efforts."

She was consumed by pleasant shivers when she should be shocked. "I highly doubt that was always the case."

"Not always." He leaned back again, his grin expanding, his dimples deepening. "Did you fall victim to the questionable antics of boarding-school boys?"

She'd fallen victim to playing the wallflower, though she hadn't exactly been playing. "My school was located in a fairly remote area, and the rules were extremely strict. The headmistress would probably have shot first and asked questions later if a boy ever dared darken our doorstep."

His eyes held a hint of amusement. "I'm certain a woman with your looks had no difficulty making up for lost time once you escaped the confines of convention."

If he only knew how far off the mark he was with that assumption, he'd probably run for the nearest exit. "Let's just say I've had my share of boys darkening my doorstep. Most had last names for first names and more money than sexual prowess, thanks to my grandfather's insistence I marry within his social circles."

"Not a decent lover among them?"

Only one, and he'd been far from decent. She imagined A.J. would be a seriously good lover. She'd seriously like to find out. "Since I'm not into kissing and telling, let's move off that subject. Do you have a significant other?"

"I did have an 'other' almost a year ago, but she is no longer significant."

"Bad breakup?"

"Let's just say it took a while to convince her we did break up."

His sour tone told Piper that topic was also off-limits. On to more generic questions. "When I first spotted you at the bar, I was sure you're Italian. Am I right?"

Luckily his pleasant demeanor returned. "No, but I am quite fond of Italy, and I do know Italian, courtesy of a former teacher."

"My second guess would be you're of French descent."

"Je ne suis pas français, mais je peux bien embrasser à la française."

A sexy devil with devastating dimples and a wry sense of humor—a deadly combination. "I'm sure the parochial girls appreciated your French-kissing expertise. But you didn't exactly answer my question about your heritage."

"I am not of French, but I am impressed you speak the language."

She laid a dramatic palm over her breast and pulled out her best Southern speak. "Why, sugar, we're not all dumb belles. I know French and German and even a little Japanese."

"Should you find yourself in need of an Italian translator, I would be happy to accommodate you."

She would be thrilled if he did more than that. "I've never been to Italy but I've always wanted to see Rome."

"You should make that a priority. I personally prefer Naples and the coast...."

As he continued, Piper became completely mesmerized by his mouth, and began to ridiculously fantasize about kissing him. Then her fantasies took major flight as she entertained thoughts of his mouth moving down her body. Slow and warm and, oh, so…

"…large pink salmon walk down the streets texting on their smartphones."

She rejoined reality following the odd declaration. "I beg your pardon?"

"Clearly I bored you into a near coma while playing the travel guide."

He'd inadvertently drawn her into a waking sex dream. "I'm so sorry," she said. "It must be the booze."

He reached over and without an invitation took a drink from her glass, then set it down with a thud. "That is bloody awful," he said. "What is in this unpalatable concoction?"

Piper turned her attention to the drink and momentarily became preoccupied with the fact his lips had caressed the glass. And that was probably as close to his lips she would get…unless she took the plunge and turned the good girl to bad. "Basically vodka and cranberry juice, but the bartender made it fairly strong. It's gone straight to my head." And so had he.

He pushed his half-full glass toward her. "Try this."

She picked up the tumbler and studied the amber liquid. "What is it?"

"Twenty-year-old Scotch. Once you've sampled it, no other drink will do."

She would really like to sample him, and if she didn't stop those thoughts in their tracks, she might derail her common sense. "I'm not sure I should. I don't want to have to crawl to the hotel room."

"If you need assistance, I'll make certain you arrive safely."

Piper returned his wily smile. "Well, in that case, I suppose I could have a small sip."

The minute the straight liquor hit her throat, she truly wanted to spit it out. Instead, she swallowed hard and handed the tumbler back to him.

"You don't like it?" he asked, sounding somewhat insulted.

"Sorry, but it's just not my cup of tea. Or cup of alcohol, I should say. But then, I can't claim to have good drinking skills."

"How are your kissing skills?" Right when she was about to suggest they find out, he straightened, looked away and cleared his throat again. "My apologies. You are too nice a woman to endure my habit of spewing innuendo."

"Why do you believe I wouldn't appreciate a little harmless innuendo?"

He streaked a hand over his jaw. "You have a certain innocence about you. Perhaps even purity."

Here we go again.... "Looks can be deceiving."

"True, but eyes do not deceive. I've noticed your growing discomfort during the course of our conversation."

"Have you considered my discomfort stems from my attraction to you?" Heavens, she hadn't really just admitted that, had she? Yes, she had. Her gal pals would be so proud. Her grandfather would lock her up and toss away the key.

"I'm flattered," he said without taking his gaze from hers. "I must admit I find you very attractive as well, and I would like to know you better. Because of that, I have a request. You are under no obligation to agree, but I hope you will."

The moment of truth had arrived. Would she be willing to hurl caution to the wind and sleep with him? Would she really take that risk when she knew so little about him, including his last name? Oh, heck yeah. "Ask away."

When A.J. stood and offered his hand, her heart vaulted into her throat. She held her breath and waited for the ultimate proposition, the word *yes* lingering on her lips.

"Piper McAdams, would you do me the honor of taking a walk with me?"

Sheikh Adan Jamal Mehdi did not take women on long walks. He took them to bed. Or he had before he'd taken that bloody vow of celibacy eight months before in order to be taken more seriously by his brothers. A vow that had suddenly lost its appeal.

Yet Piper McAdams wasn't his usual conquest. She was witty and outgoing, while he normally attracted sophisticated and somewhat cynical women. She was only slightly over five feet tall, he would estimate, were it not for the four-inch heels, when he usually preferred someone closer in height to his six feet two inches. She also had surprisingly long legs and extremely full breasts for someone so small in stature, and he'd had trouble keeping his eyes off those assets for any length of time. The oath of restraint had not silenced his libido in any sense, especially now.

They strolled along the walkway bordering the lake for a good twenty minutes, speaking mostly in generalities, until Adan felt strangely at a loss for words. Conversation had always been his forte, and so had kissing.

He thought it best to concentrate on the first. "Do you have any siblings?"

When a gust of wind swirled around them, she pulled her hem-length black cashmere sweater closer to her body. "One. A twin sister whose official name is Sunshine, but she goes by Sunny, for obvious reasons."

He was immediately struck by the familiar name. "Sunny McAdams, the renowned journalist?"

Her smile showed a certain pride. "That would be her. We're actually fraternal twins, as if you couldn't figure that out from our obvious physical differences."

Yet neither woman lacked in beauty despite the fact one was blond and the other brunette. "Piper and Sunshine are both rather unusual names. Did they hold some significance for your parents?"

Her expression turned somber. "It's my understanding my mother named Sunny. Unfortunately, we don't know our father. Actually, we don't even know who he is, and I'm not sure my mother does, either. You could say we were a thorn in her socialite side. Our grandparents basically raised us for that reason."

That explained her sudden change in demeanor. But due to his own questions about his heritage, he believed discussing family dynamics in-depth should be avoided at all costs. "You said your mother named your sister. Who named you?"

"My grandfather did," she said with a smile. "He adores bagpipes."

Her elevated mood pleased him greatly. "I learned to play the bagpipes at school, but I quickly determined the kilts weren't at all my style."

She paused to lean back against the railing. "Tell

me something. Is it true that men wear nothing under those kilts?"

"A man needs some reminder that he is still a man while wearing a skirt." Being so close to this particular woman served to remind him of his manhood at every turn.

She laughed softly. "I suppose that's true. Why did your parents send you to boarding school?"

He'd asked that question many times, and he'd always received the same answer that he'd never quite believed. "I was an incorrigible lad, or so I'm told, and my father decided I could use the structure a military academy provides."

"Guess he wasn't counting on the panty raids."

Hearing the word *panty* coming out of her pretty mouth did not help his current predicament in the least. "He never learned about them as far as I know." His father had never really been close to his youngest son, if the truth were known.

"I'm sure if you'd ask him today," Piper said, "he'd probably admit he knew everything. Fathers and grandfathers have an uncanny knack of knowing your business."

He moved to her side, faced the lake and rested his hands on the railing. "My father passed away not long ago. My mother died some time ago."

"I'm sorry, A.J.," she said. "I didn't mean to be so thoughtless."

"No need to apologize, Piper. You had no way of knowing." Nor did she know he hailed from Middle Eastern royalty, and that bothered him quite a bit. Yet she had clearly stated she loathed men with fortunes, and he had a sizable one. For that reason, he would continue to keep that information concealed.

Tonight he preferred to be only the pilot, not the prince. "Did you attend university?" he asked, keeping his attention trained on the less-interesting view in order to keep his desire for her in check.

"Yes, I did. In South Carolina. An all-women's university. Evidently my grandfather believed I couldn't handle the opposite sex. But since he was footing the bill, I put up with it long enough to get the dreaded business degree."

He shifted to face her, one elbow braced on the top of the railing. "Since business is apparently not your chosen field of expertise, what would you do if you weren't playing the ambassador?"

"Art," she said without the slightest hesitation. "Painting is my passion."

He knew all about passion, only his involved planes. "Then why not pursue that dream?"

She sighed. "I have several reasons, most having to do with obligation."

"To your grandfather?"

"Yes."

Not so unlike his obligation to his legacy. "What about remaining true to yourself and your own happiness, Piper?"

A span of silence passed before she spoke again. "It's complicated."

Family dynamics always were, especially in his case.

When he noticed Piper appeared to be shivering, Adan cursed his thoughtlessness. "Obviously you're cold. Do you wish to return to the hotel now?"

She shook her head. "I'm fine. Really."

"You're wearing little more than a glorified sweater, and I suspect your teeth are chattering behind that beautiful mouth of yours."

Her laugh drew him further into her lair, as did the pleasant scent of her perfume. "Maybe a tad. It's rather nippy for April."

"Let me remedy that for you."

When Adan began to slip the buttons on his overcoat, Piper raised both hands as if to ward him off. "Heavens, no. I don't want to be responsible for you freezing to death."

Her smile alone generated enough heat in Adan to fuel half the city of Chicago. "Are you sure? I am accustomed to extreme temperatures."

"Seriously, I'm okay."

Without waiting for another protest, he shrugged out of his coat, wrapped it around her shoulders and took a step back. "Better?"

"Much better, but now you're going to be cold."

Not likely. Not while she stood before him with her dark hair blowing in the breeze, her bright blue eyes reflecting the light above them and her coral-painted lips enticing him to kiss her. Answering the invitation was a risk he didn't dare take.

She inhaled deeply then released a slightly broken breath. "I need something else from you, A.J."

He hoped she meant something warm to drink, a good excuse to retire back inside the hotel before he hurled wisdom to the blustery wind. "What would that be?"

"I need you to kiss me."

Bloody hell, what could he to say to that? Should he answer "absolutely not" when he wanted to blurt out a resounding yes? He brushed away a strand of hair from her cheek and ran his thumb along her jaw. "I'm not certain that would be a banner idea." Many times he had heard that phrase, but never coming out of his own mouth.

Disappointment called out from her eyes. "Why not?"

"Because if I kiss you, I would not want to stop with only a kiss."

She sent him an angel's smile. "Do you have issues with maintaining control?"

He prided himself on control when it came to flying jets and yes, wooing women. Still, there was something about this particular woman that told him he could end up losing the war he now waged with his libido.

Before he could respond, she wrapped her hand around his neck and lowered his lips to hers. He immediately discovered the angel kissed like the devil, and he liked it. He liked the way she tasted and the silken glide of her tongue against his, and he definitely liked the way she pressed her entire body against him. He would like it better if they were in his hotel bed without the hindrance of clothing. He did not particularly care for the warning bells sounding inside his brain.

Gathering every ounce of strength he still possessed, Adan pulled away and stepped back before he did something they might both regret. The dejected look on Piper's face gave him pause, and the urge to come up with some viable excuse. "You, lovely lady, are too much of a temptation for even the most controlled man."

Her expression brightened. "No one has ever accused me of that before."

"Apparently you have not been with anyone who appreciates your finer points."

Now she looked somewhat coy. "But you appreciate them?"

If she could see the evidence of his appreciation, she would not have posed the question. "I more than appreciate them, as I also appreciate and respect you. Therefore I am going to escort you back to the hotel and bid you good night." Or crush his determination to refrain from sex for three more months.

Piper pretended to pout. "But the night is still young, and I'm still cold."

"All the more reason to deliver you safely inside the hotel."

"Your room or mine?"

She seemed determined to make this incredibly hard on him…in every sense of the word. "Your room, and then I will retire to mine."

She sighed. "All right, if that's what you really want."

If he said that, he would be lying. "It's not a question of if I want you. The question is, would it be wise to continue this?"

"And your answer?"

"Completely unwise."

"Maybe we should ignore wisdom and do what comes naturally. We're both of age and free to do as we please, so why not take advantage of the opportunity?"

Just as he opened his mouth to issue another unenthusiastic argument, she kissed him again. Deeper this time, more insistent. He slid his hand down her back, cupped her bottom and brought her up against his erection, hoping to discourage her. The plan failed. She made a move with her hips and sent him so close to the edge that he considered lifting her skirt, lowering his pants and dispensing with all propriety.

The last thread of his coveted self-control prevented him from acting on his desire. He refused to succumb to animal instinct. He could not discard the vow, or his common sense, for one night of unbridled passion with someone he was clearly deceiving. He would remain strong, stay grounded, ignore the fact that he had a beautiful, sensual woman at his disposal and...

Whom was he attempting to fool? "Let's retire to my room."

Two

She had always strived to be the good twin. Straight as an arrow. Boring as hell. Never before had she demonstrated such assertiveness toward a man.

Now remarkably Piper found herself alone in an elevator with that man, with only one goal in mind—ending her self-imposed celibacy in a virtual stranger's hotel room. Oddly A.J. kept his distance and remained silent as they traveled all the way to the top floor. After the doors sighed open and they stepped out of the car, she expected to see a corridor containing a line of rooms. Instead she noticed only one double mahogany door flanked by two massive, stoic guards. If a pilot warranted this much security, then he must work for an incredibly powerful family or some high-ranking politician.

A.J. lightly clasped her elbow to guide her forward

before stopping at the entry to mutter something in what she assumed to be Arabic. One of the men turned immediately, slid a card key in the lock and opened the doors. As soon as they were safely sequestered inside, Piper took a moment to survey the area—exquisite dark wood floors, towering windows revealing the Chicago skyline, even a baby grand piano in the corner. An opulent penthouse designed for the rich and infamous. Her current companion was one lucky employee.

Piper started to comment on that very thing, but her words never made it to her open mouth. A.J. did, and the kiss he gave her had the impact of a firebomb. Somehow she ended up with her back against one wall with A.J. pressed against her, her face bracketed in his palms. When he shrugged the sweater from her shoulders, slipped it away and tossed it behind him, her heart rate began to run amok. Any concerns flittered away on the heels of a heat she'd never felt before with any man. But this man knew what he was doing, right down to the way he brushed kisses along the line of her jaw and her neck before he brought his mouth to her ear. "The bedroom," he whispered. "Now."

Okay, that would be the next step. A daring step. A step Piper had never taken with a man she barely knew. "Lead the way."

No sooner had she said it than he clasped her hand and guided her toward another closed door where he paused to kiss her again. When his palms roved along her rib cage before they came to rest on her bottom, she found it very difficult to breathe.

He suddenly broke all contact and took a step back. "There is something I need to say before we go any further."

Piper managed to break through the sensual fog and back into reality. "You're married."

"Of course not."

That left only one scenario as far as she could see. "If you're worried that I'm making some alcohol-induced decision, you're wrong. Yes, I've had a couple of drinks, but I'm not drunk. And yes, this strangers-in-the night scenario is a first for me. In fact, I've only had one lover, and even calling him that is a stretch."

He seemed totally confused by that concept. "How is that possible for such an appealing woman?"

"Believe me, it is possible because I'm very particular."

"I am flattered, yet I still question whether you are giving this enough thought."

She didn't want to think, only do. "Look, in a perfect world, I'd suggest we spend a few days getting to know each other before we take this step. But unfortunately I was informed only a few hours ago that I'm traveling to some obscure Middle Eastern country to schmooze with sheikhs for the sake of trying to win a water conservation contract."

His expression went stone-cold serious. "Are you referring to the Mehdis?"

"Yes, and I realize they're your friends, but—"

"We need to talk."

That meant only one thing—party's over. "All right," she muttered, unable to mask the disappointment in her voice.

A.J. led her to the white sofa set out in the middle of the room. After they settled on the cushions side by side, he took both her hands into his. "You are one of the most beautiful, intelligent and intriguing women I have met in a very long time. Quite simply, you're special. For that reason, I do not want to take advantage of you."

Take advantage of me, dammit, she wanted to say, but opted for a more subtle debate. "I'm not special at all. However, I'm sure you normally require an experienced partner, and if it's that's your concern, I'm much more adventurous than I seem. I think my being in your hotel room is a sure sign of that."

He released her hands and leaned back. "As much as I would like to find out, I'd prefer not to complicate matters, which leads me to what I need to tell you. I pilot the Mehdis' plane."

Her eyes widened from sheer shock. "Why didn't you tell me this in the beginning?"

"It didn't matter until you said you'd be working with them. If the king learned I was bedding a prospective client, he would, simply put, go ballistic."

Figured. "Leave it to some well-heeled royal to spoil my good time. That's why I have no use for that kind of man."

His gaze wandered away. "He would be justified in his condemnation. I have a responsibility to the Mehdis and a need to be taken seriously by them."

"At all costs?"

"I'm afraid that is the case at this point in time."

In other words, thanks but no thanks, or at least that was what Piper heard. Feeling somewhat humiliated, she came to her feet. "It's been a pleasure to meet you, A.J. Thank you for a very lovely and eye-opening evening."

Before she had a meltdown, Piper headed away, only to be stopped by A.J. bracing her shoulders from behind before she could open the door.

He turned her to face him, his expression extremely solemn. "Piper, there are two things you must know about me. First, I have been taught that a man is only as good as his honor, and I am trying to honor you, even if I would like to take that black dress off you and carry you to my bed. Despite my concerns about my job, you also deserve the utmost respect and regard. And once you have time to consider my decision, you will thank me for saving you from a possible mistake."

For some reason that made Piper a little miffed. "Do you honestly believe I don't know my own mind?"

"I believe you're too trusting."

Now she was just plain mad. "I'm an adult, A.J., not some naive adolescent. And in case you're worried, I'm not a prude, I'm picky. Last, the only mistake I made tonight was thinking you could be the man who would be worth the wait. Obviously I was wrong."

He softly touched her face. "You are not wrong. When it comes to us—" he twined their fingers together, sending a message that wasn't lost on Piper "—making love, I assure you that would definitely be worth the wait. And that is what I'm proposing, waiting until we have the opportunity to know each other while you are in Bajul."

Piper's anger almost disappeared. Almost. "That would depend on whether you're everything you seem to be, because I believe honesty *and* honor go hand in hand. Now, what was the second thing you wanted me to know?"

A strange look passed over his face. "I still believe in chivalry. Will you allow me to walk you to your room?"

She shook her head. "No, thanks. I'm a big girl and I can find my way."

"As you wish." After he escorted her into the corridor, A.J. executed a slight bow. "If I don't see you tomorrow on the plane, Ms. McAdams, then I will make it a point to seek you out in Bajul."

She boarded the extremely large and lavish private plane less than five minutes before their scheduled departure, due to the rush-hour traffic and an apathetic cabdriver. When the five-man survey crew settled into the vacant beige leather seats at the front of the plane, she walked the aisle past what she assumed to be staff and press members. Despite the size of the plane, it appeared the back half had been cordoned off to passengers. Most likely it held a series of conference rooms and perhaps even living quarters. She might ask A.J. to give her the grand tour, provided she actually encountered him before they landed.

She paused in the aisle to address a middle-aged, professor-like man with sparse graying hair, wire-rimmed glasses and kind brown eyes. Hopefully he spoke English, and that the last remaining spot was available. "Is this seat taken?"

"It is reserved for Miss McAdams," he replied. "Is that you?"

Fortunately a language barrier wouldn't exist during the lengthy flight. "Yes, that's me."

"Then the seat is yours."

After sliding in next to the man and settling her red tote at her feet, she shifted toward him and stuck out her hand. "Hello, I'm Piper McAdams. I'm traveling to Bajul with the GLM engineers."

He gave her hand a soft shake. "Mr. Deeb."

Not a lot to go on there. Time for a fishing expedition. "Are you a friend of the sheikh's?"

"I am serving as his attaché on this trip."

"I'm sure that's a very interesting duty."

He pushed his glasses up on the bridge of his nose. "Managing Prince Adan's schedule can be challenging at times, evidenced by his absence at the moment."

A good thing, since she might have missed the flight if the guy had been punctual. "He has a habit of being late, does he?"

"He occasionally suffers from tardiness, among other things."

Piper wanted him to define "other things" but then she noticed a commotion toward the front of the plane. Assuming the mysterious monarch had finally arrived, she came to her feet along with the rest of the passengers and leaned slightly into the aisle to catch a glimpse. She spotted only A.J. dressed in a crisp, white shirt covered by a navy blue suit emblazoned with gold military-like insignias. Not a sheikh in sight.

She regarded Mr. Deeb again and lowered her voice. "He must be some kind of pilot to earn that reception."

He cleared his throat and glanced away. "Yes, he is quite the aviator."

After everyone settled into their seats, Piper followed suit, well aware that her pulse had unwittingly picked up speed as she noticed A.J. stopping in the aisle to speak to one man. A man who oddly addressed the pilot as Prince Adan.

Reality soon dawned, along with the sense that she might have been completely betrayed by blind faith. She turned a frown on Mr. Deeb. "He's not the plane's pilot, is he?"

Again the man refused to look at her directly. "Yes, he is the pilot, as well as commander in chief of Bajul's armed forces."

"And a Mehdi?"

Deeb gave her a contrite look. "The third Mehdi son in line to inherit the throne."

And a major liar, Piper realized as she watched the sheikh disappear into the cockpit. She thanked her lucky stars she hadn't made the mistake of climbing into bed with him. Then again, he'd been the one to put an end to that with his fake concerns over being only a royal employee, not a royal prince. And all that talk of honor. Honorable men didn't deceive unsuspecting women about their identities.

Fuming over the duplicity, Piper pulled a fashion magazine from her bag and flipped through the pages with a vengeance during takeoff. She didn't have to deal with the situation now, or ever for that matter. She didn't have to spend even one minute with A.J. or Adan or whatever his name was. He would be nothing more to her than a cute meet that had gone nowhere, a precautionary tale in the book of her life, a man she would endeavor to immediately forget....

"May I have a moment with you in the aft lounge, Ms. McAdams?"

She glanced up and immediately took in A.J.'s damnable dimples and his sexy mouth before visually traveling to his remarkable dark eyes. "Is the plane flying itself, *Prince* Mehdi?"

He tried on a contrite look. "I have turned the controls over to the copilot for the time being so we can converse."

And if she spent one second alone with him, she

might find herself caught up in his lair once more. "I do believe the seat belt sign is still on, and that means it's not safe to move about the cabin."

Of course said sign picked that moment to ding and dim, robbing her of any excuse to avoid this confrontation. Nevertheless, he happened to be resident royalty, not to mention he could hold the power to grant—or reject—her grandfather's bid. For that reason, she shoved the magazine back into the carry-on and slid out of the seat, putting her in very close proximity to the fibbing prince. "After you," she said in a tone that was borderline irritable, to say the least.

As the princely pilot started toward the rear of the plane, Piper followed behind him with her eyes lowered in an attempt to avoid the two female attendants' curious stares. He paused to open a sliding frosted-glass door and gestured her forward into a narrow corridor before he showed her into a lounge containing dark brown leather furniture.

"Make yourself comfortable," A.J. said as he closed the sliding door behind her.

Comfortable? Ha! Piper chose the lone chair to avoid inadvertent physical contact, while the sneaky sheikh settled on the opposing sofa.

He draped his arm casually over the back cushions and smiled. "Have you enjoyed your flight so far?"

In an effort to demonstrate some decorum, she bit back the harsh words clamoring to come out of her mouth. "Since it's been less than fifteen minutes into the flight, I prefer to reserve judgment until landing."

He gave her a lingering once-over. "You look very beautiful today, Piper."

She tugged the hem of her black coatdress down to

the top of her knees. Unfortunately she couldn't convert the open collar to a turtleneck. "Thank you, but if you believe compliments will put you in the clear after you lied to me, think again."

"I am being completely sincere in my admiration."

"Forgive me if I question your sincerity. And by the way, what am I supposed to call you?"

"What would you like to call me?"

He'd walked right into that one. "Jackass?"

He had the audacity to grin. "I believe I have been called that before."

She had the utterly stupid urge to kiss that grin off his face. "I don't doubt that a bit. And where did you come up with A.J.?"

"My given name is Adan Jamal. My classmates called me A.J., but as an adult I do prefer Adan."

"I would have preferred you explain all of this to me last night."

His expression turned serious. "When I discovered you were involved with the water project, I was completely thrown off-kilter."

Not a valid excuse, in her opinion. "And after learning that, did you seriously believe you could hide your identity from me indefinitely?"

He sighed. "No. I had hoped to speak with you before takeoff. Unfortunately, traffic detained our driver on the way to the airport and I had to adhere to the original flight plan."

She couldn't reject that defense when she'd experienced the same delays. Still… "You still should have told me before I left your room, at the very least."

He leaned forward, draped his elbows on his parted knees and studied the carpeted floor. "Do you know what it's like to be judged by your station in life even though it has nothing to do with who you really are?"

Actually, she did—the rich girl born to a spoiled, partying socialite and an unknown father. "I can relate to that in some ways."

He finally raised his gaze to hers. "Last night, I wanted you to see me as an average man, not a monarch."

There was absolutely nothing average about him. "I don't base my opinions on a person's social status."

He straightened and streaked a palm over his shadowed jaw. "I believe I recall you mentioning you have an aversion to wealthy men, and specifically, the Mehdis. Is that not so?"

Darned if he wasn't right. "Okay, yes, I might have said that. My apologies for making generalizations."

"And I apologize for deceiving you. I promise it will not happen again, as soon as I tell you something else I omitted last evening."

Just when she thought she might be able to trust him. "I'm listening."

"I've been celibate since my eldest brother's wedding."

"When was that?" she asked around her surprise.

"Eight months ago and approximately two months following the dissolution of my relationship."

Piper couldn't imagine such a vital, viral man could go that long without sex. "Your breakup must have been really devastating."

"Not exactly," he said. "My brothers have always seen me as being less than serious when it comes to my role in the family. I decided to prove to them that my entire life does not revolve around seeking the next conquest."

She so wanted to believe him, yet wasn't certain she could. "I admire your resolve, but I'm still having a hard time with the trust issue where you're concerned."

Adan came to his feet, crossed the small space between them, clasped her hands and pulled her off the chair. "I must see to my responsibility now as captain of this ship. But before I go, I have a request."

Who knew what that might entail? "Go ahead."

"If you will allow me to serve as your personal host in Bajul, I will prove to you that I am not only a man of my word, but I am an honorable man."

That remained to be seen. But right then, when Adan Mehdi looked at her as if she deserved his utmost attention, she couldn't manufacture one reason to refuse his hospitality. And if she didn't keep a cool head, she worried he could convince her of anything.

"Ms. Thorpe is here to see you, Emir."

Great. He'd barely walked into the palace with Piper at his side only to be greeted by an unwelcome visit from his past in the form of a persistent, self-absorbed ex-paramour.

The entire travel party scattered like rats on a sinking ship, including the turncoat Deeb. Only the messenger of doom remained, an extremely perplexed look splashed across his bearded face. "Did you know she was coming, Abdul?"

The man revealed his discomfort by wringing his hands. "No, Emir. I attempted to ask her to return tomorrow, yet she would not hear of it. She is currently in the study with…uh…those who accompanied her. It would be in your best interest to speak with her."

Leave it to Talia to bring an entourage. And if she created a scene, he would never earn Piper's trust. Therefore he had to find a way to keep the two women separated.

With that in mind, Adan turned to Piper and gestured toward the towering staircase leading to the upper floors. "This shouldn't take too long, Ms. McAdams. In the meantime, Abdul will show you to your quarters and I will meet you shortly in the third-floor sitting room. Abdul, put her things in the suite across from mine."

After Abdul picked up her luggage, she didn't make a move other than to give Adan a decidedly suspicious stare. "I have a room reserved at the inn in the village, so it's best I keep those arrangements, Your Highness," she said, prompting the houseman to set the bags back down.

He had to encourage her to stay at the palace, and he had limited time to do so. After signaling Abdul to gather the bags again, he regarded Piper. "The inn is small and will not allow you to have what you need in terms of your business. They currently do not have internet access or an office center. We have all that here."

Abdul bent slightly as if prepared to return the luggage to the floor while Adan tamped down his impatience over Piper's delay in responding. "I suppose you have a point," she finally said. "As long as it's not an inconvenience for your staff."

He would be inconvenienced if he didn't have her nearby, and in deep trouble if the old girlfriend suddenly made an appearance. "I assure you, the staff is accustomed to guests. So if you will follow Abdul—"

"It's about time you finally showed up, you inconsiderate arse."

Adan froze like an iceberg at the sound of the familiar voice. Trouble had definitely arrived.

He could pretend he hadn't heard her, or he could face the unavoidable confrontation like a man. Taking the second—and least palatable—option, he turned to discover Talia Thorpe standing at the entry to the hallway wearing a chic white dress, hands propped on her narrow hips and her green eyes alight with fury.

A compliment should help to diffuse the possible verbal bloodbath. Or so he hoped. "You're looking well, Talia."

She rolled her eyes. "Why haven't you returned my emails or calls? I've sent you at least a hundred messages over the past month alone."

He ventured a fast glance at Piper, who appeared to be somewhat taken aback, and rightfully so. "Might I remind you, Talia, we broke off our relationship a year ago."

Talia tossed a lock of her long platinum hair back over one shoulder. "*You* broke it off, and it's been ten months. If you hadn't ignored me, I wouldn't have been forced to disrupt my schedule and make this beastly trip."

When he'd told her they were done after their on-and-off six-year relationship, he'd meant it. "Perhaps we should continue this conversation somewhere more private."

She flipped a manicured hand in Piper's direction. "Are you worried your new chicky will be exposed to all the dirty details?"

As a matter of fact… "For your information, Ms. McAdams is here on business."

"Well, so am I," Talia said. "Serious business."

He wouldn't be at all surprised if she tried to sue him over the breakup. "I find that somewhat difficult to believe, Talia, yet I am curious. What business of yours would concern me?"

She turned around and clapped her hands. "Bridget, you may come in now and bring it with you."

Talia went through personal assistants as frequently as she went through money, so Adan wasn't surprised when he didn't recognize the name. He was mildly concerned over the "it" comment. But he was nothing less than astounded when the meek-looking plump brunette strolled into the room…gripping a baby carrier. Myriad concerns began rushing through his mind. Unthinkable possibilities. Unimaginable scenarios.

Yet when Talia took the carrier and turned it around, and he saw the sleeping baby with the tiny round face and the black cap of hair, he would swear his heart skipped several beats, and he began to sweat.

"Adan, meet Samuel, your new son."

Three

Piper wouldn't be a bit surprised if Adan Mehdi keeled over from shock. Instead, he assumed a rigid posture and a stern expression, hands fisted at his sides. "Talia, if you believe I will simply take you at your word about this, you are completely daft."

The woman swept her manicured hand toward the infant. "Just look at him, Adan. You can't deny he's yours. Dark hair and golden skin. He even has your dimples. Despite all that, I do have proof in the form of a DNA test."

"How did you get my bloody DNA?" he asked.

Talia crossed her arms beneath her breasts and lifted her chin. "It's all over my Paris flat, Adan. And you happened to leave your toothbrush the night you tossed me to the gutter."

The sheikh's defenses seemed to disappear right before Piper's eyes. "We were always careful to prevent pregnancy."

Talia tapped her chin. "I do recall that one night last year in Milan—"

"That was one blasted night, Talia," he replied, his tone fraught with anger.

"Once was quite enough." The woman handed the carrier off to a bewildered Bridget. "Anyway, I have a photo shoot in a remote location in Tasmania, which will give you an opportunity to get to know your kid. We'll discuss the custody particulars when I get back next month."

Adan narrowed his eyes in a menacing glare. "We will discuss this immediately."

Talia checked her watch. "My flight leaves in less than an hour."

"You will not take one step out this door until we talk," Adan demanded. "Into the study. Now."

After the sheikh and his former girlfriend exited, Piper looked around to find Abdul had disappeared, leaving her in a quandary over what to do next. She occupied her time by surveying the beige stone walls, the ornate gold statues and the unending staircase leading to the top of the massive structure. A baby's cry would definitely echo loudly throughout the building.

With that in mind, Piper sought out Bridget, who'd taken a seat on the gold brocade cushioned bench set against the wall, the carrier at her feet. She smiled at the woman, who managed a slight, albeit shaky return of the gesture. But when the baby began to fuss, the presumed au pair looked completely alarmed.

Not good. Piper launched into action, crossed to the carrier, unfolded the yellow blanket, picked up the crying infant and held him against her shoulder. After he quieted, she regarded the wide-eyed Bridget. "You aren't a nanny, are you?"

"No, I am not," she finally responded, her tone hinting at a slight British accent and a lot of disdain. "I'm Talia's personal assistant. The last nanny quit yesterday when she learned she'd have to make the trip here. Traveling with Talia isn't pleasant under normal circumstances, let alone with a child in tow."

Piper claimed the vacant spot on the bench, laid the swaddled baby in the crook of her arm and studied his cherub face. "You're beautiful, little man, although you don't look like a Samuel. Sam fits you better."

"Don't let Talia hear you call him that," Bridget warned. "She fired the first nanny over that very thing."

That didn't exactly surprise Piper after what she'd witnessed upon meeting the model. "Then she's very protective of him, huh?"

Bridget frowned. "Not really. She hasn't held him more than a handful of times since his birth."

Piper couldn't contain her contempt, a product of her own experience. "Good mothers hold and care for their babies. They certainly don't foist their children off on someone else."

Bridget reached over and touched the infant's arm. "You're right, but unfortunately Talia isn't maternal. She's consumed by her modeling career and staying in shape. All I've heard since his birth is how hard she's had to work to regain her figure. I truly believe that's why she waited four weeks to bring the baby here."

Vanity, thy name is Talia. She was beginning to like her less and less. "At least now he'll have the opportunity to bond with his father."

"I am not prepared to raise a child, Talia."

So much for bonding, Piper thought at the sound of the sheikh's irritated tone.

The self-centered supermodel breezed into the room with one impatient prince following close on her heels. "At least you didn't have to suffer through thirteen hours of horrible labor last month. And just imagine pushing a soccer ball out your todger. Besides, you have a whole staff to assist you while I had to hire several useless nannies over the past month. Good help is hard to find."

"Perhaps that's because you have no idea how to treat the help," Adan muttered as he strode into the vestibule.

Talia turned and set an oversize light blue bag next to the carrier, affording Piper only a cursory glance. "Bridget gave him a bottle three hours ago, so no doubt he'll be hungry again very soon. There's enough nappies, bottles and cans of formula in here to get you by until tomorrow, plus a few outfits. After that, you're on your own. Let's go, Bridget."

Without giving the baby even a passing glance, much less a kiss goodbye, Talia headed for the door with poor Bridget cowering behind her. Piper practically bit a hole in her tongue against the urge to deliver a seething diatribe aimed at the woman's disregard for her child. Instead, she shifted Sam back to her shoulder and remained silent as Adan followed the two women to the entry and accompanied them out the door.

When the baby began to whimper again, Piper assumed he was probably in need of another bottle. Fortunately, feeding an infant wasn't an issue, even if it had been a while since her teenage babysitting days—the one job her grandparents had allowed her to accept, but only in a limited capacity, and exclusively for those parents who'd run in their social circle.

Piper laid Sam vertically in her lap, rummaged through the bag, withdrew a bottle and uncapped it. He took the nipple without hesitation and suckled with great enthusiasm, complete with soft, yummy noises that brought about her smile. After he drained the formula in record time, she set the empty bottle beside her, returned him to her shoulder and rubbed his back to successfully burp him. Then she cradled him in the crook of her arm and stroked his cotton-soft cheek. For a time he stared at her with an unfocused gaze before planting his right thumb in his rosebud mouth.

As his eyes drifted closed, Piper experienced sheer empathy for this precious little boy. She couldn't fathom how anyone would reject such a gift. Couldn't imagine how any mother worth her salt would simply drop off her child with a man who hadn't even known he had a son. Then again, why should she be surprised? Her very own mother had abandoned her and Sunny with their grandparents shortly after their birth. As far as she was concerned, women like Talia Thorpe and Millicent McAdams should not be allowed to procreate.

Despite her poor maternal example, Piper had always dreamed of having children of her own. So far she hadn't found a suitable candidate to father her future offspring, and she certainly wasn't going to settle for anything less than a loving relationship with a man who had the same wants and desires. A gentle, caring man. Grounded. Settled...

"I am officially moving to Antarctica."

After the declaration, Adan strode past Piper and disappeared into the nearby corridor adjacent to the

towering staircase. Again. Granted, she enjoyed holding baby Sam, but she hadn't signed on to be the royal
nursemaid. And apparently the sheikh hadn't signed up
for fatherhood, either.

A few moments passed before Adan returned with a
petite, attractive older woman wearing an impeccable
navy tailored blazer and skirt, her salt-and-pepper hair
styled in a neat bob. Yet when she caught sight of Piper
and the baby, her pleasant demeanor melted into obvious confusion. "May I help you, miss?"

"This is Piper McAdams," Adan said. "She has accompanied the survey crew, and while she's here, she
will be my guest. Piper, this is Elena Battelli, my former governess who now governs the entire household."

Piper came to her feet and smiled. "It's very nice to
meet you."

"And I, you." Elena leaned over and studied the baby.
"What a lovely child you have. Boy or girl?"

"He's Talia's child," Adan interjected before Piper
had a chance to respond.

Elena's initial shock melted into an acid look. "Is
that dreadful woman here?"

"She has departed for now," Adan said. "And she left
this infant in my charge before she left the premises."

Now the governess appeared completely appalled.
"She expects you to care for her child?"

The sheikh looked somewhat contrite before he regained his commanding demeanor. "He is mine, Elena."

Piper really wanted to take the baby and bail before the verbal fireworks began. "If you two would like
some privacy—"

"You have no reason to leave," Adan said. "You have
already witnessed the worst of the situation."

Elena's features turned as stern as a practiced head-mistress. "How long have you known about this child, *cara?* And how can you be certain that woman is being truthful?"

Adan streaked a palm over his neck. "I didn't know until today, and she provided the test results that prove I am his father. Now, before you begin the lecture, I have a few things I need you to do."

The woman straightened her shoulders and stared at him. "This is your bed, Adan Mehdi, and you will lie in it. So if you expect me to raise your son—"

"I do not expect that at all," Adan replied. "In fact, I intend to take complete control over his care until his mother returns."

Provided the missing model did come back, Piper's major concern. But at the moment, she had a more pressing issue that needed to be addressed. "Do you think you might like to hold your son first, Your Highness?"

Uncertainty called out from Adan's brown eyes as he slowly approached her. "I suppose that would be the most logical next step."

Piper turned the baby around and placed him in his father's arms. "I promise he's not going to break," she added when she noted his slight look of concern.

While the sheikh held his son for the first time, the former governess stood next to him, one hand resting on Adan's shoulder. "He looks exactly like you did at his age, *cara,*" she said in a reverent tone. "Such a *bella* baby. Does he have a name?"

"Sam," Piper chimed in without thought. "Actually, Samuel, but I think he looks more like a Sam. Or maybe Sammy." When she noticed Adan's disapproving glance, she amended that decision. "Sammy definitely doesn't work. Of course, what you call him is solely up to you."

"He will eventually be renamed in accordance with tradition," Adan said, sounding very authoritative and princely. "Right now I must see to his comfort, including finding him a suitable crib."

"The nursery is still in order," Elena said. "And since your brother and Madison are currently residing at their home in the States, you may use it. We still have several bottles in the pantry, and a few items in the cupboard in the nursery, but I'm afraid we have no diapers or formula since the twins have moved past that stage. But the cribs are still there and fully equipped with blankets and such."

Adan appeared somewhat perplexed. "The nursery is down the hall from my quarters. I will not be able to hear him if he needs me during the night."

The governess took the baby without permission, and without protest, from the fledgling father, a sure sign of her close bond with the youngest Mehdi son. "There is something known as a baby monitor, *cara*. You will be able to see and hear him at any time when you are in your suite."

"Have the monitor set up in my room," he said. "I will see to the supplies tomorrow. You mentioned Zain is in Los Angeles, but you have not said anything about Rafiq."

Rafiq Mehdi, the reigning king of Bajul, and reportedly a hard case, according to her grandfather. Piper would buy tickets to see his reaction to the current scandal. Then again, maybe not. She'd had enough drama for one day.

Elena continued to stare at the baby with the reverence of a grandmother. "Rafiq has been with his wife at the resort for the past week. They will not be returning for two more days."

Adan shrugged out of his jacket and hung it on an ornately carved coat tree in the vestibule before returning to them. "Make certain Rafiq knows nothing about this until I have the opportunity to speak with him."

When she recognized a serious problem with that request, Piper decided to add her two cents. "Can you trust the household staff to keep this quiet?"

"The staff knows to exercise complete confidentially," Elena said.

"Or suffer the consequences," Adan added gruffly before turning to the governess. "Please have Abdul deliver the monitor and our bags to our rooms, and watch him while I show Ms. McAdams to her quarters."

Elena kissed the baby's forehead. "I have no reason to watch Abdul, *cara*. I trust he'll do as he's told."

After Adan muttered something in Arabic that didn't sound exactly pleasant, Piper stifled a laugh and considered an offer. "I have no problem watching the baby while you settle in, Your Highness."

"That will not be necessary, Ms. McAdams," Elena said as she handed the baby back to Adan. "If you are bent on being a good father to your son, then you should begin immediately."

Adan looked slightly panicked. "But—"

"No buts, Adan Mehdi." The governess snatched the empty bottle from the bench before addressing Piper again. "Ms. McAdams, it was certainly a pleasure to meet you, even under such unusual circumstances. I shall go instruct Abdul while the royal pilot becomes accustomed to paternity. Please let me know if you need any assistance with the boy."

Piper returned her smile. "Luckily I babysat quite a few times in my youth, so we'll be fine."

"Actually, I was referring to my former charge, the prince."

The two women shared a laugh before Elena walked away, leaving Piper alone with Adan and his son.

"She treats me as if I still wear knickers," he said, frustration evident in his tone.

Piper moved to his side and peeked at the still sleeping infant. "Evidently the two of you are very close, and I honestly believe she has your best interests at heart."

He released a rough sigh. "I suppose she does, at that. Now, if you're ready, I shall escort you to your room before I settle the baby into the nursery."

Piper almost insisted on returning to the inn, yet when she saw a trace of doubt in Adan's eyes, the touch of awkwardness as he held his child, the sympathy bug bit her. "Why don't we put him in the carrier while we climb the stairs?"

"No need," he said. "If you'll be so kind as to gather his things, I'll show you to the private elevator."

Piper couldn't help but smile over Adan's decision not to relinquish his son. Maybe she'd underestimated his ability to move into his new role after all.

He had untold riches at his disposal. He could fly jets at warp speed, navigate treacherous mountain slopes on skis and answer a woman's most secret fantasies with little effort. Yet he had no idea what to do with an infant.

As he studied the child in his arms, Adan's own paternal experience fueled his drive to succeed in this endeavor. He'd often wondered if the man who'd claimed him—and in many ways discarded him—had actually been his biological father. That question had always haunted him and always would. He vowed to give his son everything he would ever need, including his undivided attention.

His son. He'd never believed he would be in this position at this point in his life. Yet he was, and he had no one else to blame for his carelessness. No one to truly count on but himself.

"Is this where we get off, Your Highness?"

Until Piper had spoken, he hadn't noticed the car had come to a stop. "It is." After he moved through the open doors, he faced her in the corridor. "I respectfully request you call me Adan when we're in private."

She shifted the tote's strap to her shoulder. "All right, as long as you don't mind me referring to your son as Sam."

Clearly the woman was a born negotiator. "If that pleases you, I agree. I, however, will call him Samuel until he is renamed."

She sent him a satisfied smile. "It greatly pleases me, Adan."

Under different circumstances, he would definitely like to please her in other, more intimate ways. Then his son began to whimper, reminding him those carefree days were all but over. "Do you think he is hungry again?"

"I think he's probably wet," she said. "I also think we should stop by the nursery first and check it out."

A good plan. At least she could assist him when he took his first venture into diaper changing.

Piper followed behind him as he traveled the lengthy

hallway past several unoccupied guest suites. He stopped immediately right of the staircase landing and opened the door to the nursery that he had once occupied with his two brothers almost thirty years ago. The room had been left much the same, with two cribs and a small single bed set against the sand-colored walls, a large blue trunk holding the toys from his early childhood positioned in the corner. The miniature round table and chairs were still centered in the room, the place where Elena had taught the boys lessons as well as her native language, Italian. Where she had read to them nightly before bedtime in lieu of the mother Adan had never known. But that had lasted only until he'd turned six years old, when he'd been unceremoniously shipped off to boarding school.

The baby's cries began to escalate, thrusting the bittersweet memories away. He stepped aside to allow Piper entry, plagued by a sudden sense of absolute help-lessness when he couldn't think of a blasted thing to do to calm his son. He hated failure in any form, and he'd worked hard to succeed in nearly everything he'd en-deavored. Yet somehow this miniature human had left him virtually defenseless.

Piper crossed the room to the dressing table and set the tote and carrier at her feet. "Bring him over here."

"Gladly."

After he laid the infant on the white cushioned sur-face, Samuel continued to wail at a decibel that could possibly summon the palace guards. Piper seemed will-ing to speed up the process by sliding the yellow-footed pajama bottoms down the infant's legs. She then leaned down to retrieve a diaper that she set on the end of the table. "You can take it from here."

While the child continued to cry, Adan surveyed the plastic contraption and tried to recall a time when he'd watched his sister-in-law change one of the twins. Sadly, he could not. "I am not well versed in proper diaper-changing procedure."

Piper sighed. "First, you need to remove the wet diaper by releasing the tapes. But I need to warn you about something first."

He suspected it wouldn't be the last child-rearing caution he would hear. "Take care not to flip him on his head?"

She frowned. "Well, obviously that, and make sure you're ready to hold the diaper back in place if he's not done. Otherwise, you could find yourself being anointed in the face."

He certainly had never considered that. "How do you know these things?"

She withdrew a white container from the bag and opened it to reveal some sort of paper wipes. "I learned the hard way. I used to babysit for a family with three boys, and two of them were in diapers."

This woman—who had been a stranger to him twenty-four hours ago—could very well be his savior. After he lowered the diaper and didn't have to dodge, he readied for the next step. "Now what?"

"Gently grasp his ankles with one hand, lift his bottom, then slide the diaper from beneath him with your free hand."

Adan had earned a degree in aeronautics, yet this task seemed astronomical. Fortunately the boy found his thumb to pacify himself while his fumbling father figured out the process. And thankfully his hand easily circled both the infant's ankles, and raising his legs was akin to lifting a feather. Once he had the diaper removed and the baby lowered, he turned back to Piper. "Piece of cake."

She took the plastic garment from him and discarded it in the nearby bin. "True, but he's still little. Just realize there will soon come a time when he'll be much more mobile, and a lot less cooperative."

The image of his child vaulting from the dressing table assaulted him. "Will I need to strap him down?"

Piper laughed. "You'll have enough experience by then to handle him. And you'll probably want to change him in a place that's a little lower to the ground."

He shook his head. "I had no idea that caring for someone so small would require so much knowledge. I am ill equipped for the task."

"You're more than equipped, Adan." She handed him a damp paper cloth, set the container aside, then grabbed the clean diaper and unfolded it. "But right now your son requires that you finish this task. After you clean him up a bit, repeat the first step, only this time slide the diaper underneath him."

Piper displayed great patience as he followed her instructions to the letter. Once he had the infant rediapered and redressed, he noticed that his son had fallen asleep.

"Grab the bag and we'll put this little guy to bed," Piper said as she lifted the baby, crossed the room and placed him on his back in one of the two cribs.

Tote in hand, Adan came to her side. As he watched his child sleep, he experienced a strong sense of pride. "I must say he's quite something."

"Yes he is," she replied in a hushed tone. "Now let's

go so he can have a decent nap before it's feeding time again."

After one last look at his son, Adan guided Piper into the corridor, leaving the nursery room door ajar. "Do you think it's all right to leave him all alone in an unfamiliar place?"

She patted his arm and smiled. "He's going to be fine for the next hour or so. And I'm sure Elena will have the monitor in place very soon so you can track his every move. But you will need to send out for supplies tomorrow."

"I prefer to take care of the supplies myself," he said on a whim. "However, I could use some counsel on what to purchase, if you would be so kind as to accompany me into the village. I can also show you the sights while we're there."

"Aren't you afraid someone might recognize you?"

He was more afraid she would reject his plan to spend more time with her. "I have ways to disguise myself to avoid recognition. We would appear to be tourists exploring the town."

She hid a yawn behind her hands. "I could probably do that. But at the moment, I could use a nap. Jet lag has taken hold of me."

What an inconsiderate buffoon he'd become. "Of course. If you'll follow me, I will show you to your quarters."

Adan guided Piper toward the suite opposite his, situated two rooms down from the nursery. Once there, he opened the door and she breezed past him, coming to a stop at the end of the queen-size bed. He stepped inside and watched as she surveyed the room before facing the open windows that revealed the mountains in the distance.

"This is a beautiful view," she said without turning around.

"Yes, it is." And he wasn't referring to the panoramic scenery. She was beautiful. Incredibly beautiful, from the top of her hair that ruffled in the warm breeze, to her man-slaying high heels, and all points in between. What he wouldn't give to divest her of that black dress, lay her down on the purple silk bedspread and have his wicked way with her....

"That peak is really prominent."

She had no idea, and he was thankful she hadn't turned around to find out. After regaining some composure, he crossed the room and moved behind her. "The largest mountain is called Mabrúuk. Legend has it that it blesses Bajul with fertility."

She turned, putting them in close proximity. "Fertile as in crops?"

"Actually, livestock and village offspring. We've come to know it as the baby-making mountain."

She smiled. "Did its powers reach all the way to Milan?"

"Perhaps so."

Her smile disappeared, replaced by self-consciousness. "I'm sorry. I shouldn't have brought that up. Obviously you were shocked over learning you had a son."

An understatement of the first order. "Yes, but I am in part responsible. If I had answered Talia's messages, I would have known much sooner. But I frankly did not have the desire to speak with her after we broke off the relationship. Six years of Talia's antics had been quite enough."

"And that brings me to a question," she said, followed by, "if you don't mind me asking."

After all his talk of honor, she deserved to grill him as much as she would like. "Ask away."

"Why were you with Talia all that time if you found her intolerable?"

A very good question. "In all honesty, my attraction to her was purely physical. But in defense of Talia, she has not had an easy life. She practically raised herself in the back alleys of London after her mother died and her father drowned his sorrows in the local pubs. Beneath that tough and somewhat haughty exterior resides a lost little girl who fears poverty and a loss of pride."

Piper released a caustic laugh. "Sorry, but that doesn't excuse her for bringing a baby into the world and basically ignoring him after the fact."

He recalled the recent conversation he'd had with Talia in the study. "She told me she had considered giving Samuel up for adoption, but she also felt I had a right to decide if I wanted to be a part of his life."

"And she thought springing him on you was the way to handle that?"

"Talia is nothing if not spontaneous. And as I've said, I refused to answer any correspondence."

She sighed. "Look, I know it's really none of my business, but I suspect she could be using Sam as a pawn to get you back into her life."

"Or perhaps for monetary gain," he said, regretfully voicing his own suspicions.

Piper reacted with a scowl. "She wants you to buy your own son from her?"

"She did not exactly say that, but it is a possibility. And if that proves to be true, I would willingly give her any amount of money for the opportunity to raise my child without her interference."

Her features brightened. "I admire your conviction, Adan. Sam is lucky to have you as his dad."

She could have offered him an accommodation for bravery in battle and it would not have meant as much. "And I appreciate your faith in me, Piper. Yet I am well aware of the challenges ahead of me."

She favored him with a grin that traveled to her diamond-blue eyes. "Just wait until you have to give him a bath this evening."

That sent several horrific images shooting through his muddled mind. "Bloody hell, what if I drop him?"

She patted his cheek. "You won't if you're careful. And I'll be there to show you how it's done."

He caught her hand and brought it against his chest. "You have been a godsend, Piper McAdams. And you now hold the distinction of being the most attractive tutor I have ever encountered."

"Then we're even," she said, her voice soft and overtly sensuous.

He tugged her closer. "In what way?"

She wrested out of his grasp and draped her arms around his neck. "You happen to be the best kisser I've ever encountered to this point."

He wanted to kiss her now. Needed to kiss her now. And he did—without any compunction whatsoever, regardless of his responsibility to his sleeping son. With a bed very close at hand and her heady response to the thrust of his tongue, all reasoning flew out the open windows.

"Excuse me, Emir."

Abdul's voice was as effective as having ice water

poured down one's pants, thrusting Adan away from Piper. He tried to clear the uncomfortable hitch from his throat before facing the servant. "Yes, Abdul?"

"I have Ms. McAdams's luggage."

"Then bring it in."

The man set the bags at the end of the bed, then executed a slight bow before hurrying away and closing the door behind him, something Adan should have done to avoid the predicament.

He sent Piper an apologetic look. "I am very sorry I did not see to our privacy."

She touched her fingertips to her lips. "We really shouldn't be doing this."

The declaration sent his good spirits into a nosedive. "Why not?"

"Because I can't help but wonder exactly how much you really knew about Talia's pregnancy."

This time when she called his honor into question, he responded with fury. "I did not even remotely suspect she might be pregnant. Otherwise this issue would have been resolved in the beginning. And it pains me to know you hold me in such low esteem that you think I would abandon my own child."

"I'm sorry," she said quietly. "That was an unfair assumption since you seem so willing to care for your son."

His anger diminished when he noted the sincerity in her voice. "You do have every right to doubt me, Piper, in light of my initial fabrications. But I swear to you again that I will do everything in my power to prove my honor."

She answered with a slight smile. "After meeting that

man-eater, Talia, I now understand why you might be driven straight into celibacy."

That vow was the last thing on his mind after he'd kissed Piper. "As I've said before, she had little to do with that decision. I am determined to demonstrate my ability to maintain control over baser urges."

"Then we should probably avoid situations where we're going to lose our heads and do something we both might regret."

He could not argue that point, but he would have no regrets when it came to making love to her should they arrive upon that decision. He might regret any emotional entanglement. "I suppose you're correct, but chemistry is very hard to control."

"We'll just have to learn to control it for the time being."

Easier said than done. "And let us both hope we can maintain control."

"Believe me, you'll have enough distractions taking care of Sam."

Perhaps while caring for his son that would be true, but she served as his primary distraction in private, the reason why he began backing toward the door—and away from these foreign feelings for Piper that had little to do with physical attraction. "Speaking of my son, I should go see about him. In the meantime, you should rest."

She yawned again and stretched her arms above her head. "A nap would be fantastic. So would a shower. Is there one nearby?"

Old habits reared their ugly heads when he almost offered his personal facilities—and his assistance—but instead he nodded to his right. "You have an en suite bathroom through that door. And my room is right across the hall, should you find you require anything else from me."

Her grin returned. "I'm sure I'll manage, but thank you for everything."

"My pleasure, and I do hope you get some much-needed sleep filled with pleasant dreams."

No doubt he would be having a few pleasant—and inadvisable—dreams about her.

Four

At the sound of a crying baby, Piper awoke with a start. She tried to regain her bearings only to discover the room was too dark to see much of anything, leading her to fumble for the bedside lamp and snap it on.

Since she hadn't bothered to reset her watch after she showered, she didn't know the exact time, nor did she know how long she'd been sleeping. She did know that her once-damp hair had dislodged from the towel and her pink silk robe was practically wrapped around her neck.

After pushing off the bed, she immediately strode to the dresser to untangle her hair with a brush and to select appropriate clothing before setting off to see about Sam. But the continuous cries had her tightening the robe's sash as she left the room and plodded down the hall on bare feet.

She paused at the nursery to find the door ajar and a disheveled sheikh pacing the area, a very distressed son cradled in his arms. She strolled into the room, feeling slightly uneasy over her state of dress—or undress as the case might be. While she wore only a flimsy robe, he was dressed in a white T-shirt and faded jeans, his feet also bare. He looked tousled and sexy and, oh, so tempting…and she needed to shift her brain back into an appropriate gear. "Having problems?"

Adan paused the pacing to give her a forlorn look. "I have fed him twice and diapered him more times than I can possibly count, and he still continues to cry at the top of his lungs."

Taking pity on the prince, she walked up to him, took Sam from his grasp and began patting the baby's back. "Did you burp him?"

He lowered his gaze. "Actually, no, I did not."

"Then it's probably just a bubble in his tummy." She sat down in a nearby rocker, draped the baby horizontally over her knees and rubbed his back. "Did Talia happen to mention anything about colic?" she asked, and when he seemed confused, she launched into an explanation. "It's an odd occurrence that happens to some babies at the same time every night. Basically a stomachache that can't quite be explained. On a positive note, it eventually resolves itself, usually when they're around three months old."

He slid his hands into his pockets and approached her slowly. "I highly doubt Talia would have known if he had this problem. Are you certain it's not dangerous?"

He sounded so worried her heart went out to him. "No, it's not dangerous. But it's probably wise to have him checked out by a doctor as soon as possible, just to make sure he's healthy and growing at the right rate. And please tell me Talia left some sort of medical records with you."

"That much she did," he said. "My sister-in-law, who also happens to be the queen and head of our ministry of health, is a physician. I will have her examine Samuel as soon as she returns at the end of the week."

Although Sam's sobs had turned into sniffles, she continued to gently pat the baby's back in hopes of relieving his tummy distress. "It's good to have a doctor in the family. How do you think the king will take the news about Sam?"

Adan leaned a shoulder against the wall. "He is no stranger to scandal, so he has no reason to judge me."

She recalled reading a bit about that scandal during a pretravel internet search. "I remember seeing something about him marrying a divorced woman."

"Maysa is a remarkable woman," he said. "And say what you will about Rafiq's reputation for being rigid, at least he has been willing to bring the country into the twenty-first century. He had the elevator installed."

Piper thanked her lucky stars for that modern convenience. She also experienced more good fortune when the baby lifted his little head and let out a loud belch. "I believe Sam could use a warm bath now that his belly problem's solved. I can do it if you're too exhausted to take that on."

Finally, he smiled. "As long as you are there to guide me, I am a willing student."

Piper shifted Sam to her shoulder, pushed out of the chair and nodded toward the cupboard angled in the corner. "Elena said there are still some baby things in there. Take a look and see what we have available."

Adan strode to the large cabinet and opened the double doors, revealing shelves that housed numerous infant outfits and supplies. "If we do not have what we need here, then it does not exist."

She crossed the room to survey the bounty. "You could be right about that. And I see exactly what we need on the top shelf. Grab that blue tub and two towels. And next to that you'll see a small container with all the shampoo and stuff. Get that, too."

After Adan complied, he turned around, the bathing provisions balanced precariously in his arms. "Anything else?"

"Just show me to the sink and we'll bathe your little boy."

"In here," Adan said as he opened a door to his immediate right.

Piper stepped into the adjacent bath that was right out of an Arabian dream. The large double sink, with ornate gold fixtures, appeared to be made of copper. The shower to her left was composed of rich beige stones, much like the one in her guest suite, only she had access to a deep marble soaking tub. For a nursery she would deem it way over the top, but functional enough to bathe an infant.

"Lay the towels out on the vanity and put the tub in the sink," she instructed Adan. "Always make sure you have everything within reach."

"In case he climbs out of the bath?"

This time she laughed. "He won't, at least not at this age. Once he's too big for this setup, you'll bathe him in a regular tub."

He frowned. "I greatly look forward to that time."

"And it will be here before you know it." After he

had the supplies set out, she handed Sam to him. "Now lay him down and undress him while I test the water."

With the bath moderately filled and the baby undressed, she slid her hands beneath Sam and laid him gently in the tub. "You're on, Daddy."

Sam seemed to be thoroughly enjoying the process. His father—not so much. Yet Piper admired the care in which he bathed his son, though at times he seemed somewhat tentative, especially when it came to removing the infant from the tub.

"He's soaking wet," he said. "What if I drop him?"

In consideration of his inexperience, she picked up Sam beneath the arms, careful to support his head with her fingertips, and wrapped him securely in the hooded towel. "See how easy that was?"

"Easy for you," he said. "I will definitely need more practice."

"You'll definitely get that."

After carrying the baby back to the dressing table, Piper outfitted him in one-piece white footed pajamas. Sam was wide-eyed and more awake than she'd seen him to this point, and she automatically leaned over to kiss his cheek. "You're a happy baby now, aren't you, sweetie? You smell so good, too."

"And you are a natural mother, Piper McAdams."

She straightened to find Adan staring at her, a soft smile enhancing his gorgeous face. "I don't know about that, but I do love kids."

Without any prompting, he picked up his son and set him in the crook of his arm. "And I would say this lad is fairly taken with you. I cannot say that I blame him."

Piper felt heat rise to her face over the compliment and his nearness. "You're a great father, Adan. The two

of you will make a good team for many, many years
to come."

The pride in his expression was unmistakable. "I am
determined to do my best by him. Yet I already sense
bedtime could be an issue. He does not appear at all
ready to sleep."

Piper checked the clock on the wall and noted the
time at half past nine. "I had no idea it was that late. I
slept through dinner."

He gestured toward the door. "By all means, return
to your quarters and I will have a tray sent up."

She truly hated to leave him all alone on his first
night as a father. "Are you sure? I'm really not that hungry." A patent lie. Sam's half-full bottle of formula set
on the table was starting to look appetizing.

"I have to learn to do this by myself eventually," he
said. "You need food and sleep to sustain you during
our shopping trip tomorrow."

She sincerely looked forward to the outing. "All
right, but please let me know if you need help with
Sam at any point during the night."

He reached over and pushed a damp strand of hair
from her cheek. "You have done more than your share,
Piper. I cannot express how much I appreciate your
guidance."

He had no idea how much she appreciated his willingness to take on raising a baby on his own. "It was my
pleasure. And before I turn in for the night, I'll make a
list of things you'll need for the baby."

He grinned, showing his dimples to full advantage.
"Perhaps I should purchase a pack mule while we're
out."

She shrugged. "As long as you don't mind showing your ass all over town."

His laugh was gruff and extremely sexy. "I would rather show my son off all over town, so we will forgo the mule for the moment."

Piper wanted to argue against creating too much attention to his newly discovered child, but Adan seemed so proud of Sam, she didn't dare discourage him. In twenty-six years, her own mother had never expressed that devotion, nor would she ever.

Besides, the possibility of another scandal would fall on the royal family's shoulders, and they'd most likely dealt with those issues before. And if they played their cards right, no one would discover the prince in disguise in their midst.

Piper would swear the store clerk had recognized Adan, even though he wore a New York Yankees baseball cap covering his dark hair, sunglasses covering his amber eyes, khaki cargo pants, black T-shirt and heavy boots. Not to mention he hadn't shaved that morning, evident by the light blanket of whiskers along his chin, upper lip and jaw. She definitely liked that rugged, manly look. A lot. And maybe that was what had garnered the young woman's attention—Adan's sheer animal magnetism.

Yes, that had to be it. Why else would she giggle when Adan leaned over the counter and handed her the supply list? Unfortunately Piper couldn't understand a word they were saying, which left her to guess. And she'd begun to assume the sheikh might be making a date.

The baby began to stir in the stroller they'd purchased on their first stop, drawing Piper's attention and giving her a valid excuse to interrupt the exchange. "I believe Sam is going to want a bottle very soon."

He pushed away from the counter and glanced at Sam, who looked as if he might be in precrying mode. "I believe you are correct. We should be finished here soon."

After Adan spoke to the clerk again, she disappeared into a back room and returned a few moments later with a scowling, middle-aged man carrying three cardboard boxes. He set the boxes down hard on the counter, then eyed Adan suspiciously before he sent Piper a clear look of contempt. She had no idea what they had done to warrant his disdain, but she was relieved when he disappeared into the back area again. After the young woman placed the clothing, toys and other provisions they'd selected into several bags, Adan counted out cash—a lot of cash—then smiled when his admirer fumbled with the receipt before she finally set it in his open palm.

Ready for a quick escape before the love-struck clerk fainted, Piper flipped her sunglasses back into place— and immediately saw a problem with transporting the items since the driver had parked in an alley two blocks away to avoid detection. "Looks like we're going to have to make several trips to get all of this to the car."

"I'll take care of that," Adan replied as he headed out the exit, leaving her behind with a fussy baby and a smitten cashier.

Piper could easily remedy one problem by giving Sam a bottle. While she was rummaging through the diaper bag to do that very thing, she noticed the grumpy guy standing behind the counter, staring at her. She immediately glanced down to make sure the sundress hadn't slipped down and exposed too much cleavage. Not the case at all. And when she scooped the baby from the stroller to feed him, he continued to look at her as if she was a scourge on society.

Fortunately Adan returned a few moments later, three teenage boys dressed in muslin tunics and pants trailing behind him. He handed them each a few bills, barked a few orders, and like a well-oiled human machine, the trio picked up the supplies, awaiting further instruction.

After opening the door, Adan made a sweeping gesture with one hand. "After you, fair lady."

"Thank you, kind sir, and please bring the stroller and the bag."

With Sam in her arms and the secret sheikh by her side, they stepped onto the stone sidewalk and traveled past clay-colored artisan shops and small eateries. The luscious scents of a nearby restaurant reminded Piper they hadn't yet had lunch. The way people stared at them reminded her of the overly stern guy in the store. "Did you notice how that older man in the boutique kept looking at us?" she asked Adan as she handed him the empty bottle, then brought Sam up to her shoulder.

He dropped the bottle back into the bag resting in the stroller without breaking his stride. "Some of Bajul's citizens are not particularly fond of foreigners."

That made sense. Sort of. "He actually seemed angry."

"Perhaps he noticed you were not wearing a ring and assumed we are unmarried with a child."

"He would be wrong on all counts."

Piper experienced a sudden melancholy over that fact. She'd learned long ago not to chase unattainable dreams, and wanting more from Adan would definitely qualify. She still wasn't sure she could entirely trust him, although he seemed to be making an effort to earn it. Even so, she was clearly in danger of becoming too close to the baby—and the baby's father.

As they rounded the corner and entered the alley, a series of shouts startled the sleeping baby awake. Sam began to cry and Piper began to panic when a crowd of people converged upon them on the way to the car. Most members of the press, she surmised when she noticed the microphones being thrust in Adan's face. She hadn't been able to understand the questions until one lanky blond English-speaking reporter stepped forward. "Whose child is this, Sheikh Mehdi?"

Overcome with the need to protect Adan, Piper responded without thought. "He's mine."

She managed to open the car door as the driver loaded the trunk, escaping the chaos. But she'd barely settled inside before the reporter blocked the prince's path. "Is the baby your bastard child?"

Adan grabbed the journalist by the collar with both hands. "The child is not a bastard," he hissed. "He is my son."

Piper saw a disaster in the making and had to intervene. "Adan, he's not worth it."

The reporter cut a look in her direction. "Is this woman your mistress?"

Adan pointed in her direction. "That woman is... She is...my wife."

"*Your wife?* What were you thinking, Adan?"

He hadn't been thinking at all, only reacting. But after spending a good hour sitting on the veranda outside the nursery, that was all he had been doing. "The bloody imbecile insulted my child, and then he insulted you."

Piper yanked the chair opposite his back from the table and sat. "Telling the press we're married was a bit extreme, don't you agree?"

That extreme stemmed from wrath over the circumstance. "Had you not begun this debacle by claiming to be Samuel's mother, then I would not have had to defend yours and my son's honor."

She sent him a withering look. "For your information, I was simply trying to protect you from answering questions you weren't prepared to answer. I had no idea you were going tell the world you're Sam's father, nor did I have a clue you were going to have us living in wedded bliss."

"I believe that would be preferable to confirming you're nothing more than a mistress who bore my *bastard* child."

"What would have been wrong with letting everyone believe he's mine and leave it at that?"

His anger returned with the strength of a tempest. "I will not deny my son to anyone. Under any circumstance."

She blew an upward breath that ruffled her bangs. "Okay, it's obvious we're not going to get anywhere by playing the blame game. The question is, what are you going to do now? I don't think moving to Antarctica is a viable option with a month-old child."

The trip was beginning to appeal to him greatly. "If I refuse to comment further, the rumors will eventually die down."

She leaned back and released an acerbic laugh. "By the time Sam turns twenty?"

He recognized the absurdity in believing any scandal involving the Mehdi family would simply go away. "You're right. I will have to come up with some way to explain the situation. But I will not retract my statement regarding my son."

She appeared resigned. "I understand that, but you have to be worried Talia might find out someone else is pretending to be your son's mother, not to mention your wife. If she decides to come forward, everyone will know Sam's the result of a relationship out of wedlock and you lied about our marriage."

Since his ex was the consummate publicity hound, handing her that bone could prove to be problematic eventually. "To my good fortune, she's unreachable at the moment. I highly doubt she will hear any of this until she returns to France."

"Possibly, but I'm sure the king has heard by now and—" she streaked both hands down her face "—if my grandfather finds out, he'll demand I board the next plane bound for the Carolinas."

Despite what had transpired an hour ago, he still did not want her to leave for many reasons. "As far as I know, you have not yet been identified."

"I saw camera flashes."

"And you were wearing sunglasses. You could be any number of women who've crossed my path." He regretted the comment the moment it left his stupid mouth.

"All your ex-lovers?" she asked, her voice surprisingly calm.

He grasped for anything to dig himself out of the hole. "I meant any woman, whether I've slept with her or not. When you are constantly in the spotlight, your reputation becomes completely overblown. My brother Zain could attest to that. His reputation preceded him before he married Madison."

"I recall Elena mentioning they're in Los Angeles," she said. "Is his wife from the States?"

"Yes, and she is unequivocally the best thing that has ever happened to him. I sincerely never believed he would settle down with one woman."

She leaned back against the seat and began to toy with the diamond pendant dangling between her breasts. "Well, since I'm apparently just any woman, I suppose I shouldn't be worried at all. However, if I know the press, it's only a matter of time before they learn who I am."

Adan pushed out of the chair and moved to the veranda's edge to stare at the mountainous panorama he had always taken for granted. "It would be better for Samuel if everyone believed you are his mother, not Talia. She has quite a few skeletons in her dressing room closet."

Piper joined him and folded her arms atop the ledge. "Haven't we all in some way?"

He turned and leaned back against the stone wall. "I would have a difficult time believing you have anything scandalous to hide."

She smiled. "Well, apparently I gave birth and I haven't been exposed to sex in quite some time. That would be some fairly heavy fodder for the gossipmongers."

He shook his head and returned her smile. "It's good to see your wit is still intact."

"Hey, if you can't immediately fix a terrible situation, you might as well find some humor in it."

A true optimist. He added that to his ever-expanding

list of her attributes. "Do you consider the thought of being wed to me so terrible?"

"Actually, I can think of a few perks being married to you would provide."

He inched closer to her. "What perks do you have in mind?"

She faced him and folded her arms beneath her breasts. "Living in a palace immediately comes to mind."

Not at all what he'd wanted to hear. "That's it?"

"Who wouldn't want to be waited on hand and foot?"

He reached out and tucked her hair behind her ear. "I'm disappointed that's the best you can do."

She frowned. "If you want me to include your expertise as a lover, I can't speak to that because I don't know. Not that I didn't try my best to convince you to show me in your hotel room."

He still wanted to be her lover. More than he'd wanted anything in quite some time, aside from being a worthy father to his son. "Since the rest of the world now believes we've conceived a child together, perhaps we should give lovemaking serious consideration."

Her grin rivaled the sun setting on the horizon. "Procreation in reverse. I kind of like the thought of that, but…" Her words trailed off along with her gaze.

"You still doubt my honor." He hadn't been able to mask the disappointment in his tone.

"You're wrong," she said adamantly. "I realize now only an honorable man would so obviously love a child he just met. I see it every time you look at Sam."

Every time he looked at her, he felt things he could not explain, and shouldn't be feeling. "Then what would stop you from exploring our relationship on an intimate level, particularly when you were so bent on doing so in Chicago?"

"I'm taking your need for celibacy into consideration."

That vow was quickly becoming the bane of his existence. "I do not believe that to be the case."

She sighed. "Fine. Truth is, I don't want to get hurt."

He slid a fingertip along her jaw. "I would never do anything to hurt you, Piper."

"Not intentionally," she said. "But if we take that all-important step, I worry it's going to be too hard to walk away. And we both know I'll be walking away sooner than later."

Letting her walk away wouldn't be one of his finest moments, either. But he could make no promises. "I propose we continue with our original plan and learn all we can about each other while you're here. Anything beyond that will happen only if we mutually decide it's beneficial for both of us."

She tapped her chin and pretended to think. "A prince with benefits. That does sound intriguing."

He had resisted her long enough was his last thought before he reeled her into his arms and kissed her. She didn't reject the gesture at all. She didn't push him away or tense against him. She simply kissed him back like a woman who had not been kissed enough. And as usual, his body responded in a way that would merit a serious scolding from his former governess.

Bent on telling her what she was doing to him, he brought his lips to her ear. "If we had no care in the world, and all the privacy we needed, I would lift up your dress, lower your panties and take you right here."

She pulled back and stared at him with hazy eyes. "I could think of worse things."

He could think of something much better. "You deserve a bed and champagne and candles our first time."

"You're certainly not lacking in confidence."

Subtlety had never been his strongest suit. "Provided we decide to take that next step."

"Provided we could actually find the time to do it while adhering to your son's schedule."

Right on time, the sound of a crying baby filtered out through the nursery's open window. "I shall go see about him," he said without removing his hold or his gaze from her.

"I'll do it," she answered without making a single move.

"I already have."

Adan glanced to his right to see Elena strolling onto the terrace, his son in her arms, sending him away from Piper. "We were on our way."

Elena rolled her eyes. "You were on your way, all right, but that had nothing to do with the *bambino*."

Caught by the former nanny like a juvenile delinquent stealing candy from the market. "We shall take charge of him now."

Elena moved in front of him and smiled. "I will watch him for a while until you and Miss McAdams return."

"Where are we going?" Piper asked before he could respond.

"Your presence is requested in the conference room. Both of you."

Perhaps the first information from the engineers, although he had a difficult time believing they'd have anything significant to report in such a short time. "Shouldn't we wait to meet with the conservation crew until after Rafiq returns?"

"Rafiq arrived a few minutes ago," Elena said. "He called the meeting."

Damn it all to hell. He'd been summoned to take his place in the king's hot seat. "Did he happen to mention anything about water conservation?"

"I would speculate he's interested in conserving the military commander in chief's reputation." Elena cradled the baby closer and patted Adan's arm. "Good luck, *cara*. You are absolutely going to need it."

Depending on what his brother had in store for him, he could very well need to call out the royal guard.

Five

Dead silence—Piper's first impression the minute she followed Adan into the conference room for the so-called meeting. And she had no doubt she knew exactly what was on the agenda—quite possibly her head delivered to her personally by the king of Bajul.

He wore a black silk suit, dark gray tie and a definite air of authority. His coal-colored eyes and near-black hair would qualify him as darkly handsome, and somewhat intimidating. *Very* intimidating, Piper realized when he pushed back from the head of the mahogany table and came to his feet. Adan might be an inch or so taller, but his brother's aura of sheer power made him seem gigantic.

The mysterious Mr. Deeb stood nearby, absently studying his glasses before he repositioned them over his eyes. "Please join us," he said, indicating the two chairs on each side of the stoic monarch.

Adan had already settled in before Piper had gathered enough courage to walk forward. She could do this. She could face Rafiq Mehdi with a calm head and feigned confidence. Or she could turn and run.

Choosing the first option for diplomacy's sake, she claimed the chair opposite Adan as the king sat and folded his hands before him on the tabletop. "It is a pleasure to meet you, Ms. McAdams," he began, "though I would have preferred to have done so under different circumstances."

She would have preferred not to meet him at all today, if ever. Sucking up seemed like a fantastic idea. "The pleasure is all mine, Your Excellency. My grandfather has said some wonderful things about your leadership. And you may call me Piper."

"And you may address me as Rafiq, since it seems you have become a part of the royal family without my knowledge."

Piper swallowed hard around her chagrin. "Actually, that's not—"

"Are you going to jump to conclusions without hearing our side of the story, Rafiq?" Adan asked, a serious hint of impatience in his tone.

The king leaned back and studied them both for a moment. "I am giving you the opportunity now."

"I have a son," Adan said. "That whole wife issue was simply a misunderstanding, and that is all there is to the story."

Rafiq released a gruff laugh. "I fear you are wrong about that, brother. I know this because I have heard the entire sordid tale. And I do believe that included you delivering the 'wife' proclamation yourself."

Piper noticed an immediate change in Adan's demeanor. He definitely didn't appear quite as confident as he had when they'd entered the room. She had to come to his defense due to her contribution to the mess. "Your Excellency, I'm in part responsible for—"

Adan put up a hand to silence her. "It was simply an error in judgment on both our parts. We were attempting to protect each other and my son."

"Yet instead you have created a scandal at a time when we are trying to convince our people this conservation project is worthwhile," Rafiq replied. "Their attention has now been diverted from the need to relocate some of the farms to an illegitimate child born to the man in charge of protecting our borders."

"Never use that word to describe my son again," Adan hissed. "I may not have known about him, but he is every bit a Mehdi."

Rafiq looked extremely surprised. "I never thought of you as being the paternal sort, Adan. That being said, it is my understanding his true mother is the narcissistic Talia Thorpe."

Evidently the royal family and staff held the model in very low esteem. "That's true," Piper interjected before she could be cut off again. "I was simply pretending to be the baby's mother to delay the questions over his parentage."

"Yet everyone now believes you are his mother," Rafiq replied. "That has created quite the dilemma."

"I promise you I will handle this," Adan said. "I will retract the marriage statement and explain that Samuel is my child from a previous relationship."

Rafiq straightened and scowled. "You will do no such thing."

Adan exchanged a look with Piper before bringing his attention back to his brother. "You would have us continue the lie?"

"As a matter of fact, that is exactly what you will do," Rafiq began, "until you find some way to be rid of the model, for both yours and your heir's sake. Naming her as the mother will only wreak more havoc. The woman is known for posing in the nude in several photographs."

The king's condescension ruffled Piper's artistic feathers. "Some do not find nudity offensive. It would depend on what the photographer was attempting to convey."

"Centerfold photos," Adan added. "She posed for several magazines, in print and online. Some of those publications are obscure and questionable at best."

That did change everything from an artistic standpoint. "Are they widely circulated here?"

Adan looked somewhat sheepish. "After word got out that we were involved."

The king turned his full attention to her. "Ms. McAdams, if you would kindly continue the charade until your departure, then we will make certain you are compensated."

She could not believe someone was offering to pay her for a humongous fib that could alter her own life. "No offense, Your Excellency, but I can't in good conscience accept money for my silence."

"Temporary silence," the king added. "And I was not suggesting a bribe. However, I will award the contract to your corporation upon review of the bid. Once you have returned to the States, we will issue a statement saying you felt it best that the marriage be dissolved on the basis of irreconcilable differences, and that you feel your son should live in his homeland."

"And what do you propose we do with Talia?" Adan asked. "Bind and gag her before she leaks the truth to the media?"

"*She* we will have to pay," Rafiq stated. "I am certain it will cost a fortune to have her relinquish her rights as well as execute a legal document forbidding her to have any claim on the child. Fortunately, you have the means to meet her price, however high that might be."

Adan released a weary sigh. "Rafiq, this could all backfire no matter how carefully we plan. Talia could refuse to meet our terms, and furthermore, the truth may surface no matter how hard we try to conceal it."

"I trust that you and Ms. McAdams will see that does not happen."

The man was making too many impossible demands as far as Piper was concerned. "How do you propose we do that when you risk someone within these walls leaking that information?"

"The staff normally practices absolute discretion," Rafiq said, mirroring Adan's words from the day they discovered Sam existed. "Yet it would be foolish not to believe someone with lesser responsibility in the palace could sell the information to the highest bidder. Therefore it is paramount you both act as if you are a wedded couple at all times. We will issue a press release stating you were married at an undisclosed location prior to the pregnancy."

As she regarded Adan, Piper couldn't quite contain her sarcasm. "Would that be all right with you, dear?"

He shook his head. "None of this is right, but I do believe it is a viable plan, at least for the time being."

She saw her control over the situation begin to slip away. "Do I have any say in the matter?"

"Yes you do," Rafiq said. "You are free to refuse and leave immediately. With your company's crew."

A not-so-veiled threat. She mulled over a laundry list of pros and cons while Adan and the king waited for her answer. If she didn't agree, they would lose the contract, and that could send the struggling business into a free fall. If she did agree, she would have to stay on for at least a month immersed in a massive lie. And most important, she would be charged with contacting her grandparents to break the news before someone else did. She could only imagine her grandfather's reaction to either scenario. Then again, if she went along with the marriage pretense, she'd have the opportunity to stand up to him once and for all if he gave her any grief. She could finally be her own person and control her own life—for at least a month. Not a bad thing, at that.

A few more seconds ticked off while she weighed her options. The one bright spot she could see coming out of this entire debacle had directly to do with Adan. Being his make-believe spouse could come with some serious perks.

She drew in a deep breath, let it out slowly and said, "I'll do it."

Adan looked caught completely off guard. "You will?"

"I will." She rose from the chair and managed a smile. "Now, if you gentlemen would please excuse me, this pretend wife needs to make a call to her very real grandparents."

Adan stood and returned her smile. "Feel free to use my private study next door."

"Thanks. I believe I will."

Piper did an about-face, strode into the hall and prepared to lie.

"Have you totally lost your ever-lovin' mind, sweet pea?"

Oh, how she hated her grandfather's pet name for her. But Piper had to admit she was enjoying his shock. She'd never seriously shocked anyone in her sheltered life up to this point, at least not to this extreme. "No, Poppa, I'm quite sane. I would have told you sooner about the marriage but it was rather spontaneous." And pure fiction.

"When did you meet this character?"

Lie number one. "Quite a while ago, when I was in the U.K. last year."

"And you didn't bother to tell me this when you knew full well I was sending you to his country? That dog just don't hunt."

Lie number two. "We've kept our relationship quiet because we didn't want other contractors thinking I could influence the bidding process."

"And you don't have an influence over the bid now that you've gotten yourself hitched to him, sweet pea?"

Lie number three. "Not at all."

A span of silence passed before he responded. "I guess there's nothing I can do about it now, but at least it's good to know he's got royal blood and money to burn."

Of course that would be Walter McAdams's main concern when it came to her choice in a life partner. It always had been. "I'm sure when you met him back in Chicago you realized he's a very charming man."

"A charming snake," he muttered. "Of course, your grandmother's all atwitter over this. She wants to talk to you, so hang on a minute."

Piper heard him put down the receiver, followed by muffled conversation before someone picked up the phone again. "My little sugar plum is a married woman!"

Enough with the overly sweet endearments, she wanted to say, but kept her impatience in check. "Yes, Nana, I finally took the plunge." Headlong into a humongous fabricated fairy tale.

"I saw a picture of him on the internet, Piper. My, my, he's a good-looking young man. When did you two meet?"

Piper was frankly sick to death of fibbing, so she decided to try on the truth. "In a hotel bar. I attempted to seduce him but he didn't take the bait. He's quite the gentleman."

As usual, her grandmother giggled like a schoolgirl, a good indicator she didn't believe what she'd heard. "Oh, child, you are still such a cutup when it comes to boys. And you don't have to tell me any details right now."

But she did have to tell her more truths. "Nana, Adan is a very public figure, so you might hear a few rumors that aren't exactly accurate."

"What kind of rumors?" she asked with obvious concern.

She could trust her grandmother with some of the facts, even if the woman was a little too steeped in Southern society. "First, you have to promise me that whatever I tell you, it has to remain strictly confidential."

"Sugar, you know how I abhor gossip."

An advantage for Piper in this gossip game. "All right. You're probably going to hear that we've had a baby together."

Nana released an audible gasp. "Did you?"

Heavens, the woman wasn't thinking straight. "Do you recall me even remotely looking pregnant over the past few months?"

"Well, no."

"Precisely, because I wasn't. Adan does have an infant son, but obviously I'm not his mother. That said, as far as the world knows, Samuel is my baby. The biological mother's identity is a well-kept secret and has to remain so for reasons I can't reveal."

"Is she an actress? Maybe a singer? Oh, wait. Is she a call girl?"

Piper had no idea Drusilla McAdams even knew what that was. "Don't worry about it. I just need you to refuse to comment on anything if any reporters track you and Poppa down, and keep everything I've told you to yourself. Can you do that, Nana?"

"I certainly can, sugar plum," she said. "And I'm so proud of you, sweetie. It's admirable you're willing to take another woman's child and raise it as your own."

"I learned that from you, Nana."

A span of silence passed before her grandmother spoke again. "I have never regretted raising you and your sister, Piper. I do regret that Millie could never be a decent mother to you. But that's mine and your Poppa's fault. We spoiled her too much, maybe even loved her too much. She never had a care in the world aside from herself."

She still didn't as far as Piper could tell. She'd barely even seen her fly-by-night mother over the past few years, let alone established a relationship with her. "You were very good to me and Sunny, Nana. Millie is responsible for her behavior, not you. And I don't believe you can ever love anyone too much."

"Only if they can't possibly love you back, honey."

Her grandmother's words gave her some cause for concern. If she happened to stupidly fall in love with Adan, she wondered if he had the capacity to return her feelings. Probably not, and she certainly didn't intend to find out. Sadly, sometimes intentions went awry. "Look, Nana, I have a few things to do, but first, do you have any questions for me?" Piper held her breath and hoped for a no.

"Yes I do. How is the sheikh when it comes to… you know?"

Regretfully Piper hadn't experienced "you know"… yet. "Nana, a girl's gotta have her secrets, so I'll only say I'm not at all disappointed." Should she and Adan take that lovemaking step, she would wager she wouldn't be disappointed in the least.

"That's a good thing, sugar plum. What goes on between the sheets better be good if you want to sustain a relationship. Your grandfather and I have been happily going after—"

"I'd better go." Before they wandered into too-much-information territory. "I'll talk to you both real soon."

"Okay, but your grandfather told me to deliver a message before you hang up, the old grump."

Lovely. "What is it?"

"Married or not, you still have a job to do, and he expects a full report on the survey crew's progress within the next two days."

So much for spending time with father and son. For the time being, Adan would just have to go it alone.

"Congratulations, Dad. Your baby is the picture of health."

Adan turned from the crib to face Maysa Barad Mehdi—Arabian beauty, American-educated premiere physician and current queen of Bajul. "Are you absolutely certain? He seems rather small to me."

His sister-in-law sent him a sympathetic look, much to his chagrin. "He's not quite five weeks old, Adan, so he's going to be small. Fortunately Ms. Thorpe had the foresight to include copies of his medical records since his birth. He's gaining weight at a favorable pace and I expect that to continue." She paused and sent him a smile. "And before you know it, he will have a playmate."

Clearly the woman had taken leave of her senses. "I have no intention of having another child in the near future, if ever." First, he would have to have a willing partner, and his thoughts immediately turned to Piper. With her he wouldn't be seeking procreation, only practice. As much practice as she would allow, if she allowed any at all after being thrust into Rafiq's harebrained scheme.

"Let me rephrase that," Maysa said. "Samuel will have a new cousin in a little less than eight months."

Adan let that sink in for a moment before he responded, "You're pregnant?"

"Yes, I am."

He gave her a fond embrace. "Congratulations to you, as well. How is Rafiq handling impending parenthood?"

Her expression turned somber. "He is worried to death, though he tries not to show it."

"That's understandable considering the accident." The freak car accident that had claimed Rafiq's former wife and unborn child. A horrific event that had turned his brother into a temporary tyrant. "I'm certain he will relax eventually."

She frowned. "Did you only recently meet Rafiq, Adan? The man does not know the first thing about relaxing. I only hope he calms somewhat before the birth. Otherwise we'll have a fretful child."

He couldn't imagine Rafiq remaining calm under such a stressful situation. "Perhaps having Samuel around will demonstrate that tending to an infant isn't rocket science. If I can manage it, then certainly so will he."

She patted his cheek. "And you are doing very well from what I hear."

Curiosity and concern drove him to ask, "What else have you heard?"

"If you're wondering if I know about the presumed marriage, I do. My husband told me you could not have chosen a more suitable counterfeit wife." She accentuated the barb with a grin.

He found little humor in the current state of affairs. "This entire situation reeks of fraud, and I find it appalling that I've drawn Piper into that web of deceit. She's a remarkable woman and deserves much better."

Maysa inclined her head and studied him a few moments. "You sound as if you care a great deal for her."

More than he would ever let on—to Piper or to himself. "I've only known her a few days, yet I admittedly like what I do know."

"It shows," she said. "Your face lights up at the mention of her name."

A complete exaggeration. "Women always seem to imagine things that aren't there," he muttered. "Just because I am fond of her does not mean I see her as anything other than my unwitting partner in crime." But he could see her as his lover, as he had often in his fantasies. "I certainly have no plans to make this marriage real."

"We'll see," Maysa said as she covered the now-sleeping infant with the blanket. "One never knows what will transpire once intimacy is involved."

"I am not sleeping with her, Maysa," he said, a little too defensively. "And as it stands now, that is not on the to-do list." At least not on the one he wasn't hiding.

Maysa flipped a lock of her waist-length hair over one shoulder. "Adan, when you do not have an agenda that includes bedding a woman, then the world has truly spun on its axis."

If he had his way, someday people would see him as more than a womanizer. They would see him as a good father. "As always, dear queen, you are correct, at least partially. I would be telling a tale if I said I had not considered consummating our relationship. She's beautiful and intelligent and possesses a keen wit. She is also in many ways an innocent. For that reason I have vowed not to take advantage of her trusting nature."

"Perhaps you should explore the possibilities," she said. "And I do not mean in a sexual sense. You should take this time to get to know her better. You might be pleasantly surprised at what you learn."

Exactly as he had promised both himself and Piper— getting to know each other better before they took the next step. That was before he'd learned he had a son. "I see several problems with that prospect. Being charged with Samuel's care is taxing and time-consuming. Commanding the whole bloody Royal Air Force doesn't require as much attention."

Maysa began returning supplies to her black doctor's bag resting on the dressing table where she'd performed the examination on his son. "Then perhaps you will be happy to know my husband has instructed me to tell you to take your bride away for two days for a respite."

Adan firmly believed his brother had taken leave of his senses. "Why would he suggest that?"

She snapped the bag closed and turned toward him. "He's trying to buy more time, Adan. The media have already been hounding him for an interview with you, and it will only become worse once the palace releases an official statement later today. Rafiq feels that if he tells them you're away for a brief holiday, they'll let up for the time being. And considering Samuel's age, this would be the appropriate time for you to resume your husbandly duty."

He could not resume a duty he had yet to undertake. However, the prospect of spending more time with his presumed wife was greatly appealing, yet he could not ignore the obvious issues. "I cannot abandon Samuel."

"I am sure Elena would wholeheartedly step in while you're gone."

"Actually, she wouldn't," he said. "She's made it quite clear that she is handing all the responsibility to me."

"Then I will watch him until you return. And you are more than welcome to take your new wife to the resort."

He had his own secluded resort equipped with a pool where they could spend some quality time. Then again, swimming with Piper would involve very little clothing. Not a good scenario for a man who for months had engaged in sexual deprivation in order to build character. At the moment, he had enough character to rival philanthropists worldwide. "I certainly appreciate your offer, but I would not want to burden you with my responsibility."

"It's not a burden at all," Maysa said as she leaned over and touched the top of Samuel's head. "I consider it an opportunity to practice parenthood. Now, hurry along while you still have the better part of the day."

A plan began to formulate in Adan's brain. A good plan involving his favorite mode of transportation. Now all he had to do was convince Piper to come along for the ride of her life.

After the harrowing trip to the airbase, Piper would be out of her mind if she agreed to go on this little flying excursion in the miniplane built for two. "You don't really believe I'm going to climb into that sardine can, do you?"

Adan flipped his aviators up to rest atop his head and tried to grin his way out of trouble, which wasn't going to work on Piper. Much. "This happens to be a very solid aircraft," he said.

Solid, maybe. Too tiny. Definitely. "First, you make me wear a massive helmet, throw me onto the back of a motorcycle and travel at excessive speeds on skinny little back roads to get here—"

"That was designed to evade the press, and if my memory serves me correctly, you came along willingly."

Darn it, she had. "That's not the point. Now you want me to get into a plane equivalent to a golf cart with wings."

He moved in front of said wing and patted the white plane's belly as if it were a favored pet. "Do not let the propeller scare you away. This is a Royal Air Force training craft meticulously maintained by our best mechanics. And of course, you are in good hands with me as your personal pilot."

A personal pilot with great hands, and she sure would like to know how they would feel all over her body. Maybe today she might actually find out. Maybe squeezing into this plane would be well worth it. "Just show me to my seat."

He grinned and opened the miniature door. "Hand over your bag and I will assist you."

Piper relinquished the tote to Adan, as well as her coveted control. "Here you are, and be careful with it because it contains some breakable items."

His smile melted into a scowl. "This bag must weigh ten pounds. Did you pack all your worldly belongings?"

She playfully slapped at his biceps, well aware he had one heck of a muscle. "No, I did not. I just packed a swimsuit and a change of clothes, per your request. I also brought along a few toiletries and sunscreen and towels. And a small sketch pad and pencils, in case I want to immortalize our day together on paper."

His smile returned full force. "It is quite possible you will not have time to sketch."

That sounded very promising. "And why would that be, Your Highness?"

He leaned over and brushed a kiss across her cheek. "Well, my pretend princess, I have several activities planned to occupy our time."

She could think of only one activity at the moment that interested her. "Can you give me a hint?"

"No. I want you to be surprised." He executed a slight bow. "Now climb into my chariot, fair lady, and we will begin our adventure."

She managed a not-half-bad curtsy. "As you wish, good sir."

Luckily the step up into the two-seater plane wasn't all that steep, but the small space seemed somewhat claustrophobic once Adan took his place beside her.

After strapping himself in, he handed her a headset. "Put this on and we'll be able to hear each other over the engine noise."

Noisy engine—not good. "Are you sure this is safe?" she asked before she covered her ears.

"Positive. And don't look so worried. We'll barely be off the ground before it's time to land again."

"A planned landing, I hope," she muttered as she adjusted the bulky headphones.

From that point forward, Piper watched Adan in action as he guided the pitiful excuse for a plane to the airstrip adjacent to the fleet of high-powered jets. As he did a final check, the Arabic exchange between Adan and the air traffic controller sounded like gibberish to her. But once he began to taxi down the runway, she didn't care if the pilot was speaking pig Latin. She held her breath, fisted her hands in her lap, gritted her teeth and closed her eyes tightly.

During liftoff, her stomach dipped as if she were riding a roller coaster. She felt every bump and sway as they gained altitude, and even when the plane seemed to level off, she still refused to look.

"You are missing some incredible scenery."

Feeling somewhat foolish, Piper forced herself to peer out the window at the terrain now cast in the midmorning sun. She noticed only a few man-made structures dotting the landscape, but the approaching mountains looked as if she could reach out and touch them, and that did nothing for her anxiety.

As if sensing her stress, Adan reached over the controls and took her hand. "This is the best view of my country," he said. "And when I am flying, I feel completely at peace."

She wished she could say the same for herself. "I've got a swarm of butterflies in my belly."

"I had no idea you're such a nervous flier."

"Not usually," she said. "I've never been in an aircraft quite this small before."

"Try to think of this as being as close to heaven as you can possibly be."

"I'd prefer not to get too much closer."

He grinned and squeezed her hand. "I will have you earthbound in a matter of minutes. If you look straight ahead, you'll see where we are going to land."

She tried to focus on the horizon, and not the descent toward the ground. Or the fact Adan was guiding them toward what appeared to be no more than a glorified dirt road—and a rather large mountain not far away. Her stomach dipped along with the plane as they approached the makeshift runway, but this time she kept her eyes open. She still remained as tense as a tightrope when the wheels touched down and they bounced a time or two before coming to a stop.

Piper let out the breath she'd been holding and looked around to find a thick copse of odd-looking trees surrounding them, but no signs of human life. "Where are we?"

Adan removed his headset, then hers, and smiled. "I am about to show you my most favorite place on the planet, and an experience you will not soon forget."

Six

"Wow."

Piper's wide-eyed reaction to the mountain retreat greatly pleased Adan. He'd brought only one other woman there, and she'd complained incessantly about the lack of facilities. But then Talia wasn't fond of sacrificing creature comforts for nature's bounty.

"It's basically a simple structure," he explained as he led her farther into the lone living area. "It's comprised of native wood and powered by solar energy. The water comes from the nearby lake to the house through a filtering system."

She walked to the sofa and ran her fingertips along the back of the black leather cushion. "It's very comfortable and cozy."

Her code for small, he surmised. "It has all one would require in this setting. One loft bedroom and a bath upstairs, another bedroom and bath downstairs, and my study."

She turned and smiled. "No kitchen?"

He pointed to his left. "Behind the stone wall, and it's the most impressive part of the house. However, I rarely utilize the stove, but I do make good use of the refrigerator and microwave."

"No housekeeper available?"

"No, but I do have a caretaker. He and his wife look after the place when I'm away."

She dropped down onto the beige club chair and curled her legs beneath her. "What possessed you to build a place out in the middle of nowhere?"

"You will soon see." After setting her bag on the bamboo floor, Adan crossed the room and pushed aside the drapes, revealing the mountainous terrain.

"Wow again," Piper said as she came to his side. "A view and your own private pool. I'm impressed."

He slid double doors open, bringing the outdoors inside. "This greatly expands the living space. And you'll appreciate the scenery far better from the veranda."

She smiled. "Then lead the way."

When Piper followed him onto the deck containing an outdoor kitchen and several tables with matching chairs, Adan paused at the top of the steps leading to the infinity pool. "This glorified bathtub took two years to build."

"It's absolutely incredible."

So was this woman beside him. He sat on the first step and signaled her to join him. Once she complied, he attempted not to notice the way her white shorts rode up her thighs, or the cleavage showing from the rounded neck in her sleeveless coral top that formed to her breasts very nicely. "This has always been my sanctuary of sorts. A good place to escape."

She took her attention from the water and turned it on him. "Exactly what are you escaping, Adan?"

He'd asked himself that question many times, and the answers were always the same. "I suppose the drudgery of being a royal. Perhaps the responsibility of overseeing an entire military operation. At one time, my father."

The final comment brought about her frown. "Was he that hard on you?"

He sighed. "No. He wasn't particularly concerned with what I did. I once believed he'd never quite recovered from losing my mother." That was before he'd learned his father's secrets.

"You mentioned your mother when we were in Chicago," she began, "but you didn't say what happened to her. Of course, if it makes you uncomfortable to talk about it, I understand."

Oddly, he wanted to tell her about his mother, what little he knew of Cala Mehdi. He wanted to tell her many things he'd never spoken of to anyone. And eventually he would tell her their visit would be extended beyond the afternoon. "Her death was a mystery of sorts. She was found at the bottom of the mountain near the lake. Most believed she'd taken a fall. Some still wonder if she'd taken her own life due to depression following my birth. I've accepted the fact I'll never know the truth."

"Are you sure you've accepted it?"

It was as if she could see straight to his soul. "I have no choice. My father never spoke of her. But then, he rarely spoke to me. Perhaps I reminded him too much of her."

"At least you actually knew your real father."

"Not necessarily." The words spilled out of his stupid mouth before he'd had time to reel them back in.

She shifted slightly toward him and laid a palm on his arm. "Are you saying the king wasn't your biological father?"

He saw no reason to conceal his concerns now that he'd taken her into his confidence. "I only know I do not resemble him or my brothers. My hair is lighter and so are my eyes."

"That's not definitive proof, Adan," she said. "Maybe you look like your mother."

"I've seen a few photographs, and I see nothing of me in her. She had almost jet-black hair and extremely dark eyes, like Rafiq."

"If that's the case, then why would you think someone else fathered you?"

"Because my mother was reportedly very unhappy, and I suspect she could have turned to another man for comfort. Rafiq's former wife, Rima, did that very thing due to her own discontent with the marriage."

"Are you certain you're not speculating because of Rafiq's situation?"

He had valid reasons for his suspicions, namely his father's two-decade affair with the governess. Yet he had no intention of skewing Piper's opinion of Elena by revealing the truth yet. "My parents' marriage was arranged, as tradition ordained it. Marriage contracts are basically business arrangements, and in theory advantageous for both families. Unfortunately, when human emotions enter into the mix, the intent behind the agreement becomes muddled."

She frowned. "You mean emotions as in *love?*"

"Yes. The motivating force behind many of the world's ills."

"And the cure for many more."

She didn't sound pleased with his assessment. She had sounded somewhat wistful. "Spoken like a true romantic."

"Spoken like a diehard cynic," she said. "But your cynical days could soon be over now that you have a baby. There is no greater love than that which exists between parent and child, provided the parent is open to that love."

That sounded somewhat like an indictment to his character. "I have already established that bond with my son. But I have never welcomed romantic love for lack of a good example." And for fear of the inability to live up to unreasonable expectations.

She inclined her head and studied him. "Love isn't something you always have to work at, Your Highness. Sometimes it happens when you least expect it."

Piper sounded as if she spoke of her own experiences. "Have you ever been in love?" he asked.

"Not to this point." She glanced away briefly before bringing her attention back to him. "Do arranged marriages still exist in the royal family?"

Happily for him, the answer was no. "That requirement changed after Rafiq inherited the crown. Otherwise he would not have been able to marry a divorced woman. All the better. It was an illogical and worthless tradition, in my opinion."

She offered him a sunny smile that seemed somehow forced. "Well, I guess we really bucked tradition by arranging to have a fake marriage."

At the moment he'd like to have a fake honeymoon, yet he still had reservations. Piper had accommodated the king's wishes by joining in the ruse, and she'd selflessly helped care for his son. He never wanted her to believe he would take advantage of the situation. "Quite frankly, all this talk of family dysfunction is making me weary." He stood and offered his hand. "Would you care to go for a swim?"

"Yes, I most definitely would," she said as she allowed him to help her up. "But are you sure you're up to it? You look tired, and I suspect that has to do with Sam."

"He was awake quite a bit last night and I had the devil of a time getting him back to sleep after the two o'clock feeding. Yet I grew accustomed to little sleep while training for my military duties."

"Why didn't you wake me? I would have taken a shift."

"Because my child is my responsibility, not yours." He immediately regretted the somewhat callous remark and set out to make amends. "I definitely appreciate all that you've done, but I do not want to take advantage of your generosity."

She attempted a smile that failed to reach her blue eyes. "I really don't mind, Adan. What are fake mothers for?"

He could always count on her to use humor to cover her hurt. Hurt that he had caused. "We'll worry about Samuel's care when we return in two days."

Her mouth momentarily dropped open. "Two days? I thought you said this was an afternoon outing."

He endeavored to appear guileless. "Did I?"

She doomed him to hell with a look. "You did."

"My apologies. As it turns out, we have been instructed by the king to remain absent from the palace for two days to avoid the media frenzy. I do think it's best we return tomorrow before sundown. I do not want to be away from Samuel two nights."

"But my grandfather ordered me to see that the engineers finalize the—"

"Bid, and that has been handled by Rafiq. He has accepted, and the contract will be couriered to your grandfather tomorrow. He has also arranged for the engineers to be transported to the States in the morning."

She threaded her lip between her teeth as she took several moments before speaking. "Then I guess everything has been handled."

"Yes, which frees you to relax and see to your own pleasure. Nonetheless, if you insist on returning early, we shall."

This time her smile arrived fully formed. "Where should I change to get this two-day party started?"

He caught her hands and brushed a kiss across her knuckles. "Never change, Piper McAdams. I like you exactly the way you are."

She wrested away, much to his disappointment. "I meant 'change' as in clothes. I need to put on my swimsuit."

He preferred she'd go without any clothes. "You may use the bath downstairs. You'll find it between my study and the guest room, immediately past the kitchen. Or if you prefer, use the one upstairs adjacent to my bedroom. It's much larger."

"Where are you going to change?"

"I hadn't planned on wearing anything at all." He couldn't contain his laughter when he noticed her shocked expression. "I'm not serious, so do not look so concerned. My swim trunks are upstairs."

She began backing toward the entry. "I'll use the downstairs bath while you go upstairs. And I'd better not find you naked in that pool when I come back."

The word *naked* put specific parts of his anatomy on high alert. "At one time that might have been the case, but I have turned over a new leaf."

She paused at the doors and eyed him suspiciously. "A leaf from the player tree?"

He supposed he deserved that. "Believe what you will, but there have not been that many women in my life. None since I ended my relationship with Talia."

"Ah, yes. The celibacy clause. How's that working out for you?"

Not very well at the moment. Not when he knew in a matter of moments he would see her with very little covering her body. Or so he hoped. "I will let you know by day's end."

As soon as she returned to the pool, Piper found Adan staring out over the horizon. She couldn't see his face or eyes, but she sensed his mind was on something else—or someone else, namely his child. Her mind immediately sank into the gutter when she shamelessly studied all the details from his bare, well-defined back to his impressive butt concealed by a pair of navy swim trunks.

She approached him slowly, overwhelmed by the urge to run her hands over the patently male terrain. Instead, she secured the towel knotted between her breasts. "I'm fairly sure that mountain won't move no matter how long you stare at it."

He turned to her, his expression surprisingly somber. "If only I had that power."

Once she moved past the initial shock of seeing his gorgeous bare chest, she found her voice. "Are you worried about Sam?"

"I'm worried that my position will prevent me from being a good father to him. I'm also concerned that perhaps I would be wrong to ask Talia to give up all claims on him."

"No offense, Adan, but I don't see Talia as the motherly type."

"Perhaps so, but isn't any mother better than no mother at all?"

"Not really," she said without thought. "My so-called mother never cared about her daughters. Her own needs took precedence over ours. Luckily for us, my grandmother willingly stepped in and gave us all the love we could ask for, and more. Otherwise I don't know how we would have turned out."

He brushed his knuckles over her cheek. "You have turned out very well. And now if you would kindly remove that towel, we'll spend the afternoon basking in the Bajul sun."

That would be the logical next step—revealing her black bikini that left little to the imagination. A step that required some advance preparation. "Before I do that, you need to know I'm not tall and skinny like Talia. I'm short and I haven't been blessed with a lean build and—"

He flipped the knot with one smooth move and the towel immediately fell to the ground. Then he gave her a lingering once-over before raising his gaze back to her eyes. "You have been blessed with a beautiful body, Piper. You have the curves this man desires."

He desired her curves? Incredible. "Your physique is the thing fantasies are made of. But the question is, how well do you swim? I have to warn you, I'm pretty darned good at it."

And without giving her any warning, he strode to the far end of the pool and executed a perfect dive. He emerged a few moments later, slicked back his hair and smiled. "Now it's your turn to prove your expertise."

If only she could stop gaping at his dimples and get her feet to move. Finally she willed herself to follow his lead by moving to the same spot he had and doing a little diving of her own. After her eyes adjusted, she sought Adan out where he now stood in the shallow end. She remained underwater until she swam immediately in front of him and came up for air. "How's that?"

"Perfect," he said as he put his arms around her. "As are you."

She laughed even though she could barely concentrate while being up close and personal. "Not hardly, Your Majesty. I can be stubborn and I do have a little bit of a temper at times. I'm also a picky eater and I speed when I drive—"

He cut off her laundry list of faults with a kiss. A kiss so hot it rivaled the sun beating down on her shoulders. A down-and-dirty, tongue-dueling kiss that had Piper heating up in unseen places on her person. When he streamed his palms along her rib cage and grazed the side of her breast, she thought she might melt. When he returned his hands to her shoulders, she thought she might groan in protest.

He studied her eyes with an intensity that stole what was left of her breath. "Before this continues, I need to say something."

She needed him to get on with it. "I'm listening."

"I want to make love to you, more than anything I have wished for in some time. But you are under no obligation to honor that request."

Was he kidding? "If I remember correctly, I went to your hotel room in Chicago with that one goal in mind. Of course, where I wanted to end my celibacy, you were determined to hang on to yours."

"Not anymore," he said. "Not since the day I met you, actually. You are different from any woman I have ever known."

"Is that a good thing?"

"A very good thing."

"Then let's put an end to doing without right here and now."

He gave her an unmistakable bad-boy grin. "Take off your suit."

"You go first," she said, suddenly feeling self-conscious.

"All right." He quickly removed the trunks and tossed them aside, where they hit the cement deck with a splat. "Your turn."

After drawing in a deep breath, she reached back and released the clasp, then untied the bow at her neck. Once she had that accomplished, she threw the top behind her, her bare breasts no longer concealed by the water. "Better?"

"Yes, but you're not finished yet."

Time to go for broke. Piper shimmied her bottoms down her legs and kicked them away. Right then she didn't care if they were carried away by the pool pump's current and ended up in another country. "Are you satisfied now?"

"Not quite, but I will be," he said as he pulled her close, took her hand and guided it down his belly and beyond.

When Adan pressed her palm against his erection, Piper blew out a staggered breath. "I do believe I've located an impressive sea creature down below."

"Actually, it's an eel."

"Electric?"

"Highly charged." He brought her hand back to his chest. "But should you investigate further, I fear I will not be able to make it to the bed."

She stood on tiptoe and kissed the cute cleft in his chin. "What's wrong with a little water play?"

"If you're referring to water foreplay, then I am all for that." He wrapped one arm around her waist, then lowered his mouth to her breast while slipping his hand between her thighs simultaneously.

Piper gripped his shoulders and grounded herself against the heady sensations. She felt as if her legs might liquefy with every pass of his tongue over her nipple, every stroke of his fingertip in a place that needed his attention the most.

As badly as she wanted the sensations to go on forever, the climax came in record time. She inadvertently dug her nails into his flesh and unsuccessfully stopped the odd sound bubbling up from her throat.

Once the waves subsided, Piper closed her eyes and sighed. "I'm so sorry that happened so fast," she murmured without looking at him.

He tipped her chin up with a fingertip. "You have no

need to apologize. It has been a while for you, by your own admission."

"Try never."

As she predicted, he was obviously stunned by the truth. "You've never had an orgasm?"

She managed a shrug. "Not with anyone else in the room."

"You clearly have encountered nothing but fools."

Fool, singular. "I've only been intimately involved with one man, and he basically treated me like a fast-food drive-through. In and out as quickly as possible."

Adan released a low, grainy laugh. "I am glad to know you find some humor in the situation. I person-ally find it appalling when a man has no concern for his lover's pleasure."

She draped her arms around his neck and wriggled her hips. "That goes both ways, and I do believe you are greatly in need of some pleasure. Why bother with a bed when we have a perfectly good pool deck and a comfy-looking chaise at our disposal?"

He kissed her lightly. "True, but we have no con-doms."

"I see where that would be a problem."

"A very serious problem. I have already received one unexpected surprise with my son. I do not intend to have another."

Piper wasn't certain if he meant another surprise pregnancy or simply another child, period. Or he could mean he didn't care to have a baby with her. But she refused to let haywire emotions ruin this little tempo-rary piece of paradise, even if it was based on pretense. "Then I suggest you take me to bed, Your Machoness."

No sooner than the words left her mouth, Adan swept

her up into his arms and carried her into the house. She expected him to make use of the downstairs bedroom, but instead he started up the stairs with ease, as if she weighed no more than a feather. Far from the truth. Yet he had a knack for making her feel beautiful. She figured he'd probably earned pro status in the flattery department years ago.

Piper barely had time to look around before Adan deposited her in the middle of the bed covered in a lightweight beige spread. She did have time to assess all his finer details while he opened the nightstand drawer and retrieved a condom. He was evidently very proud to see her, and she was extremely happy to be there. But when he caught her watching, she grabbed the pillow from beneath her head and placed it over her fiery face.

She felt the mattress bend beside her right before he yanked the pillow away. "You're not growing shy on me, are you?" he asked.

No, but she was certainly growing hotter by the second. "I'm just feeling a bit exposed."

He smiled as he skimmed his palm down her belly and back up again. "And I am greatly enjoying the exposure." Then his expression turned oddly serious. "If you have any reservations whatsoever—"

She pressed a fingertip against his lips. "I want this, Adan. I have for a while now."

"Then say no more."

He stretched out and shifted atop her body, then eased inside her. She couldn't speak if she tried. His weight, his powerful movement, captured all her attention. The play of his muscles beneath her palms, the sound of his voice at her ear describing what he felt at that moment, sent her senses spiraling. His broken breaths, the way he tensed signaled he was barely maintaining control. When she lifted her hips to meet his thrust, he groaned and picked up the pace. Only a matter of time before he couldn't hold out, she realized. And then he shuddered with the force of his climax before collapsing against her breasts, where she could feel his heart beating rapidly.

Piper wanted to remain this way indefinitely—with a sexy, skilled man in her arms and a sense of pride that she'd taken him to the limit. She felt unusually brave, and incredibly empowered. Never before had it been this way with Keiler Farnsworth. And the fact that the jerk's name jumped into her brain made her as mad as a hornet. He couldn't hold a candle to Adan Mehdi. She suspected she'd be hard-pressed to find any man who would.

After a few blissful moments ticked off, Adan lifted his head from her shoulder and grinned. "I hope you don't judge me on the expediency of the act."

She tapped her chin and pretended to think. "I'll have to take a point off for that."

He frowned. "You are keeping score?"

"I wasn't until you mentioned it. However, I'm giving you back that point because you are just so darn cute. So no need to despair, because you've earned a perfect ten."

He rolled over onto his back, taking his weight away and leaving Piper feeling strangely bereft. "I will do much better next time," he said in a grainy voice.

Next time couldn't come soon enough for her.

Piper McAdams proved to be more enthusiastic than any woman before her. Adan had recognized that during their second heated round of lovemaking at midnight. And again a few hours ago, immediately before dawn, when she'd awakened him with a kiss before urging him to join her in the shower. They'd spent a good deal of time there bathing each other until he took her up against the tiled wall. Still he could not seem to get enough of her.

Making love to her a fourth time in twenty-four hours seemed highly improbable. He should be completely sated. Totally exhausted. Utterly spent.

"Smells like something good is cooking in the kitchen."

At the sound of her sensual morning voice, Adan glanced over one shoulder to find Piper standing in the opening, wearing his robe. The improbable became possible when his body reacted with a surprisingly spontaneous erection.

"I'm heating up the *ataif* that Ghania prepared." And attempting to hide his sins by paying more attention to the stove than his guest.

"What is *ataif*?" she asked.

Recipe recitation should aid in calming his baser urges. When goats sprouted wings. "*Ataif* is a Middle Eastern pancake dipped in honey and cinnamon and covered in walnuts. It is served with a heavy cream known as *kaymak*."

"Thank you for such a thorough description, Chef Sheikh. Now, who is Ghania?"

He was somewhat surprised she hadn't asked that question first. "Ghania is Qareeb's wife. They're the caretakers. She was kind enough to bring the food by a few moments ago."

"How nice of her."

He afforded her another fast glance before returning to his task. "I received news about my son. According to Maysa, he only awoke one time."

"You have cell towers all the way out here?"

"No. The message arrived by carrier pigeon."

"Very amusing," she said before he felt something hit the back of his head.

He looked down to see a wadded paper napkin at his feet. "No need for violence. If you care to communicate with someone, you may use the phone in my study. It's a direct line to the palace that I had installed in the event a military crisis arises."

"That's good to know, and I'd also like to know why you refuse to look at me. I know my hair's still damp and I don't have on a scrap of makeup, but it can't be all that bad. Or maybe it could."

If she only knew how badly he wanted her, with or without the feminine frills, she would not sound so unsure of herself. "For your information, you are a natural beauty, and I am trying to retain some dignity since it seems I am unable to cool my engine in your presence."

"Still revving to go, are you?"

Piper's amused tone sent him around to face her. And if matters weren't bad enough, she was seated on the high-back bar stool facing him, her shapely thighs completely uncovered due to the split in the white cloth. "Are you naked beneath the robe?"

She leaned back against the stainless steel island, using her elbows for support. "Yes, I am. I forgot to bring panties into the bath before I showered."

He was seconds away from forgetting himself and the food preparation. "Perhaps you should dress before we dine."

She crossed one leg over the other and loosened the sash enough to create a gap at her breasts, giving him a glimpse of one pale pink nipple. "Perhaps we should forgo breakfast for the time being."

That was all it took to commit a culinary cardinal sin by leaving the pan on the burner. But if the whole bloody kitchen went up in flames, it could not rival the heat he experienced at that moment.

Without giving her fair warning, Adan crossed the small space between them and kissed her with a passion that seemed to know no bounds. He untied the robe, opened it completely, pushed it down her shoulders and then left her mouth to kiss her neck. He traveled down her bare torso, delivering more openmouthed kisses, pausing briefly to pay homage to her breasts before continuing down her abdomen. What he planned next could prompt her to shove him away, but he was willing to take a chance to reap the reward—driving her to the brink of sexual insanity. A small price to pay for ultimate pleasure, as she would soon see, if she allowed it.

When Adan parted her knees, he felt her tense and noted apprehension in her eyes. "Trust me, *mon ange*," he whispered.

She smiled weakly. "Considering I'm half-naked on a bar stool, that would indicate I'm no angel, Adan. But I do trust you. So hurry."

Permission granted, all systems go. He began by lowering to his knees and kissing the insides of her thighs until he felt her tremble. As he worked his way toward his intended target, she shifted restlessly and then lifted her hips toward his mouth in undeniable encouragement. He used gentle persuasion to coax her climax with soft strokes of his tongue, the steady pull

of his lips. As she threaded her fingers through his hair
and held on firmly, he sensed he would soon achieve his
goal. He wasn't the least bit wrong. She released a low
moan as the orgasm took over, yet he refused to let up
until he was certain she'd experienced every last wave.

Only after he felt her relax did his own desires demand to be met, and so did the need to make haste. He
quickly came to his feet, grabbed the condom she'd discarded on the island and ripped open the plastic with
his teeth.

Adan had the condom in place in a matter of moments and then seated himself deep inside her. He
tried to temper his thrusts, but when Piper wrapped
her legs around his waist, restraint left the bungalow.
He couldn't readily recall feeling so driven to please a
woman. He could not remember the last time he had
felt this good. His thoughts disappeared when his own
climax came with the force of a missile and seemed to
continue for an extraordinary amount of time.

Little by little, logic began to return, including the
fact he'd probably turned the cakes into cinders. He
lifted his head and sought Piper's gaze. "I fear I have
failed in my chef duties."

She reached up and stroked his unshaven jaw. "But
you didn't fail me in your lovemaking duties, and that's
much more important than breakfast."

For the first time in his life, he'd needed to hear that
declaration from a lover. He'd never lacked in confidence or consideration of his partners' needs, yet he had
kept his emotions at arm's length with every woman—
until now.

But as much as he wanted to please this beautiful
woman in his arms, as much as he would like to give

more of himself to her, he wasn't certain he could. And if his relationship history repeated itself, he would probably fail her, too.

Seven

After they arrived back at the airbase and boarded the blasted motorcycle again, Piper feared turning prematurely gray thanks to Adan's daredevil driving. Fortunately that wasn't the case, she realized when they entered the palace foyer and she sneaked a peek in the gold-framed mirror. Granted, her hair was a tangled mess, but she couldn't wait a minute longer to see baby Sam.

Adan obviously felt the same, evidenced by his decision to forgo the elevator and take the stairs instead. She practically had to sprint to catch up with him as Abdul, who insisted on carrying her bag, trailed behind them.

Once they reached the third floor, both she and the houseman were winded, while Adan continued toward the nursery as if he possessed all the energy in the world. He actually did, something she'd learned over the past forty-eight hours in his bed. In his shower. In his kitchen and the pool.

Before Adan could open the nursery door, a striking woman with waist-length brunette hair walked out, clearly startled by the sheikh's sudden appearance. "You took years off my life, brother-in-law."

"My apologies, Maysa," he replied, confirming she was the reining queen. "I'm anxious to see about my son."

Maysa closed the door behind her before facing Adan. "I have already put him down for the night and I advise you wait until he wakes. You seem as though you could use some rest." She topped off the comment with a smile aimed at Piper.

Taking that as her cue, she stepped forward, uncertain whether to curtsy or offer her hand. She opted to let the queen make the first move. "I'm Piper McAdams, and it's a pleasure to finally meet you, Your Highness."

"Welcome to the family," she said, then drew Piper into a surprising embrace. "And please call me Maysa."

Piper experienced a fraud alert. "Actually, I'm not really—"

"Accustomed to it yet," Adan interjected. "Given time she will take to the royal treatment as an electric eel takes to water."

Leave it to the prince to joke at a time like this. "I'm not in the market to be treated royally, but I have enjoyed my time in the palace so far."

"I am glad," Maysa said. "Now, if you will both excuse me, I am starving."

Adan checked his watch. "Isn't dinner later than usual?"

Maysa shrugged. "No, but Rafiq is waiting for me in our quarters."

He winked at Piper before regarding Maysa again. "Oh, you're referring to a different kind of appetite. Do not let us keep you from our king."

"You could not if you tried."

Following a slight wave and a smile, Maysa strode down the hallway and disappeared around the corner, leaving Piper alone with the shifty, oversexed sheikh. And she liked him that way. A lot.

He caught her hand and tugged her against him. "Have I told you how much I enjoyed our time together?"

"At least ten times, but I'll never grow tired of hearing it. I'm just sad it's over."

"It doesn't have to be, Piper. You can stay with me in my suite."

She could be entering dangerous emotional territory. "Maybe it should be, Adan. I'll be leaving in a few weeks."

"I know," he said, sounding somewhat disappointed. "All the more reason to spend as much time together before you depart. I am an advocate of taking advantage of pleasure at every opportunity."

How easy it would be to say yes. "I don't know if that's a good idea."

"Since we are to give the impression we are married, what better way than to share the same quarters?"

A false impression of holy matrimony. "We could do that without sleeping in the same bed."

He rimmed the shell of her ear with the tip of his tongue. "I don't recall mentioning sleep."

And she wouldn't get much if she agreed, for several reasons. "You have to consider Sam's needs over ours."

He pulled back and frowned. "Exactly as I intend to do, but he doesn't require all our time during the night."

"He requires quite a bit."

Framing her face in his palms, Adan looked as if his world revolved around her decision. "Stay with me, Piper. Stay until you must leave."

Spending time with this gorgeous Arabian prince, quality time, would be a fantasy come to life. Yet it could never be the real stuff fairy tales were made of. If she took wisdom into account, she'd say no. If she was willing to risk a broken heart, she'd say yes. And she suddenly realized this risk would be well worth undertaking now, even if it meant crying about it later.

"All right, Adan. I'll stay."

In the silence of his private quarters, the room illuminated by the soft glow of a single table lamp, Adan had never experienced such a strong sense of peace. He had the woman curled up next to him to thank for that. Granted, he still wanted Piper in every way imaginable—he'd proved that at his mountain retreat— yet he greatly appreciated the moments they'd spent in comfortable silence after retiring to his quarters.

That lack of conversation would soon end once he told her what he'd learned from his brother upon their arrival a few hours ago. "I have to go to the base tomorrow to oversee training exercises. It will require me to stay in the barracks overnight."

For a moment he'd thought she'd fallen asleep, until she shifted and rested her cheek above his heart. "Gee, thanks. You invite me to reside in your room and then promptly leave me for a whole night."

The teasing quality to her voice gave Adan some semblance of relief. "If I had to choose between sleeping in the barracks with twenty snoring men and sleeping with you, I would choose you every time. Unless you begin snoring—then I could possibly reconsider."

She lightly elbowed him in the rib cage. "If I did happen to snore, which I don't, you'd have no right to criticize me. I thought a freight train had come through the bedroom last night."

"Are you bloody serious?"

"I'm kidding, Adan," she said as she traced a path along his arm with a fingertip. "Your snore actually sounds more like a purr."

That did not please him in the least. "I prefer a freight train to a common house cat."

"Don't worry, Prince Mehdi. Snore or no snore, you're still as macho and sexy as ever."

He pressed a kiss against the corner of her smiling, sensual mouth. "You are now forgiven for the affront to my manhood."

She yawned and briefly stretched her arms over her head. "Have you ever been in live combat before?"

The query took him aback. "Yes, I have."

"Was it dangerous?"

He smiled at the zeal in her voice. "Does that prospect appeal to your daring side?"

"I'm not sure I actually have much of a daring side. I asked because we're presumed to be husband and wife, so I believe it might be prudent for me to learn all I can about you, in case someone asks."

That sounded logical, but not all his military experiences had been favorable. "I've been involved in a skirmish or two while protecting our no-fly zone."

"Bad skirmishes?"

This was the part he didn't speak of often, yet again he felt the need to bare his soul to her. "One turned out to be extremely bad."

"What happened?"

"I killed a man."

He feared the revelation had rendered her speechless, until she said, "I'm assuming it was justified."

"That is a correct assumption. If I hadn't shot down his plane, he would have dropped a bomb over the village."

"How horrible. Was he a citizen of Bajul?"

"No. He was a known insurgent from another country. Because the files are classified, I am not at liberty to say which country."

She lifted her head and kissed his neck before settling back against him. "You don't have to say anything else if you don't want to."

Oh, but he did, though he wasn't certain why. "It happened four years ago," he continued. "That morning I received intelligence about the threat, and I decided I would enter the fray. Later I found out my father was livid, but only because if I perished, he would be without a commander."

"He told you that?" Her tone indicated her disbelief.

"Rafiq informed me, but it doesn't really matter now. I assisted in thwarting an attack that could have led to war for the first time in Bajul's history, and that is what matters. But I never realized..."

"Realized what, Adan?"

He doubted she would let up unless he provided all

the details. "I never knew how affected I would be by sending a man to his death."

"I can imagine how hard on you that must have been."

"Oddly, I had no real reaction to the incident until the following day while briefing our governing council. Midway through the report, I felt as if I couldn't draw a breath. I excused myself and walked outside to regain some composure. That night I had horrible dreams, and they continued for several months."

"I'm so sorry," she said sincerely. "For what it's worth, I think you're a very brave and honorable man. Sam is very lucky to have you as his father."

He'd longed to hear her acknowledge his honor, but he didn't deserve that praise in this situation. "There is no honor in taking another life. And now that I have a son, I will stress that very thing to him."

"That attitude is exactly what makes you honorable," she said. "You were bothered by an evil man's demise to the point of having nightmares. That means you have compassion and a conscience."

If that were the case, he wouldn't have asked her to remain in his quarters for the duration of their time together. Yet he'd not considered anything other than his own needs. And he did need her—in ways he could not have predicted. Still, he couldn't get too close to her or build her expectations beyond what he could provide aside from being her lover. He wasn't suited for a permanent relationship, as his family had told him time and again. "We should try to sleep now. I suspect Samuel will be summoning me in less than two hours."

She fitted her body closer to his side. "I'll be glad to take care of Sam tonight while you get your rest."

"Again, that's not necessary."

"Maybe not, but I really want to do it, not only for you, but for me. We barely caught a glimpse of him tonight. Besides, I'll only have him a little longer, while you'll have him the rest of your life."

Piper's words filled Adan with unexpected regret. Regret that, in a matter of weeks, he would be forced to say goodbye to an incredible woman. In the meantime, he would make the most of their remaining hours together and grant her whatever her heart desired, not only as the provisional mother to his son, but as his temporary lover.

He rolled to face Piper, leaving nothing between them but bare flesh. "Since you have presented such a convincing argument, we will see to Samuel together. Before this, could I convince you to spend the next few hours in some interesting ways?"

She laughed softly. "I thought we were going to sleep."

Bent on persuasion, he skimmed his palm along her curves and paused at the bend of her waist. "We could do that if you'd like."

She draped her arm over his hip. "Sleeping is definitely overrated, so I'm willing to go wherever you lead me."

And she was leading him to a place he'd never been before—close to crashing and burning with no safe place to land. Tonight, he wouldn't analyze the unfamiliar feelings. Tonight, she was all his, and he would treat her as if she always would be.

What an incredible night.

A week ago, Piper would never have believed she

could find a lover as unselfish as Adan. She also couldn't believe her inhibitions had all but disappeared when they made love.

As she supported her cheek with her palm and studied him in the dim light streaming through a break in the heavy gold curtains, she wanted him desperately— even if she was a bit miffed he'd failed to wake her to help care for Sam. Apparently she'd been so relaxed in the postcoitus afterglow, she hadn't heard the baby's cries through the bedside monitor. Some mother she would make.

When Adan stirred, she turned her complete focus on him as he lay sleeping on his back, one arm resting above his head on the navy satin-covered pillow, the other draped loosely across his abdomen. She loved the dark shading of whiskers surrounding his gorgeous mouth, envied the way his long dark lashes fanned beneath his eyes and admired the intricate details of his hand as he slid his palm from his sternum down to beneath the sheet and back up again. The reflexive gesture was so masculine, so sexy, she fought the urge to rip back the covers and climb on board the pleasure express.

Then he opened his eyes and blinked twice before he presented a smile as slow as the sun rising above the mountains. "Good morning, princess."

Didn't she wish. "Good morning. Did you sleep well?"

"Always with you in my bed. How did you sleep?"

"Too soundly. I didn't even hear Sam last night, and evidently you either didn't wake me to help, or couldn't."

He frowned. "I didn't hear him, either."

Simultaneous panic set in, sending them both from the bed and grabbing robes as they hurried out of the bedroom. They practically sprinted toward the nursery and tore through the door, only to find an empty crib.

Piper's hand immediately went to her mouth to cover the gasp. "Someone took him."

"That is impossible," Adan said, a hint of fear calling out from his gold-brown eyes. "The palace is a virtual fortress. If someone kidnapped him, it would have to be an inside job. And if that is the case, I will kill them with my bare hands."

"No need for that, *cara*."

They both spun around to discover Elena sitting in the rocker in the far corner of the lengthy room, the baby cradled in her arms, her expression tinged with disapproval.

Weak with relief, Piper hung back and immediately launched into explanation overdrive. "We never heard him last night. We were both very tired and—"

"The bloody monitor must not be working," Adan added. "Is he all right?"

Elena continued to calmly rock Sam in a steady rhythm. "He is quite fine. And judging from the weight of his diaper when I changed him, I would guess he simply slept all night."

Adan narrowed his eyes and glared at her. "You should have said something the moment we walked into the room."

"You should learn to be more observant of your surroundings when it comes to your son, Adan," she replied. "A hard lesson learned, but one that needed to be taught. When he is toddling, you must know where he is at all times."

Piper, in theory, didn't disagree with the governess's assertions, but she did question her tactics. "We were both expecting to find him in the crib, and needless to say we were shocked when we didn't."

Adan clasped his hands behind his neck and began to pace. "I've been in treacherous military situations less harrowing than this."

Elena pushed out of the chair and approached him. "Settle down, Adan, and hold your baby."

He looked as though he might be afraid to touch him. "I have to prepare for my duties today, but I will return to check on him before I depart for the base."

And with that, he rushed away, leaving Piper alone with the former nanny.

"Well, I suppose I should put this little one to bed for a nap," Elena said, breaking the awkward silence.

Piper approached her and held out her arms. "May I?"

"Of course."

After Elena handed her Sam, Piper kissed his cheek before carefully lowering him to the crib. She continued to study Sam's sweet face slack with sleep, his tiny lips forming a rosebud. He'd grown so much in only a matter of days, and in only a few weeks, she would say goodbye to him—and his father—for good. "He's such a beautiful little boy."

The woman came to her side and rested her slender hands on the top of the railing. "Yes, he is, as his father was at that age."

She saw the chance to learn more about Adan from one of the biggest influences in his life and took it. "Was Adan a good baby?"

"Yes. He was very little trouble, until he turned two,

and then he became quite the terror. He climbed everything available to him, and I didn't dare turn my back for more than a second or he would have dismantled something. I would try to scold him over his bad behavior, and then he would give me that charming smile, and all was forgiven."

Piper could absolutely relate to that. "He was lucky to have you after losing his mother."

Some unnamed emotion passed over Elena's careworn face. "I was fortunate to have the opportunity to raise him. All the brothers, for that matter."

Time to broach the subject of the paternal presence. "Was the king involved in his upbringing?"

Elena turned and crossed the room to reclaim the rocker, looking as if all the energy had left her. "He did the best that he could under the circumstance. Losing his wife proved to be devastating to him, yet he had no choice but to postpone his grief in order to serve his country."

Piper took the light blue club chair next to Elena. "Adan has intimated the king was a strict disciplinarian."

"He could be," she said. "He wanted his sons to be strong, independent men, despite their wealth and their station. Some might say he was too strict at times."

"Would you say that?"

"Perhaps, but it was not my place to interfere."

"I would think you had every right to state your opinion in light of your relationship."

Elena stiffened and appeared quite stunned by the statement. "Has Adan spoken to you about myself and the king?"

Piper smelled a scandal brewing. "Not at all. I only

meant that since you were in charge of the children, you should have had some say in how they were treated."

Elena relaxed somewhat, settled back against the rocker and set it in motion. "The king was stern, but fair."

"I'm not sure how fair it was for Adan when he shipped him off to boarding school at such a young age." And she'd probably just overstepped her bounds by at least a mile.

"He did so to protect him."

The defensiveness in her tone did not deter Piper. "Protect him from what?"

Elena tightened her grip on the chair's arms. "I have already said too much."

Not by a long shot, as far as she was concerned. "Look, I don't know what you know, and frankly I don't have to know it. But Adan deserves the truth."

"It would be too painful for him, and would serve no purpose at this point in time."

She wasn't getting through to the woman, which meant she would have to play the guilt card. "Have you ever asked Adan if he would prefer to be kept in the dark? I personally think he wouldn't."

"And you, Ms. McAdams, have not known him all that long."

Touché. "True, but we have spoken at length about his father. Even though he's reluctant to admit it, Adan has a lot of emotional scars, thanks to the king's careless disregard for his youngest son's needs."

She saw the first real hint of anger in Elena's topaz eyes. "Aahil...the king loved Adan. He gave him the very best of everything money could buy, and the opportunity to do what he loved the most. Fly jets."

A perfect lead-in to confront the crux of the matter, yet asking hard questions could be to her detriment. But if Adan could finally put his concerns to rest, it would be worth the risk. "I personally believe he failed to give Adan the one thing he needed most, and that would be a father who paid more attention to him, instead of shipping him far from his home. For that reason, Adan honestly believes the king isn't his biological father."

Elena glanced away, a very telling sign she could be skirting facts. "That is a wrongful assumption."

Piper wasn't ready to give up just yet. "Are you being absolutely honest with me, Elena? And before you speak, keep in mind Adan deserves to know so he could put that part of his past to rest."

"I swear on my papa's grave that the king was very much Adan's biological father."

Even though Elena sounded resolute, Piper couldn't quite help but believe the woman still had something to hide. "Then you need to tell him that, Elena. And you'll have to work hard to convince him, because he's certain something isn't right when it comes to his heritage."

Elena gave her a surprisingly meaningful look. "Do you care for Adan, Ms. McAdams?"

It was her turn to be shocked. "It's Piper, and yes, as one would care for a very good friend." Now she was the one hiding the truth.

"Then I suggest you not worry about things that do not concern you for Adan's sake."

Piper's frustration began to build. "But in some ways they do concern me. I want to see Adan happy and at peace. He can't do that when he knows full well people are protecting secrets from the past. And no offense, but I believe you're bent on protecting the king and his secrets."

"Are you not protecting Adan and Samuel by masquerading as his wife?"

She had her there. "That's true, but this pretense isn't causing either one of them pain."

"Give it time, Piper," Elena said in a gentler tone. "I can see in Adan's eyes that he cares for you, as well. Perhaps much more than he realizes at this point. But when the fantasy ends and you leave him, reality will be a bitter pill for both of you to swallow. Adan is not the kind of man to commit to one woman, or so he believes."

If Adan did care for her, but he could never be more than her lover, that would possibly shatter her heart completely. But she could still foolishly hope that the man she was dangerously close to loving might change his mind. All the more reason to give him the gift of knowledge, whether he came around or not. "Elena, if you ever cared for Adan at all, I'm imploring you to please consider telling him what you know. Isn't it time to put an end to the mystery and his misery?"

Elena sighed and stared off into space for a few moments before regarding Piper again. "This truth you are seeking will forever change him. He might never accept the mistakes the people in his life have made, even if those mistakes resulted in his very existence."

Finally they were getting somewhere. "Then it's true the queen had an extramarital affair that resulted in Adan's birth."

"No, that is not the case, but you are on the correct path."

Reality suddenly dawned on Piper. "The king had an indiscretion?"

She shook her head. "He had the desire to give the queen what she could not have. A third child. That decision required involving another woman."

"He used a surrogate?" Piper asked, unable to keep the shock from her voice.

"Yes. In a manner of speaking."

"And you know the mother," she said in a simple statement of fact.

Elena knitted her hands together and glanced away. "Very well."

She doubted she would get an answer, but she still had to ask. "Who is she, Elena?"

The woman turned a weary gaze to her and sighed. "I am."

Eight

Piper's brief time in Bajul had been fraught with misunderstanding and mysteries and more than a few surprises. But this bombshell trumped every last one of them. "Who else knows about this?" she asked when she'd finally recovered her voice.

Elena pushed slowly out of the rocker and walked to the window to peer outside. "No one else until now."

All these years, Adan had been living under the assumption that he was another man's child. A supposition that had caused him a great deal of pain, though he had downplayed his burden. But Piper had witnessed it firsthand, and now she wanted nothing more than to finally give him the answers he'd been silently seeking for years. "You have to tell him, Elena."

She turned from the window, a despondent look on

her face. "I have pondered that for many years. I still am not certain it would be wise."

Wise? Surely the former nanny wasn't serious. "Adan deserves to know the truth from the woman who gave him life."

"And he will hate me for withholding that truth for his entire life."

"Why did you withhold it?"

Elena reclaimed the chair and perched on the edge of the cushioned seat. "The king requested that Adan's parentage remain a secret, for both my sake and his."

"You mean for the king's sake, don't you?" She hadn't been able to tamp down the obvious anger in her tone, but she was angry. Livid, in fact.

"For all our sakes," Elena replied. "And for the benefit of the queen, who was already suffering from the decision Aahil made to give her another child."

"But I thought she wanted another baby."

"She did, yet after Adan was born, she could not hold him. In fact, she wanted nothing to do with him. What was meant to give her solace only drove her deeper into depression."

Piper was about to step out on a limb, even knowing it could break the revelations wide-open. "When Adan was conceived, was it through artificial means?"

Elena shook her head. "That process would have included medical staff, and we could not risk involving anyone who might reveal the truth."

"Then Adan was conceived—"

"Through natural means." Once again her gaze drifted away. "And after all was said and done, I am somewhat ashamed to say Aahil and I fell in love during the process, though he continued to be true to the queen until her demise. We remained devoted to each other until his death, and until last year, I kept our relationship a secret."

That meant the king had slept with the governess for the sake of procreation to please his queen, resulting in a decades-long affair. A twisted fairy tale that needed to be untangled. "You said 'until last year.' Does that mean Adan knows you were involved with his father?"

"Yes," she said quietly. "All the boys know. But they do not know I am Adan's true mother."

"It's not too late to rectify the deception, Elena, especially now that Adan has a son. A grandson whom you can acknowledge if you'll just tell Adan the whole story."

Elena's eyes began to mist with unshed tears. "I could not bear to tell him the rest for fear he'll hate me."

Piper leaned forward and clasped Elena's hands. "You're the only mother Adan has ever known, and it's obvious he loves you very much. He might need time to adjust, but I'm sure he'll eventually forgive you."

"It is because of my love for him that I want to protect him from more pain. And you must promise me, Piper, that you will say nothing to him."

The woman drove a hard bargain that could force a wedge between Piper and Adan should he ever learn she'd continued the ruse. "I'll allow you to tell Adan, but—"

"Tell me what?"

Startled by Adan's sudden appearance, Piper quickly shot to her feet. "We were just discussing…actually…"

"We were discussing Samuel's care," Elena said as she gave Piper a cautioning look.

"Am I doing something wrong?" Adan asked, sounding somewhat frustrated.

The lies would surely taste as bitter as brine going down. But it honestly wasn't Piper's place to enlighten him. "You're doing a great job. I basically asked Elena to keep encouraging you when I'm no longer here."

His expression turned somber. "We will discuss that following your departure. At the moment, I need to say goodbye to my son."

Piper remained rooted to her spot as Adan walked to the crib and laid a gentle hand on Sam's forehead. He looked so handsome in his navy flight suit, sunglasses perched atop his head and heavy boots on his feet. He also looked like the consummate father. And when he turned and came to her side, she desperately wanted to blurt out the truth.

Instead, she maintained an overly pleasant demeanor that inaccurately reflected her mood. "I guess we'll see you tomorrow evening, right?"

"Yes, and hopefully not too late." Then he brushed a kiss across her lips, as if this make-believe marriage had somehow become real. She knew better.

"Keep her company, Elena," he said as he kissed her cheek, unaware he was showing affection to his mother. "And do not reveal to her all my bad habits."

Elena reached up and patted his face. "Godspeed, *cara mia.*"

After Adan left the room in a rush, Piper regarded Elena again. "I'll give you my word not to say anything to him, as long as you promise you'll tell him the truth. If you don't, I will."

Elena oddly didn't seem at all upset by the threat. "I will tell him before you depart. And I sincerely hope you will tell him what you have been concealing from him, as well."

That threw Piper for a mental loop. "I'm not hiding anything from Adan."

"Yes, my dear, you are." She started for the door but turned and paused before she exited. "You love him, Piper. Tell him soon."

Long after Elena left the nursery, Piper stood there aimlessly staring at the sleeping baby as she pondered the former governess's words. Did she love Adan? Did she even dare admit it to herself, much less to him?

Yet in her heart of hearts she knew that she did love him, and she loved his son as she would have her own child. Regardless, nothing would come of it unless Adan felt the same way about her. Only time would tell, and time was slowly slipping away.

At half past midnight, Adan arrived at the palace initially exhausted from performing his duties. Yet the moment he entered the corridor leading to the living quarters, his fatigue began to dissipate as he started toward his first stop—the nursery to see his son. After that, he would retire to his bedroom in hopes of finding Piper waiting up for him. He certainly wouldn't blame her if she wasn't, considering the lateness of the hour. And if that happened to be the case, he would use creative kisses in strategic places to wake her.

He found the nursery door open and the room entirely vacant. An empty bottle on the table next to the rocker indicated someone had recently been there to tend to Samuel, and he suspected who that someone might be.

On that thought, he traveled down the hall at a quick

clip, and pulled up short at the partially ajar door when
he heard the soft, melodic sounds of a French lullaby.

*"Dodo, l'enfant do, l'enfant dormira bien vite. Dodo,
l'enfant do. L'enfant dormira bientôt."*

The lyrics alone indicated Piper could be having difficulty putting Samuel to sleep, but Adan imagined her
sweet voice would eventually do the trick. He stayed in
the hallway, immersed in faint memories of Elena singing him to sleep. Sadly he'd never had the pleasure of
recalling his own mother doing the same.

He wondered if Samuel would eventually resent him
for taking him away from Talia. Provided Talia actually
agreed to signing over her rights, and he didn't change
his mind about asking her to do that very thing.

The sudden silence thrust the concerns away and sent
Adan into the bedroom. He discovered Piper propped
up against the headboard, eyes closed, her dark hair
fanning out on the stack of white satin pillows beneath
her head, and his son, deep in slumber, cradled against
her breasts. Had she not been gently patting the baby's
back, he might have believed she'd fallen asleep, as well.

He remained in place, recognizing at that moment
how greatly he appreciated this woman who had stepped
in to care for his child without hesitation. He'd begun
to care for her deeply, more than he had any woman.
But to expect her to continue in this role much longer
would be completely unfair to both her and his child.
She had another life in another country, and she would
soon return to resume that life.

When Piper opened her eyes and caught his glance,
she smiled before holding a finger against her lips to
ensure his silence. He waited at the door as she worked
her way slowly off the bed and approached him at the

door. "I'll be right back," she whispered. "Unless he wakes again."

Unable to resist, he softly kissed the top of Samuel's head, remarkably without disturbing him, then leaned and kissed Piper's cheek, earning him another smile before she left the room.

In order to be waiting in bed for her return, Adan launched into action. He stripped out of his clothes on his way into the bathroom, turned on the water in the shower, then stepped beneath the spray and began to wash. He'd barely finished rinsing when the glass door opened—and one beautiful, naked woman with her hair piled atop her head boldly joined him.

Using his shoulders for support, she stood on tiptoe and brought her lips to his ear. "I missed you."

He framed her face in his palms. "I missed you, too."

All conversation ceased as they explored each other's bodies with eager hands as the water rained down over them. They kissed with shared passion, touched without restraint. Adan purposely kept Piper on the brink of orgasm with light pressure before he quickened the pace. She released a small moan, then raked her nails down his back with the force of her release. He soon discovered she was bent on reciprocating when she nudged him against the shower wall, lowered to her knees and took him into her mouth. He tipped his head back and gritted his teeth as she took him to the breaking point. Refusing to allow that to happen, he clasped her wrists and pulled her to her feet.

"Not here," he grated out, then swept her into his arms, carried her into the bedroom and brought her down on the sheets despite the fact they were soaking wet.

He slowed the tempo then, using his mouth to bring her more pleasure as she had done with him, until his own body demanded he hurry. In a matter of moments, he had the condom in place, and seated himself soundly inside her. She sighed when he held her closer, yet he couldn't seem to get close enough, even when she wrapped her legs around his waist.

All the unfamiliar emotions, the desperate desire, culminated in a climax that rocked him to the core. He had difficulty catching his breath as his heart beat a thunderous tempo against his chest. Piper began to stroke his back in a soothing rhythm, bringing him slowly back into reality. And that reality included an emotion he'd always rejected in the past. An expression he had never uttered to any lover. A word he dared not acknowledge now, for in doing so he would be completely vulnerable to a woman who was bound to leave.

He preferred to remain as he'd always been, immune to romantic love. Yet as Piper whispered soft words of praise, he wondered where he would find the strength to let her go. He would find it. He had no choice.

But not now. Not tonight.

Three weeks gone, one more to go.

As the first morning light filtered in from the part in the heavy gold curtains, Piper couldn't stop thinking about how little time she had left before she went home. And as she lay curled up in the empty bed, hugging a pillow, she also couldn't stop pondering Adan's abrupt change in mood.

For the past several days, he'd begun to spend more time with the baby when he wasn't at the base and a lot less time with her. She felt somewhat guilty for even questioning his paternal role, but she didn't quite understand why he'd started coming to bed in the middle of the night. Nor could she fathom why they hadn't made love in over a week when they hadn't missed a day since their first time together.

She questioned whether Elena had told him her secret, but she felt certain Adan would have told her if that had been the case. Blamed her for meddling, for that matter. Maybe the prince was simply preparing for their parting. Maybe the pretend princess would be wise to do the same. But lately she'd learned to lead with her heart, not her head. Her head told her to accept the certain end to their relationship. Her heart told her not to go down without a fight.

At the moment, her heart made more sense. For that reason, she climbed from beneath the covers to confront the missing sheikh, who she presumed was still in the nursery, tending to his son. After donning her robe, she padded down the hall to confirm her conjecture. And she did when she walked into the nursery and found Adan in the rocker, Sam cradled against his shoulder, both fast asleep.

All her previous concerns disappeared as she took in the precious sight. A scene worthy of being commemorated on canvas. Regrettably she didn't have one readily available, but she did have a sketch pad.

With that in mind, she hurried back to the bedroom she hadn't occupied in weeks, retrieved paper and pencil and then returned to the nursery. She moved closer to achieve a prime vantage point of father and son in the throes of blissful sleep. A souvenir to take with her that would enhance the wonderful memories…unless…

As she sketched the details with second-nature

strokes, a plan began brewing in her mind. A good plan. She quietly backed out the door and returned to Adan's quarters, closed the door, hid the pad in her lingerie drawer beneath her panties and picked up the palace phone. She expected Elena to answer, but instead heard an unfamiliar female voice ask, "May I help you?"

"Yes. This is…" The sheikh's fake spouse? The prince's bed buddy? She couldn't stomach lying again, even to a stranger. "With whom am I speaking?"

"My name is Kira," she said, her pleasant voice not even hinting at a Middle Eastern accent. "And you are the newest princess."

Apparently the woman thought Piper had forgotten her title. Bogus title. "Right. Is there someone available who could run an errand for me?"

"I will be up immediately."

Before she could offer to come downstairs, the line went dead, allowing her only enough time to brush her teeth and hair before she heard the knock.

After tightening the robe's sash, Piper opened the door to find a woman with golden-brown shoulder-length hair and striking cobalt eyes. She wore a navy blazer covering a white blouse and matching knee-length skirt, sensible pumps and a sunny smile. "Good morning, Princess Mehdi."

Piper would like to return the sentiment, but so far the morning hadn't started off well when she'd woken up alone. "Thank you for answering the summons so quickly, Kira, but this errand isn't really that pressing. I'm not even sure it's possible."

Kira straightened her shoulders and slightly lifted

her chin. "This is only my second day as a palace employee, and it is my duty to make this task possible."

Talk about pressure. "Okay, then. Is there a store that sells art supplies in the village?"

Kira seemed to relax from relief. "Thankfully, yes there is."

Things could be looking up after all. "Great. I need a canvas, the largest one available, and a basic set of oil paints today, if at all possible."

"I will gladly see to the purchase myself."

"Wonderful." Piper hooked a thumb over her shoulder. "I'll just grab my credit card and—"

"That is not necessary," Kira said. "The household budget covers all your expenses."

She didn't have the energy or desire to argue. "I truly appreciate that. And out of curiosity, are you from Bajul? I ask because you don't really have an accent."

"I was born and grew up here but I've been living in Montreal for the past few years. My mother was Canadian, and while she was working in Dubai, she traveled to the queen's mountain resort here one weekend, met my papa, fell madly in love and never left."

At least someone's whirlwind affair had turned out well. "That's a wonderful story. Now, if you don't mind, I have one more favor to ask."

"Whatever you wish, Princess Mehdi."

She really wished she would stop calling her that. "Please, call me Piper."

Kira looked just this side of mortified over the suggestion. "That would not be proper. I am a member of the staff and you are a member of the royal family."

Little did the woman know, nothing could be further from the truth. "How old are you, Kira, if you don't mind me asking?"

She looked a little confused by the question. "Twenty-seven."

"And I'll turn twenty-seven in three months. Since we're basically contemporaries, I'd prefer you address me by my given name while we're in private. If we're in a public forum, we'll adhere to all that ridiculous formality since it's expected. And in all honesty, I could use a friend in the palace. A female friend close to my age."

That brought the return of Kira's grin. "I suppose we could do that. A woman can never have an overabundance of friends."

Piper returned her smile. "Great. Now about that other favor." She gestured Kira inside the suite and closed the door. "Please don't say anything to anyone about the art supplies. I want to surprise Adan."

She raised her hand as if taking an oath. "I promise I will not say a word to the prince, even if it means residing in the dungeon while being subjected to torture."

"There's a dungeon?"

Kira chuckled. "Not that I have seen. And I apologize. At times I let my questionable sense of humor overtake my sound judgment."

"Well, Kira, since I'm prone to do the same, I believe that will make us fast friends. We can meet weekly and exchange smart remarks to enable us to maintain a certain amount of decorum."

They both shared in a laugh then, but all humor ceased when Adan came through the door without warning. He gave Piper a confused look before his gaze

settled on Kira—and he grinned. "Are my eyes deceiving me, or has the caretaker's daughter come home?"

"No, Your Highness, your eyes are not deceiving
you. I have returned, and I am now working in the palace with the sole intent to serve you."

He frowned. "Serve me grief no doubt, and what
is with the 'Your Highness'? If I recall, I was the first
boy to kiss you."

"And if I recall, I slugged you before you could."

This time Adan and Kira laughed, before he grabbed
her up and spun her around, indicating to Piper this pair
knew each other well. Possibly very well. She couldn't
quell the bite of jealousy, even though she sensed nothing aside from camaraderie between the two. Or maybe
she was just playing the ostrich hiding its head in the
desert sand.

After Adan let Kira go, he kept his attention on her.
"I thought you were engaged to be married."

"That didn't work out," she replied. "It's a long, sad
story that is not worth telling. Luckily Mama and Papa
mentioned my return to Elena, and here I am."

Adan finally regarded Piper. "Kira's parents were
members of the household staff for many years."

"My father tended the palace grounds," Kira added.
"My mother was the head chef at the palace."

Adan pointed at her. "And she was the resident holy
terror in her youth."

Kira frowned. "If I were not your subordinate, I
would possibly slug you again. But since I am, I will
leave you both to your privacy as I have an important
task to oversee. Princess Mehdi, it was a pleasure to
meet you." She then did an about-face and left, closing
the door behind her.

"She certainly left in a hurry," Piper said. "Evidently she had a very bad breakup."

Adan's good spirits seemed to dissolve right before Piper's eyes. "More often than not, relationships run their course and usually come to a less than favorable conclusion."

Piper's hope that he might have feelings for her beyond gratitude evaporated like early-morning fog. "I had no idea you were that cynical, Your Highness."

He disappeared into the closet and returned with khaki cargo pants, a navy T-shirt, socks and a pair of heavy boots. "I am a realist."

She leaned a shoulder against the bedpost as he shrugged out of his robe, finding it difficult to ignore his board-flat abdomen and the slight stream of hair disappearing beneath the waistband of his boxer briefs. "It seems to me both your brothers are happily married."

He tugged the shirt over his head, ruffling his dark hair in the process. "Perhaps, but they are the exception to the rule."

"Your relationship rules?"

He put on his pants one leg at a time and zipped them closed. "I didn't make the rules, Piper. I'm only acknowledging that failed relationships seem to be my forte."

"Are you referring to Talia?"

After rounding the bed, he perched on the mattress's edge to put on his boots. "Yes, among a few other nonintimate relationships, including my father."

Now they were getting somewhere. "You didn't fail him, Adan. He failed you."

"I suppose you're right. Apparently I never accomplished anything to suit him, no matter how hard I tried."

"Even learning to pilot jets wasn't good enough?"

He came to his feet and faced her. "I have no idea since he rarely mentioned my skills, even when he convinced the counsel to appoint me as the armed forces commander."

"Well, at least he had enough faith in you to believe you could handle the responsibility."

"Or he was possibly setting me up to fail. Fortunately I proved him wrong."

She smiled. "Yes, you did, at that. And if it's any consolation, I'm proud of your accomplishments, both military and paternal."

Discomfort called out from his eyes. "You never did say why Kira was here."

Time to lighten the mood. Or die trying. "She was seeking donations for the poor. I told her to take five or so of the watches in your extensive collection since I'm sure they'll go for a hefty price, and you probably wouldn't miss them."

From the sour look on his face, her efforts at levity had fallen flat. "Try again, Piper."

She folded her arms beneath her breasts and sighed. "If you must know, I sent her into the village for a few feminine unmentionables. But I'll be glad to show you the list if you're worried we were somehow plotting against you."

He held up both hands, palms forward. "That will not be necessary. I presently need to prepare for the day."

"Are you going to the base?"

"Not today. Following breakfast, I thought I would

take Samuel for a stroll around the grounds as soon as he wakes from his morning nap."

"Do you mind if I join you?"

"That is entirely up to you."

The lack of enthusiasm in his response told Piper all she needed to know—she wasn't welcome, and that stung like a bumblebee. "I'll let you and Sam have some father-and-son alone time. Besides, I have something I need to do anyway." Namely begin painting a portrait that would serve as a gift for the prince. A parting gift.

"That is your prerogative," he said in a noncommittal tone as he started to the door. "I'll tell the cook to keep your breakfast warm while you dress."

She wasn't hungry for food, but she was definitely starved for answers. "Before you leave, I have something I need to tell you."

Adan paused with his hand on the doorknob and turned to face her. "I'm listening."

She drew in a deep breath and prepared for the possibility of having her heart completely torn in two. "I'm in love with you."

He looked as if she'd slapped him. "What did you say?"

"Don't be obtuse, Adan. I love you. I didn't plan it. I really didn't want it. But it happened in spite of my resistance. My question is, how do you feel about me?"

He lowered his eyes to the floor. "I cannot be the man you need, Piper."

"That's my decision to make, not an answer."

His gaze snapped to hers. "You deserve someone who can give you the emotional support you require."

Meaning he didn't return her feelings. Or maybe he

refused to admit it. Only one way to find out. "What are you afraid of, Adan?"

"I'm not afraid, Piper. As I've said, I'm pragmatic."

"No, you're not," she said. "You're a risk taker, but you're scared to take a chance on us."

"I am only considering your well-being. I do care about you, Piper. Perhaps more than I've cared for any woman in my past. But I'll be damned if I break your heart because I cannot succeed at being faithful to one woman."

The surprising revelations took Piper aback. "Did you cheat on Talia during the six years you were together?"

"No."

"Have you cheated on any woman you've been with?"

"No, but—"

"Then why would you believe you would be unfaithful to me?"

"Because I could be genetically predisposed to adultery, compliments of my mother."

She could no longer allow him to think that his mother had taken a lover who resulted in his birth, in spite of her promise to Elena. Not when their future together could depend on the truth. "Adan, your mother was—"

The sharp rap suspended Piper's confession midsentence and caused Adan to mutter a string of Arabic words as he opened the door.

Piper expected a member of the staff. What she got was Adan's erstwhile lover, her platinum hair slicked back in a low chignon, her lithe body tightly encased in a blue silk jumpsuit, her makeup applied to perfection and her red painted lips curled into a snarl-like smile. "Surprise, you bleedin' bastard. I'm back!"

Nine

The woman in the catsuit looked ready for a catfight, but Piper wasn't about to bite. "I'll leave you two with your privacy," she said as she targeted the door as her means to escape.

Talia stormed into the room, blocking her escape. "Oh, do stay, chicky. The party is only getting started."

Adan stepped to Piper's side and moved slightly in front of her. "Calm down, Talia. If anyone has cause to be irritated, it should be me. You might have had the courtesy of notifying me of your impending arrival."

"And you might have told me you married—" she pointed a finger at Piper "—this wench."

"Piper is not a wench," Adan stated with a touch of venom in his tone. "And your argument is with me, not her. If you will join me in my study, we will discuss our son."

Talia smirked. "Here seems fine. After all, you've obviously been taking care of the bonking business in the bedroom with her for quite some time, according to the press."

And Piper had only thought they'd covered all their media bases. "You can't believe everything you hear or read, Talia. Adan has done whatever it takes to protect Sam."

The woman nailed her with a seething glare. "Our son is not your concern."

"But he is my concern," Adan said. "And I am prepared to offer you a sizable settlement in exchange for retaining full custody of Samuel."

Talia flipped a hand in dismissal. "Your attorneys have already worked that out with my attorneys."

Adan's expression was a mixture of confusion and anger. "How is that possible when I have not consulted the palace barrister?"

"Maybe you should talk to your brother about that," Talia replied.

"The king knew you were coming?" Piper chimed in, earning a quelling look from Adan.

"Yes, he did," she said. "I had Bridgette call when I arrived back in Paris. Rafiq wouldn't let me speak to you, the duffer, so I hopped on a plane and came here. He practically met me at the door with the papers. I signed them and then I had to evade the houseboy on my way up here."

Piper knew very little British slang, but it didn't take much to interpret Talia's words. "Then I assume you're okay with giving Adan full custody," she said, sticking her nose in where it obviously didn't belong.

Talia screwed up her face in a frown. It wasn't pretty.

"No. I'm giving him to Adan. What would I need with a kid?"

A litany of indictments shot into Piper's brain, threatening to spill out her mouth. Luckily Sam's cry filtered through the monitor at that exact moment, supplying an excuse to bail before she blew up. "I'll take care of him." She brushed past Talia, resisting the urge to rip the expensive designer bag from her shoulder and stomp on it for good measure.

She took a few calming breaths as she quickly made her way to the nursery to see about the baby. The minute she walked into the room, Sam's cries turned into wails, as if he somehow sensed the stressful situation brewing down the hall.

"What's wrong, sweetie?" she said as she picked him up from the crib. "Did you have a bad dream or just need some company?"

His sobs turned to sniffles as she cradled him in her arms, and then she realized he was in dire need of a diaper change. After she saw to that task, she considered instituting Adan's plan to take the baby for a stroll around the grounds. She discarded that idea when she remembered she was still wearing her robe. Nothing like giving tabloid reporters more fuel for gossip should she get caught on camera. Of course, if any of the bottom-feeders had been hanging around in the past hour, which they had been periodically known to do since she'd arrived in Bajul, they would have a field day with Toxic Talia.

Her anger came back full throttle when she considered how the woman had agreed to relinquish her child without a second thought. Couldn't she see what a precious gift she'd been given? Of course she couldn't. She wasn't concerned about anything that didn't promote her personal gain…just like her own mother.

Piper refused to make this decision easy on the selfish supermodel, and with that goal in mind, she strode back down the hall with Sam in tow. She arrived at the open door to the suite in time to hear Talia say, "Now that everything's settled, I'll be on my way."

"You're not going anywhere yet," Piper said through gritted teeth. "Not until you take a good long look at what you're giving away."

Talia spun around and rolled her eyes. "For the last time, this is none of your business, ducky."

Undeterred, Piper walked right up to her and turned the baby around in her arms. "Look at him, Talia, and think about what you're doing. It's still not too late to change your mind."

Adan took a few steps forward. "It's no use, Piper. She's made her choice, and she chooses her career. She wants no part in raising him."

Ignoring Adan, Piper kept her gaze trained on Talia. "This is a life-altering decision. There's no turning back if you walk away now. Is that what you really want?"

A spark of indecision showed in Talia's eyes. "I can't raise him," she said, an almost mournful quality to her voice.

Piper's disdain lessened as she witnessed the woman's defenses began to crumble, one fissure at a time. "Are you absolutely sure?"

"If I were a different person, perhaps I could. But I'm never going to be good at it, and it would be unfair to him if I tried." Then she surprisingly reached out and touched Sam's fisted hand. "So long, little fellow. Be good for your daddy and your new mum."

Talia hurried out the door, but not before Piper caught a glimpse of tears in her eyes. "Maybe I misjudged her," she said as she placed Sam against her shoulder. "Maybe for the first time in her life, she's doing something unselfish."

Adan shoved a hand in his pocket, rubbed his neck with the other and began to pace. "Do you find it odd that all three of us have been betrayed by our mothers?"

In a way, he was right, but not completely. Piper had intended to tell him the truth before Talia's interruption. She now recognized she walked a fine line between breaking a promise and bringing him peace. Perhaps she could avoid crossing that line by handing him only a partial truth. "There are some things you don't know about your mother, and it's high time you do."

He faced her and frowned. "What are you talking about?"

"You need to ask Elena," she said. "She holds the answers, and she's prepared to tell you."

At least that was what she hoped.

A few moments later, Adan found himself standing outside Elena's private office, his mind caught in a maze of confusion. He had no idea what Piper had been talking about, yet he suspected he would soon find out, even if he wasn't certain he wanted to know.

When he rapped on the frame surrounding the open door, Elena looked up from her position behind the desk, obviously startled before surprise melted into a smile. "Come in, *cara.*"

He entered, pulled back the chair opposite her and sat. "Am I interrupting anything?"

"Of course not. You are always welcome here."

He stretched out his legs in an attempt to affect a casual demeanor, when in truth his nerves were on edge. "Talia stopped by to sign over custody of Samuel."

"I heard," she said. "And I am very sorry that your son will not have the opportunity to know his mother. On the other hand, since I do know his mother's shortcomings, the decision she made was the best course of action in this case."

"Piper suggested it was an uncharacteristically unselfish act on Talia's part."

"Piper is correct, but then she has wisdom beyond her years."

The moment had arrived to transition into his real reason for being there. "And continuing on with the subject of motherhood, Piper also informed me you had information about my mother that she's convinced I should know."

Unmistakable panic showed in Elena's eyes. "I told her I would tell you in due time."

"Perhaps that time is now."

Elena hesitated for several moments, leading him to believe she might thwart his attempts at garnering information. "I suppose you are right."

"Then proceed," he said as he braced for the possibilities and prepared for the worst.

She picked up a stack of papers and moved them aside before folding her hands atop the desk. "First of all, I must clarify an incorrect assumption you have long held regarding your parents. Your mother always remained true to her husband during their marriage, and they both grew to love each other. Most important, Aahil Mehdi was your biological father, not some unknown man."

He had waited all his life for confirmation or a denial of his theory, yet something didn't quite ring true. "If that is a fact, then why was I the only son not raised and schooled here at the palace? Why was I the only brother sent away during my formative years?"

"To protect you, Adan."

"From what?"

"The chance someone could learn your true parentage, and you would suffer the consequences from being labeled the child of a concubine."

Anger began brewing immediately beneath the surface of his feigned calm. "Then you are saying my father was the adulterer and I am the product of his affair with a servant?"

"No. Your father was a good man, but you were the reminder of his failure to make his queen happy by giving her the baby she was not able to conceive." She sent him a wistful smile. "Yet you were the greatest joy in my life from the moment you came into this world."

Awareness barreled down on him with the force of a hundred wild horses. "*You* gave birth to me?"

"Yes, *cara,* as a favor to the king, and during the process of conception, your father and I fell in love. And as you already know, that love continued until his death, but I assure you we did not act on it until the queen's demise."

Questions continued to bombard his brain. He chose the one that took precedence over all. "Why did you wait to tell me this?"

"I promised your father I would never reveal the truth to anyone, even you."

Once the initial shock subsided, ire took its place.

"He had no right to ask that of you, and you had no right to keep this from me all these years."

"I realize that now," she said. "And had Piper not come to me and then pressed me to reveal the truth to you, I might have carried the secret to my grave."

Adan was torn between gratitude and resentment aimed toward both Elena and Piper. "How long has she known about this secret?"

"For a while."

One more betrayal in a long line of many. "She should have told me immediately."

"Do not blame Piper for not saying anything, Adan. I begged her to allow me to tell you."

"She should not have come to you in the first place."

"She did so because she loves you, Adan. She only wants what is best for you, and she believes with this information you'll find some peace."

Piper's declaration of love intruded into his thoughts, but he pushed it aside. "If that is so, then why would she subject me to this confession knowing it would cause such turmoil?"

"I suspect she recognizes that lies have the capacity to destroy relationships."

And so could the truth. His relationship with Piper had been fraught with lies from the beginning, and he wasn't certain he could trust her now.

Bent on a confrontation, he shoved the chair back and stood. "We will discuss this further after I have had time to digest this information."

Tears filled Elena's eyes. "Please tell me you do not hate me, Adan."

How could he hate the woman who had been the only

mother he had ever known? In reality, his real mother. "I could never hate you, Elena."

"But you might never forgive me," she said, resignation in her tone.

"I will try, and that is all I can promise at this moment," he said before he turned to leave.

"Where are you going, Adan?" Elena called after him.

"To have a serious conversation with my alleged wife."

"What possessed you to interfere in my life?"

Piper put down the art book she'd attempted to read in the common sitting area, moved to the edge of the uncomfortable chair and faced Adan's wrath head-on. "I assume Elena told you everything."

He released a caustic laugh. "You would be correct in that assumption, and you have yet to answer my question."

"Okay. You see it as interference, and I see it as making an effort to find the answers you've always longed for."

"I never sought those answers for a reason."

"And that reason is?"

"I knew nothing good would come of them, and nothing has."

She couldn't believe his attitude or his misdirected anger. "What's not good about finally knowing the identity of your real mother? Believe me, Sunny and I unsuccessfully tried to find our father, but we could only narrow it down to three prospects. One was in prison for insider trading, one was a money-hungry gigolo and the last was married with four children. With that field of prospects, we decided it wasn't worth pursuing. At least you now know you have a wonderful mother."

He ran a fast hand over his jaw. "I am not you, Piper. I had no desire to learn the truth. And now that I do know, I have been shown that even the most trustworthy person is capable of the ultimate betrayal."

She felt as if he'd placed her in that category, along with his biological mother. "Look, Adan, I don't agree with Elena concealing the truth for such a lengthy period of time, but on some level I did understand why she was afraid to reveal it. Seeing your reaction only validated her fears."

He paced back and forth like a caged animal before pausing before her. "How would you wish me to react, Piper? Should I be celebrating the lies I've been told my entire life? Or the fact that you knew the truth and concealed it?"

"Believe me, keeping it from you wasn't easy." A colossal understatement. "But it wasn't my place to tell you, although I would have before I left if Elena hadn't."

He narrowed his eyes into a hard glare. "It wasn't your place to go on a bloody fact-finding mission, either."

No matter how hard she tried to see it from his point of view, his condemnation hurt like the devil. Time to fight fire with fire. "Sometimes it's necessary to set a lie into motion to protect those you love, just like you're protecting Samuel by lying about our marriage."

"You are absolutely correct," he said, taking her by surprise. "And I plan to put an end to that fabrication immediately. Now that Talia has relinquished her rights, you have no cause to remain here any longer. I will make the arrangements for you to fly home as soon as possible."

As she came to her feet, she seriously wanted to cry, maybe even beg, but instead called on fury to give her strength. "So that's it, huh? I've served my purpose and now you're going to toss me out into the street like refuse?"

"I am not tossing you out," he said. "I am giving you back your freedom."

And he was going to hold her emotionally captive for a very long time. But deep down, hadn't she known all along this would happen? And she'd been an unequivocal fool to believe otherwise. "Shame on me for believing I meant more to you than just a quick fix to save your sterling reputation. And shame on you for leading me to believe you were honorable."

She could tell by the harsh look on his face she'd delivered a knockout blow. "I would be less than honorable if I kept you here any longer when we both know that I will never be able to give you what you need."

Battling the threatening tears, Piper snatched up the book and clutched it to her heart. "You're right, Your Highness. I need a man who can let down his guard and take a chance on love, even though I've recently discovered love is a risky business. But just remember, there's a little boy who's going to need all the love you can give him, since, like his father, he's never going to know his mother. Don't fail him because you're too afraid to feel."

Without giving him a chance to respond, Piper stormed down the hall to the make-believe lovers' hideaway, slammed the door behind her and started the process of packing. Only then did she let the tears fall at will and continued to cry until she was all cried out, though she inherently knew she was only temporarily done with the blubbering.

Not long after Piper finished filling the last of the suitcases, a series of knocks signaled a guest had come calling, the last thing she needed. Unless… On the way to answer the summons, she couldn't help hoping Adan had somehow come to his senses and decided to ask for a second chance. That he would appear on the threshold on bended knee with his heart in his hands and a declaration of love flowing from his gorgeous mouth. As if that fairy-tale scenario was going to happen. Most likely she'd find Abdul standing in the hall with his head slightly bowed, a live-to-serve look on his face while he declared his unwavering need to carry her luggage.

She discovered she'd been wrong on both counts when she opened the door to the ever-smiling Kira. "I'm so sorry to bother you, Your—" She sent a quick glance over her shoulder. "…Piper, but the art shop didn't have any canvases available and they only had colored chalk. They did offer to order the supplies for you."

She'd forgotten all about the painting she'd planned to give Adan. "That's okay. I won't be needing those supplies now." Or ever.

Kira appeared sorely disappointed. "But you seemed so excited over surprising your husband."

He's not my husband, she wanted to say, but opted for a partial truth. "I probably shouldn't mention this, but you'll know soon enough. The marriage isn't working out, so I'm returning home this afternoon."

Kira hid a gasp behind her hand. "I am so sorry, Piper. I was so certain seeing you and Adan together today that you were completely in love."

"Love isn't always enough, Kira," she said without thought.

"I know that all too well, Piper."

She sensed her newfound friend did, at that. "Oh, well. Nothing ventured, nothing gained, as they say. And I'm going to miss having the opportunity to get to know you."

"Surely I'll see you when you bring the baby to visit his father."

If only that were the case. Leaving Sam would be equally as difficult as leaving his father behind, never knowing what might have been. "Adan is going to have full custody. I travel a lot with my job and we both think it's important Sam grows up in his homeland with his people."

"But you'll be coming here to see him often, right?"

And now for the final, and most painful, lie. "Of course."

That prompted the return of Kira's smile. "That's wonderful. We can still have those smart-remark sessions when you're here."

"I'd offer to have one now, but I want to give Sam one last bottle before I go."

As Piper stepped into the hall to do that very thing, Kira drew her into a hug. "Goodbye for now, Piper. I wish you the best of luck."

"Same to you," she replied as she started toward the nursery, before she gave in to the temptation to tell Kira the truth.

As much as she wanted to see the cherished baby boy, Piper dreaded telling him goodbye. That didn't prevent her from lifting the sleeping Sam from his crib and holding him for the very last time. He opened his eyes slowly and didn't make a sound, as if he understood the importance of the moment. She walked around the room as one more time she sang the lullaby she'd used to put him to sleep. If only she could be his mother. If only his father had loved her back. If only…

"The car is waiting, Your Highness."

Piper wanted to tell Abdul it would just have to wait, but she saw no use in prolonging the inevitable farewell to the second love of her life. She kissed Sam's forehead, laid him back in the crib and managed a smile. "I love you, sweetie. I know you'll forget me once I'm gone, but I will never forget you."

Or the man who had given him life.

After one last look at Sam, Piper turned to go, only to discover Adan standing in the open door looking somewhat remorseful. "I did not want you to leave before I expressed my gratitude for all that you've done for myself and Samuel."

She truly wanted to tell him what he should do with that gratitude, but she couldn't. She honestly wanted to hate him, and she couldn't do that, either. "You're welcome, Your Highness. It's been quite the adventure."

He attempted a smile that didn't quite reach his eyes. "Yes, it has. And I also want to assure you that I will treat my son as he should be treated. I will make certain he has all that he desires."

Too bad he couldn't promise her the same. "Within reason, I hope. I'd hate to think you'd buy him his first plane on his first birthday."

He favored her with a dimpled grin. The same grin she'd noticed the first time she'd laid eyes on him. "Rest assured I will withhold that gesture until his second birthday."

"Good idea. We wouldn't want him to be too spoiled."

A lengthy span of silence passed as they remained quiet, as if neither knew what to say next. Piper had already said what she'd needed to say when she'd told him she loved him, even if he hadn't done the same. Now all that remained was the final goodbye. "Well, I guess I need to get my things and take to the friendly skies. I'd like to say give me a call if you're ever in need of ending your celibacy, but that wouldn't be wise."

He streaked a palm over the nape of his neck. "I suppose it wouldn't be, at that."

"And just so you know, I don't regret the time we've spent together. I only regret this little fake fairy tale didn't have a happy ending. But that's life. Goodbye, Adan."

When she tried to make a hasty exit, Adan caught her arm and pulled her into an embrace that didn't last nearly long enough. "You are a remarkable woman, Piper McAdams. I wish for you only the brightest future with a deserving man."

She was convinced he could be that man, if only he believed it, which he didn't.

Piper began backing away, determined to leave him with a smile. "I'm going to forgo the whole man-hunting thing for a while, but I've decided I am going to further pursue a career in art."

"I am pleased to hear that," he said sincerely. "Perhaps you can send me some of your work in the future. I will pay top price."

How badly she wanted to run back into his arms, but her pride had already suffered too many hits as it was. "I'll certainly give that some serious consideration. In the meantime, take care, Adan."

"I wish the same to you, Piper."

She chose not to afford Adan another look for fear she might do something foolish, like give him another kiss. But after she climbed into the black limousine a half hour later, she glanced back at the red-stone castle and caught a glimpse of someone standing at the second-floor-terrace railing—the someone who had changed her life.

The sheikh of her dreams. A prince of a guy. The one who got away...with her heart.

Ten

"This arrived for you a little while ago."

Adan turned from the nursery window to find Elena holding a large rectangular box. "More gifts from some sultan attempting to insert themselves in the government with bribes for the baby?"

She crossed the room and handed him the brown-paper-wrapped package. "This one is from the United States. South Carolina, to be exact."

He immediately knew what it contained, though he never believed she would actually honor his request. Not after the way he had regretfully treated her.

While Elena looked on, Adan tore through the wrapping and opened the box to find what appeared to be a painting, exactly as he'd expected. Yet when he pulled it from the box, he didn't expect that the painting would depict a slumbering father holding his sleeping son in remarkable detail, right down to the cleft in his chin and Samuel's prominent left dimple.

"Oh, Adan," Elena began in a reverent voice, "this is such a *bella* gift."

He would wholeheartedly agree, if he could dislodge the annoying lump in his throat. The baby began kicking his legs in rapid-fire succession against the mattress as if he appreciated the gesture.

After resting the painting against the crib, Adan picked up Samuel and held him above his head. "You are quite the noisy character these days."

His son rewarded him with a toothless smile, something he'd begun doing the past month. A milestone that had given him great joy. Bittersweet joy, because Piper had not been around to share in it.

"You should call her and thank her, Adan."

He lowered Samuel to his chest and faced Elena with a frown. "I will send her a handwritten note."

She took the baby from his arms without invitation. "You will do no such thing. She deserves to hear from you personally. She also deserves to know that you have been mourning your loss of her since she departed."

"I have not been mourning," he said, sounding too defensive. "I have been busy raising my son and seeing to my royal duty."

Elena patted his cheek. "You can deceive yourself, but you cannot deceive me. You are so sick with love you could wilt every flower in the palace courtyard with your anxiety."

He avoided her scrutiny by picking up the painting and studying the empty wall above the crib. "I believe this is the perfect spot, right above Samuel's bed so he will go to sleep knowing I am watching over him throughout the night."

"Since it is obvious you are not getting any sleep, why not watch over him in person?"

He returned the painting to the floor at his feet. "I am sleeping fine."

"Ah, yes, and I am entering the marathon in Dubai two weeks from now."

That forced Adan around. "Would you please stop assuming you know everything about me?"

She kissed Samuel's cheek before placing him back in the crib, where he began kicking again at the sight of the colorful mobile above him. "I do know you, *cara,* better than most. When you were Samuel's age, I stayed up many nights while you were teething. When you were a toddler, I put you to bed every night with a book, the reason why you were always such a grand reader. When you were six, and you broke your right arm trying to jump the hedges, I was the one who fed you until you learned to eat with your left hand. And when you were twelve, I discovered those horrid magazines beneath your bed and did not tell your father."

He'd forgotten that incident, with good reason. "I realize you've been there for me through thick and thin, but that does not give you carte blanche to lord over me now that I am an adult."

"I agree, you are an adult."

"I am pleased to know you finally acknowledge that."

"An adult who has absolutely no common sense when it counts most."

He should have expected this as soon as he opened the box. "If you're going to say I made the wrong decision by allowing Piper to leave, I would have to disagree."

"And you would be wrong." Elena leaned back against the crib's railing and donned her stern face. "As I have told both your brothers, you all have a great capacity to love, but it would take a special woman to bring that out in you. Zain and Rafiq learned that lesson by finding that special woman, and so have you. Piper is your soul mate, *cara*. Do not destroy what you could have with her by being so stubborn you cannot see what was right in front of you and you foolishly let go for good."

He hated that she had begun to make sense. "I am not being stubborn. I am being sensible. If you know me as well as you say you do, then you realize I have never stayed involved with one woman longer than six years, and we know how well that turned out."

Elena glared at him much as she had when he'd been a badly behaved boy. "Comparing Talia to Piper is like comparing a cactus to a down comforter. It's true Talia gave you a precious son, but she also gave you continuous grief. Piper gave you not only this touching portrait but also the means to heal your wounds with the truth. And you repay her by not admitting how you feel about her."

"I'm presently not certain how I feel about anything." Other than he resented Elena for pointing out the error in his ways.

"And you, *cara mia,* are guilty of propagating the biggest lie of all if you do not stop denying your love for Piper."

"I have never said I love her." He was too afraid

to leave himself open to that emotion, more so now than ever.

She pointed a finger at his face and glowered at him. "Adan Mehdi, before your obstinate behavior destroys what could be the best thing that has happened to you, listen to me, and listen well. First of all, consider how Piper selflessly cared for your son. How she protected you and Samuel by putting her life on hold while pretending to be your wife, only to be dismissed by you as one would dismiss a servant."

"But I never—"

"Furthermore," she continued without regard for his attempts to halt the tirade, "should you finally regain some semblance of wisdom befitting of royalty and decide to contact her, you will beg her forgiveness for being such a rigid *cretino*."

The woman knew how to deliver a right hook to his ego. "I take offense to my own mother calling me an idiot."

Her expression brightened over the unexpected maternal reference. "It means everything to hear you finally acknowledging me as your mother."

He laid a palm on her cheek. "I suppose I have known that all along. Only a true mother would tolerate my antics."

"And only a true mother would agree to raise a child that is not her own, and love that child's father with all her being despite his shortcomings."

He recognized the reference to Piper, yet he couldn't quell his concerns. "What if I try to contact her and she rejects me? And what do I say to her?"

"You must speak from the heart."

"Something I have never truly mastered."

She sighed. "Adan, your father also viewed revealing emotions as a sign of weakness, and in many ways you have inherited that trait from him. But in reality, it's a brave man who shows vulnerability for the sake of love. I implore you to call on your courage and tell Piper your true feelings, before it is too late."

Admittedly, Elena—his mother—was right. He had never backed away from a battle, and he shouldn't avoid this war to win Piper back. Better still, he had the perfect weapons to convince her to surrender—his well-honed charm, and his remarkable son.

When she sensed movement in the corner of her eye, Piper tore her attention away from the painting of the red-stone palace and brought it to the window that provided natural light. And after she glimpsed the tall man pushing the stroller up the guesthouse walkway, she blinked twice to make sure her imagination hadn't commandeered her vision.

But there he was, the man who'd haunted her dreams for the past four weeks. He wore a crisp tailored black shirt and casual beige slacks, his perfect jaw covered by a shading of whiskers, his slightly ruffled thick dark hair as sexy as ever. And she looked like something the cat had dragged into the garage.

She barely had time to remove the paint-dotted apron and smooth the sides of her lopsided ponytail before the bell chimed. After drawing in a cleansing breath, she opened the door and concealed her shock with a smile. "To what do I owe this honor, Your Highness?"

Adan reached into the stroller and retrieved the baby who had stolen Piper's heart from the moment she'd first held him. "This future pilot insisted on paying a personal visit to the artist who presented us with such a fine painting."

She couldn't believe how cute Sam looked in the miniature flight suit and tiny beige boots. "He really said that, huh?"

"He did."

"Wow. I had no idea three-month-old babies could talk."

"He's an exceptional child."

Born to an exceptionally charming father. A charm he'd clearly passed on to his son, evident when Sam kicked his legs and smiled, revealing his inherited dimples. "Well, don't just stand there, boys. Come inside before you both melt from the heat."

Balancing Sam in one arm, Adan leaned over, retrieved the diaper bag from the basket behind the stroller and slipped the strap over his shoulder. "We are accustomed to the heat, but this humidity is excruciating, so I will gladly accept your offer."

Once he stepped into the foyer, Piper showed him into the small living area and gestured toward the floral sofa. "Have a seat, as soon as you give me the kid."

After he handed Samuel off to her, he claimed the end of the couch and set the bag at his feet. "This is a very comfortable yet quaint abode."

"A nice way of saying *small*," she said as she sat in the club chair across from him and gently bounced the baby in her lap. "But the rent is cheap. Actually, it's free. My grandparents live in the main house and this is the guest quarters."

"Yes, I know. Your grandfather greeted me as soon as we left the car."

Great. "Not with a shotgun, I hope."

He laughed. "Actually, he wasn't armed. In fact, he was quite cordial. He's still very pleased that he's been granted the water conservation project, and that's going quite well, by the way."

"So I've heard," she said. "I spoke with Rafiq a few days ago."

"He never mentioned that to me."

"He had no reason to mention it, Adan. He's well aware that once I met the terms of our arrangement I'd go back to business as usual."

"And I presume you've done that?"

"Actually, I'm giving a few private art lessons, and I'm looking for a place to open a small gallery. Interestingly enough, my grandfather is willing to invest in the venture."

"How did you convince him to let you leave the company?"

"I told him that it was high time I had a life of my own that included pursuing my personal aspirations. And then I bribed my grandmother into taking up the cause by helping her with a fund-raiser. Between the two of us, he finally caved."

"I'm glad you're happy, Piper," he said, a solemn note to his voice.

She could think of one other thing that would make her happy, but that was only a pipe dream. "I am, for the most part. Are you?"

He rubbed a palm over his jaw. "I'm happy that I have a son and a fulfilling career. Aside from that—"

When Sam began to fuss, Adan withdrew a bottle from the tote, uncapped it and handed to her. "It seems he's getting hungry more often these days. The books

I've read clearly state that an increase in appetite in an infant signals a growth spurt."

"Spoken like the consummate father," Piper said, bringing the return of Adan's smile.

"I am certainly trying my best."

"And you're succeeding," she said as she laid the baby in the crook of her arm and watched as he downed the formula with gusto. "He's definitely grown. Before you know it, he'll be riding a bike. I can't wait to see that." The statement left her mouth before she'd considered how unrealistic she sounded.

"Perhaps he should learn to walk first."

That drew her attention back to Adan. "Yes, you're right. Time is too short to wish it away." After a bout of awkward silence, she added, "How is Elena these days?"

He leaned back against the sofa and draped an arm over the back of the cushions. "She is doing well. We've had several discussions about my father. She insists he was proud of my accomplishments, and claims he had difficulty expressing his emotions. I'm going to endeavor not to do that with Samuel. He deserves to know that his father supports him at every turn."

"And I'm positive you'll manage that just fine."

"You always have had more faith in me than most." He studied her eyes for a long moment. "I didn't realize how much I would miss your company once you left. But I have missed you. Very much."

She had no idea what to say or how to react. She certainly knew better than to hope. "That reminds me. I never saw where you released the statement outlining the reasons behind my departure."

His gaze drifted away. "That is because I never issued that particular statement. We led the press to believe you were on a sabbatical in the States, visiting family."

That made no sense to her at all. "What was the point in delaying the truth? You're eventually going to have to explain why I left and never came back."

Finally, he brought his attention back to her, some unnamed emotion in his eyes. "Perhaps that will not be necessary."

She put the now-empty bottle on the side table and set Sam upright in her lap. "You're hoping that if you sweep it under the rug, everyone will forget I ever existed?"

"I am hoping after you hear what I have to say, you will realize my mission entails alleviating that necessity."

The man insisted on speaking in riddles. "By all means, continue. I'm waiting with bated breath for clarification."

He pushed off the sofa and stood before her. "And I pray I have not waited too long to do this."

As if she'd been thrust in the middle of some surreal dream, Piper watched in awe as Adan fished a black velvet box from his pants pocket and lowered to one knee. She couldn't catch her breath when he opened that box to reveal a massive princess-cut diamond ring. "Piper McAdams, I have never met a woman quite like you, and I have never been in love until you. I probably do not deserve your forgiveness for my careless disregard, but I sincerely believe we both deserve to be together." He tugged the ring from the holder and held it up. "Now, will you do me the honor of being my real wife, and a mother to my son?"

Heaven help her, the cat that had dragged her into

the garage now had hold of her tongue. She could only stare at the glistening diamond, awed by Adan's declaration of love and the knowledge the fairy tale could soon come true. But then came the questions. Should she take this leap of faith? Could she trust that he really wanted her as his wife, not only as a mother for his child? Or was she overanalyzing everything? Then suddenly the baby reached back, grabbed a wayward tendril of hair at her nape and tugged hard, eliciting her involuntary yelp and Adan's scowl.

"That was not the reply I had hoped for," he said gruffly.

She laughed as she extracted Sam's grasp and offered him her pointer finger. "Apparently he was tired of waiting for my answer."

"And I am also growing impatient."

She pulled Sam up from her lap and turned him to face her. "What do you think about this whole thing, little boy? Should I say yes?"

When the baby squealed in response, Adan said, "I do believe he agrees that you should."

She turned Sam around in her lap to face his father and held out her left hand. "I do believe you're right."

After Adan slid the ring into place, he stood and motioned for Piper to join him. Then with baby Sam nestled between them, he kissed her softly and smiled. "I do love you, Piper. More than my MiG-20 jet."

He could be such a cad. A very cute cad. "And I love you more than my purple fluffy slippers that you always found so comical."

His ensuing smile soon disappeared. "On a serious note, as soon as we are wed, I want you to legally become Samuel's mother."

"I would be honored," she said. And she would.

His expression remained overtly somber. "He has a right to know about Talia, although I am at a loss over what to tell him."

"That's simple. When he's old enough to understand, we'll say that his mother loved him enough to give him up because she felt it was the best thing for him. And if I've learned anything at all, I suppose in some way that's what my own mother did for me and Sunny. She wasn't equipped for parenthood."

"But you are," he said. "And I've come to realize that not knowing about Elena did not discount the fact she was always the best mother a man could ask for. She's also a very good grandmother, and she is dying to have you as her daughter-in-law."

Piper couldn't ask for more. "Any idea when we're going to take care of the wedding business?"

"As soon as possible. Perhaps before we return to Bajul."

"We could always hold the ceremony in the family backyard. I provide the groom, and my grandfather provides the shotgun."

Adan laughed as if he didn't have a care in the world. "No need for that. I am a willing participant in establishing a future with you."

And very soon she would no longer be his pretend wife. She would be the real deal.

Epilogue

If a woman wanted to live in a palace, the gorgeous guy standing a few feet away could be just the man to make that come true. And three months ago he had—in a civil ceremony surrounded by her grandparents' lush gardens, sans shotgun. Now Piper McAdams was more than ready to legitimately assume her role as his princess during the elaborate reception held in their honor.

For the past twenty minutes, she'd been schmoozing with wealthy strangers while shamelessly studying her husband's assets. He wore a navy suit adorned with military insignias, a pricey watch on his wrist and a wedding band on his left hand. His usually tousled dark brown hair had been neatly styled for the occasion, but it still complemented the slight shading of whiskers framing his mouth. And those dimples. She'd spotted them the first time she'd laid eyes on him six months ago in the Chicago hotel bar.

And as it had been that night, he was currently speaking to a lithe blonde wearing a chic red sparkling dress, only she didn't see this woman as a threat. In fact, she saw her as simply Madison Foster Mehdi, her sister-in-law and recent addition to Piper's ever-expanding gal-pal club.

Speaking of expanding, a woman dressed in flowing coral chiffon that didn't completely hide a baby bump stood at the ballroom's entrance. She'd come to call her Maysa while most called her queen, and aside from the duties that came along with the title, she served as Sam's stellar doctor and Piper's confidante. The man on her arm, also known as the king, hadn't been as easy to get to know, yet he'd been warming up to his youngest brother's wife, slowly but surely.

All in all, Piper couldn't be happier with her new family. And she couldn't be more pleased when her husband started toward her with that sexy, confident gait that threatened to bring her to her knees.

Once he reached her side, he leaned over and whispered, "I have another gift for you."

"Giving it to me now would be rather inappropriate, don't you think?" she whispered back.

He straightened and smiled. "I'll reserve that gift for later when we are safely ensconced in our room. But this particular present is totally appropriate for the occasion."

Piper took a quick glance at her left hand. "I really think the boulder on my finger is quite sufficient, and so was the wonderful honeymoon in Naples."

"Have you forgotten our time on the beach?"

She faked a frown. "All right, that thing you did to me on the beach was very unforgettable."

"I thought you enjoyed that thing."

She grinned. "I did!"

He pressed a palm against the small of her back and feathered a kiss across her cheek. "Remain here while I retrieve your surprise."

As he headed across the room, Madison came to Piper's side. "Where is he going in such a hurry?"

"He says he has a gift for me."

"Oh, that," Madison replied. "I was beginning to wonder when he was going to get to that."

Piper's eyes went wide. "You know what it is?"

"Yes, I do. In fact, I assisted in acquiring it. And don't look so worried. You'll love it."

Knowing Adan, she probably would. "I'm counting on it."

Madison momentarily scanned the crowd before bringing her attention back to Piper. "I haven't seen Elena yet. She promised she'd come down once she had the babies put to bed."

"She told me she wanted to read them all a book."

"Good luck with that," Madison said, followed by a laugh. "I'm not sure year-old twins and a six-month-old will fit in her lap."

"She enlisted Kira's help," Piper added. "And believe me, Kira is amazing. I'm not sure there's anything she can't do."

"Except hold on to a man," Madison said. "At least according to her."

"A worthless man, maybe. She told me all about her broken engagement. Too bad we snatched up all the Mehdi brothers. She'd make a great sister-in-law."

Madison grinned. "Maybe there's one hiding in

the closet somewhere. Of course, there is their cousin, Rayad, although he's all into the military thing."

Piper still had a lot to learn about the family. "You'd better hope there's not a secret Mehdi hiding out somewhere. That means you'd be in charge of handling that scandal."

"True." Madison pointed at the double doors to her left, where Adan now stood. "Your husband is about to reveal your surprise, so wait and watch and get ready to be wowed."

Piper kept her gaze trained on the doors, wondering what might actually come through them. A new sports car? A pet elephant? Maybe even a...sister?

The minute Sunny caught sight of Piper, she practically ran across the room and engaged her in a voracious hug. And as if they'd been propelled back into the days of their youth, they momentarily jumped up and down until Piper realized exactly where they were and who she now was.

She stopped the girlish celebration, but she couldn't stop her smile. "Sunny McAdams, what are you doing here?"

"Answering your new husband's invitation."

She noticed they'd gained the attention of a room full of dignitaries. "Thanks to our boisterous show of affection, these people are now convinced the new princess is nuttier than a squirrel's nest."

"If the glass slipper fits," Sunny said as she stepped back and surveyed Piper from head to high heels. "You clean up good, sugar plum. Aqua is definitely your color, but I'm clearly underdressed."

Piper smoothed a hand down the bling-embellished satin strapless gown and grinned. "If you'd walked in here wearing something other than black slacks and a white silk blouse, I'd be asking you to return to the mother ship and give me back the real Sunny McAdams."

They shared in a laugh until Adan interrupted the camaraderie. "Did I succeed in surprising you, fair lady?"

She gave him a grateful hug and an enthusiastic kiss. "An excellent surprise, good sir. I do believe you've thought of everything."

"He wanted to make up for me not being at the wedding," Sunny added.

"That's okay, dear sister. You can make it up to me by staying here a few days."

"Unfortunately, I'll be leaving tomorrow. I'm meeting up with Cameron in Africa to cover a few of the most recent uprisings."

Piper hated how her sibling insisted on putting herself in danger, but she was pleased that she seemed to have found her match. "So how's it going with Cameron the cameraman?"

Sunny shrugged. "We're hanging in there. He wants to settle down in suburbia and have a few kids, but I'm not ready for that."

"Take it from me," Madison began, "you can balance career and motherhood. I've managed it with twins."

"And a very accommodating husband." All eyes turned to Zain Mehdi as he slid an arm around his wife's waist. "It's good to see you again, Sunny."

Piper momentarily gaped. "You two have met?"

"Briefly in Nigeria," Sunny said. "But I didn't know who he was until much later, since he was traveling incognito at the time."

Must run in the family, Piper thought when she considered how Adan had concealed his identity. They'd come a long way in a very short time.

As casual conversation continued, Piper noticed a man standing alone a few feet away, his attention focused on the group. "Does anyone know who that man is to my left, holding up the wall?"

"What man?" Adan asked.

"The one who keeps staring."

Sunny glanced over her shoulder before focusing on Piper again. "That's Tarek Azzmar, a corporate investor who hails from Morocco and a billionaire probably ten times over. I met him in Mexico City a few years back when he was opening an orphanage. He's a man of few words and rather reclusive. An enigma wrapped in a mystery, as they say."

"And Rafiq invited him," Zain added. "Apparently he's building a mansion not far from the palace. We'll be able to see his estate when we're standing on the west-facing veranda."

"So much for privacy," Adan muttered. "And with that in mind, if you fine people will excuse us while I have a few moments alone with my wife?"

"By all means," Zain said. "The courtyard outside provides enough protection to begin your honeymoon, if you so choose. My wife will attest to that."

Piper caught a glimpse of Madison elbowing Zain in the side, earning quite a bit of laughter as her husband led her away.

Once in the corner of the deserted vestibule, Adan turned her into his arms. "How does it feel to be an honest-to-goodness princess?"

"Unreal. Surreal. Wonderful."

"I'm glad you are up to the task, and I'm hoping you are willing to take on another."

She suspected she knew where this could be heading. "Hold it right there, hotshot. We have plenty of time to make a sibling for Sam."

"I would like to get to that in the immediate future," he said, "but this task involves your painting skills."

"What would you like me to paint, Your Highness? And please don't tell me one of your planes."

He gave her that earth-shattering, heart-melting grin. "As tempting as that might be, I'm referring to capturing the entire family on canvas. Rafiq, with the council's support, wants to commission you as the official palace artist in order to preserve history."

Piper could think of nothing she would like better. Actually, she could, but she'd take care of that later in bed. "I'm absolutely honored, and I will do my best to prove I'm up to the challenge."

"It is going to be challenging, at that. You'll have to rely on photographs of my father to capture his likeness. And we'll hang that in the foyer."

"I can do that," she said, thankful Adan had thought of it first. "What about your mother?"

"Since she's here for the sitting, that should not be a problem."

Another feat accomplished—his acceptance of Elena. "We'll hang that one in the nursery, next to yours and Sam's."

"And will you be able to paint one of all three of us?"

"Certainly, and I'll make myself look much thinner."

He frowned. "No need for that. You are perfect in every way."

So was he. So was their life, and their love. "Now

that we've taken care of the details, why don't we go up and say good-night to your son?"

"*Our* son."

"You're right. As of this morning, he's legally mine."

He brushed her hair back from her shoulder and kissed her gently. "He has been yours from the beginning, and I will be yours for all time."

In that moment, Piper realized she'd been very lucky to find the sheikh of her dreams. A prince of a guy. The one who got away…and came back, this time to give her his heart.

* * * * *

LET'S TALK
Romance

For exclusive extracts, competitions
and special offers, find us online:

- **f** facebook.com/millsandboon
- **🐦** @MillsandBoon
- **📷** @MillsandBoonUK

Get in touch on 01413 063232

For all the latest titles coming soon, visit
millsandboon.co.uk/nextmonth

MILLS & BOON

THE HEART OF ROMANCE

A ROMANCE FOR EVERY KIND OF READER

MODERN

Prepare to be swept off your feet by sophisticated, sexy and seductive heroes, in some of the world's most glamourous and romantic locations, where power and passion collide.
8 stories per month.

HISTORICAL

Escape with historical heroes from time gone by. Whether your passion is for wicked Regency Rakes, muscled Vikings or rugged Highlanders, awaken the romance of the past.
6 stories per month.

MEDICAL

Set your pulse racing with dedicated, delectable doctors in the high-pressure world of medicine, where emotions run high and passion, comfort and love are the best medicine.
6 stories per month.

True Love

Celebrate true love with tender stories of heartfelt romance, from the rush of falling in love to the joy a new baby can bring, and focus on the emotional heart of a relationship.
8 stories per month.

Desire

Indulge in secrets and scandal, intense drama and plenty of sizzling hot action with powerful and passionate heroes who have it all: wealth, status, good looks…everything but the right woman.
6 stories per month.

HEROES

Experience all the excitement of a gripping thriller, with an intense romance at its heart. Resourceful, true-to-life women and strong, fearless men face danger and desire - a killer combination!
8 stories per month.

DARE

Sensual love stories featuring smart, sassy heroines you'd want as best friend, and compelling intense heroes who are worthy of them.
4 stories per month.

To see which titles are coming soon, please visit

millsandboon.co.uk/nextmonth

JOIN US ON SOCIAL MEDIA!

Stay up to date with our latest releases, author
news and gossip, special offers and discounts, and
all the behind-the-scenes action
from Mills & Boon...

 millsandboon

 millsandboonuk

 millsandboon

It might just be true love...

MILLS & BOON

MODERN

Power and Passion

Prepare to be swept off your feet by sophisticated, sexy and seductive heroes, in some of the world's most glamourous and romantic locations, where power and passion collide.

MILLS & BOON
True Love
Romance from the Heart

Celebrate true love with tender stories of heartfelt romance, from the rush of falling in love to the joy a new baby can bring, and a focus on the emotional heart of a relationship.